Genius is a Bark Away from Insanity
The Jack Twitcher Memoirs

Jack Twitcher

M J Stadtler Productions
Mentor, Ohio
www.theothersideofinsanity.com

Edited by Brooke Baldwin & Maria Stadtler

An M J Stadtler Production

Special Thanks and Acknowledgments

To my wife Maria;

Without her support and encouragement this book would never
have been finished.

Table of Contents

Prologue

Whoever wrote the words "the pen is mightier than the sword" knew what they were talking about. I was sitting on the floor looking down at my blood-soaked shirt with a pen sticking in my heart. The ink was pumping into my veins through one side and blood was squirting out the other. The longer I sat there contemplating my predicament, the more I felt faint. The warm fluid spewing forth from my body was my life oozing out of the pen that I was supposed to be writing my life's story with. Well, damn it, I can't die now. I don't even have the first paragraph written. I thought about pulling the pen out, but then thought maybe it's best to leave it and drive myself to the hospital. The longer I thought about it the more I felt like I was going to pass out. Then it occurred to me to put a cork in it. I spit my gum out and wadded it around the end of the pen. What a genius. The bleeding stopped, at least for the moment. I pulled myself up and assessed the situation a little closer. What seemed to be a gallon or two of blood draining from my body, the very essence of life, well you get the picture. In reality it was probably little more than a test tube full. Less than they take for a blood test. With the pen still sticking out, I would survive and make it to the emergency room. I probably should have taken my car, but the sky was moonlit and clear with the temperature perfect for skate boarding. Okay, so I live in an apartment in the inner city and the hospital is only one block away. Still it was challenging trying to keep my balance while feeling queasy.

Three stitches. Three lousy stitches and a band-aid, gee whiz not even worth writing home about. It was bad enough my mortal wound wasn't, but I had to sit and tell my story of how it happened to two nurses and again to the doctor on duty. Each one left the room with a snicker. One of them didn't get out of the door fast enough before she burst out laughing. When she came back she still had tears rolling down her reddened cheeks and was holding back a smile. I think she was biting her tongue.

The final humiliation occurred when they scheduled an appointment with a psychoanalyst for the next day. I thanked them all for their services and walked humbly back to my apartment. The dirty rats even gave me the pen back, chanting, "Don't run with sharp objects," and then the laughter started again. I wasn't run - - ah, who's listening anyway? I was supposed to be writing my autobiography for Authors Weekly. It was a follow-up story after having received honorable mention for a work of fiction that I just had published. The feat of selling one thousand copies in six months was something that was now my claim to fame. If I get the gig autographing my book at the next convention, I might sell a few more and then hit the big time as an acclaimed new author. I had to keep my excitement to a minimum. I didn't want my stitches to pop. Boy what an evening. I'll have to find a way to incorporate the stab wound to the heart. Maybe instead of a boring auto-biopsy, I should write an attempted murder mystery. Every mystery doesn't have to end up with a dead body, does it?

It's almost one o'clock. I think I'll call it quits and get a fresh start in the morning. A new chapter would do wonders since my writer's cramp wasn't going away. Most of the night was lying awake creating the new story in my mind. In the morning I would put it on paper and see how it looked. I liked what I was thinking. I only hoped I could remember it all. I have a habit of thinking up great one liners and then forgetting them. Four o'clock bells and all's well. The castle clock in the hall was chiming. Now that the cat had a new home I was able to wind up the clock again without the pendulum being used as a toy. The draft of the manuscript was due in twenty eight days. One would think that was almost enough time, but the last writing took six months and then a year to edit. This one won't take as long to edit. The publishing house has agreed to do it to speed up the process. We can hit the market before Christmas. It's a big selling time, so the push is on.

By five o'clock I had enough tossing and turning. Since I couldn't sleep, it was time to get busy writing. First I would enjoy a bowl of sweet crispy flakes. I was hoping the sugar would put a few wrinkles in the old gray matter. Maybe it would even spark an idea or two.

From the hallway, I could hear some stumbling around. It must be my roommate.

"What are you doing up so early?"

"I'm going to Sarah's. We're going to the Whirlygig Festival in Pottsville."

"I thought your car was in the shop for repair?"

"It is. That's why I'm leaving early. I'm hitchhiking to her place. Her brother Joe is going to drive us to the festival."

"Why don't they just pick you up?"

"Pottsville's the opposite direction and Joe doesn't want to waste the gas. Hey, beggars can't be choosers. What are you doing today?"

"I've got to get started writing my new epic novel, so I'll be hanging around here all day. Can I ask you something?"

"Sure, fire away."

"What's with the hooded sweatshirt? You look like a gangster."

"Sarah's finishing her beautician classes and she had to do a men's hair style and cut for a test. She didn't pass, and I'm not taking this hood off until my hair grows back."

"Well, I hope you like the spooky look, because all I can see is your eyes."

"I'd rather be spooky than laughed at. What's with the band-aid? Did you cut yourself shaving your chest?"

"No! I was stabbed in the heart last night."

"What? I gotta hear about this."

Larry turned one of the kitchen chairs around and got comfortable. I suppose he thought my story was going to take more than a minute to tell. I felt a little embellishing would be necessary. I should have turned my tape recorder on, just in case the story was worth repeating.

The Story

I was gathering my thoughts for my biography. After several hours, I realized that my life's story filled only five pages and wasn't worth the paper it was written on. Who wanted to read about a guy born and raised in suburbia? People want to read about the middle child in a family of fourteen. How he had to fight his siblings for food and that made him the man he is today. The book was supposed to be non-fiction so I couldn't make up someone else's life story to tell. Another hour passed and there were more sheets of paper in the garbage than there were in the saved file. I didn't want to kill another tree, so I decided to take a break. Maybe a walk in the park, or a little skateboarding would shake a few cobwebs loose.

The park at eight was pretty much void of kids, and only a few young lovers were on the benches. It appeared to be a peaceful setting by any ones standards. So, I went over to the playground and started to skate; that's when a voice came from under the slide.

"Hey, boy, you got a lot of nerve coming around here."

"What? Are you talking to me?"

I looked around. There were only the two of us, and it was pretty obvious whom he was talking to, but I didn't understand the attitude.

"Yeah, I'm talking to you. You come around here like you own the place. Well, you don't. Take your punk board and get your butt the hell out of here."

"Hold on there, partner. This is a public park, and you can't tell me to get my butt out of here."

A body that was attached to the voice came out of the shadows of the slide. This mountain of a man could squash me like a bug if he had the desire to do so.

"I ain't your partner. You think if you talk down to me or try to make me your equal, that's gonna make things real pretty. It don't, and if you don't leave and quick, things are going to get ugly, real ugly."

Larry jumped in, "So that's when you got stabbed?"

"No, that's not when I got stabbed. When I realized that he thought I was someone else, I had to point out the error of his ways."

Larry threw in an, "Oh, boy." Then he repositioned himself on the chair with his hands folded underneath his chin and both elbows on the kitchen table.

"Do you mind if I continue?"

"Oh, no, by all means continue."

"Thank you."

This fabrication of a lie was turning into something pretty good; even I was wondering what would happen next. I had to think fast, or I would lose concentration and the story wouldn't be believable.

So, then I told the guy, "You must be mistaken me with someone else. I don't know you, and I'm sure you don't know me."

"I know you. You're a pompous, arrogant puke. You come here from your cushy apartment and write notes about what you think goes on in the life of a homeless person. I read your book. You stole my life and called it a work of fiction. You profited from what people saw as make believe. Did you ever once think about sharing the royalties with the real hero of the story, with me?"

"My story wasn't about you, or anyone that is real. It was purely a work of fiction and to my credit if I say so myself, it was brilliant."

"See what I mean, egotistical too."

"You can call me names all night, but that won't solve anything. Tell me why you think the story was about you. If you can tell me what the similarities are, I'll tell you the difference."

We talked for hours, until midnight I suppose. When finally exhausted, we parted company. I'm not sure we had come to terms or were ever going to be friends, but I wasn't dead.

Larry started to scratch his head. "I don't get it. If this guy didn't beat the snot out of you and then stab you in the heart, who, did?"

"Did I say someone stabbed me in the heart, or that I got stabbed in the heart?"

"What's the difference?"

"Well, there's a lot of ways a person can get stabbed. I went back to the apartment to write about all that had taken place. It was the start of a really good story. I would kill the autobiography until I was sixty and start a suspense thriller instead. I was so excited with all the new material that I couldn't wait to get to my desk. With pen in hand and an iced tea, I was ready to start. The phone rang, and I got up to answer it. I tripped on the throw rug, and while trying to catch my balance still holding my pen, I fell on top of it, stabbing myself in the heart."

Before Larry could throw something at me, I ran out of the kitchen. He then started laughing, so I returned.

"I'm late; I'll see you when I get back. Try putting that all on paper. It was almost believable."

"Thanks, Larry. Have a nice time and tell Sarah I said hello."

Larry headed out the door. His adventure with hitchhiking was about to begin. He just didn't know it.

Book 1

Eyes in the Rearview Mirror

The Road Isn't Lonely Anymore

It was getting late. I wanted to make the state line before ten and then find a hotel for the night. It wouldn't be more than another six hours when I got rolling in the morning from the border to my destination. I pulled over for a quick pit stop to gas up and get a snack for the final leg of today's trip. The sign at the pump said eighty-five cents. Boy, gas sure was cheap, or at least that's what I thought. I found out when I went to pay that the three had fallen off. Not such a good deal after all. The chips and soda were overpriced as well. It wasn't more than ten minutes later when I returned to the road, that I heard a whistling sound coming from the back seat of the car. I looked over to see if maybe the window was partially down. It appeared to be rolled all the way up. The sound went away, so it must have been something fluky. The radio was nothing but static. The only thing that would come in somewhat clear was the Grand Ole Opry channel. In between songs, the whistle returned. This time it was whistling the theme from the Andy of Mayberry show. I looked in my review mirror and there were two eyes looking back at me. I was so startled I dropped my pop in my lap. It was probably just as well because I think I wet myself.

"Who are you? And what do you want?"

"Never mind who I am. You don't use your rearview mirror much, do you?"

"What are you talking about?" I tried to turn to get a look at this mystery person.

"I've been watching you in the mirror for the better part of the last half hour. You eat like a pig with your mouth open. I'm surprised you don't choke on those chips while washing 'em down with your soda. You'd better keep your eyes on the road, or you may end up dying needlessly in a car crash. And that's not how I planned it."

"Planned what? The way I die?"

"No, the way I die. Look, Mr. Panic attack, I just need a ride. I thought I would hitchhike, but there were no cars going my way this time of night. Plus the fact, that I'm not . . . Let's say, not one to behold as lovely."

"Well, I won't be able to take you very far. I'm almost out of gas."

"You're not out of gas. I got in at the gas station. I thought I was going to get a free ride, but, the cheapo that you are, you only put in five bucks. I had to put in another twenty to fill it up."

I looked at my gauge, and the tank was near full. It didn't dawn on me where or when this person had entered my car. The voice was non-distinct. I couldn't tell if it was that of a man or a woman, and they were very careful not to let on. That made me think it might be a woman, and she was afraid I would pull something and overpower her.

"You can stop fiddling around looking for your Billy club. I have that in the back seat with me. Oh, and don't go looking for your Saturday night special in the glove box, 'cause, I have that too. Anything else ya got hiding to keep the bad guys away?"

"No, and I guess they aren't going to help me now. So, hey, if all you want is a ride, why all the haunting mystery. Why don't we just introduce ourselves, and we can be road warriors into the next town, or wherever?"

"You're a fool. We ain't going to be road warriors or buddies or friends or nothing. You'll be my ride and that's it. What kind of radio do you have anyway? Is that all you got is country bumpkin music? How 'bout some rock or blues or jazz? Or how 'bout, you just shut the darn thing off.

I shut the radio off. It was annoying with all the static anyway. The next few miles we drove in silence. I kept looking in the rearview mirror to see more of my hitchhiker. I thought I might get a glimpse when the headlamps of an oncoming car passed. The mystery person had a hood pulled over their head, no hair was sticking out, and they sat straight back and low, so all I could see were creepy eyes. They were formless wearing all black clothes. That kept their sexual identity a mystery as well. This was starting to get to me. No sound, no talking, and not knowing where we were going.

"Hey, hiker, do you think you should tell me where we are going so I know where to turn off if necessary?"

"You don't need to know where we're going. Just drive. There are no turns for fifty or so miles. If you would do the speed limit instead of willy-milling around, we could be there in an hour."

"There's no way that you can see the speedometer from where you're sitting, so how do you know how fast we're going?"

"I have a butt. I can feel that we're barely moving. At this "turtle's" pace, you'll be getting a slow speed ticket. If there were any traffic, you'd be holding everyone from getting to their destinations on time. Are you trying to get the sheriff's attention? You won't. He was dead when I got to the police station earlier. Someone popped him in the head. Too bad for you, he was the only trooper this side of Evansville."

"So, are you saying we're going to Evansville?"

"You don't listen very well. I didn't say anything of the sort. I said the sheriff was dead."

He or she, this was driving me nuts. What if they were the one that popped off the sheriff, but why? I was getting scared again. My cool, calm demeanor was starting to become cold and clammy. I was nervous, and they had my gun.

"I have to pull over and go to the bathroom."

"No you don't. Use the jar, that you carry with you for such occasions. I won't watch, if you're worried I'll laugh or something."

"I don't have to go now."

"Good. So you haven't asked in the last five minutes who I

17

am and where we're going. Did you lose interest?"

"I guess I don't care anymore. I don't want to end up popped in the head like the sheriff."

"Look, the sheriff was dead when I got there, I told you that. Besides, it's not my style."

"Oh, now you have a style. What style would that be?"

"You talk too much. And you think way too much. Did you ever hear of the legend of Hang Mans Tree?"

"Maybe, I'm not sure."

"Well, I'll give you the short version. . .

The Cockroach Hotel

For some reason my hiker got real quiet. I wasn't sure what was going on and why the silence. Maybe he fell asleep. I could pull over and drag him out of the car and jump back in and speed away.

"You look tired. The next exit is Evansville. There's a hotel just off the highway about a mile. You can stay the night there, then get a fresh start to wherever you were heading."

"Evansville. Ha! I knew we were going to Evansville."

"Don't get ahead of yourself. I never said "we," and the only reason you're stopping is because I think you should rest. You've got a big day from the looks of the crap you have in your briefcase. You don't really sell this stuff, do you?"

"Hey, it's a living. Who are you to judge?"

"Okay, okay. Don't get your shorts in a bunch. Look, stay at the El Cheapo hotel. They're only 19.99, and if you're lucky you'll get clean bed sheets."

The Evansville exit was coming up. I pulled off the highway as instructed, and the sign for the hotel was in view just ahead of me to the left. There was a neon vacancy light flashing with one of the letter A's in the sign missing. The price was just as Hiker said, 19.99. When I slowed to pull in the driveway I heard the door of the car open.

"Here's your gun back. Don't shoot anybody, but you may need it. This isn't the safest place in the world. Sleep fast and get out of town before the locals wake up."

"Gee, thanks, but aren't you staying?"

"What, are you nuts, in this hell hole? I've got to keep going. I'll catch the next diesel heading south and then catch you on the flip side."

The hiker, as I started to call him, her or whatever, jumped out of the car before I came to a stop. He waved good-bye in the mirror. What a crazy night. With the description of the hotel, I wasn't sure that I wanted to stay. However, being dead tired in my boots, I checked in.

It wasn't as bad as I had thought it would be. At least the cockroaches didn't seem to mind my presence; they kept to themselves under the sink. The tub was stained, and the toilet hadn't been flushed by the last tenant, so I lay on top of the covers trying not to touch anything. I thought I would use the showers at a truck stop in the morning. It would probably be less likely that I would catch some infectious disease. This was pretty stupid. I paid twenty bucks to lie awake in a hotel that by all rights should have been condemned. I could have just slept in my car for free.

I got out my laptop and started to Google "Hang Man's Tree." Hiker never told me the story, and I couldn't get it out of my head. What kind of urban legend would this turn out to be? To my surprise, there were pages and pages on the subject. It seemed like every state in the union had its own version of the story. Most were just about hanging trees and how horse thieves were strung up with no questions asked. Horse stealing in the West was a higher crime than murder.

Apparently, it was harder to replace a good horse than it was to replace a ranch hand or husband. Nothing that I read seemed to fit the story the hiker was going to tell. My thoughts were that hiker's tree was more local, and I might be heading in that direction, which is why he brought it up. Or, she, I was tired of wondering what hiker was. If I met him today in the light, I wouldn't know who he was, although I might recognize the eyes. Every time my eyes closed for a minute to rest, the eyes would come into my thoughts. They were haunting. Greenish-grey in color, with a glare that I swear could cut through a cold steak.

The image of a faceless person under a hooded sweatshirt, with no body because the black clothing blended into the car seat, gave me shivers. I couldn't get it out of my head.

I found myself waking up. I had fallen asleep out of sheer exhaustion. The sun was almost up too. It was shining through the window that only had half a curtain hanging on a bent rod that was ready to fall. No need to pack; I never unpacked. I said my good-byes to the roaches and headed for the car. Apparently the locals got up early. There were three men and a woman standing by my car, smoking a hand rolled cigarette.

"This here yer car, boy?"

One of the men started talking as he walked over towards me.

"Ye-yes, sir, that's my car alright. I'm just leaving, so if it's in your way or anything, I'll be moving it right now."

The guy talking to me was not too tall. He was dressed in jeans and a tee-shirt with a denim vest. He came over and put his arm around my shoulder and began speaking to me again.

"What's your hurry? My friends and I were hoping you would join us for breckfirst and then a little game of chance."

His breath smelled of staled booze and cigarettes. And he probably hadn't bathed anytime in recent weeks. I almost puked on his boots when he talked directly into my face.

"Gee, that sounds swell; however, I don't do breakfast, and I'm not much into games, so I hope you'll excuse me, but I have an appointment this afternoon, and I'm running late."

"Didn't your mother teach you that breckfirst is the most important meal of the day? And that it's not polite to turn down the offer of your host while visiting? Ha, Boy?"

He gave me a little shove, and I stumbled into the arms of one of the other guys. He kept me from falling but told the first fella that I had said something to him.

"Ah, what's that? Oh, yea, I agree one hunert percentile with ya. Hey, Al, this here foreigner says he thinks your breath stinks and he wouldn't eat with you ifin you were the last pig in the barn."

I tried to speak up to deny saying that, but before I could Al punched me just above the kidneys in the back. The second guy was still holding me up when Al punched me again. This time he let me fall to the ground.

"Clem, you and Joe Jr. tie him up. We're gonna teach this feller some manors and give him a proper meal before he goes off to his meetin' today. Sarah Mae, go fetch the vittles out from the truck."

Sarah had a whiny little voice, "Al honey, wouldn't you rather be sparkin' in the barn than playing with some silly city boy?"

"Nope, I like this just fine. Now do as you're told."

Whatever vittles was they were still moving inside of a burlap sack. I wasn't sure what it was, but I was darn sure I wasn't going to like it.

The Show Down at Evansville

Whatever was in the bag smelled of wet fur and feces? The outside of the burlap sack was stained with what might be blood and caked with mud. As Sarah got closer, she held the bag with her arms stretched out in front. It was almost in my face. They had hog-tied me, and I was lying on my back with my hands behind me. It wasn't comfortable at all, and I couldn't get away from the horrible smell. Al kicked me to get my attention.

"Have you ever had country fried squirrel and grits, boy?"

"No,"

I said softly while trying not to cry or puke. Al kicked me again.

"What's that? Speak up boy. I can't hear ya."

"No, Sir."

It was all I could do to get out the words without breathing. The blood and other fluids started to drip from inside the bag. A couple of drops spattered on my face.

Al responded with, "Oh look, I think he's gonna' cry. Not very manly is he? I think he's nuttin' but a girly man."

Clem and Joe Jr. started chanting.

"Girly-Man, Girly-Man, he's nothing but a girly-man."

"Stop it!"

Sarah wasn't finding much humor in the whole event.

21

Al barked back at her.

"Woman, if you ain't got the stomach for it, git in the truck. This won't take long."

A voice came from behind Al. I was hoping it was the local Sheriff.

"You should listen to the little lady. Stop the pranks and let the fellow go."

Sarah was startled. She dropped the bag with the vittles. It landed right on my chest, knocking the wind out of me. I couldn't help but take a deep breath. This time there was no holding back.

A vision of drowning in my own vomit crossed my mind. I violently started rolling back and forth until the bag rolled off me.

I rolled to the other side away from it so I could breathe again. By this time Al was facing the person giving him orders to cease and desist. The two of them stood with their legs slightly apart and arms down at their sides. It looked like they were going to draw on each other, but neither one had a gun.

Al snarled at the diminutive figure.

"No one tells me what to do. I gives the orders around these parts."

"Apparently, you don't hear so good. I said to let him go."

"And just who are you, little man, to be giving me orders?"

While the two of them were jaw-boning back and forth, I squirmed to get out of the view of Al's hairy butt. The voice of the stranger was vaguely familiar. The sun was shining from behind the hotel creating a long shadow in front of him. He was dressed all in black with a hood pulled down to his eyes. I couldn't get a clear view with the sun and a drip of blood in my eye. The stranger had his gaze fixed on Al.

"You don't need to know who I am. You just need to be prepared to meet your maker."

As Al took a step forward, I finally recognized the voice, and the eyes were unmistakable. It was the hitchhiker. Al took another step towards him. With lightning speed and accuracy, the hiker pulled out a bowie knife and threw it at Al. It landed dead center in the dirt between Al's feet.

Al laughed and then sputtered out, "Nice try, shorty. Whatcha gonna do without your big old knife?"

Al was taunting him. He bent down to grab the knife. The hitchhiker took a couple of steps towards him, spun around and landed a spinning drop kick to the side of his head. He fell to the ground. His right leg was twitching and then his body went limp. The hiker grabbed the knife and started to cut me loose.

"I thought I told you to get out of town before the locals got up?"

"You neglected to tell me they got up before the sun."

"Oops, my bad. Do you want to get a shower and clean up before we hit the road?"

"We?"

"Yes, we."

He turned to look at the other three, who were frozen in fear.

"You all better drag your big brother out of here before I cut out his heart and have it for breakfast. Then I'm going to feed his you-know-what's to the squirrels."

He tossed the open bag to Clem. The two half dead squirrels managed to run away.

"Thanks for the help, but I think we should leave before Al wakes up."

"I ain't getting in a car with anyone that smells as bad as you. Why don't you at least change your clothes and throw away what you're wearing?"

Off to a Fresh Start

I stepped back into the hotel room to say hello to my little friends, the cockroaches. As I began to change my clothes, I was feeling pretty good about the outcome of the encounter with the Evansville welcoming committee. I may have been bruised, but I wasn't dead. Even with my clothes off I still smelled. Maybe a shower wasn't such a bad idea after all.

There was no hot water. The shower was refreshing, but I made it a quick one. After putting on some fresh clothes, I stuffed my soiled shirt and pants into the cabinet under the sink. When I finished packing and gathering my stuff, I heard a lot of commotion coming from just outside of my hotel door. Looking out of the one curtain window, I saw that the boys from earlier were back. For a lack of better description, I started to call them the Evansville gang. They were attempting to take revenge out on the hitchhiker. Hiker was lying face down on the ground with his feet tied to the rear bumper of my car. Clem was in the front seat trying to hot wire the ignition to start the car. Joe Jr. and Al were high-fiving each other and singing;

"Na, Na, Na, Na, Hey hey-ey, good-bye now."

Sarah wasn't in view, but I was sure she was around. With a deep breath and a gulp, I decided it was my turn to play hero. I didn't bother to turn the door handle. After grabbing my gun out of my briefcase, I kicked the door open then fired a shot into the air as I stepped out of the room.

"There are five shots left. Who wants to play target while I practice shooting?"

It was then that I found Sarah. She had my Billy club from the back seat of the car. I raised my left hand to block getting hit in the head. With a twist of the club, I was able to grab it away from her. I gave her a poke with it.

"Back off, chick, you don't want any part of this."

Sarah ran around the car to the other side to stand by Joe Jr. and Al.

"Our beef ain't wit you, mister. We was just funning with ya. We was fixin to let you go."

Al sounded almost nervous when he spoke. He could see the wild-eyed look that I had. He may have even thought I was just crazy enough to shoot. Truth, be known, at that moment, I was not only crazy enough to shoot, but to kill.

"Get your buddy out of my car. I'm going to cut my friend loose, and we're going to get in the car and drive out of town, nice and peaceful. The first person to object gets to eat lead."

The Evansville gang backed away from the car with their hands in the air. I kept my eyes on them as I went to untie the hitchhiker.

"I thought you weren't going to take a shower."

"I thought I could trust you to stay out of trouble. Get in the car and let's get the hell outta here."

Hiker was holding his ribs but could get into the backseat on his own. I got in and started the car. We slowly backed out of the parking lot, and then I punched the gas pedal to the floor, burning rubber and leaving a cloud of dust. The sight of the gang still standing with their hands up faded from view as we approached the highway.

A moment later, still shrouded by his hood, the hiker's eyes were looking back at me in the mirror.

"For a girly-man you surprised me back there. I guess we're even."

"Yes, I suppose we are. Where to?"

"Drop me off at the truck stop in Jonstown. From there you can travel alone in peace."

"Alone, yes, but peace? I don't think so. You never told me the story of Hang Man's Tree."

"You have got to be kidding. Almost dead before ten, a murderer by noon and all you can think about is some stupid urban legend?"

The Mark

There wasn't a cloud in the sky. The sun was still burning off the morning dew, with a little mist rising from the road. I set the cruise for sixty-eight miles per hour, just a little over the limit. That way, the troopers wouldn't bother me, and Hiker would be glad that we weren't traveling at a turtle's pace. My backseat traveler was quiet again. From time to time, Hiker would go into silent mode. He would stare at me or out one of the windows. It was time to break the silence, so that I wouldn't fall asleep at the wheel.

"Hey, that was a pretty good trick you pulled back there."

"What are you talking about?"

"You know, throwing the knife into the ground to get Al to bend down, so you could kick him in the head."

"It wasn't a trick, the knife slipped out of my hand."

"Slipped?"

"Yeah, I was eating buttered popcorn watching the show"

"The show, what show?"

"The one you and the boys were putting on in the parking lot. When I realized that I had seen it before, I decided maybe I should step in."

"So you were watching the whole time, why'd you bother?"

"I've seen how it goes, and it doesn't end so well. Besides, I needed a ride. The other guy didn't have a car."

I was getting angry with the whole conversation. I couldn't believe what I had just heard.

"Why didn't you just steal the car, or something?"

The hitchhiker was getting smart with me, and his attitude was changing.

"Look, I can't drive. I don't have a license anymore."

"So, let me get this straight. If it wasn't for my car, you would have let me die back there?"

The hitchhiker snapped back irritated, "And if I would have, we wouldn't be having this conversation."

"Yeah, well, now I'm pissed off."

"Better to be pissed off than pissed on, and trust me that was coming. How 'bout turning on the radio and we cut the chatter? I'm going to take ten, no funny business. Okay."

Even though I was fuming mad, I agreed to let the hiker take a nap. With the radio tuned to the clearest broadcasting country station, I turned up the volume just enough to be irritating. I couldn't tell if the hiker was asleep or not.

His eyes were glazed over, but didn't appear to be closed. It was creepy because they looked like cataracts instead of eyelids. Looking past him in my rearview mirror, there was a cloud of dust forming in the distance.

Coming out of the cloud was a motorcycle rider, then two riders, side by side. As they got a little closer, I could see a whole bunch of motorcycles, and they were coming up fast.

"Hey, Hiker, your buddies have bikes?"

Hiker's eyes cleared as he sat up. Looking out the back window he said, "No, they don't have bikes, and don't call them my buddies."

"Oh, sorry, are we a little cranky after our nap?"

"I'm not cranky. I just know who these guys are. You're gonna want to pull over and let them pass. If we're lucky they'll keep riding."

"And what if we're not?"

"If you're a praying man, I'd suggest you start now and lock the doors."

Hiker slumped down into the seat below the window, out of view.

The roaring sound of the bikes increased as they got closer. I pulled over and off the road, just as the lead biker was about to pass. He looked in the window at me and then kicked the front fender before speeding away. Every biker that followed did the same thing. I couldn't wait to get out of there. The bikers were traveling in a pack. I wasn't counting, but if I had to guess, I'd say there were fifty or more. After what seemed to be an eternity the last bike passed. The roar of the engines faded along with the sight of them in the distance ahead.

"Gee, we must be lucky or they liked us. We're not dead, beat up, bruised or nothing."

The hitchhiker slowly sat up and looked around then added, "Not yet. They left their mark, so you can be sure that they'll be back."

"Great, so what do we do now?"

"I'd try to make it to the truck stop as fast as possible. They won't mess with us there."

Trying to impress him, I stepped all the way down on the gas pedal.

"Hold on to your hood, I'm going to open this baby up."

I rolled the windows down for effect. With the wind blowing in, it felt like we were cruising in a low flying hover craft. I got up to eighty miles an hour. I could see the sign for the truck stop. We were going to make it, or at least that's what I thought. There were clouds of dust on both sides of the road. Heading towards us were the bikers. They were coming at us riding four abreast and maybe ten deep.

"Uh, I think they're coming back. Should I pull over again?"

The hiker was cool and calm just before he went crazy and started to yell.

"What, are you nuts? Do what I say and you may live to tell your next of kin. Straddle the double yellow lines. We're going to play a game of chicken. Get your freaking seatbelt on and brace yourself with the steering wheel. When they get closer, get down low enough to see over the dash and keep the wheel straight.

DO NOT SWERVE. If you hit something or someone, keep on going and hope they don't come through the windshield.

Whatever happens, dead or alive, you have to get me to the truck stop. Keep your eyes on the road, not me, you idiot. Get ready — double yellows — Now, Now, Now!"

I did what Hiker said and started down the center of the highway. The bikers weren't moving and neither was I. We were doing almost ninety when we came head to head with the first row of bikers.

Not too Many Chickens Crossed the Road

The first two bikers to approach the car at high speed swerved at the last second, but not before we hit the back of the bikes causing them to spin into the riders next to them. All four bikers ended up sliding off the road with sparks flying all around. The next group split up to come alongside of the car.

One rider stayed back riding straight down the yellow lines towards us. When the front of his bike hit my bumper, he leaped onto the hood of the car, and his bike went sailing over the top of us. I watched as it crashed and went up in flames on the road behind us. The biker was scratching and clawing at the hood, trying to grab onto anything to keep from falling off. He wasn't able to get to the front by the windshield to grab on. He had an evil smile as he slid off. I felt a thud and a thump like speed bumps as we ran over him. We were closing in on the truck stop. The bikers were hell bent on us not making it. From behind there was one maniac that drove his chopper right up onto the rear bumper. He had six inch spikes on his shoes. When he jumped off his bike, his boots went deep into the trunk, enabling him to stick to the car.

He was a little wobbly trying to get his balance with the wind against him at the speed we were traveling. Pulling with all his strength, he managed to free a leg. He leaned forward and his foot came crashing through the rear window. It shattered into a million pieces with glass filling the back seat. He tried to free his other boot to get into the car. With his other foot free he stepped on top of the car with the spikes coming through the head liner. I thought the roof would collapse with his weight. There was a stop light up ahead. He got caught in the wires, ripping him out of his boots and hanging him like a swinging piñata.

"Are you all right back there?"

"Yeah, I think so. What about you?"

"I'm okay. We've got another quarter mile to the gate. We should be through in a minute, outside of this guy with horns growing out of his helmet heading towards us."

Hiker sat up, he looked out the front window, and then quickly got down between the seats.

"Be careful, this guy is the crazy one of the bunch."

"And just what were the other guys, the half crazies, or the brains of the operation?"

"Just shut up and listen. This guy is not going to move off the road and he's not going to let us pass. When he gets close, I want you to slam on the breaks and cut the wheel hard to the right."

"Won't that let the other guys get us if we're stopped?"

"Yeah, it probably will, but the grand pooh-bah will be lying somewhere in the middle of the road."

"What do you think it means if the gas gauge drops from three-quarters full to empty all at once?"

Hiker sat up again and looked over the seat at the gas gauge and then looked out the back window through the shattered glass.

"There's a trail of gas following the car. The line must have been cut or the tank split open when you ran the last bike over. I don't think we're going to have time for anything fancy."

One of the bikers was pointing to the ground. He was signaling to his buddies to come around to where he was. A few bikes passed us as we were slowing down. I no longer could do anything except coast to a stop or hit the brakes. That's when the hitchhiker said that we should bail as soon as the car slowed to around five miles an hour.

"Now who's the one nuttier than a fruit cake? If we get out of the car, they'll kill us."

Hiker pointed out the blue flame that was headed our way. They had ignited the trail of gasoline. It would only be a minute before it caught up to us, and we would explode with the car.

"It would be better to take our chances with them than to have them pick up our remains from the highway. Look, try to steer right to angle the car away from them, when the car catches fire, we'll get out on the other side and take cover. If we're lucky when the car explodes it won't come back down and crush us."

"Gee, I feel lucky already, just knowing that you had a backup plan."

"Three – Two – One, jump!"

There was no doubt in my mind that somewhere in the next town the sound caused a tea cup or two to vibrate off a table. The car was two hundred feet in the air and on its way back down when I heard the sound of air horns. It was a semi-truck pulling out of the truck stop and heading our way. I thought he was going to run us down, but the passenger door swung open and an arm reached out to grab me. Once inside the cab, they reached to pull the hitchhiker in too. The truck rolled past a handful of the motorcycle gang, just as the car crashed to the ground in flames. What a sight.

"Thanks, mister, we owe ya one."

Hiker was sitting in the back of the cabin of the truck with me behind two burly truckers.

"Wasn't nothing, we just wanted to see the fireworks is all, and we eat them bikers for breakfast if they get in our way. Where you boys headed?"

This time it was my turn to throw my two cents in.

"We're going south to Pottstown; I have an appointment with the owner of the Five and Dime store."

"Pottstown's fifty miles south of here. Unfortunately I have to be in Tucson by nightfall, so I'll have to drop you off in Evansville.

You can probably hitch a ride from there."

The hiker and I looked at each other and both mouthed the words.

"Oh, She—it."

Almost Heaven

The first few minutes riding in the truck were nothing short of heaven. In fact, the sign on the headliner above the windshield read, Almost Heaven. The hiker was thinking about something. He had that blank stare on his face that he would get from time to time. I was sitting uncomfortably. I had peed myself a little at the thought of going back to Evansville.

There was some chatter coming over the CB radio. The driver started talking about farming.

"The basket's full and the chickens are on their way back to the barn. Nope, no eggs are broken."

I wasn't sure what that meant, but it wasn't any of my business. The other trucker turned slightly towards us and smiled at us with the few teeth he had.

"You boys is in luck, Cousin Sarah has got her some va-can-c's at the Evansville Ho -tel. For less n twenty bucks you get the finest room this side of fifty miles. In the morning you kin eat breckfirst for free. I hear tell her vittles is to die for."

The two truckers broke out into wild laughter. Then the driver got serious for a minute.

"Ifin you boys stick around, you'll get to meetin Cousin Sarah's two Fee on says."

I was afraid to ask what he meant by two fiancées, but I just had to know.

"What do you mean by two fiancées?"

"Well, she couldn't decide between her two gentlemen callers, so she got engaged to both. That-a-ways there's no hard feelings amongst them."

"Your cousin sounds like a real sweet gal."

During the conversation about the lovely Sarah, Hiker's concentration was broken. He leaned over and whispered to me.

"We can't go back there, they kill us both."

"No Shit! So, what do you think we should do?"

"I'm working on it. Whatever I do, just follow my lead."

Hiker leaned forward with his head in between the two truckers and started a conversation.

"Boys, as nice as your cousin's hospitality sounds, we're gonna need to replace our car, so we'll just ride with you a ways further and you can drop us off in Beaver Creek. They have a little rental and used car lot right on Main Street. We should be there by five o'clock so, no worries."

The driver had a half smile and turned just enough to talk and watch the road.

"I already done called Sarah on the CB and told her we'd be bringin you boys and that you'd be needin two rooms. She'll be powerful mad if she loses the revenue on two rooms. Trust me, you fellers don't want to make her mad. She'll track you down like a hog sniffing for truffles."

"Well now, if it's the revenue, I've got a fifty spot to settle her loss."

"That would be mighty nice of you mister. I'll call her and let her know you'll be dropping by to pay her, but that you won't be staying. She'll only be insulted that you don't want no part of her vittle cookin. I'm sure that'll go over real big with her. Breaker, breaker, this is Heaven Bound looking for . . .

"Never mind, we don't want to miss out on a good home cooked meal."

Hiker sat back in his seat. He was a little disappointed that the conversation didn't go the way he'd hoped it would. He was still thinking of a way out, as he started to untie his laces and remove them from his shoes. I was wondering why, until he tied them together and then leaned forward and wrapped the laces around the throat of the one trucker choking him.

"If you don't want your buddies head handed to you, I'd suggest you pull over by the railroad crossing just ahead. We'll part company there."

The driver tried to take a swing at Hiker, but I clubbed him with a tire iron I found under the seat. The cracking sound of his forearm caused me to become nauseous. The driver was writhing in pain as he pulled over where he was told. The hitchhiker still had a hold on the other trucker, he directed me to get out and start running down the tracks. He pushed the trucker into the driver and swung himself out of the truck slamming the door shut. We were both running as fast as we could.

"Run in a zigzag back and forth across the tracks."

"Why?"

I thought it was a good question, especially since it was easier to run straight.

"If one of them has a shot gun, they won't be able to get a good shot at us."

"Do you think they have a - - gun?"

A bullet went whizzing past my head. It was so close I could hear it and feel the warmth of it against my ear and cheek. I guess that answers that.

There was a ravine, a few feet ahead. Before they could get off another shot we were sliding down and out of sight. Both of us were out of breath panting. At the bottom was a small creek. Hiker pulled up his sweatshirt and started to rip his tee-shirt. I was getting dizzy and a little light-headed. I thought it was from running.

"What are you doing, making a flag to surrender?"

"No, this is for your ear. Hold this, I'll be right back."

I put the piece of shirt to the side of my head, and immediately it turned red, blood red.

The burning I felt was the bullet glazing the side of my face. The hiker came back with some slimy clay. He put it on my ear and some on my face.

"This will take the sting out and keep it from getting infected until we can get you some medical attention. I hope you didn't have that ear pierced, 'cause, I ain't going back looking for no diamond attached to a piece of ear."

"Don't make me laugh. Pierced ears are for gays and pirates."

It was right after that, that everything went dark and I passed out.

Alone Again

My eyes were closed. For the first time in thirty-six hours, I was able to rest. Hiker was giving me instructions on how to hop a ride on a moving train. Occasionally, he would shake me to make sure I was awake and not slipping into a comma. Fear started filling my thoughts. Maybe my wound was more than a missing ear lobe. The whole left side of my face was numb. The sound of a train whistle blowing in the distance meant it would be passing in a couple of minutes. Hiker grabbed my hands and pulled me to my feet.

"Are you ready to run?"

I was too stubborn to say no.

"You just lead the way. I'll be right behind you."

The first few cars of the train passed us. Hiker was a few yards ahead, and kept waving and yelling to me;

"Hurry, hurry up, come on run, run faster."

An arm reached down from one of the box cars, and Hiker grabbed it. He was pulled onto the train. The last thing I remember was him leaning out to see where I was. Even in the distance, I could still see his eyes looking at me as I fell, face first in the dirt.

There was no light at the end of the tunnel, but I could feel two angels putting me into a horse drawn buggy. I imagined a team of pure white stallions. Time was literally floating. Everything was passing by in slow motion. After just a few minutes I fell asleep.

When I awoke, with my eyes still closed, I could hear talking.

"Where'd they find this one?"

"Down by the tracks just off the highway."

"Does he have any identification?"

"Nope, clean as a whistle."

The conversation was odd. They were talking as though I were dead. I don't know what happened to my wallet with my driver's license and credit cards, but if I had to guess, the two angels probably weren't on the short list for a promotion.

"Who else knows that he's here?"

"Just the two that brought him in, but they won't say anything."

"Are you sure?"

"Two hundred dollars says they take it with them to the grave."

"Trust me, if they say anything about this, that's exactly where they'll end up, I'll see to it personally."

"Look, Doc, let me take care of the scavengers and you just take what you need. We'll get our money and then get the hell out of here."

"Is the plane gassed and ready to go?"

"Yes sir, everything is ready. I'll get the boxes."

I was hoping that I was wrong, but it appeared that the good doctor and his partner were "black market" body snatchers. They were going to sell my parts to the highest bidder. Apparently, they had a standing order for fresh organs, and the homeless community in the area gave them an endless supply of parts.

The doctor poked me in the chest and started to slice me open. My eyes opened wide, I grabbed his hand with the quickness of a ninja then twisted his arm until he dropped the scalpel.

"Cut me again, Doc and you'll be performing surgery with a bloody stomp, or your feet."

"I - - I thought you were dead."

"Yeah, well, you thought wrong. Did you ever think about checking for a pulse?"

I pulled myself up while still applying pressure to his arm. The assistant walked in from the other room where he had been labeling the boxes and filling them with dry ice. He was preparing to pack my parts and ship them. I had the doctor strapped to the table and was going to give him a scar as long as the one he had given me.

"Unless you want to pack the doctor's heart, you'll take a seat right over there. I'll be on my way, and you two can find someone else to play operation with."

The assistant didn't say a word and did just what he was told. I took a jacket from the coat rack and slipped out the back door. There were two cars in the lot. One was a hopped-up punk mobile with a rebel flag painted on the hood; the other was a black Mercedes. I reached into the jacket pocket, as luck would have it I found the keys to the Mercedes in it. This would be fun, making my get-a-way in high fashion and style. It wouldn't be long before the car would be reported stolen, but all I hoped for was enough time to get out of town and then ditch the car somewhere. According to the radio, it was only a little after seven. I decided to find a shopping plaza. I could dump the car in the lot. From there I would look for a bus stop.

A sign for the Colonial Mall said; One Block Turn Right. That was just the place I was looking for. When I got to the parking lot, it occurred to me to look through the car for anything useful.

All eyes were on me as I pulled up to the front entrance. There was a small group of teenagers milling about. I grabbed the doctor's briefcase and a gun out from the glove box. When I got out of the car, I tossed the keys in the air.

"I've got some shopping to do. Keep the car warm; I'll be back in an hour."

Three boys scrambled to be the first to get the keys. They and a couple of girls jumped into the car and then sped away. I could hear them yelling, Party Time!

On the other side of the mall, I found another entrance. There was a bench with an older woman sitting on it.

"Excuse me, miss, do you know if there is a bus stop anywhere near by?"

"Why, yes sonny, just across the lot. You can see the sign from here. There's blood dripping on your shoes, should that be a concern?"

I had to come up with a reason why I was bleeding, and quick.

"Oh, it's nothing. I cut myself shaving."

The woman looked at me with her head cocked to one side,

"You're not one of those fairy fellows, are you?"

"If you mean, am I gay? No. My girlfriend said she thought I looked like a Neanderthal and didn't want to go to the beach this weekend unless I shaved. Well, that's the last time I do that, especially since we just broke up. She was driving and dumped me off here. My wallet must have fallen out somewhere either in her car or at the restaurant. Would it be a major imposition if I borrowed a couple dollars? I promise I'll pay it back. I'll send you a check."

She looked at me again with her head cocked to the other side.

"So, you think I'm going to give you money and then tell you where I live, so that later instead of paying me back you come over and rob me blind. That's if I'm lucky."

"What do you mean if you're lucky?"

"By the looks of you, with your hair a mess, a three day old beard and smelling like a shower isn't something that you are at all familiar with. Well, what if you're a rapist or something?"

I started to laugh. I had been through a lot and hadn't given any thought to how I must look. I wasn't sure she was buying my girlfriend story either.

"Look, I'm not a rapist or anything. I'm just a little down on my luck. To tell the truth, I was down by the tracks and got rolled by some homeless bums. They took everything I had except my pants and this jacket."

The old lady's eyes were fixed on me and the jacket. I asked, "Are you waiting for the bus, because there it is?"

"You couldn't get me on one of those things, they're un-safe."

"Are you worried about getting mugged or raped on the bus or that the clientele may not be suitable company for a lady of your apparent upper class standards?"

"Oh heavens no. They don't have seat belts. You'd think in this day and age with all the air bags in cars and the safety features they put in vehicles, the damn RTA would put seat belts on their bus. Excuse my language, things like that bother the sh - -oops. Things bother me, that's all. Don't tell anyone, but I carry a gun."

"Your secret's safe with me, miss. I guess I'll have to hurry, if I'm going to catch the bus. Did you think anymore about that couple of bucks?"

"Oh, here, you'll probably blow it up your nose or shoot it up your arm. But, whatever you do with it, I hope you take a bath and wash your hair."

Opening her purse, I saw she had a roll of bills, enough to buy the damn bus and get the freaking seat belts she was so concerned about. She peeled off a hundred and two fifties.

"Take this. I was planning on losing it at bingo Saturday night anyway."

"Thanks. This means the world to me, and I will pay it back by giving the same amount to someone else who needs it too."

"Yeah, yeah, hurry up and catch the bus, unless you want to wait for my son. He's picking me up any minute, and we can drop you off wherever you want."

"You're too kind. I'll just take the bus. I may be heading out of town. I'm supposed to be in Pottsville two days ago. My car - - and this is the truth now, my car was totaled in an accident, and I was going to the nearest town to buy another one. That's when I got rolled and lost my wallet and credit cards. You wouldn't believe what happened next."

"Well, I have time to listen. The bus just left."

"Oh, Shit." I mean shoot."

"I know what you mean. Oh, here comes my son. He's about your age, you two might hit it off and go have a drink and pick up some women. That's after you take a bath, of course."

"Yes, of course."

I looked out the door into the parking lot. A hopped up punk mobile with a rebel flag on the hood was pulling up.

"There's my Bobby now."

This Hotel was Clean and Smelled of Fresh Linen

As I watched Bobby get out of the car, a chill ran up and down my spine. I needed to get out of the situation, and quick.

"Well, thanks again for everything. I'm going to get a bite of something to eat in the food court while I wait for the next bus to arrive."

I got up from the bench. The nice old lady suddenly turned nasty.

"Sit back down, buster, and don't give me any lip about it."

At first I thought she was kidding until I turned around and saw her pointing a pistol at me. She didn't even care if anyone saw her waving it around.

"You seemed like such a nice young man, but I bought the jacket you're wearing for a dear friend. I know it's his because I had his initials sewn onto the right breast pocket. If you killed the

Doc to steal his coat and briefcase, you'll be dead where you sit."

She stood up to yell to her son, all the while keeping her focus on me.

"Bobby, get your butt over here."

Standing in front of me she was blocking Bobby's view of me sitting on the bench. She asked Bobby, "Where's Doc?"

"He's at the office finishing up, why?"

"Because one of your cadavers is walking around talking about the fun times the three of you had together, and showing off his scar."

After saying that, she stepped aside so Bobby could see me.

"Oh, shit!"

"You better believe, oh shit. Your operations are supposed to be on dead people."

"When he was brought in, he was dead, but then he wasn't. It's some kind of miracle momma, I swear."

The old lady whacked Bobby on the forehead.

"You're an idiot. We'll have to take him back to the office and finish him off. The shipment is due tomorrow, and they already advanced me the money."

"What should we do?"

"It looks like I'll be cleaning up another mess of yours. If we don't deliver, they'll fill the order with the two of us instead. Call Doc and let him know we're coming in with a live one, and to have the ether ready."

Bobby started towards the car, calling the doctor on his cell phone. Momma motioned with her gun for me to get up and go to the car.

"You'll ride in front where I can keep a close watch on you."

She opened the passenger side door and shoved me in. She got in the backseat. Bobby was already sitting behind the wheel ready to go.

"What did you do with Doc's briefcase?"

"I left it on the bench. I can go get it if you'd like?"

"Funny, you're a real funny guy. Death is staring you in the face and you still make jokes. Bobby, take this while I get the case."

As she handed Bobby the gun, I reached for it too. I pushed up and a shot went off into the roof of the car. The three of us were struggling for control of the gun. I turned and took my right elbow and cracked Bobby in the nose. He fell back holding his face. Now it was just me and the feisty old broad. She had the strength of a much younger person. I thought I was wrestling with a man. When she leaned forward to get a better position, I gave her a sharp head butt. She dropped into the back into the seat.

Grabbing the gun, I opened the door and slowly got out of the car. There was another bus coming, and I wasn't going to miss it. I shot all four tires and the radiator then ran to catch the bus.

Apparently no one was paying attention or cared because not one person including the driver said a word when I got on. Once again I knew it wouldn't be long before they, or the police would track me down. I was confident that Bobby and his mother weren't going to be calling the cops, but the doctor might.

As we headed down the street, I saw lights flashing. I started to sweat and got real nervous. I could see through the front window three patrol cars. All six cops were out with their guns drawn. As we passed the flashing lights, the cops were arresting the kids that had taken the Mercedes for a joy ride. I felt bad, but figured they would get off with on a misdemeanor. I needed to get off the bus as soon as it came to the next stop to avoid getting caught.

We pulled in front of a small diner. Dinner sounded good, so I got off the bus and went in to order something to eat. After placing my order, I noticed that almost everyone had a jacket or sweater hanging on the post next to their booth. When one guy got up to go to the bathroom, I swapped jackets and then went out the back through the kitchen.

In the parking lot there was a uniform cleaning service making a delivery. I was in luck. I could get fresh clothes and a new identity of sorts. All I wanted now was a bath, shave and a car. The money wasn't going to last long, so tonight I would call home and have some money wired to whatever hotel I would find.

If I were to rent a car, I would need to call the bank in the morning and get my credit cards replaced. Thoughts of stealing a car or hitchhiking entered my mind, but both were risky. After finding an outfit that was close to my size, I slipped out of the van before the driver came back.

He must have been in the diner or something because no one was coming. I slapped myself in the head. Sure enough the keys for the van were in the ignition.

This would be the perfect get-a-way car. The driver probably would call the company, the company would then call the cops, and by that time I'll have dropped it off somewhere. There was an itinerary on a clipboard. The next stop was at a hotel just up the street. Talk about a lucky guy. I parked the van in the back of the hotel near a service entrance and then walked around to the front to check in for the night.

The Beaver Creek Hotel was the name on the sign over the desk. Beaver Creek was where Hiker wanted to be dropped off by the truckers. There's supposed to be a used car lot somewhere in town. That would be the first thing I'd look for in the morning. After a rather quick but refreshing shower, I hopped into bed. It felt so good to close my eyes and relax. I was thinking of the events of this last week. If I were to write this all into a story, no one would believe it was true.

There was a double click at the door. The light from the hall came shining in. Someone had opened the door. They were quietly and slowly making their way into the room.

A Quickie A Hanging and the Rescue

The sound was of two voices whispering as the door widened and they entered the room.

"Are you sure there's nobody in here?"

"There's no sign on the door, plus I kept the key from Saturday night. They can't rent a room without a key."

Oh good, a real smart guy that thinks the hotel only has one key for each room.

"Get yourself ready. I have to use the toilet."

What a relief. It was just some dumb couple stealing the use of the room for a midnight quickie. As the woman headed towards the bed in the dark, she still hadn't noticed me. She took her clothes off and neatly placed them in a pile on the floor. It wasn't until she got under the covers and rolled over on her side that she discovered I was there. We were face to face when she let out a scream loud enough to wake the dead at the cemetery down the street. My left ear popped, I was almost deaf on that side. Since I had gotten used to sleeping with my clothes on, all I had to do was grab my shoes and run out.

"What the hell is going on in there?"

A sheriff came out of the bathroom pulling up his pants, trying to tuck in his shirt at the same time. I felt like my luck had run out. The sheriff and his blonde bimbo were having an affair, and I was in the middle with no way out.

"Boy, we have got ourselves a little problem. This story can't be told the way you think it happened. Sarah, cover up, I can't concentrate."

"But, Daryl, this is our special time."

"Not gonna happen tonight. You might as well get dressed and go on home."

I can't believe it. Is Sarah like the only woman in this area of the southern hemisphere? She owns the hotel in Evansville. She's the truck driver's cousin and also engaged to two thugs. She must have something going on, because here she is again on a night out with the sheriff of Beaver Creek. There's just no getting away from this woman. She's like a bad cold or a dirty penny that keeps coming back.

"Now Sheriff, we can resolve this like gentlemen. You don't need to be pointing your gun. As I see it, this whole evening never took place. I'll just leave quietly and you'll never see me again."

"Nope, I don't see it like that at all. You created quite a stir, and people will see us leaving. So, here's how it's coming down. We take breaking and entering as a serious crime. However attempted rape is a hanging offense. Don't need no judge or jury either. Oh, and you shouldn't been messing with the Mayor's daughter. You just in the wrong place at the wrong time, boy."

Geez, it just kept getting worse by the minute. When Sarah was dressed, she left the room. The sheriff marched me out at gun point like a hardened criminal. As he put me into the back of the patrol car, he pushed my head down to avoid hitting the door and then clubbed me with his gun. I was out cold. When my eyes opened, I was barely standing on an orange crate. There was one end of a rope tightly tied around my throat and the other tied to a barren oak tree. My hands were untied. If I fell it would look like a suicide hanging and not murder. I guess I was supposed to fall before I came to. There was no good way to keep my balance and try to get the rope off. To top things off the wind was kicking up and I was starting to sway a little.

Just off the road there was a dust cloud heading my way. I thought it was a twister until I saw a red Jeep coming through it. The Jeep pulled up in front of me and a familiar person got out.

"Hey, bud, if you're hanging around waiting for a bus, it don't come this way."

With the rope constricting my throat, I could barely get out the words, "Screw you and the horse you rode in on."

"Just a little crabby are we? And such language towards the only guy around that might save your sorry ass."

I had my hands around the rope and was pressing hard on the crate with my feet, trying to relieve the pressure.

"You can go to blazes; I'll hang around until the next white knight comes along."

"Suit yourself."

"Wait, wait I was kidding. Get me down already."

"Your wish is my command."

Hiker cut me down and helped me into his Jeep. After drinking a twenty ounce bottle of water, I had to ask, "How in the world did you find me?"

"I didn't find you. I was driving down the highway when I spotted a body hanging on a tree. I thought I'd check to see if it was dead or alive. I guess you're lucky I was curious."

"Yeah, one lucky guy, I feel like I owe you my life."

"Nah, keep it, I've got one of my own. Besides, I told you I would catch you on the flip side to tell you the story of Hang Mans Tree. Looks like I don't have to anymore."

"No, I lived it. I certainly don't need to hear about it. Can you get me to Pottsville?"

"You're either crazy as a loon, or one dedicated salesman. What's so important in Pottsville?"

"The Five and Dime in Pottsville is my largest account. I sell out my entire inventory every year when I go there."

"I hate to break this to ya, but the Five and Dime had a going out of business sale, their last day was Tuesday. Wasn't that when you had your appointment?"

"Sure was."

"Gee, if you would have said something, I could have told you and saved you a lot of hassle."

"Thanks, now what am I going to do?"

"Maybe you should go home and write a book. I'll bet it'd be a real hoot to read."

THE END

Well, I think that turned out better than the original. I'll send it off to the editor in the morning and get an initial reaction. If they like it, I'll start a second, and maybe the book will be a collection of short stories instead of a novel. It sounded like a plan. Now all I needed was a good second story.

Book 2

Jack Goes On a Holiday Adventure

Man Ain't Supposed to Fly

An Adventure to Remember. . . The Thrill of a Life Time. . .

These were just a few of the descriptions that headlined the advertisement for Parasailing. In just three days the entire family would be flying to five islands for a month long vacation. Well deserved, I might say. The best part was, just one business meeting on Wednesday of the first week. After that I was to do whatever I wanted, and the whole thing was going to be picked up by the company. Only one catch, I had to write about the trip in diary form and find someone to publish it within a year. If I didn't accomplish that, the company was going to payroll deduct whatever I spent. With that thought hanging over my head, I almost didn't want to go.

As a man gets older, the fear of dying enters his thoughts from time to time. Not that it will eventually happen, but that it will happen before he does something he has never done before. Something so crazy, people will be talking about it for years. It should be part of his eulogy. My vision was to go parasailing. This was the only thing that I was looking forward to doing on vacation. I even had a picture from the travel company on the refrigerator.

Three hundred dollars for a one hour lesson, equipment rental and twenty-five minutes over the ocean blue. For an additional seventy-five bucks, they would film the whole event and make a

CD complete with my choice of theme music and a voice-over describing the activities. For another thirty they would throw in an eight by ten color glossy inserted in a driftwood frame of me in flight.

"Sign me up, boys, I want the deluxe package."

For those of you new to the thrill seeker's life, parasailing is strapping on a parachute and being pulled by a boat instead of jumping out of a plane.

I was totally nuts at my age to attempt this, but I wasn't crazy enough to sky dive. I rather liked the idea of having water for a landing and not some field of clay or rock.

Friday at 4pm we were scheduled to leave. At 8:37 we would land. The hotel was only twenty-three minutes away. With any luck, I would be in bed by midnight. Seven o'clock the alarm was to go off and I would be at the docks by eight.

Friday night arrived and everything went as planned. My wife decided she didn't want to be embarrassed watching me fly. She said that I should duct tape my driver's license to my A, um my buttock and that way if anything happened, she could claim me at the morgue after shopping. Ha ha.

Molly, our oldest of two thought the male bonding between her brother and me was a little too syrupy. She said the testosterone levels were way past being safe, so she decided shopping would be relaxing and help settle her stomach. (Fingers in her mouth, feigning a gag)

Griff (my son) was all man. He was ready to watch his father fly or die. I'm not sure that was a comforting thought, but he was coming with me. He was going to make his own recording, in case the experts missed something. I told Molly to remember that her credit limit was three thousand dollars and not to spend it all in one place. I added that the best shopping was in St. Maarten and we wouldn't be there until our third week. I was hoping that maybe she'd save a little.

Off to the pier for training. The shuttle couldn't move fast enough for my liking even though the driver didn't slow around turns and only stopped when it was absolutely necessary. We arrived in one piece, I think. I had to check to be sure. Griff was in hysterics and couldn't wait for the ride back. He hoped we would get the same driver.

The equipment was spread all over. Brightly colored silks were gently blowing in the wind.

The first thing we learned was how to assemble our chute and how to steer while in the air. Next was landing in the water and how to get out from under it so that we wouldn't drown. Last was how to make a hard landing on the ground. They had us jump off a small hill and roll. Exactly the scenario I didn't want to happen.

Finally we were all ready to take flight. Three people were assigned to a boat with an instructor and a driver. My boat was the last in the fleet of seven. My nerves were jumping, and I didn't care if I were the very last to fly. In fact I was wishing and praying that would be the case. Each boat headed to different parts of the bay area so that there wouldn't be any accidents of people getting too close to each other. That meant my turn was coming up sooner than expected. The driver turned around and asked if anyone had changed their mind yet.

As the boat slowed just a little ways off shore, we tossed our gear over the side and waded to the beach. Each of us strapped ourselves in. When the task was complete, the instructor came by and checked our belts and buckles. We then waded back into the water and squatted with our knees bent and leaned back. It was the same position one would be in if they were getting ready to ski. One wave of the right arm by Enrique, (our instructor) and we were dragged just a few feet until the boat was safely away from the shallow water.

I must have blinked. When the driver hit the throttle, I was in the air before I could take a second breath. Whew boy, what a feeling. It was exhilarating, frightening and fantastic all at the same time. The faster the boat went, the higher I went in the air. I was bird high in the sky, soaring with the seagulls.

The birds looked over and one, I swear said, "Are you nuts, old man? You should be on the beach baking like the rest of the tourists. We have enough traffic up here with the planes, now you yahoos think you can fly too."

Actually the birds didn't seem to care. I was just practicing some lines for the diary.

From one hundred and seventy-five feet in the air, the beach was a myriad of color. The umbrellas, blankets and bodies all speckled the sand. Now I wish that I had purchased the twenty dollar one time use camera. Pictures from here would be spectacular. As I looked down towards the boat, I noticed a school of fish swimming just under the surface of the water. They were moving so fast some of them were passing the boat.

A few of the fish were leaping out of the water. It appeared that they were being chased by something. It was probably a larger fish maybe a barracuda or a shark. The driver made an extra wide turn, and we were heading back. That was the fastest twenty-five minutes of my life. Or it would have been until time stopped.

There was a shadow under the water. It was longer and bigger than the boat, and was heading towards it with the fish still trying to get out of its way. Since everything from here was but half its size, this thing must be huge. The instructor signaled for us to start our descent. I was watching the hand signals as the shadow came up and bumped the boat. Enrique fell over the side. The driver turned to see what happened, and the boat was hit a second time, which caused my cable to snap. I was free falling and with little experience, I had no control. Out of nowhere there was a sharp gust of wind, and I went sailing farther away from the beach. I was no longer able to see the boat and what was happening below.

Flying Without a Rope

If I had just paid a little more attention during the class, I might not be in this predicament. The anticipation of flying had me so excited I barely heard anything other than how to strap myself into the harness. It never occurred to me that I might get separated from the boat. In the back of my mind I could hear Enrique saying, "Pull left to go left, pull right to go right and pull on both to rise." Pull what I asked myself? I guess it didn't matter. There was no way my hands were letting go of the harness straps.

The wind continued to push me out to sea. I crossed the break wall separating the bay from the ocean. Things were starting to get a bit turbulent, and I was being jostled about.

There was a deep pitched humming sound coming from somewhere. It was getting louder by the second. With every ounce of strength in my body and contorting into a pretzel, I could finally see behind me. This is going to sound very cliché, but I wish I didn't know now, what I didn't know a minute ago.

The sound I was hearing was a small commuter jet. I was right in the middle of its flight path. You would think that the pilot would be able to see a bright yellow, red and blue sail with an eighteen foot wing span. Apparently they were hoping I knew some kind of evasive maneuver. They would be wrong about that. As the plane got closer, the jet engines started to pull me in. I was being sucked towards the plane, and they weren't moving. I was now able to see the pilots. One was looking down at the water and the other, assuming he was the co-pilot was waving his arms for me to get out of the way. I started yelling at him, things I would never repeat.

The nose of the plane was within a few feet of me, with its speed and swirling winds, I dropped like a brick on top of it. My sail was pulling me along towards the rear of the plane, and I was deposited off the back. I survived the suction of the engines, and now all I had to do was safely float to the water and wait for a cruise ship. These waters were infested with every cruise line known to man, so I stood a real good chance of rescue within a short period of time.

I was gliding along finally able to relax and enjoy the ride. It was peaceful and serene.

A few birds were alongside of me. I believe this time instead of gulls they were pelicans. The wings were broader and the bodies were bigger. Okay a moment of levity. You know that part that hangs down on a pelican? I believe it's called the gullet. Well, I'll bet you've never heard it flapping in the wind. I was laughing so hard I forgot where I was for the moment.

Reality has a way of bringing a person around rather quickly. The sky started to cloud, over and it was growing dark. It wasn't noon yet, but it looked like evening. With the wind kicking up again, instead of a soft water landing, I was headed upwards. Now all I needed was some rain and a clap of thunder. I was a flying lightning rod with the aluminum poll framing holding the sail together. Fortunately I wasn't very good at predicting the weather. The clouds rolled through and the sky turned blue.

I was still fidgeting with the straps and trying to figure out the controls when something below caught my attention. It was the fish jumping out of the water again in schools and swimming as fast as possible to get away from the evil of the deep. And there it was again. Just below the surface was the shadow. I couldn't make out the shape of it, but it seemed to follow me like stink on a skunk. Then it broke the surface. This mammoth beast was longer wider and bigger than any cruise ship on the ocean. I had seen pictures of Navy ships that were as big as a city. This thing was every bit the size of one of those.

Oh, boy. I didn't want to see what I was seeing, and I was hoping it didn't see me. It wasn't a fish or a whale. It was a submarine of sorts.

I couldn't read the writing from my angle above it, but I could tell it wasn't of US origin. When I spotted a hatch starting to open, all I could think was, I needed to hide. Someone was almost out when the wind blew me backwards and hopefully out of sight for the moment. Then the most unbelievable sight took place right in front of me.

The ship opened up a large hatch, and eight small aircraft flew out from it. They were black oval shaped crafts, once out of the sub, they flew almost straight up and disappeared from view. Then the submarine closed up and submerged. The whirl pool it created on its way down pulled me with it. I was in the water with the silken sail on top of me.

I needed to release from the harness or drown.

Up to My Neck in Hot Water

The water was hot. I could understand why the fish were trying to get away from the sub and leaping in the air. They were afraid of being boiled alive. I started to have the same fear as I became

50

increasingly more uncomfortable under the canopy of my parachute.

If I could crawl out of my skin to escape, I would. This little pocket between the frames was my bubble of air to stay alive. The steam rising from the water was burning the insides of my nostrils. The very bubble that saved me by providing air was soon to be my death trap. I had to get out of here and quick.

Even though all my life I had been around water, boating, fishing and skiing, I wouldn't consider myself to be a very good swimmer. I took a deep breath and dipped under the water. In a fraction of a second I popped back up. The air was so hot it was burning inside my chest. The frantic panting wasn't helping at all.

Two months ago when the company awarded me with this trip, I joined a weight loss and jazzercise class to get in shape. "No Pain, No Gain" had become my adopted philosophy on life. However, this was beyond breaking a sweat and a few body aches. This was flipping hell. I promise you, I didn't just say that.

Upon my second attempt I drew a slow deep breath and closed my eyes tight so they wouldn't boil out of their sockets. Once submerged, I pulled myself along the tubular frame of the parachute. Occasionally, I would feel with one hand for the water's surface. As soon as I felt a breeze blowing across my fingers, I pushed off and poked my head out of the water gasping for air. Now it was time to do my best Olympic free style swim to get to cooler water. I didn't have to go far. Thirty, maybe forty yards away and I could feel a change in the temperature. A little further and thoroughly exhausted, I came to rest. While floating on my back, I began to think about our first lesson of our class on parasailing. Enrique told us, in the event of a water landing to stay with our parachute.

He said it was easier to spot a large brightly colored object from the air, than a bobbing head in open water. I thought to myself, I'd rather be a bobbing head . . . than dead.

After a few minutes, I felt my body temperature dropping. It felt so good nothing short of ice water would have been better. I started to smell an odd but vaguely familiar aroma emanating from a source nearby. I looked all around to discover the origin of the smell. It was me. I wasn't beet red. I wasn't red as a lobster. I was Prime Rib rare. Bleeding red, with a soft pink center, some areas were light brown around the edges. In other words, I was cooking. I screamed out in pain and while crying out loud I let myself sink into the water. The sea salt would cauterize my wounds. When I got back to the surface, a sound like music to my ears was heading towards me. It was the sound of twin outboard motors on a small boat.

The boat approaching me was white with a red cross on the side. There were three guys on board. Two were life guards from the resort, and the third was Enrique. Apparently they had picked him up on their way to search for me. He was pacing back and forth like a caged lion. When they got close they cut the engines.

Enrique yelled, "Mr. Jack. Mr. Jack, we found your equipment."

With deadly accuracy he threw a preserver over my head. The two life guards pulled me into the boat. Enrique continued with excitement in his voice.

"Your son, he, tell us, he see you fly over the wall. You are lucky the wind is low today. One guy we never find. Grief, he say, he go back to the hotel to play his games in the room."

What a relief. Everyone was safe. Enrique wasn't finished, though.

"We find your equipment, Mr. Jack, so you no lose your deposit. And don't you worry. If there is any damage, we will deduct it from your security deposit."

I smiled as best I could and thanked him.

One of the life guards gave me a stern warning.

"Next time stay over the bay area. Especially with those open sores. The locals have spotted some Great Whites just past the break wall. Did you know they can smell blood in the water over a mile away? You're one lucky guy, that's for sure. What hotel are you staying at?"

"I'm at the Porpoise and Gulls on Beach Dr."

"Oh, yeah, that's a real nice place. How long will you be there?"

I looked at the life guard with the "what's it to you attitude."

"Uhm, I guess we'll be here till Thursday."

"Great! I hope you enjoy the rest of your visit, and don't worry about coming to the station. We'll forward your search and rescue bill to the hotel and you can settle up when you check out."

"Gee, thanks. You're very kind."

Sure enough when I got back to the hotel, Grief, I mean Griff was on the bed, his feet up on the headboard. He was oblivious to the world playing his video game.

I slathered loads of aloe all over my aching body then covered the red glowing areas with sun tan lotion. The last thing I wanted to hear when my wife got back from shopping was, "I told you so."

What seemed to be hours, or more than a day, in actuality was less than three. The whole terrifying near death experience took less time than it did to buy a new purse and a pair of sandals.

When my wife and Molly walked into the room, I was propped up in a lounge chair on the patio reading a magazine.

"How was your shopping, dear?"

"Oh, it was wonderful. We had the best time, and they have such great deals. Look, I got this straw purse and matching sandals. They were less than $300.00 dollars, and you know they would be twice that back home. So, you owe me a nice dinner for being so thrifty. How was your little adventure? Did you have fun?"

"Let's just say, Man Ain't Supposed to Fly."

THE END

Book 3

A Memory That Chills the Soul

To this day I can't go near the ocean, any large body of water for that matter. It's a shame too, because as a youngster and even well into adulthood I loved the water. Most of my fondest memories were of vacationing somewhere along the ocean with a sandy beach.

As a family growing up we would Jet Ski, water ski, snorkel, and in the cool of the evening we would sail. As an adult, my friends and I followed that tradition. When I married, my wife and I did the same, only we did it with class traveling all over the world.

We would plan two years in advance and charter a trip to some tropical locale. Every vacation was better than the last, and we were fortunate enough to afford all the memories money could buy. Then something happened, and I've tried hard to forget it. I've even tried believing that I imagined the whole event. My wife, friends and therapist all said the same thing.

"There's no way that could have happened, and why only you? Don't you think if it were real at least one other person would have seen it too?"

For five years I kept the story bottled up inside and never told another living soul; until now.

It was a nine hour flight to paradise. The accommodations were minimal, and the seats were small and squished together. This was a private airline. Only thirty people were on board including the flight attendants and two pilots.

We left Honolulu for destinations unknown. The vacation was on a small island in the South Pacific that was privately owned. In order to stay there, you had to be invited.

It didn't cost as much as one would think because most of the expense was pre-paid by the owner including the flight.

We arrived in the middle of the night. After a restless three hours, I decided to take a walk along the beach. The sand felt good on the bottoms of my feet. The waves were lapping my feet, and the foam tickled my toes. I was collecting shells and things, putting them all in a nylon sack that I carried to put my treasures in. Up ahead in the water there was something floating. It was bobbing up and down. When I got closer, the sea tossed it out of the water where it landed right in front of me.

Picking it up, I discovered it was a cell phone sealed in a zip-lock bag. Probably a sailor that didn't want to get his phone wet. There was nothing else in the bag, so I tossed them both into my sack. It was seven o'clock, time to meet my wife for breakfast. The hotel's restaurant's name was The Coconut Bar and Grill. A palm leaf covered affair with wicker chairs. Breakfast was buffet style with what I would soon discover was the world's worst coffee. I like coffee, all kinds of coffee. In the morning I like it hot and black. This stuff was oil. There is no other way to describe it. It was thick, it was hot, and it was nasty. When I took my first sip, it was so hot I got third degree burns on my lips just blowing on it. After the coffee cooled, it thickened and a stir straw could stick straight up in it.

"What, Jack? You don't like the coffee? You're making that face you make when you don't like something."

"The coffee is a bit strong."

"This isn't going to be another one of those vacations where all you do, is complain about the food, is it?"

"No. I'm not complaining. I'm merely making an observation. How is your omelet?"

"The eggs are as artificial as the butter. I don't think those are real blue berries either."

"My dear, and who's complaining now?"

"Jack, you asked, and I commented. I'm not complaining."

There was a moment of silence while we both choked down our coffee and eggs.

"What's the plan for today? Did you bring the itinerary?"

I was as anxious as a school kid in line at the ice cream shop. I wanted to get going onto whatever thrilling thing we would do.

"I thought we would go to the beach and tan. Tomorrow we have the island tour on the yacht. If we don't get some color, we'll burn."

"Oh."

I loved the ocean and the beach and all that, but I hated lying around "tanning". It was boring. I decided to get my metal detector and go treasure hunting, while Nancy lay in the sun.

It was my hobby, and once in awhile I would find something that could be characterized as treasure. Once I found a silver spoon. I was sure it was part of a place setting for the King and Queen of France. I didn't care if it said "Made in China".

There were a lot of trade ships between Europe and the Far East, so it was possible. Maybe not, but who uses silverware for a picnic on the beach?

The sun was beating down, but compared to the weather we left fourteen days ago, this was heaven. Most of the time walking I had my head looking at the sand. From time to time, I would look around on the beach or at the water. I stopped dead in my tracks. There it was. I couldn't believe my eyes. This thing was massive. The last time I saw it, it was half way around the world off the coast of Africa. I couldn't believe it was the same beast, although I didn't want to believe there was more than one. My heart was pounding, and a cold sweat broke out across my brow. I rubbed my eyes in disbelief. When I looked up it was gone. No one in the nearby area reacted like anything strange had just occurred.

People were swimming and playing volley ball, and I was shaking like a leaf. I sat down in the sand at the edge of the water. The waves were more than warm, they were hot. It was just as I remembered when I fell into the water when my parasail separated from the tow rope of the boat pulling me. I ran back to the blanket where my wife had fallen asleep. Oh, boy, she was lobster red and only on one side.

"Honey, you're not going to believe what I just saw. Here, let me put this on. You're baking and don't have enough oil."

"What did you see, that cute couple jogging nude?"

"No, not the cute couple, it was - - what cute couple, where?"

"You get so easily distracted, what did you see?"

"It's gone now, so I guess it doesn't matter."

"Would you mind getting me a drink? I'm thirsty."

The next day we were to go sailing. Nancy was so burned from the beach she decided to pass.

"You go ahead and have fun. I'm staying indoors, probably do some shopping."

"How am I supposed to have fun, knowing you're alone shopping with the credit card?"

"Ha, ha. But not very funny."

The ship didn't set sail for another hour, so we both went down for breakfast. I passed on the buffet and just ordered some grits and toast. While waiting, I pulled out from my treasure bag the cell phone. I decided to see if it worked. The chime went on as the menu screen opened.

The greeting said, "Hi! Jack."

"Look, the greeting is the same as my old phone. Remember you said it was corny. I wonder if this guy's wife thought the same thing. Well, gotta scoot. Put this stuff in the room will ya?"

I went down to the docks to catch the boat. It was a sixty-three foot ship, the largest in the area. Soon, we would be out to sea for a day of fishing, diving, and pure relaxation. At least that's what I thought.

Aboard the Nordic Prince

There were three islands that made up the resort. The private island that we were on was two miles long by a little less wide. The only thing there was the small hotel, beach front all around, two restaurants and a Texas hold em tournament hall. Fifty seats are all it held, and only high stakes players could enter.

The largest of the three islands had all the shopping, eateries, casinos and nightclubs. The only marina was also on the big island. You could get there by walking over a bridge that was connected to the private island or you could take a water bus. The only way to the third island was by boat. It was a half hour trip in a power boat, or an hour by sail, depending on the wind.

This island was mostly a nature preserve. There were pure white sand beaches and a tropical rain forest. If you went for the day you had to bring your own lunch. There were no food or beverage stands anywhere. Most of the naturalists liked the white sand and privacy. A patrol boat kept away curiosity seekers. They would confiscate all photographic equipment if they found any. This was a place the rich and famous could literally let it all hang out and not worry about seeing themselves the next day on the internet or the front page of the globe.

I rented a moped for the week, so I rode it to the harbor. The ship was black with gold trim and could be seen from almost anywhere on the two islands. It was enormous. The name on the back of the ship was "Foolish Pleasure." There was a sign below the name that read, "My other boat is the Queen Mary." I believed it too.

A British seaman stopped me as I approached the gangway.

"Good Morning, Sir. If you were scheduled for the Island tour today, we've been detained. Due to issues we are having with our electronic systems, particularly the GPS, we have put off travel until the morrow. We hope to have her up and running first thing in the Am. If you would still like to go for an outing today, there is a sail boat at the end of the pier that is taking all comers."

I looked in the direction of the seaman's finger and spotted the vessel he was referring to. It was one of the most unique ships I had ever seen in my life, and I'd seen a lot of watercrafts, but this was a beauty. I thought it to be a replica of a Viking ship. When I got on board, I learned that it was an original ship with modifications and a whole lot of restoration. The ship proudly proclaimed it to be the "NORDIC PRINCE." It was a handsome ship to be sure. I got caught up in its history and didn't realize we had set sail.

If we were to take the same tour, we would stop for a walk

through the rain forest and then, head out to sea for fishing snorkeling, diving and treasure hunting. It was all that I lived for on this vacation. My hope was to find a piece of gold or silver, something more valuable than the spoon I found three vacations ago.

It had just now occurred to me that this antique of a boat could float, unlike the other that had all the high tech stuff on it and was still tied to the dock. I was glad it was too. This was way more fun. I took on the persona of Jack Twitcher, Capt'n Jack Twitcher that is, aye mate and a bottle of rum.

I got permission to climb up to the crow's nest to get a look around. It was twenty one feet tall. The ocean was green-blue and clear. I could see schools of fish and a line of lobsters on the march. I was hoping we could catch dinner, there's nothing better out of the see than fresh lobster. As the waters got deeper, the color changed to dark blue and then almost black. This was where we would anchor to go coral diving and treasure hunting. I tied my nylon sack to my waist and jumped in the water. The water was icy, but refreshing.

One thing I learned about coral reefs was to never stick your hand in a hole. Moray eel like to hide in them waiting for a meal or a free "hand" out. I knew this like I knew my name, yet when seeing something sparkle from within the coral, while shining a light I forgot my safety lesson and reached right in. I was careful not to disturb the natural landscape while picking up the object. It was some sort of jeweled ornate looking thing-a-ma-bob. It didn't appear to be anything that I recognized, so it went into my sack and I moved on. My watch alarm went off, which meant it was time to return up top.

I was leisurely heading in the direction of the boat, when an explosion pushed me backwards. I almost lost my oxygen tank and had to hold on to my mask with both hands. The sound created a ringing sensation in my head.

I was dazed, and I didn't know which way was up. I stopped myself from drifting deeper. In a moment I regained my composure and saw light. Thinking it was the sun, I headed towards it. What I found when I got to the surface was a burning ship. There was debris all over. Floating near me was a box. I climbed on top and took off my mask and tanks.

There was carnage floating all around me. It didn't take long for the sharks and barracuda to find a bounty of blood and bodies. I started calling out to see if anyone else had survived. There was no response. It appeared that the boat had been blown out of the water by a missile or a torpedo.

The water started to warm up. When it got hot, the fish and sharks all retreated from the area. It was getting so hot that I hoped my box wouldn't burn, or I'd be boiled alive. I found a small piece of the ship that could be used as a paddle and started to maneuver away from the area. No more than a hundred yards in front of me, it appeared. The black beast from the beach two days ago was here. I could only pray it didn't see me. What the hell was this thing?

Panic in the Pacific

The shock of the situation was starting to take hold of my emotions. I was beginning to freak out and had nowhere to go or anyone to console me. I sat and screamed at the top of my lungs. It didn't help. Every time I saw a bobbing head or body part, I'd lean over the side of the box and throw up.

I was sickened by all that was around me. Paddling as fast as I could to get away only helped a little. It seemed like the sea was pushing the debris along towards me. The beast was still floating nearby. There was no movement from it. I wondered if it had been stunned by the blast, and that's why it surfaced. It was frightening to behold, yet I was curious to find out what it was. If it were a whale, there probably wasn't anything to fear, other than getting knocked over by its tail, of course. Then there's that issue of being swallowed, but, I had to get closer.

Evening was approaching. My wife was waiting at the hotel. We were supposed to go to dinner with some folks we became friends with on the beach. It was the couple that liked to jog in the nude. Don't ask me how my wife does it, but she'll talk to anyone. Frankly, I found it uncomfortable to look at them and engage in conversation. I made sure that we were going to dinner in a clothing required restaurant.

"Why, Jack, are you embarrassed of the human body?"

"No. I just don't need to eat with two people that obviously like to show off their stuff."

"Well, if I had her body, I'd be flashing it around the beach too. And if you had his, I wouldn't hide you in a cabana."

The thought now crossed my mind that she may start to worry about me. I think I should have been back two hours ago. I wished that I hadn't put my cell phone in the foot locker that they gave us. Even though it was sealed in a zip lock bag to stay dry, I couldn't bring it diving. So, I guess all I could do was wait for a rescue to find me. We were supposed to be only five miles out. It seemed to me that we were close enough to shore, someone would have seen the black cloud of smoke and the flames from the explosion.

Even a cruise ship should have seen something as they were passing. These waters were normally full of cruise liners as well as smaller craft. It amazed me that the area wasn't swarming with onlookers and the coast guard. As far as I could see, there was nothing around except me, the debris and the beast.

Back on the Island:

While my wife was getting ready for dinner, she heard the ring tone of a phone she didn't recognize. She looked around for the sound and found it was the cell phone that was in the sack of shells from the beach. It was muffled because it was still in the zip lock bag. When she took it out of the bag, it stopped ringing, but there was a message indicator flashing. Being the clever woman she was and curious too, she figured out how to retrieve the message.

"Nancy, we're under attack. I don't know what or who, but half the ship has been blown to pieces, and the other half won't be floating much longer. There were several flying crafts that were shooting rockets at us, we caught fire and, I gotta go, someone is getting out of a small boat and I think it's the enemy.

I'll call back when it's clear."

My wife took the phone to ask at the hotel and asked if they knew if anyone had reported losing a phone. They told her that no one had reported it to them, but that it could belong to a guest at one of the other hotels or fallen overboard from a passing cruise ship. The message was so disturbing that she went to the Coast Guard station to have them listen to it.

"How in the world would a stranger know my name, and leave a message on a lost phone? It must have been missing for more than a day or two before my husband found it on the beach. What's even creepier is that it sounds like his voice. But, that just can't be."

"Ma'am, it's obviously a prank or something. There have been no reports of any wrong doing out to sea, much less flying craft shooting at ships. Where is your husband now?"

"He went out on an Island tour aboard the Foolish Pleasure. The tour was only supposed to be four hours. When he got back we were going to dinner with the Johnston's from Rhode Island."

"Well now, that's a problem."

"How so officer, is that what people call you guys."

"Yes, I'm Chief Petty officer Patterson, and this is officer Reilly."

"My name is Nancy Twitcher, you were saying?"

"I was saying that the Foolish Pleasure had technical difficulties with their electronics and didn't leave port. That means your husband didn't go out on the tour. Has he ever gone off somewhere without telling you before?"

"What are you implying?"

"I'm not implying anything, just asking a question, that's all."

Nancy picked up the phone and cut the conversation short. She requested that they notify her if they heard of any strange events out in the open waters. They agreed and then started writing a report about the phone call. On her way to the restaurant the phone rang again. She was reluctant to answer it. It was in the bottom of her purse, so as before by the time she opened it to speak; the message was already in voice mail.

"Nancy, you're not going to believe me, that black beast isn't alive. It's an atomic submarine. The flying crafts landed on top of it and then went inside of a hatch. Two riders on Jet-Skis are out patrolling the area checking for survivors. I am hiding in a crate that I found floating in the water. It's full of supplies and canned food. Most of the people on board with me were either killed when the ship exploded or they were shot when they were discovered alive. I'm scared half out of my wits. You've got to send help, or. . ."

The phone went dead. Now more than before Nancy was in a panic and frightened. She wanted to go back to the Coast Guard station, but she knew they didn't believe her story. She went to meet with the Johnstons. She would tell them all about the calls and see if they could come up with a plan. Mr. Johnston, Ken was his first name said he had a friend that had a small private plane. They wouldn't be able to go out until morning because there was a tropical storm brewing and it would be too risky.

"Risky bullshit, my husband's out in the middle of the ocean under siege by some weirdo group of assassins and you're worried about a little rain"

"Calm down, if it is your husband by some strange coincidence, we'll find him."

"Don't tell me to calm down. What do you mean, by coincidence?"

"Well, how did your husband find his own phone two days ago on the beach and then start calling you from a wrecked ship? If he were on board, wouldn't he still have his phone? If he went overboard during the attack, it's not likely that he would have his phone or that it would work after getting wet. So . . ."

"I don't like what you're saying. You don't believe it either. Where should we meet in the morning?"

"The air strip is on the big island just passed the harbor, take the water taxi and we'll meet you at seven."

"Thank you. Good night."

One Sleepless Night for Two

Nancy went back to the hotel. She sat out on the patio staring at the ocean. It was quiet other than the sound of the waves crashing against the retaining wall of the pier. The moon had a cloudy haze, making the sea dark with haunting reflections of light from the passing boats that were coming in to dock for the night. Many were fishing, some snorkeling, while others were just enjoying a day in the sun. She started to feel guilty about not going on the boating trip, but then, who would save Jack? The phone rang while she was clutching to it tightly. It was the only thing she had of Jack, even if it was only his voice.

"Hello, hello. Can you hear me? Hello."

There was no answer from the caller. She looked at the screen and tried to re-dial the missed call. The screen was blank and the phone was turned off. It seemed strange. How did the phone ring, if it were off?

My only hope of survival was to hide in the floating debris of the boat and keep moving. These guys were on a mission to find something, and they weren't letting up the search for whatever it was. I was curious as to what could be so valuable that they would blow up a ship and kill more than thirty people? At the moment it didn't matter; I had to try and stay alive. When the last of the surveillance teams returned to the sub, it was time to get busy. If I were going to make an attempt to depart from the general area, I would have to camouflage myself. In the supply box that I was using for a raft, there were two roles of twine and one line of heavy rope. I gathered pieces of the ship and tied them around the box. This would give me an opportunity to paddle away and not stick out like a sore thumb. I found part of the mast with the ships flag. That would be my signal if any Coast Guard ship or plane would come in search for the Nordic Prince. After assembling my cover, sheer exhaustion took over, and I fell asleep.

Nancy had fallen asleep too. She awoke to the sound of the phone. This was really creepy. She opened the phone and the message light appeared. She pressed the button to retrieve the call.

"I can't talk long. These guys are well armed. They have more fire power than a military installment during war time. I'm afraid if someone comes looking for me, they'll be blown out of the water or shot out of the sky. I am hiding in a box with pieces of the ship covering me so I hope to float away undetected. They want something badly, and they will stop at nothing to get it."

"Jack, it's me. I'm coming in the morning to find you. Hold on, Jack, please, hold on."

Nancy was talking to herself. There was no one on the other end of the phone. It would ring and then turn off to save its own battery power, then when it was turned on, only a message would play. She tried to check the phone log, nothing was in it. No numbers to missed calls were listed. When she tried to re-dial the last number, the phone rang in her hands. Totally freaked out she dropped the phone and ran inside crying. The rest of the night was spent in a wicker chair rocking back and forth like a child.

I woke up to a knocking sound. The box was hitting up against something. I was hoping it was rocks along the island shore. I pushed the lid up with my head. I was careful to try to see without being seen. There was nothing but open water in front of me, to my right the view was the same, but to my left was a black metallic - - oh shit, I was hitting against the sub. A creaking sound was made when the hatch opened. Two or more of the subs crew were coming out. They started towards me and my pile of wreckage. I wanted to see my enemy, but I also wanted to live to tell about it. I closed the lid on the box.

"Esto oped dous not tome."

"Neyt. Dous esto de, fletsoun en sjink."

They were speaking no language I had ever heard before. It sounded German, but I knew a little, and it wasn't that. Maybe some Spanish, but I took that as a second language in college and it wasn't that either. The only thing I could make of it was that they were talking about the box and the debris floating against the ship. I had to hope they didn't have their flame throwers. If they did, I'd be cooked.

"Ken, I have to warn you and your pilot, I got another call last night. There's a submarine armed with all kinds of assault weapons including missiles that can take the plane down if we get to close."

"Thanks, Nancy. You don't have to worry about us; we'll fly high enough to stay out of their radar. Do you have your own phone?"

"Sure, why"

"If we see anything, I want to be able to let you know. And of course if you hear anything you can give us a call."

"That won't be necessary, I'm going too."

"I'm sure there's no way to talk you out of it, so let's get a move on. Here's a parachute, just in case."

"Thanks, Ken."

Ken's friend was a pilot. It appeared from the calls that the sub might be nuclear. If that were the case, it would explain some of the radio frequency disturbance on the island. He suggested that we head towards an area where the sound of the disturbance was coming from.

The jibber jabber stopped. I peeked out as they were walking back to the hatch and entered the sub. I felt the water stirring. The ship was starting to submerge. I was safe.

Somehow I had survived the night and the living hell of the day before. As it was going under, the water was heating up again. It went down a few feet then accelerated with such thrust it created a whirlpool effect. I was spinning and sinking all at the same time.

Thinking Outside the Box

The swirling trip to the oceans floor wasn't a long one. That meant the water wasn't very deep. The box was filling rapidly with water. I wasn't going to have much air, so I felt around the box for my scuba gear. One of the classes was on putting your tank and mask on with your eyes closed. It was to simulate being in the dark waters of the ocean, or if you were in a cave under water. The tank was light. There wasn't much air left in it. Once I got everything on I tried to push open the lid. It wasn't budging. Even though it was pitch black inside, I could feel around. I realized the box had flipped over. Something heavy was on top, probably the pieces of wreckage that I tied to the box for camouflage. Instead of hiding me to stay alive, it might be the cause of my death. My heart was racing. I needed to slow it down to save air. Crossing my legs, I sat on the bottom and began to meditate and pray. I calmed myself to the point; I could count the beats of my heart.

The pilot turned to Nancy and started his conversation with,

"I've got good news and bad news. Which would you like first?"

"Give me the bad news. I'll need good news after hearing it."

"The static that was causing the radio and electronics to go screwy is gone."

"Gee, that sounds like good news to me. We should be able to contact the shore patrol and Coast Guard."

"Normally, Nancy, I would agree, but I was using the static to track the sub. Now that it's gone, we have nothing to go by."

Nancy's mouth dropped in dismay. She couldn't hold back her tears any longer.

"Now what do we do?"

"If the sub is gone, we can fly a little closer to the water and get a better look around. We should be able to find the wreck by following the map of the tour that the ship would have been taking."

"Ken, look over to your left. What's that floating? Do you see it?"

"I don't quite know, Dan. See if you can get over that floating pile of debris."

They spotted a piece of the back of the ship. It had part of the name showing. It was definitely the Nordic Prince. Nancy was frantic and couldn't sit still.

"Can't you slow down so we can see if there are any survivors? We need to find Jack."

"Not if we don't want to become part of the wreck. I'll call the Coast Guard. They'll send a cruiser along with a chopper."

Nancy told them she needed to get in the water to search for me. Before they could stop her from parachuting out of the plane, she had the door open and jumped. After hitting the water, she got out from under the chute and swam to the piece of the ship they had seen from the air. She ripped off her top and pants without unbuttoning anything. Nancy was prepared to dive with her swim

67

suit already on under her clothes. She waved to the two guys in the plane and then dove under the water to take a look around.

She could hear something but wasn't sure what it was. It didn't matter. She had to go up for air. Climbing back on the back end of the ship to take a break, she looked for the plane with Ken and Dan. She wanted to signal that she was okay. It wasn't long before the appearance of a few aquatic visitors was noted. The area was still fresh with the scent of death, and the barracudas and sharks were moving in. That put an end to Nancy's diving and rescue attempt. Any minute she thought the Coast Guard would be coming. After all, it didn't take long for her and Ken to find the wreckage. Surely they had been given the coordinates to the area.

An hour passed, the smell of decay was making her sick. She was afraid to vomit, because that would attract the sharks. It didn't make any sense that no one was coming. From her pants pocket that was floating nearby she heard the phone ring. The sound was very faint. She had wrapped it tightly in plastic, but brought it along just for this reason. Jack might try to call.

"I'm at my last few ounces of air. There's one corner of my watery tomb that hasn't completely filled and I am using it as best I - - ulp, hic, - - can. I fear I will die here, Nancy, if you can hear me, I lov- - -"

"NO, you can't die, not now, not yet. YOU CAN'T DIE!"

The sound of a helicopter was nearing. She stood-up and started waving her arms. They hovered over head, and a couple of divers jumped into the water.

"Are you alright? Have you seen anything or anyone?"

"I'm fine. I believe my husband is in a storage box with the ship's mast tied to it. If you find the mast, you'll find him. Hurry, he's barely alive."

They looked at her as though she were crazy, but dived into the depths of the water anyway. A rope ladder was sent down to pull Nancy out of the water.

A Storm is Brewing

There was a disturbance in the water. The winds must have

been kicking up; the box was starting to move. I couldn't tell what was happening, but if there was a storm, that would impede any rescue attempts. I was hoping there was a rescue attempt. The water was starting to warm up. That could only mean one thing, the sub was returning. That would definitely be a problem, a big problem for anyone on the surface. I felt confident they wouldn't be looking for wreckage under water, so I wasn't worried about myself.

"Ma'am, we have to get back to the base before the gusting winds blow us into the water. We can't stay any longer. It looks like we're in for a tropical storm. When these things set in, it's no longer safe for us to be flying low."

"Can't we look for a just a few more minutes? I'm sure my husband's just below. They should be able to find him."

"I can't risk my crew, ma'am, we're pulling out now. The Coast Guard should be here any minute. They can handle the rough waters. I'll let them know the coordinates, and if your husband's down there, they'll get him. "

Once again, Nancy was listening to no one. Before they could close the cargo door of the helicopter, she jumped into the water.

"Crazy bitch, she must have a death wish or something. Let's get this thing outta here before we join her and we all die together.

The clouds were darker than ever and the winds were steadily picking up. Even the Coast Guard ship was having a hard time negotiating the waves. Nancy was clinging to a piece of the wreckage. She wanted to dive but was afraid the current would carry her past the area. She kept praying the divers from the Coast Guard would make it in time to save me.

My box was edging towards a precipice and was about to fall into a deep crater. The water temperature was creeping up towards being uncomfortable. The hotter the water temperature, the closer the sub was in proximity to me. I didn't know that Nancy was in the water and the sub was heading towards her. I only knew that my tank was almost out of air, and I couldn't escape with the weight of the ship's mast on top of me.

The sound of an air horn alerted Nancy, who was now sitting on top of a floating piece of ship's wreckage. She had crawled out of the water when she felt the temperature rising as well. She started waving and screaming for help when she saw the Coast Guard cutter heading right for her.

"Hold, on and we'll get a line to you."

One of the crewmen was yelling through a megaphone to Nancy.

"Thank God, you found me. If you have an extra tank, I can show you were the crate that has my husband in it is."

"I'm afraid we can't do that, ma'am. The seas are too rough. By now your husband could be one hundred yards away with the under tow carrying him. I suggest you join us up top and let the professionals do the diving."

That was the wrong thing to say to a frightened, upset woman, who had already risked her life twice. She dove deep into the waters, and the divers followed. Without the lights that the divers had, she couldn't see where she was going, but at least she knew they were with her. She stopped and signaled for air. One of the divers took off his mouth piece to share a couple gulps. She then pointed up. Nancy had done all she could. Now it was the Coast Guard's turn. When she surfaced she let them pull her into the boat.

"That was awfully brave of you lady."

The supply box titled and threw me against the side as we went over the cliff. I was on my side when I realized that the lid was free of debris and I could finally get out of my would-be coffin. I had to hope I wasn't too deep because I didn't want to drown getting the bends swimming to the top as fast as I could. The water in the crater was so cold I almost took a deep breath but contained my chilling shock for the surface. The water was changing rapidly from cold to hot. By the time I got to the surface I felt like I was on fire. I climbed aboard the first thing I found floating in the water.

"Welcome aboard."

A hand was stretched out to help me up. I detected a slight accent, but we were in the tropics, so it wasn't unusual for someone to have an accent, usually French, British, or Bahamian. Not having heard more than two words, the accent wasn't clear.

"Thanks, the water was getting hot, and I had to get out before par boiling."

"Yes, I know. That is the one thing we haven't quite figured out. We have to keep moving to stay cool."

I looked around. I wasn't on what I had hoped would be a rescue ship. I was standing on the upper deck of the sub. The very freaking sub, that for all this time I had been hiding from. I swam right up and on to it. This was to become an interesting conversation to say the least. The captain seemed like a nice guy, but I knew better. However, I wasn't going to let on. I told him I was part of the rescue team looking into a mysterious explosion of a wooden vessel called the Nordic Prince.

"You don't say. I haven't heard of that ship in these waters, and I know most of them. We've been in this part of the ocean for the better part of five years, so most of the water craft including the cruise lines are familiar. I don't recall any explosions either. We would have felt that for several miles under the water."

"Gee, I don't know what to say."

"Where's the ship that you were on when you made your dive, Mister? I didn't get your name."

"I didn't give one. And I must have been off course; my boat is just over there between your sub and the islands."

Another man came out of the sub and joined the captain. The two were speaking to each other in the odd language that I heard them speaking before. This wasn't going to be good. A third crewman came on deck and said something that sounded like he spotted a ship nearby.

Nancy's phone rang. This time was the same as every other time, only a message.

"Nancy, I was able to get out of the box when it drifted over an underwater cliff. If you get this message, call the Coast Guard and the Navy along with anyone else. The sub has returned and it is armed with nuclear weapons. They must evacuate the area at once or they will be attacked. They won't have the fire power that this thing has. I pray you aren't with them trying to rescue me. I only hope you'll be safe and I can figure a way out of this mess."

Nancy went to the Captain to tell him about her call. She was frantic. No one could understand why she didn't want to pursue finding her husband after all the heroics of just a few moments earlier. She was afraid to tell them she got a phone call from her husband on a phone that didn't seem to work most of the time. There appeared to be a lot of scurrying around and yelling this and that. One of the crewmen spotted the sub. It was heading full speed towards them. Panic was in all the crew's faces. They wouldn't be able to steer clear, no time to fire up the engines to turn about. Nancy looked over the rail at the black beast heading their way . . .

From Under the Water They Came

What I didn't know at the time, was two of the Coast Guard divers were still searching for me. The captain and his second in command started down the stairs in through the hatch of the sub. I was being directed at gun point to follow. When I got to the hand rail, I swung around kicking the sailor overboard.

I pushed hard on the hatch and then jumped in the water. I swam as fast and as far away as I could. I turned back while catching my breath. The sailor in the water was hanging onto the side of the sub for his life. The sub had a full head of steam and was heading in the direct path of an oncoming ship. I could see the colors and stripes. It was the Coast Guard cutter. They didn't appear to be moving or taking any evasive actions to get away.

The two divers had given up hope of finding me and started back to the surface. When they saw from below the two ships on collision course, they drifted back down to a safe distance near the ocean's floor. I witnessed the whole thing. The ship was about to be destroyed by the submarine ramming into it head on.

I closed my eyes on the impact and then had to go under to avoid getting hit by flying debris. If I never lived to see it again, this was twice in as many days that a ship was destroyed by the sub. The only difference was they weren't hit with missiles.

The submarine started to dive and go out to deeper waters. This was the opportunity for me to check for survivors and do whatever I could to help the victims keep from drowning.

A chopper was flying low overhead. It dropped a ladder to the water. One of the crewmen yelled out to me.

"Grab on, we'll pull you up."

I did so with joy and appreciation in my heart. When I got on board the air craft, huddled in a corner crying, was my wife Nancy.

She was wrapped in a blanket trying to dry and stay warm. I couldn't believe my eyes. When she looked up and saw me, she threw the blanket off and crawled over to give me a hug. I hadn't cleared the door yet. Together we almost went back in the water. One of the crewmen caught us and pulled us back to safety. They waited for the divers to return to the surface and pulled them up into the helicopter, then took off as fast as they could to get out of sight, if the submarine were to return.

When we got back to the island base, I was questioned about the sub, the Nordic Prince and anything else they could think of relating to the incident. Nancy was also questioned. We were separated, so they could see if our stories matched. They released us, but said to stay on the island for a few days in case they had more questions. We went back to the hotel. The whirlpool bath was just what we both needed. A glass of champagne to celebrate being alive and reunited, it was such an emotional moment, we both sat and cried in each other's arms.

"Nancy, how in the world did you find me?"

"I just followed the messages that you sent on the cell phone."

"What cell phone?"

"The one you found on the beach the first day here. Remember, it had your name in the welcome screen."

"Oh, yeah, that phone. I took out the battery to charge it because it kept turning off. I wanted to find out who owned it and return it to them. I'm still not sure how I told you where I was. I didn't have a phone."

We looked at each other and then towards the wall. Next to the TV was the battery charger with the battery from the phone still in it. Each of us grabbed our cheeks and screamed. To this day, I have no answers to what happened. I haven't gone anywhere near an open body of water, so I don't know what became of the sub. What's more, I don't care. I say a prayer every so often for the men and woman that died aboard the Nordic Prince. That day haunts me, and there are times I wake up in the middle of the night with cold sweats screaming. Nancy always reminds me that everything is alright, but it's not. It's not alright. It's been five years since I bottled away my secret of that day to my friends. It's been five years and nothing was ever printed about the demise of the Nordic Prince or the Coast Guard ship. I had to wonder why it was hushed and kept a secret.

I went down to the basement to look at my treasures that I had collected over the years. There was one thing that stood out among all the rest. It was a key-shaped object about eighteen inches long by five inches wide. It was ocean green with diamonds incrusted all throughout and it glowed in the dark.

THE END

Book 4

A Hole in the Earth

New Findings

My interest in caves started when I was between the age of eight and ten. Our family was on vacation. One stop during the week away from home was to a small cave in Bellevue, Ohio. The cave is called Seneca Caverns and is one of Ohio's treasures. It's the largest cavern in Ohio and goes to a depth of one hundred and ten feet stopping at an underground river. The water travels for miles and ends up at another tourist trap called Castalia's Blue Hole. The Blue Hole is surrounded by trout streams that are illegal to fish. It didn't make much sense as a kid, still doesn't.

The next cave was enormous in comparison. It's Kentucky's Mammoth Caves. It is said that the caves have been explored for more than four thousand years. I can't doubt the statement, but who's keeping track? These two caves got me into the world of Spelunking. A strange name for the exploration of caves, but it sounds cool when you tell someone what you do for a hobby, and they don't know what it is. Some people think you like doing something kinky, and you're open about it. Those people think cave diving is metaphoric for something else as well.

Today, I'm headed to the western plains. There are a few holes in the earth that are said to have been explored, but only to about one hundred and fifty feet. It's believed that some of these caverns may go far past two hundred feet, but nobody has dared digging their way past the posted signs. I was willing to go, and I got the permits to do so. Not just anyone can crawl into a national park cave and explore beyond the stated safety points. I had connections with the governor's office, so, well, here I go.

At four o'clock on Saturday afternoon I headed south, literally. The tours of the cave ended at five-thirty. There would be plenty of time for me to get to the end of the public trail. I would have to wait for the last patron to leave before I could enter the "forbidden" zone. At the end of the trail there was a sign hanging that simply stated, No Trespassing, Visitors are prohibited beyond this point.

The entrance to the next level had a rope hanging across it. That was the deterrent to keep people from further exploration and possible danger. According to sources the lower level of the caverns had not been entered for nearly one hundred years. The last known explorer never returned, and that's when they decided it was unsafe for the public to go any further than the posted sign.

When the last tour headed up, I took a gulp and ducked under the rope to start my descent into the underworld. I put on my head set and started to record my journey. In addition to the tape recorder, I had a helmet with a video camera. With both film and tape, I would have total documentation, which I hoped to sell to PBS or the National Geographic channel.

The first few feet were easily walked standing straight up. The moist ceiling from the humidity started to get lower to a point where I was crawling. The color, for the most part, was mossy, green and gray. The floor was solid rock and the ceiling was the same. I guess I was expecting dirt or clay for the base, and maybe the same for the top. I placed fluorescent markers along the way, just in case there were any turns; I wanted to come back the same way I came. The walls of the cave were starting to close in on me.

The path was so narrow I could no longer turn around. I would have to push backwards to retreat. But, that wasn't in the plans. A drop into a hole wasn't in the plans either, yet I was free falling with nothing to grab onto to stop myself. The temperature was changing as rapid as my fall. First it was cold, then it started to warm a little. I held on to my helmet and hoped the video was getting all of this. I knew the tape of my screaming would come out loud and clear.

There was no way of knowing how far I dropped before hitting bottom. I felt a sharp pain in my left foot. I must have twisted my ankle when I landed. The sound of water echoed all around me. I had fallen into the middle of a shallow underground stream. The warm water felt good against the cooler air of the cavern. I looked full circle to film my surroundings.

The vibrant colors and enormous stalagmites entranced and amazed me. I'd estimate them as several thousands of years old. I trudged closer to take some still pictures with a digital camera that I had in my back pack. Nothing seemed damaged during the fall. The formations were a veil of ice similar to a water fall. As I got away from the moving water, I could see another tunnel behind the veil. I carefully marked my trail, although I didn't know how I would get back up the hole that dropped me here.

Behind the veil, I saw a tropical paradise. Trees and shrubs grew everywhere and a sandy beach lined the water. I couldn't believe my eyes. Near the pool of water on the opposite shore from where I stood, I saw a wooden lounge chair with a small table next to it. This area of the cave would compare in size to a small ball park. I was in total awe of this place. The chair and table meant that I wasn't the first one here. I had to wonder if others remained. It wouldn't be long before I got my answer.

Life in Middle Earth

My mind was racing with the possibilities of a subterranean culture. The lounge chair fascinated me. I had to cross the lake to see if I could detect its age. With the temperature down here and humidity, wood could stay without rotting for hundreds of years. On the other hand if it were new, then someone had access to this underground paradise. Feeling something brush against my legs, I fell to the ground. It startled the living hell out of me. I only caught a glimpse of the tail as it rushed into the water, then disappeared.

Apparently there were reptiles or something aquatic in nature. What if I were to discover a new species? I'd get to name it and become famous for it. Exhaustion was setting in. I looked at my watch to see how long I had been down under. It was eight-thirty. I couldn't believe that three hours had passed. The hole must have been deeper than I thought. During the fall there was a definite lapse in cognitive time. What I didn't know was the reason I was so fatigued. I didn't realize that it was eight-thirty in the morning. My journey was almost fifteen hours deep into the Earth's core.

My leg was in full throb. I needed to sit and find something in my backpack to wrap my ankle. The lounge chair would be perfect. Directly across the lake would be a much shorter distance than walking around it. The only thing, I didn't account for its depth or what else besides the little lizard might dwell within. I started to wade in the water. When I was waist deep I began to float, taking the pressure off of my ankle. Occasionally I would touch bottom to check the depth.

Midway across I could feel a pulling effect on my legs. It was as though I had stepped in quicksand within the water. I noticed a whirlpool swirling around my body. Thrashing with my arms, I made every attempt to swim. It was no use. I was going under. My hope was that the camera equipment was still functioning to keep record of my demise, that is, should someone find it.

I could still see the surface from under the clear blue water. Something really strange was taking place. The water was so highly oxygenated that I could breathe while being completely submerged. I let myself sink to the bottom of the lake and then walked to the other side gradually coming to the surface and then to the shore. Now that was one wild experience to be sure.

When I got to the chair, all I could do was sit and stare back at the water. It occurred to me to check my equipment. I took off my backpack and started to assemble all my gear. While setting up a small camp, I started to rewind the recorder. It was digital so no tapes to get ruined by the water, and it was tightly sealed in a waterproof pouch. I was pretty sure that it would still work. What I wanted to see, more than anything, was the video.

When I looked down at my shoes, getting ready to remove them, I noticed a small trace of blood. My pants across the back had two fine slices near my calves on both legs. The only thing that came to mind was when the creature brushed against me. It must have had a razor-sharp tail that cut me. I was only guessing, but it seemed feasible.

Two bandages later along with downing the contents of a juice box, I was ready to start exploring again. A strange feeling of being watched started to become a concern.

The Eyes Have It

My ankle was still a little tender, but with the ace bandage nice and tight, it was manageable. I started to walk to the far side of the water in the opposite direction from where I had entered this area. I decided to name it the "Lost Lake." It seemed fitting. I couldn't tell how far it was to the end of the body of water. It was a lot larger than I had first suspected. It certainly wasn't a pond. It was definitely lake size. There were short trees and lots of foliage along both sides. I was afraid to venture into the brush, preferring to stay in the open where I could see my surroundings. I felt safe near the water. I still had the feeling of being watched.

When I sat down to tie my boot lace, I discovered why. In the bushes ahead of me, green glowing circular orbs blinked. They were the shape of cat's eyes. When they opened wide they were a florescent green. They would close and it would become dark, all but the light from my helmet and lantern. Each time I would turn slightly away, the eyes would open. I had to be fast to catch them open. I believe I counted up to ten eyes. I was hoping that it was five of something and not one creature with ten wild glowing eyes.

I turned out my lights and sat directly across from the bush. I got out my camera and turned off the flash so that I could take a picture and not scare my foundlings. I wanted to discover a new species of something, anything.

I didn't care what it was. The branches started to bend forward. It was coming out to get a better look at me. Apparently it too was curious. I sat perfectly still, barely breathing. I could see a shape starting to form, followed by two other shapes of the same size and dimension.

Something splashed in the water, and my visitors retreated back into the bush. For now my picture of the glowing eyed creature had been spoiled. I waited for a few minutes, but no blinking and nothing was coming out from hiding. It was time to move along and hope for another opportunity later.

Silly me, I wonder what was splashing around in the water, and why it scared the foundlings. A few feet ahead I came upon a rock formation. It went from several feet in the water into a dense wooded area. The top of the formation was covered with ice. It could be the melting ice that fed the body of water, or there might be another source flowing from above ground and down into the cavern. I started to walk into the water to get around the rocks.

The water rippled towards the rocks, and it wasn't caused by my entering the water. Something was under the surface and was circling nearby. Just as I was about to make the edge of the formation, I found myself on an escarpment almost falling head first into another body of water.

The fall would have taken me twenty or more feet below where I stood. I had caught my balance just long enough to be knocked into the water by the tale of a serpent. If this were Loch Ness, then I just found Nessie. No one believes that Cryptids still exist, and until a moment ago, neither did I. This monster of the lake must be what scared the foundlings. I climbed as high and as fast up the rocks as possible.

When I felt safe, I turned around to see if I could spot it. I got my camera ready, and it wasn't long before I got a shot of it. It came right up to the edge of the rock formation and looked me squarely in the eyes. A puff of steam from the cold air blew out of its nostrils. It was as close as I'd ever want to be to a living Pleciosaurs. I snapped a picture, forgetting to turn off the flash. The monster made a screeching sound that almost popped my ears. It dove into the water and was gone. I didn't waste any time climbing to the other side.

This side was quite different. It was jagged rocks, no sand, shrubs or other greenery. It was colder too. The water had a covering of ice. I wanted to turn back, but I didn't feel it was the best of my options, so I ventured forward.

Creepy Crawly Things that go Crunch

Standing on the edge of the precipice, my back was against the cave wall. It was cold and damp. I inched my way forward still thinking it would be safer to turn back, but my fear of the Lake Monster kept me moving away. There was a break in the ledge, and one foot slipped. I almost fell into the dark abyss, but somehow maintained my balance.

Now I was facing the end of the trail. I would have to make a short leap or take a slide down a rocky slope to another level. I guess the slide rather than a fall sounded better. I sat down on the slimy rock ledge and then gave myself a push.

I was sliding down so fast it was as though I had a rocket strapped to my back. My eyes were tearing from the speed and wind that was created during my dissent. When I hit bottom, the landing was soft. Somewhat surprised that I didn't hit rock, I looked down and pointed my flash light in the direction of my bottom.

I was in the middle of some kind of mushy, gooey, yucky smelly gunk. Geez, I have never had the displeasure of breathing in something so putrid and fowl that it made me want to vomit. This stuff was sickening. With every fiber of my being I tried to get up and get away from this horrible gunk.

Out of seemingly nowhere the gunk erupted, and I was catapulted across the cavern landing in the middle of the frozen lake. All I wanted to do was try to clean off the stench from my body and my clothes. I started to stomp on the ice to break through and get to some water. It worked. I made a hole big enough to dip my clothes in.

I stripped and dipped. When the clothes were fresh smelling again, I gathered my stuff and went to the opposite shore. I found a rock to sit on to get dressed. That feeling of being watched came over me once more. I peered around, and sure enough, the green eyes of the foundlings were behind me.

The glowing green of their eyes was intriguing more than spooky, yet they weren't making themselves visible, and that creeped me out a little. What the heck were these creatures that had no visible form with glowing eyes? They all blinked in succession and then one at a time. The blinking started to take on a rhythm almost like Morse code.

I glanced to the other side of the water. The same thing was happening with another set of eyes. Now I was getting nervous. This was definitely a form of communication.

When I tried to get up to move, the ice cracked in the water in front of me. The Plesiosaurs was back. Fortunately he was facing the wrong way. Clothes on or not, I made a run for a tunnel to make my getaway.

The safety of my hiding place was not to last. Something deeper in the tunnel had a sinus problem and was breathing heavy. The deep breath followed by a whistle through the nasal canal made me want to laugh out loud. I covered my mouth while looking outside.

The Plesiosaurs was gone again. I carefully and ever so slowly stepped towards the water and out of the tunnel. Making my way further into the cavern, the lake ended, and it was nothing but sedimentary rocks to walk on. I was relieved thinking that the Monster of the Lake was behind me and all I'd have to deal with was finding a way out.

There was an odd crunching sound as I walked. It wasn't quite like egg shells. It was a harder material with a distinct crack and then squish.

The sound was distracting my attention from trying to make an exit from this level of the cavern. I shined my light towards my feet to see what I was walking on. The jagged edge of the surface of rocks, or what I thought were rocks, appeared to be more like scallops. In the center of each open shell was a brilliant red colored material. I was guessing it to be a sea scallop, but why wouldn't they be under water instead of out in the open? A thought occurred to me. What if this was low tide? If it were, then high tide would be following. I just didn't know when.

Both Water and Anxiety Are Rising

My mind was starting to play ticks on me. I was beginning to believe that whatever I thought would come to fruition. First I felt like I was being watched, then the discovery of the glowing green eyes. Next I wondered if the lake contained any creatures to be concerned about when crossing and the Plesiosaur appeared. Now I'm wondering how much time I had before high tide came. It wasn't a moment later that I was standing in water ankle deep. The sound of flowing water was getting louder. The lake above was spilling over the side of the cliff and filling the frozen body of water which was expanding into the area which I was in.

At the rate the water was rising, I'd be in over my head in less than ten minutes. Along with the water, the lake monster would be back. I desperately needed a way up to higher ground. The sides of the cavern were almost straight up, jagged and moss covered. They weren't going to be an easy climb. In fact, they couldn't be navigated even if I had the proper climbing gear.

Moving farther into the cavern I had hopes of finding an uninhabited tunnel as my way out. The water was now up to my waist. It was freezing as it combined with the frozen pond.

I could barely feel my legs as I walked. My toes felt as though they would fall off if I didn't warm up soon. The spotlight on my helmet was growing dim. All my spare batteries were in my backpack, which was still by the lounge chair about two levels up and a long way in the wrong direction. Although, maybe it wasn't the wrong way, I needed to go back to the tropical paradise, get warm and get out. I changed my course and tried to return to the first level. I thought if I could swim or just float maybe I could get back.

That wasn't going to happen or at least not easily. A tall fin sticking out of the water was on its way towards me. This wasn't what I had hoped for. It wasn't even a thought, so I didn't know what to make of it. The lake monster didn't have a fin. This was something new. The fin was followed by two more fins. These shark-like creatures were circling around me and with each pass they got closer. I felt one brush against my legs, and I screamed. They swam away for a minute. Apparently they were frightened by the strange sound of a loud shrill voice. They were heading back. I knew instinctively they would figure out that the sound wasn't harmful. I had to find another way to scare them off.

The green eyes were everywhere watching the event unfold before them. A lot of blinking was going on, and then the sound of heavy breathing with a nasal whistle came into the scene. A large dark shadowy figure walked boldly into the water. As my light got weaker I could see it thrashing about in the water by the sharks. The next thing I saw was the beast holding one of the fish over his head, and then he let it drop. In one gulp he swallowed it whole and then started the process over again.

This wasn't how I expected to get out of my predicament, but it was fine by me. I walked passed as the fishing expedition continued, totally unnoticed. When the beast finished his dinner he returned to the tunnel. If I didn't know better, I'd swear he was a relative of the Sasquatch from the mountain regions of the northwest. Well, I lived through another creature of the deep and still I wasn't out of the water or to my destination. However, I was near the stinky grotesque goop thing. Accidently I slipped and ended back in the middle of it.

This time I wasn't able to contain myself. The moment I puked, it erupted catapulting me up to the higher level. It was a stinky escape, but I was happy to be back with only the frozen veil to find. I'd be back in the underground paradise.

Inside Paradise Caverns

The frozen veil, or actually the frozen water fall, was at the far end of the lake in the mid section of the cave. I was somewhat familiar with the surroundings, having been here just hours earlier. I found a rock to sit on. I needed a rest after all the running and hiding. It started to occur to me that going back was not the way out. I had gotten back to where I was after falling in the hole. I wasn't going to be able to get out the same way. I listened to the water.

It was soothing and making me drowsy. As I started to doze off, I felt my body being lifted off the ground. I thought I was in a dream state levitating just a few inches in the air and moving along the shore line. I opened my eyes fully to realize I was being taken somewhere by the foundlings. There were ten of them carrying me. It was a very uniform cadence that they marched. All together they turned and headed towards the bushes leading into a dense forest area.

I should have been frightened, but they were very gentle creatures and handling me with the utmost care. I felt safe with them, and I really didn't have a good reason to do so. For all I knew they could have been taking me to their leader to eat me for dinner. I kept still and watched more of the foundlings come out of hiding. There were some in front of the processional and a few behind, along with others walking on either side. I wished I knew what these things were. I also wanted badly to get a picture. All at once and rather abruptly they stopped. There was a moment of silence followed by a lot of blinking of their glowing eyes, and then I was dropped to the ground. They scampered into the woods and disappeared. Now, I was afraid. I didn't know what scared them off, but I thought I'd better take cover and hide too.

Good thing there were all sorts of trees and bushes. A flame of fire shot out from behind me, singeing the bark of the tree where I was hiding. My attempt to take cover was on the wrong side of the tree. The fire breathing monster was close enough to roast me, if it had better aim. Another blast of fire hit the tree causing it to burst into flames. I ran as fast as I could back to the water.

Thunderous footsteps followed me. One more snort of the monster's fiery breath and I could feel my shirt burning on my back. I pulled it off and threw it to the ground. The water was only another few yards. This time instead of flames the beast was close enough to take a bite.

With his head lowered to the ground, he snapped at my butt, clenching my jeans with his teeth. They ripped through the fabric and settled deep into my flesh. He lifted me high over his head and started shaking me.

I was getting dizzy and sick to my stomach when he tossed me sailing into the water. I let myself sink to the bottom. The salty water was stinging, but at the same time felt good. I rose to the surface slowly trying to get an eye on my enemy. There wasn't a trace of him anywhere. The green glow of the eyes from the foundlings started to reappear. I felt it was safe to return to the shore once more. It was time to make a decision to go back or go forward.

Foundlings, Friend or Foe

The foundlings were as curious about me as I was about them. I slowly waded towards the shore, trying not to frighten them. Their glowing green eyes started blinking. It was a silent form of communication. I was finally close enough to get a good look at my shy little friends. They were no bigger than a koala bear with no discernible hair or fur. They had the hide of a reptile, kind of greenish-gray color and were able to stand erect or run on all four legs. Their ears were kind of long and floppy but would perk up at the slightest sound.

I almost started laughing out loud when the ears would go up and down and the eyes were blinking in constant rhythm. It was quite a sight to behold. When I was to the shore, I lay straight out to stay about head height. I thought a position of submission would show them I meant them no harm. They shied away from the water, but gathered as close as they could to examine their new found creature. (Me)

The entire shore-line was filling up. As far as I could see, the area was covered to capacity with foundlings.

I looked behind me, and the foundlings were on the opposite shore as well. With all the blinking going on the cave was aglow. It was just like a stadium concert with everybody's cell phone on to light the place up. There wasn't an apparent leader of the pack, but there was an order of assembly. The larger ones were standing towards the front protecting the smaller, possibly the younger ones. When I had crawled almost all the way out of the water, one by one the largest to the smallest lined all around me.

They had a flattened nose that was a flap of skin with one hole on the end. As they came sniffing, the snout stiffened. This process of smelling me was reminiscent of a dog acquainting itself with another dog or stranger. The noise was building into a crescendo of wind and wheezing. I couldn't help it. I laughed so hard and loud, the closest foundling fell over, while the rest scrambled into the forest to hide. It was over.

They were gone in an instant. I got up and found all my belongings packed neatly into my back pack. It wasn't how I had left things, but after a quick examination, it appeared everything was there. Now I had to figure a way out. I sat on the lounge chair, lay back and took a long, well deserved nap.

An Unexplained Occurrence

I felt more rested than I ever had before. Sitting up, I thought about the whole reason I had crossed the lake in the first place. It was to examine this chair and see if I could tell how long it had been down here.

The first thing I found out was it was plastic wood, which is why it hadn't rotted from the humidity. I flipped the chair over. The factory tag was still attached. Manufactured in May 2011, that didn't seem possible. I left for my exploration of the cave in May of 2007. That would mean I've been down here for over four years. It seemed to me that it was only two maybe three days at best, although it would explain my beard growing down to my chest and my hair touching my shoulders. I gathered everything and stuffed it all in my backpack.

I followed the water's edge until I reached the area that I had fallen from into the water. Looking up, I could see a faint light and the luminescent paint marks that I used to lead me back the way I came. I waded into the water directly below the hole in the ceiling of the cavern. The water started to gurgle and bubble all around me. I had a sensation of rising. When I looked down, the floor of the cave was twenty feet below me. I was being pushed up by some force and was heading to the top of the hole. When I got to the floor of the cave level where I had fallen, the water started to recede. I grabbed for the side and pulled myself up before falling again into the lake below.

It was a slow crawl out, but eventually I was able to stand and walk again. I got to the area where the restricted sign was. The sign had fallen and was lying on the ground. When I got to the surface, everything was closed. I don't mean just for the weekend, the souvenir shop was boarded up, and the ticket booth was falling apart. There was nothing but dust, dirt and debris with a few tumbleweeds in the parking lot.

I was surprised to see my Jeep was still there. It had several inches of dust on it. As I approached my car, I dropped my bag and started looking for my keys. A few vultures flew over head. They looked hungry.

I got into the Jeep and thought to myself, "What are the chances this thing will start?" I turned the key and the lights came on. The engine cranked slowly, but fired up. I guess that's why they call them Die Hard batteries. The date on the radio panel said 5/18/2019. I left on May 15, 2007. The only thing I was right about was the three days. I couldn't believe I had been down in the cave and lower levels of the cavern for twelve years.

I cleaned the windshield of my car and started heading for what I hoped would be home. The gates of the park had been knocked over. The black top highway was nothing but rubble. There were no land marks, no trees no grass. I was in total desolation. What in the world happened while exploring? I stopped my Jeep. I was a heartbeat away from sobbing. Apparently the Mayans were right about 2012. It was quite possible that I was the only surviving human.

The End (or not)

What in the World Happened?

I woke up. I was soaking wet, in a cold sweat. I was trembling with fear. Sitting up I looked around. I was still in the cavern on the lounge chair where I had fallen asleep.

My dream of the world as I had known it was so real, that it had me terrified. I stared into the water for a short spell. While calming myself, I remembered the reason I had crossed the lake in the first place. I came to examine the chair. It was a poplar wood with a white stain. With the constant temperature of the cave, the chair was in remarkably good shape. I flipped it over to see if there were any manufacturer's marks on it.

A silver plate had the name of the company on it.

Bench Craft since 1909
California Leisure
Mfg. date 1963

Wow, forty-four years old and it looked brand new. I wondered how it got down here, but my concern was how I was going to get back up to the ground level on earth. This hole in the ground was starting to grow tiresome. I just wanted to get out and go home.

With a new goal and a song in my heart, I whistled while I walked to the end of the lake where I had first arrived by falling through a hole in the upper level. I was looking at the ceiling. The hole was nowhere to be found. I knew it was some place near the far end of the cavern and just above the water, because when I landed, it was in the water. I started to wade across while still looking up. When I got more than mid-way, I spotted a glow in the ceiling. It was my florescent paint that I used to mark my way. From the left side looking up I could see the hole. It wasn't visible from the other side. Now, how in the world am I going to jump fifty feet in the air and then grab on to the floor of the upper level?

The water started to gurgle and bubble all around me. I had a sensation of rising. When I looked down, the floor of the cave was twenty feet below me. I was being pushed upward and was heading to the top of the hole. When I got to the floor of the cave level where I had fallen, the water started to recede. I grabbed for the side and pulled myself up before falling again into the lake below.

It was a slow crawl back. I followed my paint marks and eventually I was able to stand. In the distance ahead I could hear talking. If I were right, it was Tuesday, or maybe Wednesday. That would mean there was a cave tour. Marching straight ahead, when I came to the no trespass sign, I ducked under the yellow tape and got in line. I followed the last person of the tour as though I had been with the group all along. When the guide brought us safely to the top, before entering the souvenir shop, I stopped and kissed the ground. I ran to my Jeep and turned on the radio,

"It's sun, sun, sunny today with a high of 104. Tomorrow. . ."

I shut it off. No news of the end of the world. In fact, the date and clock were three days and seven hours after I had left. It was May 18, 2007. I think this is a day I shall always remember. Now I need to prepare my notes and develop some pictures and get them in the mail to the National Geographic Society. I started down the road when my backpack fell off the front seat. Something was rolling around inside of it, trying to get out. Pulling over to the side of the road, I grabbed the sack and opened it. Without a peep, a baby foundling jumped into my lap.

I guess if the pictures don't turn out, this little fellow is all the evidence I need to validate my journey to middle earth.

THE END

Book 5

No Justice

Young Jack Twitcher writes an autobiographical story of his teenage years.

I hated my parents. I hated this hick town we moved to. I hated this house with the barn in the backyard. Why don't they just call it a tool shed? That's what it is. A barn has horses, cows, pigs and chickens. The tool shed has the riding lawn mower, snow blower,
(yelling)
"AND TOOLS, it has tools, not farm animals, IT'S NOT A BARN!"

I was angry and I hated the school I was attending. Three months into my JR. year of High School, and my dad, whom I no longer talk to, uprooted the family and we moved to Hicksville, USA.

All my life we had lived in Oakland, New Jersey. Dad made good money, and I guess you could say we lacked for nothing.

The Company wanted to open a Midwest manufacturing facility. They offered my father a management position and a substantial raise. Before the next beat of his heart, he was shaking hands accepting the job. I hated him for that.

At the new school I was a nobody. I wasn't special, I wasn't cool. I was the "New Kid."

No one even knew my name. In Oakland, my name was my claim to fame. I was the captain on the basketball team. I was the leading scorer from the outside and virtually unstoppable when charging the net.

I was King of the Home Coming Court and never had less than two girlfriends at one time. I had my main squeeze and an alternate.

Number two was always trying to be number one. The competition was good for me, especially on a Saturday night at the drive-in movies. Everyone from sophomore to senior knew my reputation on the b-ball court and with the ladies. Even in my own mind, I was the "Shit."

In the new school, Burhill High, get that, even the school has a hick name, I wasn't even on the basketball team. The coach said it was mid-season and there was no room on the roster. I asked her, that's right, a woman coach. I said, "Do you know who I am?"

She said, "No."

I was going to try out for the swim team next month until I found out "She" coached swimming too. They say your first impression is a lasting impression. Believe me; she wasn't going to forget our first meeting. I hated her too.

The icing on the cake came on my 16th birthday. I was to get my Mom's car. She was going to get a new one. My hand-me down first car was to be a brilliant black metallic two door Lexus coupe. I used to wet myself just dreaming about driving it. When we moved, my parents sold the car. Dad was getting a company car; Mom was taking his. There was no need for two cars anymore.

My father drove a Chevy, a tan four door sedan, which I may or may not share with my mom. I hated her for giving up "my car." And I hated my father for driving a Geek Mobile. Everything I ever loved I had to leave behind. The thing that hurt the most was kissing Rosie good-bye. Mom said it was puppy love and those things never last.

My older sister made it out. She was lucky. She was nineteen and got a job, then found an apartment. I offered to work part time after school to help her with the expenses. She said, Jeff was moving in and she didn't need my support. I hated her now too, but not as much. I knew that I would just be in the way, and if they wanted to run around naked, I would have to stay away.

Besides Mom and Dad said, "NO!" and that was the end of the conversation. My little sister wanted a pony; she was just gullible enough to think we could keep one in the tool shed. What a Goof.

Burhill, Iowa, not my idea of any place on earth that I wanted to live, and I sure as hell didn't want to die here either. I told my parents at one minute after midnight on my eighteenth birthday that I would be moving out. They could save the money for a cake. I wouldn't be around to eat it. I hated this place. The only teen hang-out within fifty miles was the Burhill Burger and Suds.

They still had drive-in service with the big fat microphones like you'd see in the movies, the real old movies. The place was a shining example of a greasy spoon. If you ate inside you would need a bath afterwards. I figured that's where the suds came in. At first I didn't know that meant soda pop. I hated the name soda pop instead of Coke.

The California Connection

My birthday was June fourth. In Oakland, most years that would be around the last day of school. To celebrate both events, the family would pack up and go to Ocean City for the weekend. That would be the start of summer vacation. I looked forward to it ever year. This year school was to be extended through the tenth because of "Snow Days." I hated the fact that the school year was going long, and I hated the weather that caused it to do so.

I asked my mother if we would be going to Ocean City this year when school let out. She gave me a look that chilled my spine then said, "I hardly think so."

I hated the look and the response. Somehow I made it through the school year with no basketball, no swim meets, and I didn't even try out for baseball. My life had gone from the pinnacle of success to licking the slime off the belly of worms. In plain English, my life SUCKED and I hated it.

It was at this point in my life that I think my mother wished she had just two kids instead of three. I was pretty sure of the two, one of them wasn't me. If my parents weren't so deeply religious, abortion may have been an option, but even in Hicksville at age sixteen it would be considered murder. As much as my parents were not thrilled with my attitude towards my current life's existence, neither was capable of murder. Besides, it was their fault.

The buzz around the school was that the fair was coming for ten days in July. Did I say Fair? I meant to say "The Big Fair." Big whoop, a stupid Hicksville fair, nothing but greasy fries, cow chunks roasted on a stick and the fresh smell of droppings from the equine. Gee, I can hardly wait. Half of the class was in the 4-H club. They would be sheep shearing and showing off their skill raising rabbits. What a talent that is, I mean, the rabbits don't need a lot of coaxing to reproduce. Anyone with half a brain can feed, water and clean a cage. The other half, or as I called them, the "Smart" ones, were going to work the carny and food stands to earn pin money. I didn't even know what "Pin" money was.

I've always gotten an allowance. Twenty bucks a week. Three fifty for a fine nutritious hearty school cafeteria lunch and I got to keep the change. By the end of the week I had enough left over to buy a pack of smokes. At night I would take a break from the world and practice blowing smoke rings. It was peaceful behind the tool barn. I found an old wooden folding chair that had been left in the barn by a previous owner. It wasn't comfortable, but it beat sitting on the ground. After my blood pressure dropped a few degrees, I'd head back to the house. I would rub fresh grass on my clothes to disguise the odor along with a tester cologne spray and mints. In spite of everything, my momma didn't raise no fool.

"Oh, My God, I'm starting to talk like a hick."

The only shining light in my life was Sylvania. She was a California transplant. If we compared notes, I think she hated living in Burhill more than I did, and I didn't think that was possible. Sylvania was very vocal. In just one week she was on a first name basis with the school principal.

I likened him to a headmaster at a witch and warlock seminary.

He was old enough to have taught school when Lincoln wasn't the face on a penny.

Sylvania liked to be called Sky. I understood why too. Who wanted to have the name of a light bulb? From the moment our eyes met, we were connected. She had a kickass attitude and took no shit from anyone. Just knowing she could beat me with her California karate was cause for fear and excitement at the same time.

The last Saturday before the end of school we were going white water rafting with some of the kids that weren't as dorky as the rest. I planned in my mind how I would flip the raft and then show off my swimming prowess by saving Sylvania. She would be so thankful I'd be able to make a move and get away with it, without worrying about getting kicked.

Graduation Day

It was Friday, the day before our white water adventure. All day the only thing I could think about was how I would save Sky and be a hero. Finally I would be a "somebody" again. It would be my first step to rebuilding my reputation. The only thing I hadn't given much thought to, were the rapids themselves. I had done a little body surfing while on vacation in Ocean City. At swim meets I could do the 100 meter free style as smooth as a dolphin, but I never considered the speed of the water and the undertow. I hadn't thought about the possibility of hitting the rocks below. As these things flashed in my mind; the prospects of disaster loomed as large as success.

I reassured myself, saying, "Hey, I can swim and that's all that matters, right? Sure that's right, that's all that matters and I get the girl in the end."

Twelve fifteen rolled around, and it was time for lunch. With the nice weather a lot of the kids ate their lunches outside. I was surprised the school was so liberal, although they did take a head count of how many went out and how many came back. There was also a security guard; I think it was to protect us from a rogue Guernsey that might stampede the playground or something. There sure was no threat of an actual crime going to happen around this place.

I spotted Sky sitting on contemplation rock. It was the focal point of the court yard in front of the school. As I approached, I noticed something very different about her. She was sullen, and I could tell one wrong word, and I would find myself standing in a puddle of tears. She was a heartbeat from breaking down. This was the first time I saw her with any emotion other than anger. She was acting like a . . . a girl.

"Sup, Sky? How's things? Ya ready for the big day?

"Big day? Oh, yeah, sure."

"You don't sound too excited about the trip. I can hardly wait."

"Trip, what the hell are you talking about?"

Apparently Sky was talking about something totally different in the way of big days.

"Well, we're supposed to be going rafting tomorrow, remember?"

"I'm not going."

"Why?"

"You wouldn't understand."

"Try me."

"Okay, but if you breathe a word of this to anyone, it'll be your last."

"You don't have to worry. You're the only person I talk to."

"When my family moved here a few months ago they sat down with the principal to discuss my options for graduation. I didn't have a high enough GPA for the standards testing here, so they agreed to hold me back. Since I'm only seventeen, I wouldn't be that old when I graduate. They didn't even ask if I cared. All my friends back home are graduating tomorrow, and I won't be unless. . ."

"Unless what?"

"Unless I pass the stupid math test this afternoon; all the kids think I've been spending time with the principal being punished. The truth is he's been helping me graduate this year instead of next. And my detentions have all been for extra credits."

"Gee, I never knew. I thought you were just some tough chick that was always getting in trouble for speaking your mind."

"I know. On my first meeting with the dude I threatened to kick his wooden teeth into the back of his skull. I think he liked me for my enthusiasm towards my goal."

For the first time during the conversation a smile and half a laugh came over Sky's face. Now I just had to figure out how to help her with her test.

"What time's the test?"

"One thirty. Why?"

"I have a plan. How close are you to the window?"

"I sit right by it. I made it clear to everyone I had to sit near a window to see the sun to remind me of California. Some fat pork butt thought he'd get a date by giving up his seat."

"Alright, whatever, the point is, I've already taken the test this year. I aced it, so if you can get it out the window, I'll fill in enough for you to get a C. That way they won't suspect anything."

"Wow, if we pull this off, I'll owe you big time. But, ah, maybe just a D+, I ain't a C student. I just want to graduate and get the hell out of this place."

"You got it, a D+."

We left with the plan ready to be executed. All I had to do was feign an illness during English and slip out the back door of the school, take the test and then slide back in. Sounded simple except for the hall monitor, she didn't like me, and I would have to bribe her to get outside.

"Hi ya, sweet cheeks."

I tried to use as much believable charm as I could. This chick was a rock and not a real pretty one either.

"What do you want?"

Oh, boy. This was going about the way I expected, and time was running short.

"Well, I- I thought maybe if you aren't doing anything tomorrow you'd like to go rafting with me and some of the gang. My date canceled, and I thought maybe. . ."

Before I could finish my sentence she was answering.

"I'll go, but you better not try any funny stuff in the car."

"Oh, great, no funny stuff I promise."

Instead of heading back to class I went the other way to get outside. She was so excited about the invitation that she never paid attention to which way I went.

Sky was breathing heavy and sweating like the proverbial pig by the window. When she saw me coming, I saw a sigh of relief.

"We've only got ten minutes. Where've you been?"

"Long story, give me the papers and don't worry. Ten minutes is more than enough time for a D."

"I need a D+, you ninny!

"Yeah, whatever."

I finished the test with about a half minute to spare and then ran back to class. I was totally confident Sky was going to pass, even if it was by the patch on her britches. When the bell rang for the end of school, I searched all over for her so she could give me the news.

Sky was nowhere to be found. I even poked my head into the principals' office, but she wasn't there either. I went home on the bus hoping she would call to let me know what happened. The phone never rang. At midnight, I fell asleep with my cell phone next to my pillow. I had a nightmare that Mildred, my substitute date, put the moves on me, and the whole class laughed me out of town.

We were to be in the school yard by seven. My mom had to drive me because I wouldn't be able to get my license for another week, since school wasn't over. My birthday was Thursday, and we went to the Burhill Burger and Suds. Whoopee. Mom made me a tray of brownies. She knows I love her brownies. I got a new cell phone and some cash, so it wasn't a total waste of a night.

At the school Saturday some of the kids were already there getting gear loaded into a suburban that Kendal (the cool dude) borrowed from his old man. As I got out of the car, my mother said; "Be safe, I love you."

"I'd like to say I love you too, but you know that would be lying."

I closed the car door without looking back. What a mean thing to say. I wanted to turn around and apologize, but I heard the sound of the car leaving. I better say something as soon as I get back. I've been mad, I've been angry, but I never considered myself to be mean, that was as rotten as anything. I heard my name called from behind. I turned around to see Mildred heading my way.

"I didn't think you were going to show. I was ready to slug you on Monday. But, here you are. Shall we load your stuff?"

With one hand she picked up my backpack, and with the other she wrapped her arm around mine and dragged me to the van. She was a strong gal, and I wasn't in the mood to argue. Everything was loaded and all six of us were in the van when a car came into the lot and blocked the exit.

"Hey, shithead Twitcher, get your scraggly ass out here."

I thought who the hell could that be? I got out of the van. The door of the car opened and a voice yelled.

"Get in, Twitcher. I've got a score to settle with you."

Everyone in the van was watching. I approached the car slowly and looked in . . .

A Surprise Visit

Let me back up for a second. A black Cadillac with smoked glass windows pulls up and someone calls me out and starts yelling obscenities. What in the world was I thinking by walking over to the car? I thought for a moment it could be an enemy, but I hadn't made any. For that matter, I hadn't made very many friends either. For all I knew it could have been a hit man hired by my parents to do the nasty deed. After all, this kind of car certainly wasn't from any neighborhood around here. I looked into the front seat. Behind the wheel was a familiar face.

"JD, what the hell are you doing here?"

I couldn't belie e my eyes. It was my best friend from Oakland that I grew up with. In the back seat were Sticks, and Bird, two of my other teammates and friends.

Sticks, was Al Corry's nickname. He was six-two and about one hundred and fifty pounds. That pretty much says it all. Bird was Jimmy Kern. He literally could fly. He was the fastest base runner on the baseball team, and he could out run anyone on the court with a rebound, so we called him Bird. JD was the leader of the pack, "Get in and shut the door. We're going to be late."

I did as I was told. JD hit the gas, and we left the parking lot in a cloud of dust with the wheels spinning and throwing cinders all over. I was so thrilled to see the guys, I asked, "So, what are you guys doing here? Did you drive all the way or what?"

Bird leaned over the front seat.

"We flew in last night and your mom put us up in the hotel downtown. That burger joint sure makes a great shake, and the fries ain't half bad either."

"Whoa, wait a minute, my mother?"

"Yeah, your mom called my mom and made all the arrangements. What do we do the first weekend after school every year? Our families all go to the cottages in Ocean City, right?"

"Yeah, right, so what are you saying?"

"I'm saying your mother is sending us to Ocean City first class. she thought she would surprise you for your birthday. Somehow she even got you out of the last week of school. If you weren't such a genius, the principal probably wouldn't have gone along with it. You sure have the best mother in the world."

Bird added, "I'll trade ya my mom for your mom any day, man."

They all concluded I was the luckiest kid on earth. And I would have felt that way too, but all I could feel was guilt for the way I had left my mother in the parking lot a short while ago.

I made up my mind to call her as soon as we got to the airport and I had a moment alone. I needed to apologize, big time. When we arrived at the airport, we got in line for the check in. My mom had packed a bag for me for a full week's stay. Of course being at the beach didn't require a lot of clothes.

I told the guys I needed to use the restroom, but I just wanted to get away for a minute to call home. The phone rang and my sister answered,

"Hello, oh you, what'd ya say to Mom? She's been in her room crying ever since she got back."

"I need to talk to her. Get her on the phone will ya?"

"Are you going to make her cry some more?"

"Look, I don't have much time, just please get her, please."

My sister proceeded to yell up the stairs.

"Mom, phone, someone you don't want to talk to ever again as long as you both shall live."

My mother answered the phone.

"Hello."

"Mom, you don't have to say anything. I'm sorry for the way I've been acting since we moved, and I am really sorry for the mean things I said. I can't believe you are sending the four of us guys on vacation. Thanks, I'll wash your car every week and mow the lawn without complaining. I love you."

There was silence on the other end of the line. My mother didn't say a word. She just hung up the phone. Now I really felt like a creep.

"JD, I need you to drive me home. If you miss the flight, I'll pay to get you a ticket for a later flight. I'll see you guys again - - soon, I promise. Have a good time in Ocean City."

As we approached the car I noticed the plate. The letters were MK MY DA. I imagined it to say Make My Day. My mother had made my day, now I had to figure out what I was going to do to make hers. Just past the airport on the corner of 73 and route 8, I spotted a florist.

"JD, stop here I have to get something for my mother."

I went in and bought two dozen yellow roses. They're her favorite. When we got to the house, my sister and mother greeted JD with a hug and a kiss on the cheek. My father was home from work, and he even shook his hand, which I think was a first. I got the glare and the cold shoulder from all three. I pulled the flowers from behind my back and presented them. It was a bit tentative, but my mother took them, thanked me and then put them in some water. I looked at her and asked, "So are we good?"

She looked at me and then offered a hug.

"I know how JD drives. If you two hurry you can still catch the flight to OC. Behave yourself. I love you,"

"I love you too. Once in awhile you should just slap me when I'm acting like a jerk."

"Okay. Now go on and get!"

We made it just before they were ready to raise the stairs to the plane.

Sometimes the best made plans are in my dreams. In Reality;

Something Different Takes Place

"Hey, shithead Twitcher, get your scraggly ass out here."

I thought who the hell could that be? I got out of the van. The door of the car opened and a voice yelled.

"Get in, Twitcher. I've got a score to settle with you."

Everyone in the van was watching. I approached the car slowly and looked in . . .

Let me back up for a second. A stranger pulls up in a car blocking the van. A voice calls me out and yells obscenities, and I walk over. What in the world was I thinking? It was a black Mustang GT with smoked glass windows. The chrome rims glistened in the sun and the mirror finish of the paint made it hard to look directly at it. I sauntered over to the car as if I had no fear. Truth be known, I was shaking in my boots. I looked in the front seat. The body behind the wheel with the loud booming voice was a well tanned pro-wrestler type. I couldn't figure out how he crammed himself into this little of a car.

"Get in, Punk."

Instead of running away screaming like a little girl, I followed his instructions and got in the car.

"Shut the door, the air around here smells like the backside of a horse."

As soon as the door closed, he turned up the stereo. The car started to vibrate and rattle with some hip-hop music. The bass was thumping, I felt like I was in the middle of the drum section of a marching band. The big fellow glanced over at me, put the car in reverse and we left in a cloud of dust. I could see the faces in the van. They were all horrified. A few moments after our get-a-way an open hand was shoved in my direction,

"The name's Trevor Dalton. Sky sent me to fetch you."

I shook his hand.

"A pleasure I'm sure. My name is Jack."

"Yeah, I gathered that when you were the only one to get out of the van and respond to my call."

"I didn't think about that. So, how do you know Sky? And where'd she get off to after school?"

"We used to hang together before her family moved to cow-town USA."

"Oh, were you like a couple?"

"Couple of what?"

I must have had a strange look on my face because Trevor laughed.

"I'm bustin ya, man. Sky and I were always just good friends, nothing more and nothing less. I told her I would attend her graduation if she was able to pass. She called me last night, and here I am. I understand you had a hand in helping her through math."

"I did what I could."

We pulled into the lot at the Burhill Burgers and Suds. Sitting on one of the outdoor tables was Sky. I could tell as I got out of the car and approached her that she had been crying. I looked to see if Trevor was coming too, but he was reaching to close the car door and slowly pulled away. His mission in fetching me had been accomplished. I walked not too eager to engage in a conversation that instinctively I could tell was not going to be a happy one.

"Sup, Sky?"

"Hey."

She turned her head, wiping away the last of her tears. She was dressed in an outfit suitable for the commencement ceremony. I looked at my watch. It was almost nine and the graduation was to take place at the fairgrounds at ten-thirty. The fair stadium was the only place around that could hold a crowd the size of the senior class and their families. Something was wrong, and I knew it.

"So, I guess you did it. You went ahead and graduated and everything. You look real nice. I don't think I've seen you in a dress before."

"I didn't pass math."

"What are you talking about?"

"I didn't pass math, but the teacher graded on a curve…

"And"

"And I got a D+"

"You should be careful what you wish for. I could have gotten you an A."

At this point she finally broke into a smile and then punched me in the arm.

"You're some kind of flipping genius, and a shit head aren't you."

"And good lookin. You forgot good lookin."

She looked at me, laughed out loud then punched me in the shoulder again. The fun and frivolity didn't last long. Sky got quiet and real serious. The look of tears welling up was coming across her face.

"I'm not going to the graduation ceremony."

"What are you talking about? You're all dressed up and you worked hard for it all year."

"Yeah, well, my parents said it wasn't a real graduation and that I was scheming behind their backs. They said they wouldn't come to see a liar and a cheat get a piece of worthless paper. They said they will go next year when I'm of age and have earned the diploma. They added that I was a disgrace to the family and to society."

"I can't believe that. They didn't find out about the math test, did they?"

"No, of course not, I never told them about the arrangement with the principal and the tutoring I was getting so that I could get out and be with my friends. Now it looks like I'll be with them after all."

"How's that?"

"I've had my last fight with my mother, and my dad isn't going to yell and threaten me anymore. I'm moving back to Cali, to live with a friend. I want you to come with me."

I had my heart in my throat. I took a gulp while trying to think of something to say. It wasn't my battle, even though I had disagreements with my folks too, I didn't have the nerve to pull up stakes and walk out on them.

"I'll tell you what. I'll come with you if you'll go to your ceremony and get your diploma, Deal?"

Sky wasn't in the mood to make deals, but I had to buy some time. There was no way I could just leave. Suddenly I felt a sense of family and the importance of being part of one. My family had always been supportive of me, even when I was being a jerk. I felt like such a creep for treating everyone the way I had. After all, it was just a move, and a good one for my mom and dad. I wouldn't be with them for more than another couple of years through college and, well anyway, I knew it was the right thing in the end for all of us.

All I really had to do was ask for plane fare and I could see my buddies almost any time I wanted. I was too busy making my parents feel guilty that I didn't give them the satisfaction of sending me. Sky finally made a decision.

"Deal, I'll call Trevor and he can take us to the fairgrounds. We have time. Aren't you going to wear a suit or something?"

Boy was that a change of attitude. We stopped back at my house for a change of clothes. I introduced my mom and dad to Sky and Trevor. While we were there I pulled my mother aside and explained the conversation and commitment. She said that I was doing the right thing in being supportive, and that maybe a week or two and things would settle down. She asked how we were getting to California, and I told her at this point I wasn't sure.

Then out of nowhere she gave me a hug.

"Jack, you're growing up, and there will always be tough decisions to make. I'll give you some cash and increase the line on your credit card. Consider it an advance on your allowance and a summer vacation. You call if you need anything or get in trouble."

"Thanks, Mom, you're the best. I promise you I won't get in trouble and I'll call when I find out how and where we're going."

All Grown Up

California was amazing. The waves were bigger, the cars were faster, and the traffic in L.A. was ridicules. I absolutely loved it. This was the life. I envisioned never going back. Sky started spending more and more time with her friends and less time with me. When she wasn't with her friends, she was looking for a job. One morning I woke up and realized how much I missed home and my family. I left a note on the microwave door and took a bus back to Burhill. That summer I signed up for basketball and made the team. These kids were darn good too. I had a whole new respect for my teammates that would eventually become my new best of friends.

I graduated summa cum laude in 1973. Twenty years later I found myself stuck in a dead-end job. I fell into the promise of corporate America. The company my father had worked for all his life hired me the day after I graduated from Lexington Community College. I was a junior executive in the products development division. I hated it.

I spent the first five years with the company in that capacity before moving into sales and marketing. I liked the traveling part and the creative writing of the ads. Today I was on my way to New York for a sales convention. While sitting in the airport, I was reading an article on my laptop. It was, "These troubled times" written during the riots of the sixties. There was a lot of civil unrest and protests of the Vietnam War.

I looked up for a moment to rest my eyes and check the time. Standing in front of me was a woman that looked like she had been there for a few minutes trying to decide to wait or interrupt my reading.

"Geez, I thought you were glued to that thing. How ya been, shithead?"

I couldn't believe my eyes. It was Sky. I hadn't seen her since the summer she moved to California.

"Well, glory be if it isn't Sky Paddington. What on earth are you doing around these parts?"

"I go by Sylvia B. now. And I'm heading to New York for an assignment."

"Sylvia B? What's that, some sort of stage name?"

"Well, not exactly. I'm a fashion designer, and these days it's in to wear domestic instead of French or Italian."

"Oh, well, congratulations. Are you on the 2:30 flight? Maybe we can get our seats exchanged and do some catching up."

"That sounds wonderful."

"Give me your ticket and I'll see what I can do."

Sky gave me her ticket. Apparently she was a big deal in Hollywood, but I didn't follow the scene, so I hadn't a clue. She had a first class ticket and mine was in coach.

"I see you're in first class. Should I trade up or do you mind sitting with the commoners?"

"Whatever is available, my service books my flights. It doesn't really matter to me."

Her service makes her reservations, maybe I let this one go too soon. If I would have stayed in California maybe I'd be somebody too, instead of just a traveling salesman. The ticket agent was about as crabby as any person on earth. I could see her tortured face cringe even before I asked her to punch a few buttons on her keyboard.

"And what can I do for you, sir? The flight is about to leave."

She intimidated me to the point I started to stutter, and that almost never happens.

"I - - um, I

"Step aside, sir, while I wait on someone who knows what they want. Miss, may I help you?"

"Yes, I believe your idiot agent at the front counter gave me the wrong reservations. I was supposed to have two first class seats together, not one. I won't put up with this crap. One of your agents with an insouciant attitude towards your clients can get it right or get another job. And trust me, I can make both happen."

Now it was the agent's turn to stammer. She was beginning to perspire and was getting red in the face. Her fingers were flying across the keyboard while she was checking the screen. The woman in front of me snapping commands was Sky. She put her hand behind her, reaching for the tickets. She then threw them on the desk at the agent.

"If you call this customer service, I'd rather be baggage. At least the bags get on the plane without an attitude from their handler. While you're standing there trying to look like you know what you are doing, why don't you call a manager over so I can get something accomplished before my next birthday?"

"That won't be necessary, Miss B. I have your seats and you may board at once. Complimentary champagne will be served once you get settled. Do you need a taxi when you get to New York? I can make a reservation."

Not only did I feel totally emasculated by what just happened, I felt bad for the crabby lady. I sure was glad I was on Sky's side, because if I weren't, I think she'd rip me a new one and I wouldn't be able to sit for a week.

"I don't think I've ever sat in first class before. You were pretty amazing back there. Who was the second seat for? Did someone cancel out on you?"

"What are you talking about? There were never two seats together. You can't just go up and beg like a puppy. They'll whack you on the nose with a newspaper and tell you to sit. Geez, I remember when you were a tough guy full of himself and no one pushed you around. What happened?"

"I guess I grew up and realized that not everything has to be a battle and that you have to pick and choose which ones are worth fighting and which ones to let go."

The flight to New York was two hours and twenty-three minutes. It passed so fast I didn't know we had left the airport. We talked the whole way there and then promised after our appointments that we would get together for dinner and a show. I left my cell phone on even during the seminar, but I never heard from her again.

I guess she found glamour and fame. I found life on a forty acre ranch with a few cows in the barn along with two horses, some chickens and some stray cats wasn't such a bad life after all. I even had a riding lawn mower in the tool shed next to the barn.

THE END

Book 6

Fear and a Little Imagination

Jack Buys his First Motorcycle

Most people would consider me to be a mild-mannered borderline geek. Rest assured it's not because I wear bifocals, or have a buzz cut that sticks up in the front and waves. I think they form that opinion based on the first few minutes of conversation. I tend to stutter when in the company of woman, especially if they are more intelligent than me. I have a hard time talking to men as well. The men tend to dominate the conversation and say things like, "What do you think, Nerdly? Or, so, little man, any thoughts on the subject?"

I usually shrug my shoulders and then run to the restroom and cry like a little girl. Just because I'm sensitive, it doesn't mean I'm gay or nerdy or a freak-a-zoid of some sort. It just means that I'm emotionally challenged when engaging conversation in the social arts.

No one in their wildest dreams would have imagined that I would buy a bike. We're not talking about a ten-speed, or a cross country racer bike. Oh, no, we're talking the real deal, a motorbike. That's right! A motorized, two wheel, high performance, rubber burning, head turning roadster. I told everyone at work to conserve gas I was buying a moped. I even brought one in to have the mechanic take a look. Like an idiot I bought a fixer-upper, and I don't know how to do either?

Then I decided I would buy a euro-style scooter. I could hear the roaring hum of the 50cc engine and feel the wind blowing gently against my face as I raced down the street at thirty miles an hour. In the middle of the country's highest gas prices, I would be the envy of everyone at work. I could go in and brag about getting seventy miles a gallon and how one tank would last me ten days. Oh, man, I felt cool just thinking about it.

When I found out that you needed an operator's license, the same as if you rode a motorcycle, my mind was made up. I was buying a bike. I started searching for one on the internet. I wanted an old school style. Black with chrome and a lot of vroom vroom. I found a beauty of a bike on the other side of town. The fellow selling it showed me all about it, but I didn't have my license or even my temps, so I wasn't able to ride it. I didn't want to tell him that I never rode before and feel stupid. After all, I wasn't a kid anymore. I was a few years past my prime, oh alright, I'm middle aged and never had a motor anything before outside of a car. I had the bike delivered to my work, and of course everybody had to come out and see it.

"Hey, Nerdly, how ya gonna get it home?"

"I don't know."

"Have you even ever ridden one before?"

"No."

With every question I was getting more nervous, and I started to sweat. Before they could say anything else I ran to the bathroom. I flushed a couple of times so on one could hear my tears.

When I came out, everyone was back to work and some had gone home for the day. Now, all I had to do was, wait in the parking lot for the last of them to leave and I could try out my 1983 Vintage Suzuki GS450E. Okay, so it's older than my kids, but it's mine and it's not a scooter or a moped. When the area was void of all manner of man, I hopped on my bike and tried to remember how to start it. Okay, now how do I get it to move?

It wasn't more than a couple of tries and I was heading towards the street. My work was on an industrial parkway, so after hours there was very little traffic. I was so nervous, I was afraid of rusting the chain on the way home.

I turned down a side street that I knew made a loop with a few stop signs. I felt the stopping and starting would build confidence and then I would start my six mile journey home. I stopped and called my wife. I told her I would be late and not to hold up dinner. She was so proud of me for climbing out of my shell and doing something daring for a change. She even told everyone including the insurance agent who insisted that she take out an extra policy for just in case.

"Mrs. Twitcher, I'm sure Jack will be a safe rider, but you just can't tell about those crazy drivers out there these days. Now just sign here and you and the kids will be secure in the knowledge that if old Jack don't make it back, you won't have to go to work or starve. Oh, ah sign here, here, initials, and that's it. Keep in touch."

"Thanks, Carl, I'll see you at mom's for dinner on Sunday."

Carl was Janet's brother. He always looked after his little sister and me. He was more like a brother to me than an in-law.

The evening sky was starting to appear as the sun was setting. Oh, boy, if I didn't conquer my fear of riding pretty soon, it would be dark before I got home. I got off the bike and parked it on the side of the street. At the corner there was a big rock. I sat on it and stared at the bike. It was only six miles to home. It might as well have been a million. I was alone, I didn't know how to ride my bike, and I was afraid of the whole thing. The word stupid kept coming into my mind. How could I be so stupid? I closed my eyes just for a second. I thought I could talk myself into some confidence and get on my horse and ride.

"Eureka! That's it!"

I hopped onto my trusty stead and rode well into the forest, weaving through the trees along a path and up the mountainside. Many a knight in armor had traveled this path in search of the dragon's lair. But, it was I that knew his secret hiding place. I alone knew where, the devil's beast rested until it was his time to terrorize the villagers and burn their cottages with his fiery breath.

I was on a mission to save my family and my countrymen. I would slay the dragon and drag his carcass back to show one and all that they had nothing to fear, as long as Jack was here.

Going Home

The sun was shining in just the right way that its reflection on the headlamp bezel created a smile. The red tone on the lower chrome was like ruby lips. The smile, however, turned to a devilish grin. The bike started to mock me.

"Hey, Girly-man, who's your daddy?"

"I'm not a girly-man."

"He speaks. I can't believe it. The girly-man can talk. So, you gonna ride, or what, Butch?"

"My name is not Butch. I'll ride when I'm good and ready."

"Sure you will. Is that before you cry or after you wet yourself, Butch?"

"Stop calling me that."

"Ooh, I'm shaking. I'm shaking."

"Shut up!"

"Make me."

I stood in front of the bike blocking the sun's reflection. The smile disappeared. I walked over to the side of the bike and kicked the front tire. I think I heard a groan. I then squeezed the brake handle and swung my right leg over the saddle styled seat. I sat with a thud. The bike moaned. With the turn of the key, I attempted to start it up.

"Wimp, wimp wimp wimp wimp wimp wimp."

Now even the motor was mocking me.

"Shut up", I said, as I pulled out the choke and tried again.

Grrr Vroom, Grrrr, Vroom Vroom. I gave it some gas and let out the clutch just a little too fast. We went fish tailing all the way to the corner. I slowed but didn't stop as I turned onto the main road. Shifting into second and then third, we were cruising.

"Yeah, who's the daddy now?"

I accelerated to warp speed. We were hovering over the ground, riding down the boulevard in stealth mode. To the passers-by we were virtually invisible. At this speed the traffic seemed to be standing still. I was glad to be wearing my thermal gloves, a lined leather jacket and that the bike had a windshield to divert the air stream. Riding through the neighborhood, I kept an eye out for possible evil doers or any danger that might befall the good citizens our fair city. When I was satisfied that all was well with the world I headed for the underground tunnel that would take me to my safe haven of rest.

The cavern below Liberty Mansion was my secret hide-away. No one knew it existed except the butler and me.

I slipped out of my super suit and returned to being my mild-mannered self. I decided then and there that I would no longer be known as the one they call Jack. I was changing my name to JT. The sound of it was so much cooler. And I was one cool dude now.

Still exhilarated from my first ride, I was sitting at the kitchen table. There was a muffled sound coming from somewhere. It sounded distant.

"Jack? Jack, is that you?"

It was someone calling my name. From behind I felt a thump on the back of my head, then a knocking.

"Jack, you're home early. I wasn't expecting you. I haven't . . . can you hear me in there?"

I lifted the visor on my helmet. My wife had been talking, but I couldn't understand a thing she said. I took my helmet off.

"Were you saying something?"

"Yes, you're home early. I thought you weren't going to be home until later. I haven't started dinner. Do you mind if we just order a pizza?"

"Oh, no, that will be fine, dear."

"How was your ride?"

"It was great. All is safe and well with the world."

"What?"

"Never mind, you wouldn't understand."

"I'm sure you're right. What would you like on the pizza?"

The Ride

Morning came after a restless night. I had dreams of motorcycles dancing in my head. The handle bars were like arms. They were doing disco to Nights on Broadway by the Bee Gees.

It was nightmarish the way they were carrying on. It gave a whole new meaning to the term "Biker Bar". After a quick juice and a piece of burnt toast, I headed for the garage to see my friend. I named the bike Andy. Don't ask why because I don't know myself. I don't even know anyone named Andy, other than the comedian, but my bike didn't have the same sense of humor. In fact, the bike wasn't that funny. It had more of a sardonic humor with a bit of a temper.

"Good morning, Andy."

"What's so good about it?"

"Well, for one thing, the sun is shining and it's going to be in the mid seventies all day. It's the perfect day to go for a ride."

"Sez you. You don't have to feel the hot tar under your wheels, or have someone's sweaty butt sitting on your back all day. Oh, no, you get to feel the wind and enjoy the scenery, while I do all the work."

"Well, gee, I'm sorry you feel that way. I suppose I could just leave you sit in the garage while I go to the beach."

"The Beach, huh? Will there be any other bikes there?"

"Lots and lots of bikes, are you with me or not?"

The engine started all by itself. It was purring like a kitten. I'm not sure, but I think the headlamp winked at me as I got on. The garage door opened with the push of a button, and we were on our way. Ocean Boulevard was ten miles from home. This would be my first experience riding more than five miles and with day traffic. I was shaking so much that the few pounds I was hoping to lose were falling off like melted butter on a hot potato.

THE END

Book 7

Between Floors

Investigative research isn't exactly a glamorous job, but it pays the bills. I worked for a company that did investigations of everything under the sun. We'd investigate low level crime, from auto theft to home robbery. We'd get a few high profile cases of museum art theft, and an occasional murder mystery. My end of the bargain was computer espionage. Computer theft was on the rise.

Criminals were learning how to hack systems as fast as safety blocks were being developed to stop them. Bank fraud was at an all time high. Fake deposits to off shore accounts were cashing in for real money. We got the assignment and I jumped at the chance to track these high tech geeks down and turn them over for prosecution. These guys, whoever they were, made the crimes of Bernie Madoff look like petty theft. This was grand scale and global. The Feds were pretty sure it was either one sharp cookie or a small group. They were pretty sure they weren't just random occurrences.

My first stop was to the High Towers bank building in New York. I hated high rise buildings, especially in NY. The elevators were slow and seemed like they were broken down half the time. If it wasn't thirty-five floors up, I would take the stairs. Everyone knows that all towers have a missing thirteenth floor. I am sure no one really knows who started the superstition, but the only one who asks why, is a ten year old. They ask once, get the usual answer and then forget about it for the rest of their lives. Not me.

That was one of the questions that nagged me all my life. Maybe that's what got me into this business in the first place.

I pushed the up button. The indicator display showed the elevator car to be on the thirty-first floor and on its way down. Every thirty seconds it would move. If I calculated the time by the approximate number of stops, I could figure it would be almost fifteen minutes for the elevator to reach the ground. I couldn't imagine a building this size having only one service elevator.

The front hall had a dozen high speed units. Any given moment a door was opening or closing. The super speed always upset my stomach, so I waited for the service elevator in the back, plus it was close to the parking garage. I started to wonder about the thirteenth floor. Did they count from the first floor which was actually three levels below the ground floor, or did they count from there, which would make thirteen the tenth floor? Here I go thinking again.

Finally the arrival bell rang. I got onto the elevator and pressed number thirty-five. My only hope was that it wouldn't make twenty stops before I got to my floor. I was alone in the elevator until the eleventh floor. A young couple got in. They were giggling and doing a whole lot of touchy-feely stuff along with some sloppy kisses. I would have told them to get a room, but I think I was invading their secret place. After all, who takes the service elevator anyway?

When I arrived at my client's office for the initial interview, there was a sign on the door.

"Closed for renovations"

This not only irritated me, because I had called to confirm the appointment, only an hour before, but it intrigued me as well. I made a mental note and also a voice recording of the circumstance. Out of habit, I tried the door. It was unlocked, so naturally I proceeded to enter into the office. There were no lights on and the switch wasn't working. All the windows were covered with newspaper blocking the light from outside.

Just in front of one of the larger windows, there was a desk and an oversized leather recliner. The solid oak desk had a glass protector on top. I walked around to the window. If they were doing renovations, why wasn't the furniture removed? I was starting my investigation without the help of the branch manager, whom I had scheduled the meeting with. Also, where were the workers? I snooped around for about ten minutes, uninterrupted by anyone. I heard voices outside of the door. Suddenly I felt like a criminal. It occurred to me that I shouldn't have come in without the presence of the party I planned to meet. When two well dressed men walked in, they looked surprised to see me.

"Who are you? And what are you doing snooping around my office?"

"Mister Jacobs? I'm Alan Fellows with the Finders Group. We were to meet at ten."

"Oh, yes. I got detained in the coffee shop catching up on some Wall Street news. This is Leonard Gretsky. He's one of our branch managers from the central building in the Bronx."

We all shook hands during the introductions. Leo had shifty eyes and never looked directly at me when talking. I always distrusted people who didn't look at me when talking.

"You'll have to excuse the mess. The painters have been coming out for three days, but never show. I have everything covered and ready. It's a pain in the ass working in these conditions. To top it off, the electricity is out on this floor, all except the elevator."

"It's not a problem for me. Shall we get down to business? Or is there something we shouldn't talk about in front of Mr. Gretsky?"

"Leonard and I have been close friends in business and socially for over twenty years. There is nothing we can talk about that he doesn't already know."

We talked for just short of an hour. I was convinced that one or both of these guys knew more about this case than they were telling me. I couldn't figure out why Jacobs would hire our firm and then withhold evidence. Just another piece of the puzzle to fit together, I thanked them for their time. Heading back to the elevator, I heard one of them say,

"Do you think he suspects anything?"

I pressed the button and stepped back to hear the rest of the conversation.

"No, it doesn't matter anyway. He's not a cop. He's just some jerk with a private firm doing some investigations for the stiff."

"Where's the body anyway?"

"It's outside the window waiting to have an accident."

"What do ya mean an accident?"

"The scaffolding for the window cleaners is going to snap. It could happen any time between now and rush hour."

"Gee, I feel sorry for anyone standing below when he hits. It's going to be a big splat."

The bell for the elevator rang. As I got in, both men came out of the office. They came running towards me as the doors closed.

I heard far more than I wanted to. I was praying that they couldn't press the up button and reverse the direction of the elevator. There was no way out for me if they could. My worst fear was realized when the elevator stopped on the thirtieth floor. No one got on, but instead of continuing down, I was heading back up. I pressed the stop button. I needed time to think.

30 Seconds Between Floors

I knew there was only thirty seconds between floors. I had to think fast. Everyone knows about the service hatch, so that's the first place they would look for me. I remembered from a movie that old elevators didn't have safety latches on the doors, so they could be opened while moving. All I would have to do is release the stop button, open the door at the next level and get out while it was moving. The guys waiting wouldn't know what floor I got off, and they would find the empty elevator. I was feeling like a genius detective for the moment.

"What just happened?"

"Our Mr. Fellows didn't get off the elevator at the thirtieth."

"How do you know that?"

"I know that, because he assumed after it stopped it would continue down and he would get away. If he were smart he would have just gotten off, ran to the front elevators and made his way downstairs. Instead when the elevator started going up, he panicked and hit the stop button."

"That makes sense. What do you think he's going to do?"

"It doesn't matter. We have five floors between us. There's no way to cover every floor, so we won't."

"I don't get it?"

"While the genius is making his plans of escape, we take the front elevators down to the lobby, catch a cab to the airport and head to Miami as planned. With a little luck he was the only one seen getting on the service elevator. He then takes the wrap for the murder of the old man. It couldn't have worked better if we spent all night thinking about it."

"That's what I like about you. You have the luck of the Irish."

The two men walked casually through the building to the front. Meanwhile I got off by opening the doors of the elevator while it was still moving. I managed to open them while passing the thirty-second floor. I quickly ran to the front and pressed the button for the next car down. The front elevators were busy and people were pushing to get on.

I had to wait for the third set of doors to open before I could find room on one to head down. In the back of the elevator, I hadn't noticed, the two men from the office were riding down in the same car. At each stop people were getting on and off, so the elevator stayed full all the way to the lobby. I needed to get to the parking garage.

As I waited for everyone to exit, the two guys bumped into me on their way off. Leo apologized. Just as the door was ready to close I think he realized it was me. At the same time I recognized his face, I looked out to see Jacobs waiting for him. The doors closed and I was on my way once more.

I was sweating from what I perceived to be a near death experience.

I got on my cell phone as soon as I got in the garage to call 911. I reported the possibility of a murder and gave a description of the suspects. Since I had no idea of where they were going, it wasn't going to be easy to track them down. I went to my office on the lower side of Manhattan. When I turned on my computer, there was an email waiting for me to open. It started out with,

"My only regret is not writing to you sooner. The bank is missing another four hundred and fifty thousand dollars. It was deposited in an account somewhere in the Virgin Islands. I received a death threat this morning, that if I reported the theft, I wouldn't live to see the next sunrise over the Hudson. I have been shot and left to die, please try to find Skyler Tarrington, that's the name on the . . ."

When the email ended abruptly, I could only assume one thing. I wondered if this was Mr. Jacobs. There was no ISP address on the email, so I wasn't able to trace it back to its origin. I had to ask myself; why would anyone dying leave me an email message instead of calling for help?

The Criminal Element

My trip to the 401 was less than enjoyable. I was treated like a criminal from the moment I walked into the station. I started to recount the events of the morning to the Captain and a couple of his on duty patrolmen. The worse thing about the treatment I received was that I knew all these guys. The Captain and I had been friends for over ten years. He was in my wedding party, and every year at Christmas I make a generous donation to the policemen's benevolence fund.

Before I finished my story, they whisked me into the interrogation room to wait for the FBI. Two agents, both dressed in gray suits came in. They each had on a pair of dark sunglasses. This was getting ugly. After ten minutes of rapid fire questions, agent Sanders said;

"Let's go to the alleged scene of the crime. You can walk us through the event, and tell us everything you remember. We're going to need it all."

You would have thought I was suspect number one. In fact, I felt as though I was being accused of committing the crime instead of reporting it. The bank building was only a few blocks away. The three of us got into a black four door Ford with deep tinted windows all the way around, and a bullet proof glass partition between the front and rear seat. I was in the back and couldn't hear the conversation of the agents. When we got to the parking garage, the window partition was lowered allowing me to talk to them.

"Where did you park, Mr. Fellows?"

"I parked near the rear entrance on the second floor below street level."

"Why did you park in the rear instead of up front where most of the patrons and bankers enter?"

"I had an appointment as I've already told you with Mr. Jacobs. His office is on the top floor of the building. I don't like the high speed elevators, but it's too high to take the stairs. I find the service elevator to be a little more comfortable way to travel."

"And likely, no one would see you coming or going?"

"Hey, I'm trying to help you guys solve a possible murder. Why do I feel like I'm on trial?"

"Sorry, I meant if the suspects came this way, they wouldn't have been noticed."

I wasn't getting along with either agent, but I especially didn't like Agent Sanders. He was getting under my skin. The other Agent was quiet, although even with the dark glasses I could see he was thinking about all that was said, and calculating his theory on the case. We followed the exact path that I took in the morning. Since I had been taking notes and dictating into my tape recorder, we could instant replay the whole thing.

When we got to the thirty-fifth floor, there was something different about the hallway. None of the office doors were facing towards the elevator as they had earlier. I kept my mouth shut about that detail for the moment. We went around the corner to Mr. Jacob's office. The door was open. There was a breeze from a window blowing into the hallway. Other than some papers and an empty trash can, the office was abandoned. It appeared to have been cleaned and white washed. We could smell fresh paint. I touched one of the walls. It was damp and cool to the touch.

"What the hell is going on here? This better not be a wild goose chase."

Sanders was angry, stomping his feet and kicking the papers.

"Chamber call the precinct, and get a finger print kit up here.

I want this place dusted floor to ceiling, and I want it NOW!"

Agent Chamber walked into the hallway. I could hear him on his cell phone making the request.

I continued to look about the room. The number on the door and the name was the same, even the gold letters, but this wasn't the same room. I was in a room at the end of the hall opposite the service elevator. This room was more centered, almost midway down the hall and closer to the front where the main elevators are.

"If you two don't need me, I'll just find my way to the little boy's room."

"Come right back. We'll need to get a description of all the office furniture you say was here this morning."

"No problem, I'll be back in two shakes."

I left casually. Walking at a faster pace, I went back to what I thought was the room I was in originally. There was a door with letters that had been freshly cleaned off. I tried the handle, but this time the door was locked. In my wallet, I carried a pick for just such occasions. One left, one right, a couple of clicks; I was in. Everything was exactly as I had left it. I had an urge to call Agents Sanders and Chamber, but I held off. Walking to the window, I peeked through the paper to see if the scaffolding was still hanging. Sure enough it was. I could see a pair of shoes, the body of whoever was still there. Now it was time to prove my case.

"Hey, come over here, I found something. Agent Sanders come over here. I'm just around the corner."

The two agents came running. Both had their guns drawn.

"This is the room I was in this morning. Someone just changed the name on the doors to cover up. There's a body on the scaffolding hanging outside of the window."

No one wanted to disturb the evidence. They both looked through a rip in the paper to verify what I had told them. I was thinking I was off the hook finally and we could start the investigation properly instead of them investigating me.

"You'd better get some Blues up here along with the coroner."

"You got it."

"Agent Sanders, I think you have enough to go on. I need to get back to tracing the computer hackers and find the missing money."

I had barely finished speaking when there was a loud cracking sound and then a snap. We knew immediately what just happened. Running to the window, all we could do was watch the scaffold fall to the ground and pray no one was under it when it hit.

One loud crash, a little dust rising, and it was done. We didn't know if the body was Jacobs or not, but we would find out soon enough. I felt like I was going to puke, but kept my composure.

"Ah, hey Fellows, sorry about the hard time I was giving you. I have to admit, I didn't believe your story. Actually, I still don't. So, don't leave town for seventy-two hours. And don't leave the country at all, ever. Understand?"

"Yes sir, I got ya. You have all my numbers if you need me. And trust me, I have yours too."

He looked at me a little strange, but he knew what I meant. I was going to walk back to the 401, that's where my car was, and everyone was so busy no one was offering a ride.

I looked at the hole in the ground from the scaffolding. It was more than five feet deep and every bit as wide. The police already had the area taped off. It was strange to me, I didn't see a body.

Who's Who and What Now?

The office door pushed open when I attempted to put in my key. I know it was locked when I left, I always lock it. Someone broke in. For all I knew they could still be in there. My days of walking through a door unannounced were over. The last time I did that I was shot in the shoulder. Eighteen years as a cop and that night ended it for me. I was lead man on raids and drug busts. I had a strong leg and would kick the door in then enter while my back up waited for the "All Clear" sign.

If the door didn't cave, I'd put a shoulder to it. There was never a time that I didn't make it through a front door. I was hit in the shoulder by a crack dealer with fortunately for me, bad aim. A little to the right and the bullet would have pierced my heart. A little higher and I would have had it between the eyes.

After that incident I could still kick in a door physically, but mentally I couldn't break the threshold. I stayed on the force as a desk jockey to get my twenty years in and a partial retirement package. I signed up with The Finders Group because I liked investigative work, and for the most part I was behind a desk hacking computer codes. Today was one of the few times I went to meet a client face to face. I wasn't sure who I had met, but I was pretty sure it wasn't Mr. Jacobs.

I decided it was best to announce my arrival so I wouldn't startle a trigger happy thief. I reached for the gun in my shoulder holster. Shit, it was at the police station. It would be easier to buy a new one than go through the hassle of all the red tape and ten day waiting period.

"I'm unarmed. If you want to leave without me seeing you, I'll close my eyes and count to ten. One, two. . . No one came out, so I went in and had a look around. The office looked undisturbed and just the way I left it. I looked in the closet and then in the bathroom. No one was there. My laptop was open to the banks' page with my notes. Someone figured out my password. They were taking a few notes of their own. I made it a habit to back my files up on both a compact disc and a mini-flash drive that I would carry with me whenever I left the office. If anyone tried to copy my files, they were encrypted, so all they would get was a bunch of gibberish.

As I sat down, the phone rang. I was still shaken from entering the office and having flashbacks of when I was shot. The call went into voice mail.

"Alan, I know you're there. Don't pick up. Meet me at Beans over Broadway for coffee, say around five-thirty."

It was Bill MacFarland, the Chief of police, my alleged friend. He sounded emotional or overstressed. It was rare that he would call me from the precinct. Something had to be very wrong, and to request a meeting over coffee. He doesn't even drink coffee.

The one thing that was stressing me was the two bankers knew who I was and where I worked. I had given them both one my business cards. They could have come here while I was with the police and tried to recover the information on the case.

I had no idea they weren't legit. My only goal until five was to find out what they viewed on my laptop and if they used the internet. I could download the history of wherever they had been. I also played back my phone records. There was a call made to a number in Florida. I didn't make it, so whoever broke in did. I jotted it down and then erased it from the phone log.

The perpetrator that broke in spent some time browsing through an ad for theater tickets from a local broker. Why would a crook be buying tickets and risk getting caught while doing so? This was a good one. The idiot booked two tickets for the Phantom, using his credit card. All his information was logged on a secure site. I would be able to retrieve that in less than a heartbeat.

I downloaded the information onto my backup systems then ran out of the office. I was late for my date with Bill. The door had been jimmied open and wouldn't lock. I went back in quickly. I got a piece of tape and stuck it on the top corner of the door. If anyone else went in, the tape would be broken when I got back.

Bill was sitting at a table in the front window. I waved at him as I walked in. He had two hot cups of coffee sitting in front of him.

"Alan, hi, I was afraid after the rough treatment at the station today that you wouldn't show. I had to be a jerk in front of the FBI agents. If they knew we were friends, it could jeopardize the investigation."

"I understand. You did a fine job of convincing everybody including me that you were an ass."

"Okay, I deserve that. You need to back off this case. It's not just a few lousy bucks being stolen in computer fraud. It's bigger than that and it's getting dangerous."

"How so?"

"Did you actually see the body today on the scaffolding outside the window before it fell?"

"No. I didn't want to disturb any evidence, so I just peeked through a tear in the paper."

"Alan, this was a Miami style murder. There was no body."

"But, I saw the shoes. What do you mean Miami style, and if

there wasn't a body, how do you know there was a murder?"

"We have positive ID that what you saw was Mr. Jacobs."

"I'm not following."

"Mrs. Jacobs identified her husband's feet. They were still in the shoes. We're pretty sure he's dead. He was probably tortured first. When they didn't get what they wanted . . . I think you can fill in the blanks. Get yourself as far away from this case as possible. Leave tonight if you can. In fact, buy some clothes and don't go home. If they went to your office, they'll find where you live too."

"How do you know they were at my office?"

"When you called with the information about a possible murder, we set up surveillance of your office and home. Two guys went into your office. Neither matched the description of the bankers you met. So far they haven't shown up at your house, but rest assured they will. Sooner or later, they always do."

After throwing up in my mouth when I heard what happened to Jacobs, I thanked Bill for the warning. I went back to my car and drove non-stop to New Jersey. From there I took a Grey Hound bus to Ocean City Maryland. It was an all night bus ride. I didn't sleep much. I was afraid and my mind was racing with the thoughts of the day.

Scared and Alone

Wal-Mart shoppers after midnight are an all together different breed of people. Some of them were on leashes being led by either a boyfriend or girlfriend. I guess it depended on who was wearing the collar. Then there were the usual transvestites, the gay couples sharing changing booths and a guy in a Santa suit that forgot his trousers.

I tried to stay clear of him, but he kept popping out in the aisles. I can't remember ever finishing a shopping spree in less than twenty minutes. I was able to buy a week's worth of clothing for less than a hundred bucks. The nice part about the Wal, is that I could also get a laptop computer and a revolver. I didn't have to go searching all over town for another store to be open at one am.

It was a little scary that I could buy a gun with very little identification and no waiting period.

I walked to the Surfside. It was a little motel on the beach. My wife and I had stayed there many times with the kids for summer vacations.

I hadn't seen my wife since the night I got shot. She couldn't handle seeing me lying in a hospital bed almost dead, with wires and tubes coming out of my body. She also couldn't say to me in person that she was leaving me and taking the kids. She left a note on the nightstand for me to find.

"Alan, we both knew this day would come. Every time you didn't come home from work on time, if the phone rang, I would jump out of my skin thinking I was going to get bad news. Tonight is close enough. I won't be the one to tell your son and daughter that Daddy isn't coming home. I'll be gone by the time you heal. I'll always love you, but not like this. I don't expect you to quit the force, your work is too important, but, well, when the children are old enough to make a decision for themselves, I'll let them know how to find you. Don't look for us, we won't be there."

She didn't even sign the fricken note. I hated her for that. Yet I understood perfectly. I just wish she had been there through the seemingly endless nightmares. I wished that she would have stayed for my retirement. I could have used the loving support of a wife during the hardest days of my life. It was then that I wished the dope addict had been a better shot. Whew, enough of the past. I had a lot of work to do. I set up the laptop and started downloading programs to start my search. This was going to be a challenge. I had to run a trace without being traced. It was possible, but not easy. I was up against some sharp computer hacks. These guys were capable of erasing IP addresses, which would enable them to become ghosts. I needed to be better than them.

It was six the next morning. I was set and ready. Before pushing the enter button, I decided to go across the street to the diner for breakfast. It was a little joint that had the best eggs and hot cakes this side of the Atlantic. My eyes widened and my jaw dropped.

I couldn't believe Dotty was still working in the kitchen. She was older than dirt when we used to come here years ago. I walked with a little skip in my step.

"Dotty, I can't believe you haven't retired yet."

"Yeah, well, I can't believe you ain't dead yet."

"Come here. Let me give you a hug."

"Okay, but no copping a feel."

We both laughed and enjoyed the moment. She shared with me about her husband passing on to glory just a year this past September, and I told her I lost my wife. I didn't have to tell her how; she could read between the lines and see it in my eyes.

"I'd ask you if ya wanted to do some sparkin tonight, seeing that we're both single, but I am sort of committed to a fellow at the Old Aged Home. You know me, I like my men mature. At my age the only place to find one is at the cemetery or the home."

I blushed at the suggestion and snickered about her liking older men. When we finished with our chat, I got a cup of Jo to go and went back to my room.

Kat Calls

The first thing on my to do list was to find out who the credit card belonged to that was used to buy the Broadway tickets on line. The last four numbers didn't mean anything. That was the individual's account number. I wouldn't need all seventeen either, unless I wanted to buy something and charge it to my friendly burglar.

I went to the online ticket site. The Phantom tickets were purchased through a high priced ticket agency. The show has been sold out for weeks. There was a confirmation of schedule section. I put in the credit card numbers. I have to admit I was pretty good at this. I closed my eyes, counted to three then checked the screen. Gretsky, Leonard. Now that was the last person I would have suspected. I tracked the order. He paid $1,175.00 for each ticket plus $250.00 handling and gratuity.

The show was an eight pm start time. Fourth row center stage, one more click and I would have the seat numbers too.

"Nice job, Leo. From the fourth row you'll be able to smell the stars as well as see them up close."

I was talking to myself out loud. Goal number one was complete. Later, I would buy a Go Phone at Wal-Mart to call Bill. Throw away phones are hard to track. My next objective in finding these guys would be more of a challenge. Before I got started with that, I would need to cover my tracks. I set up a dummy IP address in Singapore under the name Lee Chen.

If someone were to find Lee, they would be directed to another IP using the name Kai Chek in communist Red China. Kai's address would bounce them to Amir Hussar of India. My favorite is to have anyone that's gotten through the maze of IP's to end up at Disney World in Cinderella's Castle. As far as I know, no one has ever made it past the castle.

Confident my cover was secure, I started to search for Gretsky. It bothered me that I didn't know who his partner was. I wondered if I had met the real Arthur Jacobs and if Leo was the one that killed him. I needed to establish a time line of events.

10:10am I met with the two bankers. We talked for one hour then parted company.

11:12am the evasive elevator tactics took fifteen minutes. I bumped into Gretsky on the ground floor.

11:30am back at my car I was in the garage making a 911 call to report a possible murder. Once I arrived at my office, I checked my emails. I got the "I've been shot" then went to the police station to be grilled.

1:15pm the FBI and I went to the scene of the crime. We followed the path of my original trip to the bank entering through the basement service doors of the building. When we finished up our investigation together, the scaffolding fell to the ground.

2:30pm I walked back to the station to get my car. From the station to my office was ten minutes. Phone call from Bill, we met at

5:30pm. 6pm I drive to the bus depot. At midnight I arrived here.

Somewhere between 12:30pm when I left to fill out a police report and 3pm when I got back, Gretsky was buying big buck theater tickets and making a phone call to Florida. Shit, I forgot the phone call. The number was on a scrap piece of paper stuffed in my wallet.

A reverse look up, and voila.

What the - -. The number was registered to none other than the late Arthur Jacobs. I slumped back in my chair and took a sip of coffee.

All this, and my coffee was still warm.

How could I find out who Leo talked to for eleven minutes? It couldn't have been the fake Jacobs. He was with him earlier. It couldn't be the dead Jacobs, - - well 'cause he was dead. Or was he? Maybe the ID from the wife was phony and a cover up. In that case I may have met the real Arthur Jacobs at the meeting.

I ran my back-ups then pulled out the flash drive and disc. I was heading across the street to get the disposable phone when it occurred to me to call the Florida number to see who would answer. I bought a thirty minute calling card, thinking that would suffice. After all, I was only making a couple of calls.

My first call was to Bill MacFarland, I told him where to apprehend Leonard Gretsky for questioning. Then I called the Jacobs Family of sixty-three Coral Drive, Miami FL.

"Hello, may I please speak to Mr. Jacobs."

"This is he."

"Arthur Jacobs?"

"Yes, who's this?"

"Alan Fellows, sir. We met yesterday at the bank."

"Impossible. They're renovating the 35th floor. I've been here all week. The paint fumes make me sick."

"We'll I guess I had my appointments mixed. Oops, I see it now, I met with Leonard Gretsky. My notes indicate that you're not back until next week, sorry about that. I didn't mean to disturb your vacation."

Before I could hang up the phone. . .

"What was on the agenda of our alleged meeting?"

"I was hired to help find who defrauded the bank of four hundred and fifty large, along with maybe another one point two million dollars on top of that."

"I see, well this is the first I'm hearing all this. I'll call you Tuesday when I get back. What's your number?"

"You can reach me at 212-646-1955. I can't wait to meet you."

"Same here. Good-Bye now."

"Good-Bye."

I felt like I had just been set up. My instincts said the whole thing was an elaborate hoax to get me out of town and off the trail. I was ready to give Bill another call with the latest scoop. I decided to hold off. After all, he was the one that told me Jacobs was dead. And he was the one that said I should leave town even though the FBI agents warned me not to. Thinking back, I was never shown their badges. How could I be so stupid?

I needed to get back. It was four hours by bus or forty-five minutes by plane. However, it could be two or three hours before a plane departed for JFK. My car was still at the bus station in Queens. That made my decision easy, take the bus. I grabbed all my stuff from the hotel and walked to the station.

After getting my ticket, I carefully stepped over the inhabitants that were already claiming stake to prime real estate for the night. With restrooms and showers right in the terminal, it amazed me how bad these homeless people smelled. The fact that they would rather soil themselves than lose their spot and walk thirty feet was a sad commentary on their existence and lack of self esteem.

The bus was right on time; thirty-five minutes late. Unfortunately I've been on enough buses to know that if it's scheduled for one time, it will leave thirty to forty minutes later. I would have to plan my strategy with a pencil and paper.

There is no such thing as Wi-Fi on the bus. I had done my homework on the details of the bank's hours of operation. The front doors were locked by security at 6pm. The elevators to the upper floors were shut down at 9pm.

If an employee was working later than that, they would have to use one of the four emergency stair cases. I was hoping, even counting on the service elevator working later for the maintenance crews to use throughout the night. Since I would be working non stop when I got back, I decided to take a nap for the next couple hours of my trip.

I'm not sure how long I was asleep. I awoke to the sound of my cell phone ringing.

"I'd like to speak with Mr. Alan Fellows. Is he in?"

It was a soft, weak, nervous-sounding voice.

"Look lady, you're calling a cell phone. I don't appreciate solicitations costing me minutes on my plan."

I was ready to hang up when I heard the voice say;

"Daddy, its Katarina, your daughter."

"Katz?"

Father and Daughter Reconciled

"Katarina, could it really be you?"

"Yes, Daddy, it's me."

"How did you get my number? It's not listed."

"Mom told AJ and me that when we came of age, she would tell us how to contact you."

"AJ?"

"Alan Jr. your son."

"How stupid, it's just that I always called him little Al."

"Well, he's not so little any more. The fact is he's six foot one and a hundred and seventy-five pounds. He's been an all star linebacker in high school two years in a row."

I was playing dumb with her. I followed both of their academic achievements through the years. I knew she was an honor student and was on the debate team. I just wanted to hear her tell me. I couldn't believe it had been eight years. She sounded just like her mother.

"Wow! That's terrific."

"Daddy, I've tried to find you since I was thirteen. Mom told us that after 911 you were called back into the military. She said you were in special operations and couldn't be contacted."

"Your mother was always good at secrets and hiding things. Remember the Easter when she hid your basket in the yard and when you couldn't find it, we had to buy one from the grocery. It finally showed up when the weather warmed up and the eggs spoiled. I spotted the neighborhood skunk digging around the bushes. I don't know what smelled worse, the rotten eggs or the backside of the skunk."

"Daddy, I'd like to reminisce some more, but Mommy's dying and you have to come home as soon as possible."

"What happened?"

"A few weeks ago she contracted the H1N1 virus. She wasn't able to shake it and then caught pneumonia. AJ and I took her to the hospital on Saturday. She was doing okay until last night. She slipped into a coma. Daddy, I'm scared. Please can you catch a plane or something and come home?"

"I'm on my way. What hospital is she in?"

"She's at Metro Mercy."

"That's just around the corner from me."

"Daddy, it's the Metro in New York City, not in Nova Scotia."

"Nova - -, your mother must have told you that. Honey, I still live in the same house you grew up in. I never moved away or went into special ops. Your mother left me, and said if I ever tried to contact her or you kids, she would move so far away, I would never find you or her, for so long as I lived."

"So you live in New York?"

"Yep, I'm on a Grey Hound heading for the station in Queens. Do you drive?"

"Of course I do."

"Meet me at the Central Perk in about an hour. If I'm late, just wait. These damn buses are never on schedule, but they're always on time."

"What?"

"Never mind, just meet me, and bring your brother if you can."

We hung up our phones. That was the last person on Earth I ever thought I would hear from. Maybe that's the reason I've never changed phone plans or services. I can't believe my wife had kept the number of my cell to give to the kids on their eighteenth birthday. I didn't know what to do with the investigation. It would have to be put on hold. I rolled my wedding band nervously around on my finger. I would always do that when I was troubled or thinking. Tonight it was both.

"You are quite the actress, little lady. I do believe your father bought the mom dying story hook line and sinker."

"Okay, so the bastard's on his way. You said you would let me and my brother go if I did as you asked. So cut these fricken damn ropes off me. And one more thing, if my brother dies, you'll have hell to pay."

"Do tell. I was going to cut you loose and let you take your little bro to the hospital, but now I feel threatened, so in order to save myself, you'll just have to stay here."

Katarina spit at her captor. Gretsky spit back, he slapped her face knocking Kat along with her chair to the floor.

"Hey jerk face, Gretsky. Stop playing with the children and get your ass over here. Someone's trying to hack into our account in Switzerland. Just a few minutes ago we got wiped clean in the Bahamas. That was half a mill easy. What the hell do you think is going on?"

"I'll tell you what's going on. Somebody tipped off the bank and they're taking their, OUR money back. I wouldn't doubt that it's the little slut's daddy. Get the car and pull it around. We've got a latte to score and a daddy to pop."

That Sixth Sense and Voices

I was nervous getting off the bus. What if I didn't recognize my own daughter? After all, it's been eight years. She's a woman now, not a little girl. For all I knew she could be a dainty young woman or a tattooed biker chick. I should have asked her what she would be wearing so I could find her in the coffee shop. I was ready to dial, when something inside told me to hold off.

When I got to my car, there was a note on the windshield.

"You weren't supposed to go anywhere, but welcome back. If it's after 8pm when you get this, call me. We need to talk."

It was signed by agent Sanders. How did he know I was gone and where to find my car. I was asking myself a hundred questions without answers.

I was being tailed and I didn't like it. They probably went to Ocean City with me on the bus, and I didn't even know it.

Looking around before getting into the car, I didn't see anyone I recognized. The drive to Manhattan was only twenty minutes. I was putting together what I would say to Kat. This was going to be very emotional for me, and I had to somehow keep my composure. I couldn't let my little girl see me cry.

It was 12:35 when I arrived at the Central Perk coffee shop. There were only two tables with people sitting at them. I hesitated to walk in. I hung out in the shadows of the foyer and looked for someone that might be my daughter. At one table towards the back, the guy facing the door looked vaguely familiar. I just couldn't quite place him. At the other table there was a lady and her friend. I was pretty sure they were both too old to be Katarina. As a couple brushed past me to get inside, they were laughing and making a ruckus. The gentleman with his back to me turned to see what all the commotion was about.

"Oh, Shit."

I put my hand over my mouth as I blurted out in shock. It was none other than Leo Gretsky. That meant the guy across from him was either the real Jacobs or the fake one. Whichever it was, it was the same guy who claimed to be Arthur Jacobs when we met at the bank two days ago. It was 1am, and no daughter yet. She should have been here before me.

Something was wrong. I backed out of the foyer. There was a bus stop across the street. I could watch the shop from there, with the street lamp out, I wouldn't be easily seen.

It was now 1:30 and still a no show. Jacobs and Gretsky were both checking their watches. At 2 O'clock they must have decided to call it a night.

There was no reason for me to think they were waiting for me or my daughter, but I wasn't going to go over and say "Hi" like we were all best buddies either.

I decided to call Kat. Maybe she had been called to the hospital if her mother had taken a turn for the worse. I hit the re-dial button on my phone. Gretsky and Jacobs were out front hailing a cab. I could hear Jacob's phone ring, and mine was ringing in my ear at the very same time. It was his phone, not Kat's that was ringing. I hung up before he could answer. I immediately hit star sixty-nine so the call couldn't be traced.

"Who was that?"

"I don't know. Wrong number I guess. They hung up before I

could answer. Why do you think that Fellows dude didn't show?"

"He must have been tipped off by someone. Or he's smarter than he looks."

A cab came while they were still talking. I didn't get to hear the rest of the conversation, but just knowing that they were waiting for me said Kat knew they were going to be there. Maybe that's why she didn't show, or maybe she was put up to it, which would mean she could be in some sort of trouble. I decided since the hospital was only a couple blocks away, I would check out the story about my wife being there and in a coma since Saturday.

"Excuse me. Do you know what room Mrs. Alan Fellows is in?"

"Visiting hours, are over for the day. Come back in the morning after 9:30."

"You don't understand. I have been away for awhile and my daughter called and told me that my wife is near death. I must see her right away."

"NO! YOU DON"T UNDERSTAND. I said visiting hours are over. Now leave or I will call security."

"I'll leave. Thank you for your compassion. I hope when you have a family member dying that they lock the door and throw away the key, so you won't ever get to see them breathing again."

Another nurse was listening. She stepped over,

"What's your wife's name? I'll check on her for you."

"Thank you. Her name is Nancy Fellows."

"Nan, now you must be pulling a girl's leg. She worked the third shift and left about a half hour ago. She had got herself some overtime and called off tomorrow. If that's near death, I want to see what she look like in a coffin."

"She works here and isn't a patient. Is that what you're telling me?"

"That's right. Now if you are her husband, you'd be the jackass she walked out on. The cop that would rather be dead than wed. The sick son-of-a-bitch that let her get away and take the kids then never so much as picked up the fricken phone to wish his babies happy birthday. Is that you?"

"That would be me. I guess I'll go now."

"Oh, yeah, you better be goin, or I'll throw you out on the street like a stray cat."

I think I just met Angel. She was always one of my wife's dearest friends. I went to my car to digest the last few hours. My daughter was in trouble, I could feel it, and my wife still hated me, but wasn't sick or dying, and apparently didn't know about Katarina trying to call. Or did she? I drove to the last known address that I had on my wife and kids.

There were lights on in the front room. I thought it was kind of odd for three in the morning. I drove by the house real slow then parked the car five houses away. As I got closer I could hear crying and yelling and the sound of something breaking. From behind the hedges I was able to look in the window. Jacobs was leaning over someone sitting in a chair. Gretsky wasn't in the immediate view of the window, but he was probably there too.

"So, what did you say to your father to tip him off?"

"I didn't say anything."

 Kat was crying. I peeked in just far enough that I could see my wife lying sprawled out on the floor. She looked as though she might be unconscious.

"You must have said something. We need him to figure out the code for the vault. He's a geek, and with your help, we'll get it. Start thinking, I don't know how much longer your brother can live in a bucket of ice water."

"I can get him to come here."

"Yeah sure, tell me how you're gonna do that?"

"He loves his son more than anything in this world. I'll just tell him the truth. He'd be willing to do anything you want to save him, and as a bonus his wife and me."

"You're either pretty smart of pretty dumb. Wipe your face then call him. No funny business or I'll be happy to make the family reunion one less starting with momsy. She's about useless anyway, and I don't like her attitude. Hopefully when she wakes up she'll adjust the feisty ball kicking down a notch."

"Your Freak of a friend deserved it, and the slap with nails across the face was a bonus. I hope it leaves a nice scar."

"Can't you tell her to shut the hell up? She's getting on my nerves."

"After she gets her daddy here, you can shut her up yourself."

The Set Up

"Daddy, where are you? I've been waiting for hours."

"I'm sorry, honey. The bus broke down outside of Newark. I didn't have your number so I couldn't call to let you know what happened."

"I thought this guy was supposed to be some kind of genius. He doesn't know to press the redial?"

"Leo, shut up. You go on with your story."

Jacobs was pointing at Gretsky and then Katarina. I was watching everything that was happening through the window.

"You're not still at the coffee shop are you?"

"No Daddy. I thought you changed your mind and weren't coming so I left and came home."

"Oh, well it's late. They're supposed to have the bus up and ready any minute. I'm only twenty-five miles away. Hell, I could have walked there by now. Why don't you get some sleep? I'll meet you at the hospital in the morning. We can go see your mother together."

"Daddy I have some bad news to tell you."

"She didn't take a turn for the worse, did she? Don't tell me she died before I could say good-bye."

"No, Mom's resting, She's fine. AJ and I were abducted this evening. We're being held hostage."

"What? I don't have any money to speak of. What could anyone want from me?"

"I don't know. They said you can get them into some sort of vault."

"They are there with you, aren't they?"

"Yes. Daddy, they plan to kill AJ if you don't comply with their demands."

"Tell them to meet me at the bank. I'm not sure what they want, but I'll figure it out. Don't worry, baby girl, I'll get you and AJ. At least your mother is safe at the hospital."

"Uhm, she's not at the hospital anymore. She's home with us."

There was the sound of a little scuffle followed by,

"I think that's about enough."

Jacobs grabbed the phone and walked towards the window. I ducked below the sill so he couldn't see me. I was afraid he might be able to hear me through the window. I crawled to the side of the house then ran into the neighbor's yard.

"Mr. Fellows, it's so nice of you to volunteer your services. If you can't meet us within thirty minutes, your son will be frozen alive. He's already turned a nice shade of blue."

"But, the bus is broken down. Even if it were running, I'm still at least forty-five minutes outside of Manhattan."

"Have you ever stolen a car before?"

"No. I've never stolen a thing in my entire life."

"Well, make tonight a first and get your ass to the bank. Be at the lower level service entrance of the bank in twenty-eight minutes. No excuses if you want to see your son thawed and your pretty little girl without a scar across her throat."

He hung up before I could plead for a little more time. I went out front to watch to see if they would leave together or if just one of them was going to meet me. While I waited for some sort of activity I called Agent Sanders. Even though I wasn't sure he was really with the FBI, I had to go with my gut instincts on this one.

I told him everything and when to meet Jacobs or Gretsky or hopefully both. I then called my buddy Bill. I was going to give him one last chance to prove his friendship.

The front door opened and the lights went out in the house. Both men got in the front seat of their car and drove quietly away so that they would not disturb the neighbors on either side.

When they got to the stop sign, they stepped on the gas a little harder and squealed the tires as they turned onto Fifth Avenue.

These two guys thought I was the idiot. I played them like a fiddle and all was going as planned. They would walk right into the hands of the FBI and a few Blues from New York's finest. I walked into the house, which they had forgotten to lock. The first person I came up to was my daughter. This isn't the way I hopped our reunion would go, but at least she was alive.

I pulled the duct tape from her mouth.

"Ouch! Could you be a little more careful, asshole? Hey! Who the hell are you?"

"I'm your father, so watch your mouth, little lady."

Tears welled up in her eyes. As soon as I untied her, she gave me a hug so tight I thought we would melt together.

"Daddy, Alan Jr. is in the basement. I think they knocked him out and put him in the freezer. It's been like forever. Go and see if you can get him. I'll tend to Mom."

I looked over and saw Nancy on the floor unconscious. She had duct tape around her ankles, wrists and across her mouth. I almost cried. I wanted to go over to help her and hug her, but my first duty was to get my boy out of the freezer.

I went down the stairs with caution. I didn't know this house, and I wasn't sure where the freezer would be. Against the wall near the washer and dryer, there was a big white chest. That had to be it. I ran over the lid had a lock on it. Without hesitation, I grabbed the first thing that looked like it would knock the lock off. It was a small folding chair, but it worked.

I opened the freezer door. My son was in the bottom stuffed like a sardine. At the moment I couldn't tell if he were dead or alive.

I pulled on his arms with all my strength to lift his lifeless body out.

I noticed that the body was warm instead of ice cold. Before I set him down on the floor, he began to kick and tried to break free.

"Alan, stop. Let me cut the tape off before you hurt yourself. You don't know me, but I'm your father."

He looked into my eyes as I wiped tears from them. I couldn't have been happier. I had feared the worst from the moment I got the call. We went upstairs. I had to hold him up because his legs were all cramped from being in the box for a couple of hours. He let go of me when he saw his sister. The two sat trembling in each other's arms. A third head joined them. It was my wife. I stood and watched the scene. To me, it was just like Christmas morning. After the gifts were all opened the three would hug, and I would take pictures. It was that moment in the middle of my recollections that Nancy looked up.

"Are you going to stand there like a goofball, or will you come and give us all a hug?"

"This isn't how I envisioned our family reunion. We need to get out of here you know, the sooner the better."

"Not so fast."

I knew that voice, but I didn't like the sound of it. I turned to see none other than Captain Bill MacFarland. He had his gun out of his holster.

"Is everyone alright?"

"Yes, as good as we can be for what's just happened."

"Do you know if anyone else is in the house?"

"No, but I haven't seen anyone since Jacobs and Gretsky left. What's going on?"

"Alan, the FBI apprehended the both of them and they're down at the station. We won't get much out of them. They are both screaming for their attorney."

Bill put his gun away and called the waiting officers that were outside with an all clear. Finally we could all relax and enjoy the moment together.

"Alan?"

"Yes Bill?"

"Have you figured out where the bank's money went to?"

"Yep"

A Trip to the Hospital

"Paging Doctor Weiss, Paging Doctor Weiss."

Between pacing and sitting in the emergency room waiting, I was trying to hold back my emotions and keep from passing out. The pain was throbbing. Every fiber of my being was trying to shut down to compensate for it. The x-rays were due from radiology any minute. After which the doctor would determine the necessary treatment. They wouldn't prescribe any pain medication until the results were back. I could tell them my wrist was broken. I didn't even need an x-ray to figure that out. I heard it crack when I punched the living room wall, hitting a support beam behind the drywall.

My anger had gotten the best of me after receiving bad news. As a trained professional I should have known better. Every cop knows when it comes to family, emotions can affect decisions, and it's likely you may do something you'll regret for the rest of your life. The rule is, call for backup then step aside.

I was so caught up in the moment with saving my family that I forgot all my training. It was my cleverness getting Gretsky and Jacobs out of the house that enabled them to get away free and clear.

All the police could charge them with was loitering. They hadn't gone into the bank because they were waiting for me. They couldn't be charged with assault and battery or abduction because they weren't caught in the house with my wife and kids tied up.

When I got the call that Gretsky and Jacobs had been released, I punched the wall. Shit! How could I have been so stupid? For two days after the incident, we were a family again. I stayed with my wife, son and daughter in their house. Nights were spent in the guest room, but I was with them, and a warm fuzzy feeling of unity was shared by all.

The News of Gretsky and Jacobs being let go wasn't anything that I wanted to deliver tonight at the dinner table. However, it might be hard to cover a cast up to my shoulder. I almost couldn't get in the car with the damned thing on. Driving with my left hand trying to shift the transmission was a real challenge.

No Place Safe

There were two cars in the drive. That meant my wife and daughter were both home, most likely my son was too. I took a deep breath as I walked through the front door. I looked around, then, said in a loud voice.

"Get ready for dinner. I'm taking everybody out tonight."

"Is that you, Alan?"

"Yes, get a sweater, it's a little chilly. I made reservations at Lady Saigon's for seven o'clock."

"What's the occa - -

Nancy was in mid sentence when she walked into the front room and spotted my cast.

"Holly Hell, what happened to you?"

"It looks a lot worse than it really is. I broke my wrist, is all."

"You broke your wrist and they put your arm in a cast up to your shoulder?"

"It's supposed to stay in one place to set. I have to have it on for six weeks."

"You've got to be kidding."

"That's what I said when the doctor finished putting it on. Now enough about me, round up Kat and little Al. We don't want to be late or we'll lose our table."

"AJ, your son likes to be called AJ. He's not little Al anymore."

"Right, old habits are hard to break."

I didn't want to scare anyone if they saw how I had to drive, so I had my wife do the honors. As usual dinner was fabulous. There's no place on the planet that makes Sesame Chicken like they do at Lady Saigon's.

"So, what's with the dinner out tonight?"

"I've just been commissioned on a new job. Whenever I get paid, I go out to eat. Tonight I thought we'd all go out together."

"Thanks, Daddy."

"Yeah, thanks, Dad, it was real good."

And then the inevitable question came from my wife.

"What's on your mind, Alan? I can tell something's wrong."

Nancy had a sixth sense about things and was always very perceptive when it came to reading the lines on my face. She could tell whenever I was keeping something troubling from her. Her easy going demeanor changed to one of concern.

"I was hoping we could discuss this later when the kids weren't with us."

"If there's something that includes them, they need to hear it."

All eating stopped. A silence fell thick as fog between the four of us. I cleared my throat before I began.

"The police were holding Jacobs and Gretsky on possible charges of Grand Theft, Bank Fraud, and International Espionage along with alleged Abduction, Assault and threat to do bodily harm."

"What do you mean "were holding"?"

"They were let go this morning, pending further investigation."

"So, you're telling me those two bastards are back on the street."

"Well, yes, but . . .

"No buts. Alan, you son of a bitch, it's not enough that you don't give a shit about yourself, you go head first into alleys and doorways and get shot at on a daily basis, now you've gotten me and your children involved."

"Bill said he'd get us into a 'safe house'."

"F Bill and you, I've seen enough movies to know the families that go to a "safe house" never live to see how the movie ends. Damn you.

Nancy stood up and pounded the table. Everyone in the restaurant turned to look in our direction. She threw her napkin on the table.

"Katarina, AJ, we're leaving. Your father will not be coming home and staying with us tonight, or any other night, for that matter."

She was looking at me with fire and tears in her eyes.

"I thought things were going to be different. I even prayed that they would be. How could you bring this on us, how could you? Get yourself a cab. When you get home your clothes will be in the driveway. Take your shit, and don't come back. Damn you, Alan. Don't you ever come back."

I couldn't think of anything to say to stop them. They walked out and never looked back at me. I covered my face with my napkin and wept like a baby. After a few minutes when things settled and no one was staring anymore, I left a hundred dollar bill on the table then went outside and hailed a cab.

When I got to the house both cars were gone. My clothes were strewn all over the front lawn. It wasn't much, so I told the driver to keep going and take me home.

The cabbie dropped me off at home. I was devastated. This time I may have lost my family for good. In my heart I knew it wasn't my fault. How could I conceive that they would go after my wife and children? Nancy was wrong thinking that I invited these two goons into our house to threaten their lives. She was being mother hen protecting her chicks, and I respected her for that.

I walked into the kitchen to grab a beer out of the fridge. Before sitting at the table I reached for a fifth of Jack from the liquor cabinet. If I were going to be discouraged, disgusted, disgruntled and depressed, I might as well be drunk too.

The first beer tasted good. The J.D. was smooth with a warmth that was comforting. After the fourth round any flavor from the beer had disappeared. When I finished my sixth shot of whiskey, I had to hold on to the table while the room started circling around me. Two more rounds and it was time to go to the bathroom. I got up and made it as far as the kitchen floor. I was down and out.

I woke up the next morning with the sun shining through the window on my face. It was hard to focus; the light was blinding me. My first attempt to get up was futile.

I forgot about the anchor attached to my arm. I rolled over and pulled myself up using a chair. Without giving it a lot of thought I went downstairs to the basement to cut off my cast.

There was no way I would be able to function for six weeks with a cast up to my shoulder. This was going to be a real trick. Using my left hand, I cut just below the elbow. It hadn't occurred to me how I was going to get the upper portion off without severely injuring myself. I heard the sound of a power mower coming from my backyard. I was in luck. The kid I had mow my lawn could cut me free.

Johnny was a good kid. During summer vacation he did yard work to earn cash for college tuition and books. He drove me to my wife's house so I could get my car. She parked it in front of a fire hydrant, probably hoping I would get a ticket or the car would be towed away. Knowing her, she probably was hoping for both. There were no cars in the drive, so I assumed they had left for the day or forever. Noticing the front door was left open, I went up the walkway to close it. In their haste to leave, the last one out forgot to lock up.

I peeked in and was horrified with what I saw. Someone had sliced all the sofa cushions then smashed all the furniture in the front room. The stuffing was all over. Lamps were broken, tables were sawed in two. The only thing I could think was that Jacobs and Gretsky came back and no one was home.

They were pissed that they had been apprehended and now no one was here to seek revenge. I made sure that there wasn't any evidence of the family being home while the mayhem was taking place.

Closing the door behind me, I got into my car. I was madder than a hornet. Nothing that I could say to myself was going to calm me down. I pressed the redial button on my cell phone calling Jacobs. It rang three times before he picked up.

"Hey, Asshole, we don't need any more attention drawn to ourselves. The little mishap with the arrest was disconcerting, but I'm willing to let that one slide. However, breaking and entering along with property damage charges; now that would just be stupid. It might even be cause for termination."

"Who is this?"

"It's your boss. Shut up and listen to what I have to say."

"I don't work for anyone except myself. I'd suggest you listen to me. If you're smart, Alan, you'll hang up the phone, join your fricken family and hide."

"Good Guess, but you have short term memory. You need me to fetch something to the tune of Six hundred mil and change. If you and your partner want half, you'll follow my instructions."

"If you don't want to be dead, you'll stick a sock in it."

The bastard hung up on me. I wasn't sure what to do next. I tried playing hard ball, but he threw me a curve and I fouled out. Shit! I was still sitting in my car in front of my wife's house when my cell phone rang. I was thinking it was Jacobs calling back to negotiate.

"Mr. Fellows, we need to talk. I don't want there to be any funny business. No cops. No FBI, just you and me alone."

I wanted him to talk a little. The voice was familiar, but it wasn't Jacobs or Gretsky. This voice was different; it was slow and succinct with a bit of an accent and very soft.

"I'm listening, who's calling?"

While I waited for his response I checked the caller ID. The call was from a phone registered with a Florida area code.

"Arthur Jacobs. You told me to call when I got back in town. We were to arrange a meeting. Someone is impersonating me and using my office to perpetrate a crime. I need to see you as soon as possible. Where can we meet to discuss things?"

"Do you know where Sweet Jo's is?"

"If that's the gourmet coffee shop near the square, I know the place."

"Yeah, that's the place. How about we meet in an hour?"

"Sure, fine, sooner if possible."

"I'll be there in twenty minutes wearing blue jeans and a NY Yankees jacket."

"That sounds like a thousand other guys in New York."

"I guess you're right. What will you be wearing? I'll find you."

"I'm wearing a gray pinstriped suit with a yellow tie."

"Gee, that could be a problem too. Let's say when we get there we just call each other."

"Sounds good, I'll see you there."

My gut said this could be a set-up. If this were the real Jacobs, then he wasn't dead after all, and now he's back in NY. I wondered who else knew about him being in town. There was only one way to find out. The coffee shop was only ten minutes away. I wanted to get there early to assess the situation and look out for the phony Jacobs or Gretsky, just in case they were in on the meeting.

The Set-Up

At this point, fifteen or maybe twenty minutes had passed since I talked to the Jacobs imposter. I felt like yanking his chain again, this time with a different strategy. Three rings again. He was checking the caller ID before answering.

"Alan, what took you so long to call back? You've pissed me off once already. The longer I wait, the angrier I become."

"Look, Arthur, my mother called and I couldn't get her off the phone. You and I got off to a bad start. We don't have to work for each other. We just have to work together."

"Okay, say that I agree? What do you have in mind?"

"This is what I think we can do, and we'll both come out with a surmountable degree of satisfaction. You have the locations of the drops right?"

"That's right."

"Okay. I have the master security codes to withdraw and transfer funds. All we have to do is get together and make it happen."

"Okay, smart guy, how do we do it, and how do I know we can trust you? Last time we were to meet, I ended up in jail."

"We don't have to trust each other at all. I keep my secret and you keep yours. All I have to do is link the access code to the drops. We both get a share of $640,435,010."

"Where'd you come up with that number? I was told a few hundred thousand?"

"You were told wrong. Jacobs didn't want you and Gretsky or whatever your partner's name is to know just how much money there really is to grab. He thought you two could convince me as a securities agent to make the drop, but something went south. He was bumped off, and I'm beginning to think you two were supposed to be the patsies."

"You're a pretty smart guy. Wayne and I were only supposed to get some information from the banker dude, rough him up a little and then get you to spill the beans. When we got to the bank, someone had chilled Jacobs and put him out on the scaffold with the rope sliced so he would drop to the ground creating his own grave."

"Yeah, I surmised as much, but that's all water under the bridge. Jacobs gave me his security codes to guard while he thought someone was trying to get them. Apparently they figured they were getting nowhere and they iced him. Go to the Tri-State Camera shop. It's at 150 Sullivan Street in Brooklyn. They have a Wi-Fi café in the back of the store. I'll set up three laptops with wireless connections. We can communicate without talking. Once we establish a link we can start the money transfers. Be there around seven. Look for a laptop with a floating dollar sign for a screen saver. Your partner will do the same. You don't have to look for me. I'll be there."

"Let me just say this, if there's any funny business this time, you will be a dead man, and I will personally see to it."

"Not to worry. In the mean time I have to figure out who's the double cross and pay him or her, a visit. Don't be late or the whole thing will blow up in our faces."

That went better than expected. I pulled down a side street and walked around the corner to the coffee shop where I was to meet Jacobs. I was hoping this guy was the real deal and not another scammer. I purposely wore a Cleveland Indians cap and jacket so I would look like a tourist. No one looked suspicious, so I got a latte and sat watching customers come in and out.

One older guy in a pinstripe suit entered carrying a brief case. He wouldn't have been set apart from the crowd, except that he was in a wheelchair. From the looks of things, he may be a double amputee. I turned my back to him and dialed the number stored in my cell phone. I could hear a phone ringing nearby in the shop. Then it stopped.

"Hello, is this Alan? Where are you?"

It was the man in the wheelchair talking to me. I had to get out of there without becoming suspicious. Jacobs' wife testified that she could identify her husband by his severed feet. The two of them must be in on the scam, or at least one of them is. I took my coffee cup and threw it at the wall then started yelling.

"Why you son-of-a-bitch, I ought to drop you where you stand. There's no way them damn Yankees are going to beat Cleveland in the series. Why don't we step outside and settle this once and for all."

Oops. I wasn't talking to anyone directly, but three guys were willing to take my challenge. I walked passed Jacobs, and once I broke the doorway I ran like hell with the three Yankee fans at my heels. I spotted a mounted policeman and headed right for him. As we approached I stopped to pet the horse and talk to the officer. The three fans kept walking. That was too close for comfort. I went back down the side street, got in my car and took off for the camera store.

Transferring the Funds

The first thing I did when I got to the camera shop was go to the back where they had the computers. There was a Wi-Fi lounge where people were sitting at the available desks. Most of them were oblivious to anyone around them. They all had their laptops fired up and were into whatever they were doing. There were several laptops for sale that were demo models. I took out my pre-programmed flash cards and put them into two machines. I would be able to save all of our communications on the cards. I wirelessly connected my laptop to the two designated computers that would be for Jacobs and Gretsky. From a remote location, I would be able to give them information and control the whole operation. I told the Jacobs impersonator not to look for me.

After I got everything set up, I left. I went across the street to a little Italian restaurant. I could watch them go into the shop from there. Mama Laurella made the best calamari with linguini in the world. I was starved, so I was going to eat while I worked. The smell of garlic and pasta sauce filled the air. I loved coming to this place every time I was on this side of town.

It was nearing seven. I spotted Jacobs entering the camera shop. He was alone. I thought it was a little strange until Gretsky showed up. I guess they didn't want to be seen together if something came down like last time.

I started the floating dollar signs on the designated laptops. They were pass-coded so no one else could use them. I was hoping they would be smart enough to put in their names. I called Jacobs.

"Hey, I'm running a few minutes behind. The computers are all set. I can talk to you remotely on the screen. Look for the laptops with the floating dollar signs. When you press enter it will ask for a personal code. Just enter 123. That's it. Once you and Gretsky have signed on, I'll give you instructions."

"I don't like the fact that you aren't here. I smell a double cross. I think we'll just wait for you."

"You can wait if you like. I'm tied up in traffic. I should be there in a few. In the meantime, my car broke down, so I'm in a cab. We can still do this if you want. We have a limited window of opportunity if we want to make this happen tonight."

"What are you talking about?"

"It's four hours from coast to coast. We have to complete the transactions before midnight. The postings at each bank don't occur until the following day. Since tomorrow is a Saturday, no one will do the end of the month statements until Monday. Each end of month the banks allow for a floating loss or gain of about a hundred thousand dollars. In the larger branches that number jumps to a quarter million."

"So, how many banks are we talking about? I thought we were just hitting the New York Central Savings and Loan."

"That's petty cash. We are transferring from six thousand two hundred and thirty banks all over the country. I hope your off shore depositories can handle a billion dollars hard cash. If all goes well we can do securities next."

"You said earlier six hundred million, not a billion."

"You heard me right the first time, but I did a little research while I had some time. The record in cash and securities theft is just under a billion dollars. No one has ever done one point two billion in cash. If we're going to do this, I want the record, or die trying."

"Hey, none of that die trying stuff. We're gonna get the money all right, and live to tell our grand kids about it. So what do we do now?"

"Okay. Tell Wayne to log in. I need both machines on. Good. Stand-by. I have a weak signal, probably the tunnel."

They were falling for it. I had them both on-line. Now all I had to do was get them to enter the off shore account number. I wasn't transferring into them, I was transferring out.

By midnight, they will be flat broke. The international police, FBI, and bank securities all over the Virgin Islands will be on them like stink on shit. I was feeling pretty good until the other Jacobs rolled into the restaurant and found a table next to me. He leaned over;

"Aren't you the fellow from the coffee shop? I thought you were going to get the living hell beat out of you by those Yankee fans. It was pretty clever how you got away by talking to the mounted police officer. So, Alan, what ya got cooking on your computer?"

"How'd you know my name and who I am?"

"Easy, when we hired you, we ran your photo and credentials. I know everything there is to know about you, from where and when you were born, to where and when you will die. You may not know where your wife and children are, but I do."

"You leave my family out of this."

"If you think you are going to double cross me, I'll have them cut up and flash frozen then delivered to McDonalds to be fried."

"Look, the only double cross going on is getting the bank its money back. When the two yo-yo's across the street put in their security codes, I'll be pulling money out faster than you can blink."

"And what about the bank heist, the one billion dollar withdrawal?"

"That's a line of bull I fed them to set the bait. They're so greedy they fell for it hook, line and sinker."

"I see. However, it is possible to do, isn't it?"

"I suppose, with the right information, but it would take a lot to set it up."

"How about we do it? If we don't need the idiots across the street, I'll have them removed, and you will never have to worry about them bothering you or your family again."

This was getting out of control. The real, at least I think the real Jacobs, was greedier than the other two, and killing wasn't out of the question. I had proposed such a believable scheme, he wanted in. I couldn't back out now and tell him the whole thing was pure fiction, the stuff movies are made of. I had to play my cards and hope to find a way out.

Is the Real Arthur Jacobs Dead or Alive?

It hadn't occurred to me that I might need a plan of escape. Should things fall apart, I was up a creek in a cement box. I had to do some fast thinking. Unfortunately, not a lot was coming to mind. Only thing was to not let Arthur know that the whole scheme was nothing more than a flimflam to get Jacobs and Gretsky arrested.

"Arthur, do you have the off shore deposit account security codes?"

"Of course, why do you ask?"

"I just needed to know whether we should part company with the two clowns across the street. They think I'm in a cab stuck in the tunnel. I put them on hold with a low reception cut off. The two of them are waiting for me to come back on line."

"Go ahead with your plan to get my money back. Let them get arrested for grand theft if you think you can make it stick."

"I'll call a friend on the force. He can swing by and pick them up."

"Okay, but if I suspect foul play, (Arthur tapped his side indicating that he had a gun) I'll put a cap between your eyes."

I emailed Jacobs and Gretsky to start the download. I told them I would be setting up the withdrawals starting at eleven. What they saw happening on their screens was a pre-programmed Excel spread sheet. It was a lot of numbers flashing so fast they had no idea what was going on. When their download was complete, the program stopped, and the floating dollar sign reappeared on the two laptops. I waited for a couple of minutes. I could see from the restaurant window both Jacobs and Gretsky leaving the store together. They had the look of success on their faces.

"Well, that's that. The FBI should be here any minute to pick them up before they can get away."

"Good, then I won't have to have to knock them off before they go to jail. I have a couple of guys on the inside that can handle it for me, and no one will be the wiser. What's next?"

"We need to go to the bank. I need a larger capacity computer to hold all the data that we'll be collecting."

"We can go in my van."

I needed a reason to go alone. Shit! Nothing good was coming to mind.

"I've got to get the memory cards from the laptops across the street. It would probably be best if we're not seen going into the bank together after hours. Why don't we meet in your office first thing tomorrow morning?"

"You're an idiot. Did you forget that I'm dead? I can't go back to the bank for a meeting. You must think I'm some sort of a fool if you think I'm going to let you out of my sight."

With a little sleight of hand and some distraction, I was able to get the memory card from my laptop.

"Look, Arthur, you don't have to see me to know where I'm at twenty-four/seven. Take my laptop. It has a GPS locked onto my cell phone. You can follow me anywhere with it. I'm sure you're smart enough to operate the system."

"Yeah, give me that thing, I'll figure it out. I still don't like the plan, but, if you have to go to the bank to use their computer, I can't go with you. However, my grieving widow can. Go get your memory cards from the laptops. You got five minutes. My wife will be here when you get back."

"Fine, I'll be no more than three, start the count down."

Arthur was greedier than he was smart. At least that's what he led me to believe. He inadvertently answered all my questions. He was dead to the world. Only his wife knew he was alive, well, now me. That meant no one knew he was in NY either. My plan of escape was developing for me. All I had to do was convince Arthur's wife that there was no reason to split the money with a dead guy. I had to assume she had a partner, so I needed to be careful not to give her an excuse to no longer need my service to pull off the caper.

I got back to the restaurant in time to catch the "loving couple" in a warm embrace. Arthur looked at me then gave his wife directions;

"Watch him, Ethel, he's a slippery bastard. The kind you can't trust. He thinks I don't know what he's up to, but I do."

"Arthur, please, you flatter me. Introduce me to your lovely bride. If she's going to play warden, I'd at least like to know her name."

"Alan, Ethel. Ethel, Alan."

"Hi, Ethel, are you ready to be a Billionaire?"

"Shut the hell up and let's get this over with already."

As we headed towards a black Cadillac De Ville, I couldn't help but think; "What a bitch, they deserve each other." The bank was fifteen minutes away. The ride over was quiet. The only thing I could hear was a whistle sound coming through the driver's deviated septum. I was hoping this goon wasn't the wife's partner, yet I had my suspicions.

"Pull around the back. We'll go in through the service entrance on the basement floor of the parking garage."

Our driver stopped the car in front of the bank doors then got out to escort Ethel and myself to the entrance.

"Stay with the car Gerald. We may be awhile so take a nap."

"Yes, Ma'am"

Good, the goon was just the driver. It was time to turn on the charm to get the lovely Mrs. Jacobs on my side. My only wish was that I hadn't skipped charm school.

"We need to access the main frame of the banks computer system. Do you know where it is?"

"I know this bank better than my fat ass husband. He came here seven days a week and pressed the button on the elevator for the top floor then he'd go to his office. If he wasn't drinking a toast with his slut of the month, he'd be counting his money. For almost ten years I've had the opportunity to walk every fricking floor of this hell hole of a bank. One floor at a time, day after day for ten fricking years, I learned all the offices and where the secrets are kept. We don't need a fancy computer to be rich; I know the combination to the vault."

I was totally shocked by all that Ethel just told me. She spilled her guts like a can of beans, and I didn't even begin to pry. Getting her on my side seemed like it would be as easy as just asking. Her cell phone rang.

"Yeah Bill, I'm with the twit that is gonna make you and me worth more than the old man. No, he don't know nothing. He thinks we're gonna rob the bank. Shhh! gotta go. Sorry, I didn't mean to call you a twit, but my boyfriend gets jealous when I'm with another guy that ain't my dead husband."

"Not to worry, I wasn't paying attention. I have this little thing called a robbery on my mind."

The Secret that Lies Within

Ethel was a character in her own right. She appeared to be twenty plus years younger than Arthur. The lack of makeup didn't detract from her youthful appearance, although the facelift and a nip-tuck here and there certainly helped her keep a picture perfect image.

She was the typical well kept and adorned rich man's wife. Most, older men with money like arm candy to show off when they go out on the town. The problem was she had been neglected at home. I could see she needed a lot of attention. Since she wasn't getting it from Arthur, she found Bill to fill the void. I didn't know how he fit into the robbery yet, but it wouldn't take much to get Ethel to confess all I needed to know.

At the moment nothing mattered except the plan to foil the robbery attempt and get these two in jail along with the other Jacobs and Gretsky. I wasn't sure how the arrest of an alleged dead guy would go down, but that too, was not my worry.

While we waited for the elevator to come down to the basement, I started to ask Ethel the burning question;

"Ethel, you said you didn't need to hack the main frame because you had the combination to the vault. How much did Arthur say you would be getting from this caper?"

"It's none of your business. If you want to live to enjoy any of your share; you'll shut up and get busy."

"I'm just wondering what amount of money, does a guy pay his wife to amputate his feet and then suffer through the pain to fake his own death."

"What the hell are you talking about? Arty had diabetes all his life. It got so bad, he had to have both feet taken or die from the disease. What sick twisted thought did you have?"

"The story was, your husband was tortured, had his feet cut off and then murdered. They had you identify the only parts of his body that were found at the scene of the crime."

"That's the most ridiculous thing I've ever heard. They brought me his feet and I identified them. When Arty had his surgery, he asked the doctor if he could keep his feet. They pickled them in a jar for him, and he brought the disgusting things home. He used to bring them out at parties after dinner just to see if he could make somebody puke."

"Nice."

The elevator door opened and we got in. I watched Ethel hit three numbers two up and one down. Most elevators would stop at the lowest floor number, so the combination didn't make any sense. I didn't say a word. I just watched and waited. The lights on the side panel lit up at each floor. Ethel was talking under her breath;

"First floor: Bank Tellers open 9:30 to 4:30

Second floor: Accounts receivable

Third floor: Accounts payable. . .

This went on all the way up. She would state the floor number then say what the operation was on that floor. It only got interesting around the twelfth;

"Twelfth floor: Foreign securities

Thirteenth floor: Bank Vault, Main Computer, Bank Security Cameras.

Fourteenth Floor: Marketing

Fif . . .

"Wait a minute, there is no thirteenth floor."

"Weren't you listening, I said thirteenth floor."

"I heard everything, but, look, no building has a thirteenth floor its bad luck. Besides look at the light board, the numbers go 10-11-12-14 fifteen and so on."

"Men, you only see what you want to see, and you have selective hearing. The thirteenth floor is between twelve and fourteen. Every building has one, but it usually houses non-essentials like housekeeping. In this case, the bank has all its secrets on lucky 13."

"Huh. How do we get there?"

"I'm not stupid. I know you watched me put in the code. If you hold your shorts up, you'll see. Better yet, you tell me, you're supposed to be the genius."

"Okay, you punched in 15 – 20 then 18. The car should stop at 18 then go to 20 not 20 and back down. I guess I'm not so smart. Fill me in."

"Sheesh, they call me the dumb blonde. 15 and 20 equals 35. When you subtract, in this case, go back down, you get to 13. Watch and learn."

The elevator as always was slow. The door had already opened and closed at fifteen. We were almost to the twentieth floor. The bell rang and the door opened.

"Get out, wait five seconds, then get in before the door closes."

I did as I was instructed with Ethel at my heels. We got back in, and without touching a thing, the door closed and headed downwards. I was astounded by the way this worked. I dare say, I would have never thought of it.

But there was still no 13 on the light board, so I was curious as to where the elevator would stop. I started doing the math again and wondering if basement floors counted in the equation. The light at 15 flashed twice, we were on our way to 13, I was still thinking it would be the number 12 or 11, but I would be wrong on both counts.

The Thirteenth Floor

The elevator slowed to a crawl and then stopped. The lights on the panel started to flash in succession one through twenty-five and back down. When the flashing finished, the board went dark. A few seconds later, three lights appeared simultaneously, the 15, 20 and 18. When they went out, the 1 and 3 flashed. Ethel pushed both buttons at the same time, and the door opened.

"Welcome to Never Land."

"Never Land?"

"No one believes in Never Land, and you don't believe there's a thirteenth floor, so this must be Never Land. To your right is the bank's vault, on your left is the main frame for the computer system, and straight ahead are the security cameras."

"Security Cameras, have we been on camera this whole time?"

"No. The cameras only video tape the first floor where they

can watch the front and back, any place where there's public contact."

"Okay, I get the front with the public and would-be robbers, but what's the back?"

"I can't believe you are supposed to be a securities agent. The back is to watch for sticky fingers of the employees."

"So, none of the other floors have surveillance?"

"You gotta listen more and ask less, I just said the only floor with cameras is the first. I know it's late, but don't fall asleep on me."

"I'm not sleeping. I just can't believe that this place is so lackadaisical about security. How do you know all this anyway?"

"A couple years ago when Arty was upstairs bonking some babe, I came to pick him up. He called down to security to tell them to send me away, and that I shouldn't wait up for him, he was in a meeting. The guard and I both knew what was going on. I asked if he would take me for a tour. I told him all the times I'd been to the bank; I had never been past the foyer where I pick up the cheatin bastard. He told me, they had a different name for Arty. I didn't ask what it was, and I guess it didn't matter. We hit it off, and over the course of a few months he took me from top to bottom with a complete story of the activities on each floor. He was the perfect tour guide."

"He sounds like a heck of a guy, and one day he just blurted out the combination to the vault?"

"It didn't go down quite like that. I used to bring him a sandwich and a beer. One night I brought in a picnic basket with a bottle of wine. Sven couldn't handle alcohol very well. He was drunk as a skunk. I had to finish his shift and drive him home. On the way home he blathered on about everything under the sun. That's when I started to realize he could help me with my finances."

"I don't get it."

"Sven would get drunk and spill his guts about bank secrets. One night he asked me if I could keep a secret, I said sure. He told me to close my eyes, and he walked me to the service side of the building. I know this because I opened one eye."

"Very clever"

"Thanks. We got on the elevator, and he punched in the code. We were on our way to 13. He again advised me to not peek. Sven told me all about the activities on the floor. Once we got there, I spiked his drink with some hard stuff. He got real silly and thought that night would be the night to make his move on me. Have you ever had sex on a bed of one hundred dollar bills?"

"No, I can't say that I have."

"He walked me to the vault. Sven was very thorough with his instructions for me to not watch when he dialed the combination. If you've been following, I cheated and watched the whole process. We had the best time of my life. I miss him a lot."

"You make his absence sound more than he left for a new job?"

"Sven was called upstairs to meet with Arty. Arty told him his services were no longer needed and that he should pack his stuff and get it out. That's when Sven got stupid. He told Arty that he couldn't be fired because he knew of the affairs with the secretaries and he would make it public if he ever lost his job at the bank. Arty told him to shut the office door so that they could talk in confidence. When Sven came back, to sit down, Arty shot him in the head."

"I can't believe it. How do you know all this?"

Artie's a big shot with a big ego. He's another one that can't hold his liquor. When he gets a little wine, he starts to sing like a canary. He was proud of himself and the direct hit. He said he wasn't even nervous nor was he a bit regretful. "The little puke had it comin to him. He screws my wife and then he thinks he's gonna screw me too. No way was I going to let that happen." That's what he told me the night it happened. I miss Sven. Now I'm going to pay Arty back by stealing money from his precious bank. Screw him!"

"Well, that was quite a story. How much money is in there anyway?"

"There's never less than $500 thou, and on pay days there can be over two million smak-a-roos."

"You really don't know how much Arty, I mean Arthur is trying to get his hands on, do you?"

"You keep asking me that. I don't know and I don't care. You can play with the computer if you want, but I'm fillin my pockets with hundred dollar bills."

Ethel headed to the vault. I watched as she started to turn the dial on the safe's lock.

"One point two billion"

She turned and almost fell over her purse that was sitting on the floor.

"What, are you serious? That rat was trying to pay me off with chump change while he was holding the biggest pay day in bank history. And with him allegedly being dead, he thinks he can get away with it."

"Yep, that's what I thought. Would you like to continue opening the safe, or take your chances with me in a little high stakes, high tech robbery for some real cash?"

Two Plus Two Doesn't Equal Four

I was starting to figure things out, but there were still a few things that didn't add up. Nothing from the start of my investigation was the same. The characters involved kept increasing. First it was the Bank Tycoon, Arthur Jacobs. He was swindled by some computer hacks that stole from his offshore accounts somewhere in the Virgin Islands. Arthur is supposedly murdered by someone, but not the fake Jacobs or his partner Gretsky. They alluded to a third party that might be involved. The alleged dead Jacobs show's up after a week in Florida, where he has a summer home. It appeared to be an elaborate scheme to cover up a robbery of the bank here in Manhattan and nothing at all with the offshore accounts. In all actuality, I didn't even know if those accounts were real.

The perfect criminal in all this is dead, so no one will suspect him. His wife isn't a suspect. She doesn't work at the bank, although she hates her husband, so she could be a suspect in the murder case. Okay, no one knew about the prospects of millions until I brought it up. All of them were in for a few hundred thousand. When I told them of the plan to scam banks all across the country, they all started coming out of the woodwork and were willing to off each other in the process. I needed to pump Ethel a little more to put the rest of the puzzle together.

"So, what do you think, are you in or out?"

"My husband said you're not to be trusted. What's to say if we join forces that you won't double cross me?

"There's nothing that I'm going to tell you that you're going to believe. Arthur's right. I'm not to be trusted. I had plans on turning the whole operation over to the Feds, but when you're dead husband showed up alive, it kinda threw a wrench in the works."

"Well, let me say this, if you cross Arty, you won't live to see the sun rise tomorrow morning."

"Do you honestly think that I don't know that?"

"I suppose you do, but I gotta ask ya something. Why do you keep saying my dead husband when he ain't dead? At first I thought it was kind of funny, but now I don't."

"It's a bit of a long story, so I'll shorten it up. I was hired to check into a bank theft by a computer hack. I set up a meeting to see your husband. When I got to the bank at the appointed time, no one was there. I snooped around the office just long enough for an imposter of your husband and his partner Gretsky to catch me. They were as surprised as I was but covered nicely. When I left the office, I heard them talking about a stiff out on the ledge. They spotted me listening and chased me into the elevator, and I got away."

"What's this Gretsky guy's first name?"

"I think Jacobs called him Wayne. I don't know the identity of the fake Jacobs. Your husband hired them to take the fall for the bank robbery and his murder."

"But he was never murdered, was he?"

"No, and I'm starting to think that I'm the only one that was led to believe he died when the scaffolding fell. I was told that even though they didn't find a body, that you identified his feet. That's why I thought you knew he was dead."

"Like I told you, they asked if they were Arties feet and I said yea. He used to take them on the plane with him to put on the mantle in Florida."

"Nice. Anyway, the two goons ransacked my office then abducted my family when I was sent out of town. I managed to have them arrested, but they beat the rap and got out."

"I think we may have a little problem."

"What's that?"

"Wayne Gretsky is Sven's older brother. I met him at Sven's funeral."

"Does Arthur know that?"

"Arty didn't go to the funeral. Why would he? He shot the guy."

"Do you think Wayne knows your husband killed his brother?"

"Oh, well- -"

"Oh, well, what?"

"I may have said I missed the great sex we had, and that if my husband had found out he would have popped him."

"I'll take that as a yes. Why would your husband hire Sven's brother?"

"He didn't. He always had a guy he knows on the police force hire everyone. It's beneath him to hire the help and thugs."

"Who's his contact on the force?'

"You're gonna die when I tell you. He does all his hiring through the chief, the same guy I'm dating. Isn't that a hoot?"

"Wait a minute, back up. Your Bill is the chief of police."

"Yep, he's my ace in the hole."

"Yeah, and he's my best . . . was my best friend."

"Ooh, this is getting hot, don't ya think? The kind of stuff movies are made of. I'm getting chills just thinking of the possibilities."

Random Thoughts Come Together

Bill was the one that hired me. Now that I think about it, I had no contact with Arthur Jacobs until the phone call to him in Florida. His number was left on my outgoing phone list. It was the same time my office had been ransacked by- - well, I thought by Jacobs and Gretsky. It was starting to bother me that I didn't

163

know who the Jacobs imposter was. The other thing I didn't know was who else was involved on the force besides Bill. Or maybe he wasn't really involved, he was just dating Ethel. Yeah, but if that were true, why the cover up with the phony death of Arthur and then send me out of town, as if he were protecting me? I think he's in it up to his eyes and is playing both sides to see who gets the money first.

The other burning question was who were the two detectives? Were they in on it too, or just doing what they thought was an investigation?

No, if they weren't in on it then there would have been some news about the event and possible murder. Those two were definitely in. We were up to eight people that were involved in one way or another. Only half knew there was more money than in the safe.

"Ethel, does Arthur know the combination to the safe?"

"No one that works at the bank is allowed to know the safes combination. It is only opened by security and with at least one or two witnesses."

"That's why your husband sent you instead of coming himself. How did he know that you knew the combination?"

"That's a good question. I certainly didn't tell him."

"What about the 13th floor? Does he know about the existence of this floor?"

"No, you, me and security is the only ones."

"Okay, I think I'm starting to put this all together. How much time do we have until security starts in the morning?"

"They start at six, so that gives us four and a half hours."

"That should be more than enough time to pull this off. I need you to call your husband and tell him I've run into a road block with hacking into the main frame, but I think that I can overcome it with a little time, and that he should be patient. Can you do that for me?"

"Sure. No problem."

I was still working on a plan to come out of this alive and hopefully have a family waiting for me with a hero's welcome. I couldn't believe my best friend could ever betray me and shack up with a – well woman like Ethel. He was never the cheating type, but his wife passed away a few years ago.

He always said that if anything ever happened between Nancy and me, he would make his move on her. He always was jealous that I got her and not him. Shit, that was twenty years ago at a high school dance. I can remember it like it was yesterday.

I had a chill run down my spine. There were no charges filed against the phony Jacobs and Gretsky when they abducted my wife and kids. It was Bill that was the arresting officer, and it was also Bill that gave me the bad news that they were let go. Nancy was pissed at me because she felt threatened that the two were let off with nothing more than trespass charges by the bank. I was wondering why she didn't file a complaint as well having been the one that was beaten and kicked and having watched our daughter get slapped around. Oh, my God! It was all staged to get me to rob the bank for them. The only one not coming out of this alive is me.

Trapped

The firewall security that the bank had installed on their computers was pretty sophisticated. I was slowly hacking my way through the layers to get into the accounting programs. I was just about to yell out, "I'm in" when I heard Ethel in a heated conversation with her husband. The only part I could make out was the final expletives and the phone being thrown across the room. No sooner did it hit the floor when the phone started ringing.

"WHAT!" Oh, I'm sorry, baby. I thought you were my bastard husband. We just had a big fight. I told him where to go and what to do when he got there."

About three seconds elapsed before Ethel belted out;

"No I won't calm down. He's trying to cheat us out of Fifty million dollars."

There was another pause of silence while the party on the other end spoke to her.

"That's right, fifty million - - no, I'm still with the geek, why? He's getting ready to pull of the biggest scam in history since

Bernie Madoff."

I was trying to work and listen at the same time. I was downloading as much information on Jacobs that I could. The only problem was there were no off-shore accounts in his name. There were no holdings or withdrawals of any kind other than payroll. He was pretty much a blank slate. I couldn't imagine him going along with me and not having an account for the deposit. Nothing made any sense. Ethel came over to the computer where I had my laptop set up. She was eating a candy bar that she found in a desk somewhere. She plopped herself on the floor instead of in a chair. I looked over at her, without saying a word. She replied;

"It's more comfortable on the floor. Plus if this is going to take a while, I can lie down and take a nap."

"We may have a situation."

"What do you mean- - a situation?"

"There are no off shore accounts in your husband's name. I was supposed to find out first who was stealing from the bank and then who was putting the money back in the bank. There are no transaction logs of any activity going to the Virgin Islands. That would be noted somewhere. Wait a minute, this looks suspicious. What's your maiden name?"

"Morenkowski"

"Spell that for me."

"M o r e n k o w s k i, don't tell me the money's in my account and the ratfink kept it from me?"

"Not yet. But there is an account in Barbados under an Ethel Morenkowski. It was opened two weeks ago with a bank transfer of $500.00 dollars."

"Five hundred measly dollars, that ain't getting a plane ticket over there."

"It's probably the minimum that the bank will take on an international transfer. I think this whole thing up to this point has been one big test to see if it's possible to move money and not be noticed."

The elevator door closed. The antique floor indicator showed the needle going down. I had to ask a question that up to now I had been avoiding. We were both watching the needle.

"Ethel, don't think, just answer the question. Did Sven have an open or closed casket at his funeral?"

"You are one sick individual. They had to scrape half his brains off the wall. Of course it was a closed casket."

"Who helped Arthur with the cover up? I'm sure he didn't take care of it himself."

"His buddy Bill helped. He always helps."

"The same Bill that you're dating, that used to be my friend?"

"You got it, one in the same. Do you think we should be concerned that the elevator stopped in the basement?"

We both knew how long the door stayed open and were mouthing silently, one-two-three until we got to fifteen and the elevator started moving up.

'I think we shouldn't panic yet. It might just be the cleaning crew."

"They don't come in until seven after the bank closes."

"Are there any stairs?"

"Nope, the stairwell goes past this floor and right to the next."

"We have to get out of here somehow. Up to this point, no one has stolen anything and no one is dead, except maybe Sven."

"I miss Sven."

"I know you do, but that's not helping. If we can get to another floor, even if we get caught it's only a misdemeanor for breaking and entering. I'll even settle for battery charges if I have to hit someone over the head with a chair to get out of here."

"I'm not leaving without a purse full of hundred dollar bills."

Ethel started towards the vault. I watched as the elevator stopped at the 15th floor. Fifteen seconds and it headed upward to the 25th floor.

"Ethel, I can't let you do that. You'll go to jail, or worse."

I started to try to stop her from dialing the combination.

"Touch me again and I'll drop you where you stand."

Ethel pulled out a 9mm hand gun from her purse. She was all business. I backed away with my hands up. I looked back and the elevator was coming back down. It stopped at the eighteenth floor.

"Ethel, we can still get out of here. You can't think they'll let you walk out of here with a few hundred thousand and not say anything. Come on, think about it."

"Okay, I know a way down. . .

The Great Escape

"What are you doing? I told you, Ethel, you can't take the money. They'll kill you."

"I heard you, but if you want to get out, we have to go in."

"You're not making any sense."

"Look, I told you I know all the secrets. The vault has a dumb waiter in the back. It's how they transport the cash up and down without using the main elevators. It's part of the bank's security. The downstairs safe behind the tellers never has more than ten grand, when it goes over, it's sent up. Now, do you want to follow me or bash somebody with a chair?"

"I'm with you. How much time do we have?"

We both looked at the elevator dial as it was leaving the 18th floor.

"I'd say we got thirty seconds. Hurry up, will ya? I can only keep this door open for a short while before every alarm in the place goes off."

"I've got to leave my lap top. It'll keep em guessing until we can make our escape."

I slid the lap top across the floor. It stopped right in front of the elevator. Ethel was about ready to close the vault.

"Wait, I have to see who gets off. I need to know who all the players are in this game."

The elevator doors opened. The first person out was Wayne Gretsky. He was pointing a gun ready to shoot anything that moved. The next one out was the imposter Jacobs. Ethel gasped and almost called out to him. I covered her mouth and then watched as a third person got out. This time I gasped and quietly shut the vault.

"Okay, boys search the floor and be thorough. I don't want any evidence that anyone's been up here; that includes the two of them and us."

My wife was snapping out orders like an Army drill sergeant.

If I hadn't seen her with my own eyes, I wouldn't have believed it.

We crawled onto the dumb waiter. It was just big enough for us to squat and close the sliding door.

"Oops, the button's on the outside. You'll have to raise the door to get it sent down to the first floor."

"Are there any stops in between?"

"I don't think so, but I've never been in this thing. Kind of cozy, isn't it."

"Yeah, sure, cozy."

I raised the door and pressed the down button just as the vault door opened. A gun shot fired and the bullet hit the door. We were on our way down. I was hoping this thing didn't have a stop and reverse on it.

"Whew, that was close. Now how are we going to get out of the safe?"

Ethel had a twinkle in her eye. She started to grin.

"Silly man, the safe is made to not be broken into. They put a safety release inside in case one of the dumb blondes locked themselves in."

"I forgot this bank isn't like the rest I've run security for. Wait, you said the first floor is under constant surveillance front and back. How are we going to get out of the safe and not be caught on camera?"

"The only security that's going to see the tape was supposed to have been shot in the head. If I ever see him again, he'll have a real bullet between his eyes. I can't believe that he let me suffer and then knew I was dating someone else and never came out of hiding to tell me what was going on."

"I don't know what to tell you Ethel. Men are pigs."

The dumb waiter stopped, we just about fell out onto the floor when the door opened.

"Can your driver be trusted?"

"Yes, with his life. He's the most faithful person I know."

"Call and tell him to take the car around the building to the Coffee Cabana. Tell him to keep the motor running. You'll need him to haul ass as soon as you get in the car."

"No problem. I got it handled."

Ethel made the call while we were exiting the safe. I followed her closely. She took me into a broom closet and then looked me in both eyes and grabbed my face. I didn't know what was happening. It was so unexpected and fast. She kissed me right on the lips.

"There, that's all the celebration you get. Pull that drain cover up. We're going to a place the rats don't even know about."

I did as I was told. There was a ladder leading into the sewer. When she climbed down ahead of me, I followed and pulled the cover back in place. It was just in time too. I could hear the voices of the Gretsky brothers.

"Don't worry. Sven didn't show me the drain. I found it by myself one night."

"That's nice. I'll want to hear all about it some other time. Where does this take us?"

"It takes us anywhere in the city that we want to go. I used to like to go under Cavello's restaurant. They have the best smelling garbage in all of Manhattan. But, if we want to get away, we should drop off into the sixth street subway and head into Queens."

"Ethel, you are an amazing woman. By now the boys and Arthur are watching your car and following it from a safe distance. Tell what's his name…

"Maurice."

"Tell Maurice to wait five minutes and then take off and leave some rubber on the road. We won't be able to go to either airport or the bus station. They'll be watching those. We need to get some wheels and somehow get to Buffalo. We can cross into Canada and catch a flight to San Diego."

"Why are we going to San Diego?"

"Because I've never been there, and I've heard it's nice this time of year. Are you coming with me?"

"No, but I'll keep your secret. Here's my card. Call me sometime and let me know how things work out."

"But, they might kill you."

"I'll take my chances. I'm going back to Arty. I can't wait to see the look on his face when I tell him Sven's alive and I've been bonking Bill. If I die right then and there, it'll be worth it. Now go on and get. I'll take the heat for awhile, and you'll have time to get to Buffalo."

It's been five years since I last saw Ethel. The sun shines every day on my Island in the South Pacific. I have a little straw hut, and I fish and swim every day. No cares. No worries. I have an automatic deposit set up with wire transfers from all over the world, just small amounts, never more than ten or twenty dollars from each account. I've never bothered to total it, but coming from five thousand accounts, it adds up to a tidy sum.

THE END

Book 8

The Hunted

The Rain Never Stopped

I was alone,
I was cold,
I was wet,
I was afraid.

The lightning and thunder hadn't ceased since I left the car on the side of the road. It wasn't out of gas, it just quit running and wouldn't start. The worst was, before the car stopped, I was already lost. My only hope was that maybe I was heading towards a town or someplace where I could get help.

Has anyone ever wondered why bad things only happen after dark and in the rain? Nothing ever happens to a car on a bright sun-shiny day or when you're a stone's throw away from a gas station. But, let the rain and thunder begin, and zap, your car has engine failure. Add to that a hundred miles from the nearest town in either direction and you have the start of a real thriller.

Another lightning bolt, this one struck a tree just ahead, and one of the limbs fell blocking the road. I trudged forward. My clothes soaking wet felt heavy on my body. I needed to shed a few pounds, so I took off my jacket and then my shirt. I didn't want to carry them. After I climbed over the tree, I hung my clothes neatly and kept moving onward. At times the rain was coming down so hard the road was barely visible. Sheesh, could things get any worse?

Oh, sure they could. I heard the cry of a wolf nearby, and then the reply of its mate. In what light was available from the moon as dark clouds passed over, I saw a set of eyes in front of me. Don't ask why, but I turned and looked behind me and those same eyes were staring at me. Both sets were low to the ground. Instinctively, I knew these were the two wolves I had heard. Un-instinctively I had no idea what to do. I moved slowly. The rain wasn't bothersome anymore. I was sweating bullets.

I stopped dead in my tracks, thinking it wasn't very wise to go toward a growling beast. He was ready to pounce. With his front feet forward, his rear legs propelled him into the air. He was one leap away when I heard a single gunshot, then a yelp. My would-be attacker went off into the woods. I couldn't tell if he had been hit or not.

"Hello, who's out there?"

There was no response from the gun man to my call. I called a couple more times to no avail. I was looking in all directions, but there was no one in sight. The rain was still pounding on the ground and it was the only sound I could hear until from behind there was a loud growl. Then the front paws of the animal clawed into my shoulders, pushing me to the pavement.

I lay in the middle of the road with this ravenous creature ready to rip into my flesh. Turning to the side, all I could see was the gnashing of teeth. I could feel his hot breath on my face.

"That's enough, boy, get down. That's a good boy, now sit."

I heard the click of a chain onto the beast's collar. Apparently, wolf number two was someone's pet. I got up slowly to thank the person who had just rescued me. Possibly this was the same person who had shot at the first wolf. Once again there was no one around. It was just me and the beast sitting before me with his leash hanging off his neck to the ground. He was calmly looking in my direction.

"I guess it's just you and me. Where's your master?"

"Bark, grrrr bark, bark."

"I don't know what that means. Are you trying to tell me something?"

The wolf/dog stood up. He began to pace and then started

barking.

"Bark, bark, bark, bark, bark."

"What is it, boy? You want to tell me something don't you, or do you want me to follow you?"

"Bark, grrrr, bark."

It sounded to me like that was a bark of confirmation. I picked up the leash and told him to lead the way.

He took off running, and I was doing my best to keep up. A short distance up the road there was an opening in the trees. It appeared to be an unpaved driveway. We headed up the drive to a small cabin. It was set deep into the woods, far enough that it couldn't be seen from the road. I froze in my tracks. How could I know that the dog's master wasn't having me brought to him, and that he wasn't the one in trouble, but, that I was? The only thing for sure, was that someone had a gun and it wasn't me, and someone had this dog well trained and they were nowhere to be found. Or for whatever reason they were not responsive or willing to show themselves.

"I think this is the end of the road for me. If this is your home fella, well, here you are. I'll find my way back to the highway and just continue on my way."

When I let go of the leash, I started to back away. I got a puzzled look from the dog. Then he started slowly towards me. He was showing his teeth and growling. It appeared that I was being disobedient. He picked up his leash, and then still growling, walked it over to me and dropped it at my feet.

"You want me to pick it up and follow you again, don't you?"

"Grrr Bark."

"I'll take that as a yes."

I picked up the leash, and he practically pulled me to the cabin and onto the front porch. The front door opened...

Inside the Cabin

When the door creaked fully open, there were more than a dozen eyes staring in my direction. As I was led into the cabin, the eyes belonged to a wolf pack. They separated to the left and to the right, forming a circle around me.

The windows of the cabin were all boarded shut. It was small with just one room which appeared to have been abandoned some time ago. There were rotting boards and a few missing from the back wall making a second entrance for the wolves. The smell of wet fur, urine and feces was overwhelming. I felt as though I was going to puke any minute.

There were glowing embers in a fireplace behind the wolves off to the right. My master, the lead dog, directed me to a chair in the middle of the room. He nudged me to sit. Each of the pack came around and gave me a good sniff. I was frightened beyond belief. A couple of the wolves dragged in some wood to add to the burning embers, and before long there was a roaring fire. The smoke filling the room was a welcome aroma. I could now clearly see my captors. There were grey and black wolves along with some larger breeds of dog. Looked like mostly Shepherds and Rottweiler's.

More canine creatures were entering the cabin through the back and the front. The room was filling to capacity. As the rain continued, there was a crack of lightning followed by thunder, and then a voice spoke softly to the pack. It was a deep resonating sound that I will never forget, if I live to tell about it.

"What did you boys find for me tonight?"

I tried to turn and look at the person talking.

"Keep your eyes forward or closed. When I want you to see me, I'll come around."

He was stern with me and had very little patience.

"I just want to know what you are planning to do with me. That's all."

"If you can't figure it out, you're just plain stupid - - Hey, did I tell you to move? Sit back down and don't get up again or else."

The wolf/dog master was distracted by the movement of one of the pack. It appeared that some of them were growing restless. I'm guessing hungry too.

My head was pulled back by my hair. I was looking into the nostrils of a beastly man.

"I told you boys to be chubby chasers. This poor sap will barely feed half of yuns. What are the rest of you going to do? If you don't find another meal you'll be nothing but skin and bones, or dead."

The dogs cowered whenever he spoke to them, but when he turned away they would growl and flash their teeth. There wasn't any doubt left as to what was going to happen. It was just a question of when and how he was going to kill me. He pulled a hunting knife and held it to my throat.

"You wanna die quick or be eaten alive? The choice is yours."

With the next clap of thunder I soiled my pants.

"Why are you doing this to me? I haven't done anything to deserve such harsh and inhumane treatment."

"SHUT UP! I don't want to hear your whiney little voice. The only thing I want to hear from you is how loud you can scream."

He took the knife and sliced my neck just enough to draw blood, and then he called one of the dogs over.

"Butch, you can have the first dibs on the Au Jus."

One of the Rottweiler's trotted over to lick the blood that had started dripping from my neck. As instructed, a couple others meandered over and tugged on my shoes until they came off. One by one a wolf or dog would bite and rip at my clothes until my pants had been completely removed. They didn't care whether they got cloth or flesh. I had teeth marks all over. I was naked and bleeding, lying on the floor after being knocked off the chair.

"Okay, that's enough for now."

A few more logs were dragged into the fire. The flames grew and spread beyond the fireplace. The heat was growing in intensity. It felt like my flesh was cooking. Every time I tried to sit up or roll away, one of the wolves stepped on me, growled and bit me. I was penned down. Curiously, though, the mystery man had disappeared.

The front door creaked as it opened. The light of the fire revealed a shadowy image on the wall of someone new that entered the cabin. They stood in front of the fireplace drying off from the storm. . .

Just In Time for Dinner

Without addressing any one in particular, the stranger began speaking. They were walking back and forth with a limp. Under their right arm they used a cane or a walking stick for support.

"Dinner looks to me to be a bit rare. I like my meat well done"

The voice was that of a woman, although the way she was dressed you couldn't tell. She didn't sound all that ladylike either. Finally she turned from the fire and looked down upon my naked, bloody body. I rolled over in shame.

"You ain't hidden anything I haven't seen or eaten before."

She laughed then removed the walking stick from under her arm. She fired a shot into the ceiling of the cabin. In rapid succession the dogs scattered and ran out through any available opening. Her stick was a rifle that she had been using to hobble with.

"Well, son-of-a-bitch, you're still alive. I can't believe it. Old George has usually got his man carved up by now. Guess he wasn't liken' that you wasn't one of his."

I was afraid to ask what she was talking about, but curiosity got the best of me.

"What are you talking about, and who's George?"

"If we're going to have a civilized conversation, you might want to put some pants on."

She picked my half shredded pants up and started to hand them to me so I could get dressed. After getting a whiff,

"Well, maybe not these. Here, wrap this blanket around yourself. You'll probably get fleas, but it's better than sitting in what ever happened in your shorts."

She was feisty with a poor sense of humor, just what I needed. I hoped she had something funny to say about the blood I was leaving all over the place.

"You don't appear to be one of them. Who are you?"

"Mister, I ain't ever been called "one of them" before. Thanks for not associating me with them. We need to get out of here before the wolves figure out I don't have another round to fire. Can you give me a hand? I think I busted up my ankle pretty good when I tripped over a fallen tree stump back in the woods."

"Was that you that shot at the wolf on the highway?"

"One in the same mister, now let's get a move on. George don't take kindly to his dinner leaving before he's had a chance to eat it."

I was directed towards the back to make our escape through one of the broken boards. We were running a three-legged race down the side of a hill into the woods and settled down on a rock in a small stream. While catching our breath, my Knight-tress in shining camouflage began to tell me a story.

"Old George is a prison guard for the county facility just up the road a piece. He's always had a love for animals, all kinds, but specially the dog type. Well, every night after dinner he would walk a tray of leftover food and toss it over the fence. He could hear the dogs enjoying their meal, but he couldn't see em. One day he was caught on camera throwing out the food, and the county commissioner threatened to fire him if he did it again. After that the dogs would still come by and howl all through the night as they were starving to death. This made George crazy and angry. He decided he wouldn't let his beloved animals suffer and die, so he came up with a scheme to feed them. Shhh, I think I heard something. . ."

The Hunt Begins

Silence fell heavy as the rain. The only thing I could hear was the rush of the stream and the splashing of water against the rocks.

"Are you sure you heard something?"

I asked in a whisper. I didn't want to talk loudly because there might have been someone or something in the woods.

"Yes, I heard a twig snap."

This woman that had saved me from a fate, which was worse than death, well actually saved me from deaths door, was more like an army drill sergeant than any lady I'd ever met. She gave orders and had no patience if they weren't followed at once. She also looked like she could snap me like a twig if provoked to do so.

"Look over there between the two trees. There's a clump of tall grass. See the eyes looking this way? That's Butch. If he howls, Buddy and Sierra will come a running. It won't take long for the rest of them to find us - - and then George."

"So what do we do?"

"I've got to stop Butch. I'll be the decoy. You stay in the stream and keep walking north. The dogs can't smell you in the water, although with the odor you're wearing they might. NO MATTER WHAT don't look back and don't stop moving. Run if you can."

"But—"

"But, nothing, get a move on, mister. I'll catch up to you soon as I can. Try to get to that little car on the road and lock the doors. I put some gas in and jumped it to see if it would start. It does. You might want to get your gauges fixed. They ain't so good. NOW GET."

She pulled the wet blanket off me and cracked my backside with it to get me moving. Not that I didn't have good reason before, but being naked I had all the more reason to run. I can't believe I was out of gas. The gauge read full. Guess it doesn't matter. I would still have been walking trying to get help.

Geez, is this rain ever going to stop? I wondered what time it was. It seems like daylight should be coming soon. In the distance, I heard a loud, tortured scream, I wanted to turn back, then I heard a dog yelp, followed by silence. I wasn't sure what had just happened. My imagination was filling in the blanks.

I was hoping it wasn't what I thought. Exhaustion was taking its toll, and I had to stop and rest for a minute. I heard a sloshing sound coming towards me. Fear of who or what froze me to the rock I was sitting on. It wasn't clear to me by the sound, but they weren't moving very fast, more like a trudge than a trot. The slosh was followed by heavy breathing. Now I could make out the figure. It was the drill Sergeant.

"Boy I'm glad to see it's you, and not somebody else."

"I thought I told you to keep moving. You should have been to the car by now."

Maybe I wasn't so happy to see her. When she got close enough to me, she collapsed in my arms. Her leg was twisted at the ankle, and both arms were bleeding. She had had quite a tussle with Butch. By the looks of her, I wasn't sure who won. She apparently passed out from the pain. It was my turn to save her. I wrapped both her arms around my neck so I could drag her through the water. It helped that she wasn't as big as her bad-ass attitude.

The water was deep enough that her legs floated a little and that aided in the rescue run. I saw a clearing and a flashing light. There was a tow truck in front of my car getting ready to haul it away. Now this was going to be embarrassing. How was I going to claim my car while in the buff? Since I couldn't carry my package up the embankment, I laid her gently on the side of the stream and removed her pants so that I could get my car. In the trunk was my suitcase with all the necessities for a change.

"Gee, couldn't you have been just a little bigger? Now don't run away, I'll be right back."

"Hey mister, that's my car. I got lost in the woods trying to find help."

"You say this is your car? Ya got any identification?"

"No. Not on me. I fell in the water and lost my wallet and my keys. Do you think you can jump it and get it started for me? I have money in my suitcase, so I can pay you if you can get the trunk open too."

"I won't have any problem with any of that. The key was in the ignition."

"Great, then I can pay you right away. How much do I owe you for your trouble?"

"It's no trouble. I'm up and down this highway all the time. I was just here pulling that branch off the road so traffic could get through in the morning. You look a little roughed up. Was ya in a fight or something?"

"No, just scraped up from the brush. Let me have the keys, I'll pay ya anyway. Will a fifty be enough?"

"That's right nice of ya mister. My name's George, and who do I have the pleasure of this fine evening?

No Animals were injured in the writing of this story. All are well trained actors, and the sound effects, were previously written for the scene.

A Failed Rescue Attempt

With that deep resonating voice and the name George, I finally made the connection. My body was covered in a blanket of fear. I was sweating ice. He couldn't tell in the rain that I was shaking in my boots, that's if I were wearing em. I hoped, since he only saw me from behind, that he didn't recognize me. The still bleeding neck, dog bites and claw marks might have been a giveaway; however, once again the rain helped hide most of it.

George was waiting for me to introduce myself. He had his hand held straight out. I was afraid to shake it, but . . .

"The name's Jack, Jack Twitcher, and the pleasure is all mine to be sure."

We shook hands. He squeezed hard, pulled me close. While looking me square in the eyes, he said;

"You'll want to get yourself outta here right quick. I hear tell the wolves in these parts enjoy hunting in the rain."

"Thanks, thanks for all your help. I'll be out of here as soon as you get my car off the tow hooks."

While George disconnected the car, I went into the trunk for a change of clothes. He signaled me with a wave and took off down the road. When I saw his tail lights disappear into the night, I went back down the embankment.

Shit, I thought I told her to stay put. Where the hell could she be?

I was frantic, fearing the worst. Where could she have gotten off to? Or did someone take her away. I softly called for her.

"Hey, lady, where are you? I told you not to go anywhere, I'd be right back"

"Psst, shithead, I'm over here. You left me in plain view of the road. If George were to see me without my pants on, he would have first shot you in the head and then asked questions. You didn't sex me while I was passed out, did you?"

"Sex - - sex you, why no, no of course not."

"Why not, don't you like me?"

"I like you well enough, it's just that, well, I couldn't go claim my car with no pants on, so I borrowed yours. Here, you can put them back on."

"Are you sure you want me to?"

"Look, I don't even know your name. Besides this is hardly the time or the place. We need to get you to a doctor to look at that leg of yours."

"You're so caring, always thinking of the other person."

"Okay, now I think you're just delirious from the pain and talking crazy. Let me help you get to the car."

She put her pants on and I carried her to the car. As soon as the engine started, she looked over at me.

"My name is Sarah Louise Parker."

She passed out again before I could tell her mine. I was just passing the fallen tree when I saw two wolves standing in the middle of the road in my rearview mirror. I started to step on the gas when two more wolves jumped onto the road in front of me. I slammed on my brakes and swerved to avoid hitting any of them. I spun the car around and floored it in an attempt to get away. I heard a thump on the roof. Then a dog came from the woods and managed to leap onto the hood of the car. I had to slow down. My vision was blocked.

The rain was coming down harder than ever, and the animals were coming out of the woods, jumping from behind bushes. I was stuck now in the mud with my tires spinning. This was turning into nightmare number two, maybe three. I had lost count.

I could see head lamps coming towards us. As long as it wasn't George, I might get lucky and get a little help from someone. The car had a siren with blue flashing lights. That meant a sheriff or a patrolman of some sort. When the patrol car was about a hundred feet in front of us, the officer stopped, stepped out onto the road with a shotgun and fired a shot in the air.

"Go on, get out of here or the next shot will be at your mangy flea bitten butt. Damn animals, I'd like to shoot the whole lot yuns."

He walked slowly towards the car. With the headlights of the patrol car and his flashlight shining in my face, I was practically blind. He knocked on the glass of my driver's door.

"Ya got yourself good and stuck, boy. Roll down that window

so's I can see who I'm talking to. You got your license and registration, mister?"

"I have the registration, but I lost my wallet."

"Well, ain't that convenient."

"Pardon me."

"Oh, nothing, I was just talking to myself."

He peered into the window shining the flash light on Sarah trying to assess the situation.

"Mister, is your girlfriend dead or alive?"

"She's alive of course. She's just exhausted that's all."

"What's with all the blood, you two have a fight? That's a nasty cut on your neck there. Did your girl cut you while you was beaten her up?"

"No, she didn't cut me, and I didn't beat her up."

"Step out the car and put your hands behind your back."

While doing everything the officer said, he slammed me hard against the hood of the car and then cuffed me. He took a step back and got on his walkie-talkie.

"Jimmy, it looks like we got ourselves a domestic out on highway nine. I need backup and a tow truck. See if you can get that rascal George out of bed and send him over."

I thought to myself, "This just keeps getting better as the night rolls on." Another clap of thunder and the clouds parted one more time.

No Bail

Before the back-up car arrived, the officer continued to rough me up. He directed me to the patrol car and then prodded me with the barrel of his shot gun. With the rain and the wet pavement I guess I wasn't moving fast enough.

"What's a matter, mister? Can't get your footing with them flops on?

He pushed me and I started to trip. I was able to maintain my balance, so next he cracked me behind the knees and I went down. While on my knees he taunted me and then pretended to hear something. As he turned quickly to look behind, he purposely hit me in the head. I went face first into the road.

Being cuffed I couldn't do anything but eat the dirt. I broke a tooth which I spit out along with a mouthful of blood and may have broken my nose as that was the first thing to hit. I wouldn't give him the satisfaction of screaming in agony, and I had to man up not to cry.

When the lights from the back-up patrol car came shining around the bend, he pulled me up by my hair and shoved me into the backseat of his car.

"You shut up and don't say a word. I can make it go real easy on you, or real hard. You make the call."

There was nothing for me to say. The two officers were talking when they walked over to my car to check on Sarah. I couldn't make out what they were saying from that distance, but when the second guy was close to my door, he said,

"I'll call for an ambulance to take the little lady to Mercer Hospital. George Hollens is on his way with the tow."

I was kept sitting in the back seat of the patrol car while the two officers told jokes and smoked cigars. Once the ambulance was on its way to the hospital with Sarah, we were on our way to the police station where they promptly threw me in jail.

"Do I get to make a phone call?"

"Sure you do, it's your right to do so. However, with the storm and all, the lines are down. When they come back on, that's when you can call. I tell you this, though, we're a small town, and last big storm it was two weeks before power came back and three days more before phone service was restored. A fancy man like you outta have himself one of them cell phones."

The officer laughed and started to walk away.

I mumbled to myself, "No towers, no signal, no phone service, dead battery."

"What's that you're saying?"

"Nothing, do you know what they intend to charge me with. After all, I was just stuck in the mud, not causing a ruckus or anything."

"I think Officer Gentile is drawing up the papers even as we speak. I'm sure he'll be right along to read you your charges. You might want to remind him to read you your rights; he forgets that all the time."

I sat on the only chair provided. It was three legs of one length and one leg broken. I was nervously rocking. Daybreak arrived with a mix of sun and rain. I hadn't slept a wink. Mostly from fear of something else happening that might cause me bodily harm. I started to assess my wounds.

The rotten bastard that broke my nose and tooth still hadn't charged me with anything. He hadn't removed the cuffs either. You'd have thought they caught some master criminal that had been on America's most wanted for the last twenty-five years.

There were some strange sounding footsteps accompanied by some heavier boots heading towards my cell. I would have gotten up to look, but it would have been difficult at best. Worse, it would have been painful, and lastly, I didn't want to risk falling on my face. At this point I was hoping for the best, but the truth was, I didn't even care.

"Jack, Jack Twitcher the book writer?"

It was Sarah. She had a cast on her leg almost up to her hip. She was a sight for sore eyes.

"How did you know my name?"

"It was in your wallet, on all your credit cards and driver's license."

"Looks like you did a real number on your leg."

"Yeah, the doctor said after I fractured my ankle it wasn't a good idea to go running through the woods. He said I'll be able to play soccer in about six months."

"Soccer?"

"I'd kick your ass up the field and back down."

"I'm sure you could. Do you know when they might let me out?"

"From what I hear tell, you could be in here a long time."

"What? Why?"

"Well, for starters, Grand theft Auto …"

"But, it was my car."

"You got any I.D.? No, I didn't think so."

"But, you said you found my wallet, right?"

"Shut up and let me finish. Next, kidnapping, assault, attempted murder, rape, driving without a valid license, loitering and finally, operating an un-safe vehicle."

"You have got to be kidding. I can't believe it. But, you found my wallet. That should identify me and help, right."

"You betcha, I told them what happened and they dropped all charges except the driving without a license, which is only a misdemeanor."

"I have to ask, where'd you find my wallet?"

"It's a long story. I'll tell you on the way to my place to get you cleaned up. Nice nose job, did Larry do that to ya? I wouldn't say anything. He gets powerful mad at ratfinks."

THE END

Book 9

Those Glorious Golden Years

When I retire, they'll be no senior home for me
Just put me out to pasture, where I can roam free
"Hmm, not a bad start, at least I've got ten to fifteen years to finish it."

That's what I was thinking when I penned the first stanza of a poem I would title, "The Glory Years."

My mind drifted out the window. I was staring into the wide open spaces of my backyard in upper Manhattan. The open space encompassed a whopping ten by ten plot of artificial turf. There was a clothes line that blocked the view of the graffiti painted on the building across from ours. Looking back to my keyboard, I hit the save button and went to the internet.

I started a search for Real Estate out West. There were pages and pages of all types of land offers and bargains and how to get free land from the Government. Gee, it was hard to tell the real sites from the scams. The one that caught my attention read like it was talking directly to me. It was as though the agent was on the other side of the screen and talking to me while reading my mind.

"All your life you've dreamed of living the life of a cowboy."

"Yes, that's right."

"Retirement is just around the corner. Now's the time to make the investment that will take you through your Glorious Golden Years."

"Where do I sign?"

I called the agent for a development down in the valley overshadowed by a gorgeous white crested mountain. The property at one time was owned by a fifth generation cattle rancher. When he hung up his spurs, he sold everything he owned to a local investment company. They in turn sold it to a real estate development firm. The two thousand plus acres was parceled off into prime lots for residential homes. The smallest of which was thirty acres. At a ridiculously low price of thirty-five hundred an acre, how could anyone pass it up? The best part, we didn't have to build for ten years. We could be the first to pick our plot of land if we acted soon.

I ran downstairs more excited than our daughter at Christmas.

"Honey, pack your bag. We're going to pick out our country home site. If we buy while we're there, they'll pay for our airfare. I figure if it's free we might as well go first class."

"John, that sounds wonderful. What weekend are we talking about?"

"Well, this weekend is the special offer. In addition to the airfare, they put us up in a luxury hotel for our stay including a champagne breakfast."

"Great! I can't go. Take your camera and send me some pictures. And DON'T sign anything."

"What are you talking about, you can't go?"

"The ice cream social at church is this weekend. You know how hard I've worked to get from cashier to head scooper. I won't miss it for the world."

"But - - if we don't buy this weekend - - we won't get the free airfare and hotel."

"Then I would suggest you fly coach and stay at a Holiday Inn."

"But - - the champagne. . ."

"John Alan Fellows, if you buy property without my seeing it, you won't have to worry about retirement property because you won't live long enough to retire. The last scheme you got us into took five years to pay off, and did you learn to golf? No. And did we use the Jacuzzi, hot tub, swimming pool or tennis courts at the "All Inclusive Vacation Resort" NO WE DIDN'T.

Now I don't mind if you go and snoop around, get the information, take some pictures and bring back the champagne so we can talk about it, but if you buy so much as anything more than a hamburger, your ass will be served at the next social."

"Yes, dear, maybe I'll take a bus and save some money."

"That's my good little man. Are you ready for dinner? It'll be on the table in five minutes."

She always had a way of winning a discussion that had to do with spending money. I guess that's why we still have a few bucks in the bank. Instead of being mad, I should be thankful. I just have to figure a way to get the property and not tell her.

Friday night at seven, I headed for the airport. Saturday I was to get on a shuttle to see the development. It was so aptly named, Wilderness Passage Estates. I couldn't wait to get there. Eight O'clock couldn't arrive soon enough, I was up at six with the sun and looking at the most beautiful countryside I had ever seen. At the end of my view was a mountain. Snow-covered just like the picture in the brochure. I went down to the gift shop and bought a straw cowboy hat. I'd get a real one someday but this wasn't that day. A small shuttle bus with a magnetic sign pulled in front of the hotel. I looked to see how many of us bargain hunters there would be going to "The Land." No one else showed up. I suspected that maybe the other people were staying at the free luxury hotel, so I wasn't all that worried or concerned when I got on the bus alone.

"All aboard, next stop Wilderness Passage Estates."

The Land

I was sitting on the bus, moving from seat to seat, checking out the view from every window. I didn't want to miss anything. I kept checking my watch. It was almost eight-thirty and we were supposed to leave at eight. I stepped out of the bus to speak to the driver. I wondered what the holdup was. To my surprise, he was nowhere to be found. He wasn't on either side of the bus, so I went inside the hotel to ask if they knew where he went. There was a young fellow at the far end of the check-in counter. He was talking to someone in the back office. As he looked over, I waved to him to come over. He turned away.

"Yeah, some clown is waving at me, like I want to talk to him or something?"

"Excuse me, I can hear you."

"Yeah, like I can hear you too, so, what?"

"Well, I just have a question."

"You're gonna make an issue of this, aren't you, mister?"

"Look, all I want to know . . ."

The bellhop or whoever this rude employee was started to slowly saunter in my direction.

"Good Morning, Sir, welcome to Mountains View Hotel. How may I be of service? Will you be staying for the night or longer?"

Wow, a complete one hundred and sixty-five degree turnaround in attitude. I could hardly believe I was talking to the same person of a minute ago.

"Oh no, I already have a room. I was just wondering what happened to the bus driver?"

"Look, mister, I only do the check-ins. I don't keep watch over the help. Go ask the concierge service."

Now that's the fellow I recognized from before. I looked over at the travel and information desk. There was no one there.

"But, there's . . ."

The bellhop was back at the far end of the desk talking again to the person in the back room. He looked in my direction, and again I waved for him to come over.

"Can you believe this guy, I can't believe this guy. He don't want to check in and still he wants to jabber jaw all morning."

"I can still hear you, and I speak English you know?"

"I can still hear you too, and your English will come in handy with the couple in 512. They're on their honey moon from London."

Great more sarcasm, I looked outside and the bus was gone. I went out and kicked the dirt. This was just my luck. I was P.O.'d to the max. I pushed the front doors to the hotel open with such force that they hit the walls. Not one person so much as flinched. My grandstanding didn't even get the attention of the staff member cleaning the lobby.

I sat in a guest chair in front of the information desk. A little sign on the desk said, "Be right back." The hours were listed of being open from 7:30am until 3pm. I waited for a half hour. No one showed up. Back I went to the front desk. Oh yeah, you guessed it, the same fellow was in his usual spot. I didn't want to get confrontational. All I wanted was an answer on how to get to the development.

"Yo. Hey buddy. Come here. I want to talk to you, and I want a straight answer."

"Oh, boy this guy seems a little pissed. Maybe we should call security."

"I can hear you, and you don't have to call security. I just want to know when the next bus comes to take me to the *Wilderness Passage Estates*."

Laughter erupted in stereo from the guy at the far end of the desk and from whoever was in the office. This secret person peered around the corner to see who the funny man was.

"See, I told you he was a clown. Now he's making jokes."

"I can still hear you. Can you please just give me a little help? There's been no one at the information desk for the better part of an hour, the bus driver disappeared and then the bus left. I have an appointment for a showing of property at the *Wilderness Passage Estates* and I-I-. . ."

"Look mister, I just do the check-ins. Go sit, have a cup of coffee, calm down and I'll find someone to help you."

"Well, that's better."

As I headed for the coffee in the little breakfast nook, laughter again broke out, this time louder than before. I may have even heard the guy in the back fall out of his chair onto the floor. I knew instantly while stirring the cream and sugar into my coffee that no one was coming. I got on my cell phone to call the real estate agent.

"Hello, this is John Fellows. Yes, good morning to you too. No, no I'm in town. I just got up a little late and missed the bus. Oh, you're kidding, that would be great. You're sure it's not a problem? Yes, of course I'll be ready to go. Fifteen minutes, that's terrific. Thank you, thank you very much."

The agent himself was going to pick me up. I thumbed my nose and stuck my tongue out at the little puke with the attitude. He laughed then turned his back to me as I went outside to wait. The heat of the mid-day sun was starting to take hold. According to the forecast it was going to hit 104. Now that wasn't bothersome because I heard out West it's a dry heat and the humidity is very low. By the time the agent came, I was soaked to the bone in my own sweat.

I felt a shower was necessary. I sniffed my armpits. Not too bad I thought. The agent was driving a white Cadillac with white leather, white wall tires and the obligatory bull horns on the hood.

"Mr. Fellows, I presume."

"Yes, just call me John."

"John it is. I'm Alonso Morning. Most folks call me Al."

"Alright Al, shall we go off to see my new property?"

"Sounds like you're ready to take advantage of our big bonus bonanza. All new home sites are fifty percent off on the wood siding, a, cabin models. That's providing you buy thirty acres or more."

"Well, Al, if all goes well and I find the perfect site, you can bet your bottom dollar we'll be writing a deal tonight."

I think I imagined Al rubbing his hands together. Dollar signs appeared in his eyes. Al was a robust fellow to say the least. He wore a ten gallon white Stetson hat, blue wrangler jeans with a leather dude jacket. This guy was slicker than snake oil. He was a long cool breeze of selling machine, and I was buying whatever he had to offer. We got into his car. He offered me a cigar and a jigger of hooch. I don't even know what hooch is, but it was refreshing and sure tasted good. My cell phone rang.

"Hey honey, yeppers, on my way wif the agent now."

"John, you sound funny. It's ten in the morning. Have you been drinking?

"Drinking? No. It must be the mountain air or a bad connection."

"You haven't bought anything or signed any papers have you?"

"No. Of horse-snot."

"What?"

"What?"

"John, you're not making any sense. I think you should leave before you get us in trouble."

"Not to worry, I won't pay double, the house is half off. I think -

Do the Hustle

We drove for maybe twenty-five miles and then turned down a dirt road. There was a sign swinging from one side of the entrance poles to the estate. One good gust of wind and the whole thing would be on the ground. Just inside the welcome sign was a mobile trailer. It had a wood-sided fascia to give it a rustic look. There was sage brush and cactus mixed with a few dried up pine trees. I was surveying the entirety of the situation when a tumble weed rolled past the car. Al pulled right up to the front of the trailer, almost touching it with the bull horns.

"Well, here we are. Shall we go in and look at a map of the development? We can freshen up before we head out and look at the landscape. Here ya go, my friend, you look a little parched."

Al handed me another jigger of hooch. This stuff was wet and wild, unlike the dry desert we were standing in the middle of.

"Say, Al, where they putting the oasis swimming pool and bass lake?"

I stumbled getting out of the car and almost fell on my face before Al grabbed my arm. He helped me up the two steps into the mobile office.

"The Bass Lake is going to be dead center of the town we're building. Here, I'll show you on the map. See, that blue spot is the lake."

"It looks a little like someone spilled a drink and the ink smeared."

"Ha, ha. John you are quite the comedian. Now over here is the club house. All the streets run into it, so where ever you are, you're never too far from the pool and indoor tennis courts."

"Indoor tennis, I don't remember reading about that."

"The civic council just approved it, last night as a matter of fact. You do play tennis don't you?"

"I took a lesson once. Does that count?"

"Why sure it does, John. Everything counts."

"I'd like to take a look at Little Mountain Lane."

"Gee, John, I don't know if we have time to go anywhere else. Where's it at?"

"See the circle at the base of the mountain that looks like a coffee stain? That's where I want to go."

"Oh Yeah, Little Mountain Lane, it's probably my favorite of all the streets in the development. You can't find a better place anywhere on the map. You can trust me on that."

Al poured me another cup of hooch. It was cool and refreshing and had a hint of lemon, or some kind of fruit. It quenched the thirst like nothing I've ever drunk before. This time when I got up from the table I landed on the floor and started laughing uncontrollably. Al's face started to take on funny shapes, and I started laughing even more, so much so I thought I was going to crack a rib.

"Here ya go, up and at um. Now don't judge too much by the dirt roads. All the paving is scheduled for the fall when the weather cools. You can't pour concrete when it's blistering hot or it'll crack and then ya just gotta keep patching it with tar. We here run a first class operation. We do it right, or we don't do it at all."

"Thash tha kina thing ah like to hear. Coo-ality workmanship ish the name of the game."

"John, you don't drink much, do you?"

"Why, I don't drink any at all. I haven't drank a drink since the time I bought a mebershit in a con-tree club. My wife won't let me liv that down. I'll take that mistake to the grave. Wha-I do you ask?"

"Oh, uh, no reason. It's just that I've never seen anyone enjoy the hooch like you seem to."

"Hooch, that's af unnie name. What's in this stuff any way?"

I started laughing again at the sound of the name, hooch. Tears were rolling down my cheeks. When we got to Little Mountain Lane, it was like nothing I had ever seen in my life. The mountain had a white cap just like in the picture. We drove to what was alleged as the end where there was to be a cul-de-sac. I picked dead center where the property butted right to the base of the mountain.

"Thas, it Al, I want this one. Writer up, I- I- I'll take er."

"You got it, my friend. We'll go back and you can celebrate while I draw up all the papers. Have you decided if you want the Lincoln log house or the Davy Crockett?"

"I'll know it when I she it. Shay, do you have anynor of tha Hooch? I'm awful thirty, I mean thisrty, Oh, what the hell, I need a drink!"

My cell phone rang, I was about to answer it when the battery died.

Sign Here, and Here, and It's Yours

The trip to the office was nothing short of a blur. When we got into the trailer, I had to piss like a race horse; I thought I would wet myself before I got to the bathroom. Al went straight to his desk and started drawing up some preliminary paperwork.

Stumbling back out of the bathroom, it was all I could do to make it into a chair and not land my ass on the floor.

"Shay, am I gonta get the fwee airfare and staaa at tha lux-yourie hotel?"

"John, you just relax, I'm going to take care of you. I'll see what freebies I can throw in without getting fired by the agency."

"Shanx Al, you ara goo-urp, excuse me. You ara a goo-urp, good maahn."

"Yes I am. And you'll thank me when you see the sweet deal I'm making you on the estate property and cabin. Now remember, you have ten years to build, or the property reverts back to the seller and all upfront fees collected are forfeited. But, you don't have to worry about that. I'm sure you're a responsible citizen and will complete the obligation on or before the contract due date. Okay, here we go. . .

The land ....$3500.00 an acre 30 acres.......... Total $105,000.00

The Deluxe Lincoln Log Cabin......................Total $275,000.00
     Optional Basement $80,000.00
     Water to the home site $45,000.00
     Electricity to the home $33,500.00
     Natural Gas to the home $28,950.00
Annual association fee first year $1800.00
Pool and recreation fee first year $3,200.00
Shuttle from the hotel.. $225.00
Private Tour $75.00
Two days in Deluxe Hotel.. $465.00
     Room Tax $32.55
     Occupancy Tax $46.50
Round Trip First Class Airfare................................. $749.00
Baggage $40.00
Grand Total **$574,083.05**

X _____

John, all I need is your authorization by the X. Will you be financing or paying cash?"

"Al, I shink ur tryin ta cheet me."

"John, I'm giving you the deal of a life time. Why would you say such a thing?"

"Cause, I didn't say at da lux hotel. And I flown couch."

"Gee, John you should have said something, sorry about that. How much was your hotel?"

"Shixty-five a night. Chimes two nights."

"Okay, that's $130.00. I'll take that off the bottom. Now how much was the airfare, I don't want to hoodwink you on that."

"My fo-lite wuss $299.00."

"Fine, I'll deduct that as well. Now I just need you to sign here and then I'll take you back to the hotel. I'll make some copies for you and pop them in the mail. You should have them in a week or two. So, if you'll just sign at the X, we can be on our way."

I grabbed the pen, read over the document and promptly passed out. Whatever was in the hooch, it was the most powerful stuff I had ever had in my life. I was out for the entire afternoon. I don't remember getting to the hotel, let alone undressing and crawling under the covers. I woke up to see the angelic look of my wife standing by my bedside.

"John, are you okay? I was worried when you didn't answer your phone. I'm lucky the information on the hotel was still up on the screen of your computer. When I got here, I thought you were dead. John, can you hear me?"

Saved From a Fate Worse Than Death

"Honey, is that you?"

"Yes, John. Who did you think it was?"

"I thought I died and went to heaven and you were an angel welcoming me home."

"You had better come up with some other line; you've used that one before."

"Oh."

"John, I swear you should consider yourself the luckiest man on the face of the planet."

"I don't feel lucky. Do you have a couple of aspirins?"

"Here, sit up. There's a glass of water on the nightstand."

I felt horrible. The room was spinning, the bed was moving up and down like a boat rolling on three foot waves. Uup - - down. Uup - - down. Up - - I ran to the bathroom.

"BARRF! Boo-agh - - Oh, oh, Barrf."

I stumbled back and sat down. My wife was calmly sitting in a chair opposite the bed.

"I feel like shit."

"I've got news for you, John. You look worse than you feel."

"I need coffee."

"You need a shower, and then coffee. There's a cute little place across the street. You're not going to believe what happened."

Just what the "doctor" ordered, a nice hot shower. The steam helped clear my head. I was starting to feel almost human again. Maybe this is what it's like to be a Zombie. I was more dead than alive. My wife called to me from the bedroom.

"If we check out before two, we won't have to pay for another day. I have complimentary reservations for a room at the Bellagio in Vegas. We can stay three nights with dinner and a show on the strip each night. Your Al is a real sweetheart."

My Al, Sweetheart? I turned the water on full cold and sobered up in an instant. I got dressed while half wet, shaved most of my face, skipped brushing my teeth and just gargled.

"What's that, honey? I didn't pack much, so all I have to do is put my dirty stuff into the laundry bag. Are you going to tell me how you got us a free stay in Vegas, and at the Bellagio?"

"It's kind of a long story."

As I started to sit on the bed to listen, I said,

"I've got time."

She grabbed me by my arm before I hit the bed.

"I'll tell you at the coffee shop. Right now we have to get out of here. While we're waiting for the bus to the airport, I'll tell you all about it. Boy, you should have seen the look on that guy's face when I walked in on you two . . ."

After checking out of the hotel, we crossed the street to the Dixie Café. It was a quaint little place. We ordered our usual, Vanilla Carmel Latte's. All at once the strangest face came over my wife.

The angelic glow that I knew and loved disappeared, the smile that she wore, even her soft lilting voice changed. A devilish grin came over her as she started to tell the story of how she got the trip to Vegas, and more.

She Said He Said

My loving wife settled into her chair. She took a sip of her brew. Looking me straight in the eye she began her tale. It started with hopping on the next flight out of JFK and arriving here. The flight was three hours long, so she wasn't in a very good mood, having sat next to a guy that snored the whole way. In addition to that, her seat back wouldn't recline, a young child kept kicking the seat and then looked over and giggled. The topping on the cake was a baby crying from start to finish. She was absolutely beside herself when she got off the plane. But nothing compared to the confrontation she had with the bellhop at the front desk.

It was almost four in the afternoon, and Mr. Attitude was still working the day shift. Somewhat disheveled and not in a mood to wait for him to finish his conversation with the mystery person in the other room, she rang the bell. Oh, yeah, I know what you're thinking, she rang the bell.

"I can see you, Miss, but I am having a conversation over here. I'll be with you in a minute, so don't get your panties all in a bunch."

As my wife was telling the story, I could see the fire in her eyes starting to rekindle.

"Excuse me, I know you can see me, and I know you are conversing with another staff member, but your insouciant attitude towards your guest is unacceptable, so before we have to take this outside, I'd suggest you trot your lazy ass over here and give me some help."

There was dead silence. Not a word was spoken by either of them as he walked over and stopped front and center.

"Good afternoon. Welcome. How may I of service?"

"Thank you, that's better. My husband has a room here. I would like a key so I may freshen up and then I'll need a rental car for just one day. I would like it delivered here in half an hour. There's fifty bucks in it for you if you can handle that for me."

"Miss, I can handle it, no problem. What name is the room under?"

"The last name is Fellows. It should be registered under John A. Fellows."

We later found out the clerk/bell hop's name was Jeremy and the secret person was the shift supervisor Shirley. When Jeremy heard the last name and realized who she was talking about, it was all he could do to keep from laughing out loud. Hysteria was on the loose in the back office. The way the story followed, Shirley was rolling on the floor howling.

"Mrs. Fellows, ha-ahem, may I take your bag to your room? You'll find, ha ha, ahem I mean, I think you'll find the accommodations most acceptable."

"I'm not sure what's so funny, but if you recognized my

husband by just the mention of his name, I can only imagine."

The car was ready on time and Jeremy earned his tip. The next stop was to the office of none other than, Mr. Alonso Morning. When my wife stepped into the trailer, Al was hovering over me trying to put a pen in my hand to have me sign the contract.

"Excuse me, I'm looking for the general manager of the Wilderness Estates sales and leasing. What's wrong with that fellow? Is he dead from the heat, or bored with your presentation?"

"Miss, I'll have to ask you to wait your turn. I'm just finishing up a deal with my client. He's legally blind, so he has to get his face almost into the paper. We'll be just a minute. If you want to make pretty, you can sit over there."

That was strike number one. Al should have never used chauvinistic tactics on my wife. She sat and put on a smile while Al was still trying to get a pen to stay in my lifeless hand.

"Now, John, if you'll sign write here, we can wrap this up. All I--

"All you need is to sit down and shut up. That's my husband you're trying to hustle. If you want to sell someone something today, you'd better slow down and talk to me, Mr. Fancy pants."

She took the chair I was sitting in and rolled it away from the desk. Sitting down slowly while watching in shock was Al. Standing directly in front of the desk, my wife opened up her purse. . .

"Don't shoot. We can work this out. I swear I wasn't trying to cheat nobody."

"Oh, don't get your feathers ruffled. I'm looking for my glasses to see what my husband is trying to get us into. Can I see the property first?"

Al's color started to come back and his heart dropped back into his chest.

"Well, of course we can. Your John picked out the best piece of property in the whole community. He told me he wanted to make his wife happy and he was picking out the finest for the love of his life. He told me you were pretty, but he didn't tell me he married a much younger gal than himself. Care for a little refreshment?"

Al was pouring on the charm along with a jigger of hooch. It was still scorching hot, so the drink was cool and soothing as it went down.

"Just what is this stuff, grain alcohol with a twist of lemon? You didn't give this to John, did you? He can't hold his liquor. One sip of even Nyquil and he goes all loopy. Did you make this yourself? It's pretty good? I'll have another if you can spare it."

"Mam, you can have all you like. I've got another gallon in the trunk. Now, if you will, imagine a freshly poured concrete road leading up to a rustic log cabin sitting at the base of this here mountain. Right there is where Johnny boy wants to build you two a love nest. He's probably the most romantic man I've ever met. Is he that way at home too? I can see in your eyes why he loves you so much."

"You can?"

"Oh, yes. Your eyes sparkle like diamonds, yet they're blue as the ocean."

"Really?"

"I'm telling you, if your husband wasn't up in that trailer, I'd have to make a pass at you. Why you're just as lovely as the day is long."

"Okay, Al, cut the crap. Less go over that contract. I hold the keez to thish deal, that is to shay, if you want to see the color of our money, you've got to shell me. Doo you gots anymore of that hooch, I'm parched. Damn, how hot dosh it get around thish plash?"

By the way the story was going, I wasn't sure I was going to like the ending. My wife's speech pattern was starting to slur and Al's eyes were beginning to twinkle. Every sip my wife would take, Al would start counting dollar signs. When they arrived back at the trailer, the fun and games were over. Jillian put on her game face. The same one she had when she started to tell me the story. I knew what was coming, and if Al weren't such a swindling, conniving skunk, snake in the grass, I would have felt sorry for him. But, he deserved all she could dish.

First she handed Al one of her business cards. Jillian was a certified public accountant working for an attorney that had offices in both New York and Washington, D.C. Al slumped into his chair. He handed her the agreement and just watched as she scratched with red ink all over the page. She was adding and subtracting faster than he could blink. When she had finished, she turned the paper around and said,

"I'll sign it after you sign it."

She handed Al a pen. Almost weeping, Al looked over the contract and then signed at the bottom where the sales person authorized the agreement.

"Now one thing more, we were to get round trip airfare if we bought today. While I'm getting out my check book, you get on the phone. I want two tickets to Las Vegas. I want a penthouse suite at the Bellagio with dinner and a show on the strip. Make that for three nights all inclusive. And I know John would want a cowboy hat. Yours will do."

"Tell me again why I'm doing all this?"

"Because while I was sitting over there "making pretty" I was filming you with my cell phone as you were trying to forge my husband's signature. I'm not sure, but in some states getting a person drunk to sell them something is against the law. Of course you've heard the saying, "What happens in Vegas stays in Vegas." We'll be out of here on the first flight tomorrow afternoon. Your secret is safe with me. Have the tickets sent to our hotel by noon tomorrow and I'll have a certified check for 193,657.98 waiting for you or your currier. Are we agreed?"

"Agreed"

"Oh, and Al, have a nice day."

Al sat back in his chair. He was wondering what freight train just ran him over. Jillian helped me to my feet and practically dragged me to the car. When we got to the hotel, Jeremy gave her a hand getting me to the room and into bed. The rest as they say; is history.

THE END

Book 10

The Legend of White Smoke

Three months to the day, I opened the mail box and the deed to our property was there in a big yellow envelope. I went rushing into the house to tell my wife, we were finally the owners of a retirement plot of land complete with its very own mountain.

"John, if I hadn't seen it for myself, you would be waving divorce papers right about now instead of the deed to an estate. I fell in love with it the moment I set eyes on that mountain. And it's in our backyard. You did good for a change."

"Well, if it weren't for you, we would have overpaid by three hundred thousand."

"Three Hundred thousand, seven hundred and thirty four dollars to be exact, but that's all water under the bridge so to speak."

"Yes, and I'm sure I'll never hear about it again. Say, do you want to go see it this weekend and plant a stake or a flag or something in the front lawn?"

"John, there's no lawn, and this weekend is going to be nightmare city for me. I have to prepare documents for Larry to take to court. It's probably going to take a minimum of twenty hours. You, go. Just stay out of trouble, will ya?"

She always has to end every conversation with, "Stay out of trouble." Just one time I wish we could have a chat about something and it end with, "Good job, John, or boy I didn't think you had it in you."

She has a way of making me feel like a little kid. I went to the garage to pack the tent and all my camping gear. I was heading out West to be in the wilderness with nothing but Mother Nature all around me.

The Jeep was so tightly packed I couldn't get one more thing in it if I tried. I called into work to take a vacation day and left Thursday evening instead of Friday. Monday was a holiday, so I would have a long weekend. I checked to make sure I had my cell phone and car charger. I always forget one or the other, and it makes Jillian jump on a plane feeling a need to bail me out of a jam. This trip was going to be different. No human contact should mean there would be no problems.

From five miles away I could see our mountain. It was majestic and had a white cap of snow. The sides were pine trees, firs and a few hardwood maples. The first thing I wanted to do was walk the perimeter of the land and stake off our claim. I drove up to the entrance of the estate. Things were different. The sign was up straight, and in place of the trailer there was a small rustic cabin. I pulled up to check things out. I was greeted at the door by Al, my salesman.

"Greetings, my friend, welcome to the Wilderness Estates."

"Al, it's me. John. John Fellows"

Al looked all around like he had seen a ghost or was about to.

"You come alone, or's your wife stuffed in that Jeep somewhere?"

"Oh, gee Al, you don't have to worry. She stayed home this time. I can assure you that there will be no negotiations this weekend."

We both laughed as he shook my hand. He told me about all the progress that had been made since the weekend I was here last. They were going to start pouring the concrete for the streets next week. I asked if it would be all right to camp on my property for a couple of days.

"You stay as long as you want, John. Nobody will bother you. When you get back there you'll see that your thirty acres have been marked with yellow stakes. There's a sign that says Sub Lot 132. That's you."

"Cool beans, I'll see you on my way out."

What a nice guy. He seemed different than the first time, still friendly, but less of a shyster. The anticipation of camping out was welling up within me. I felt like a nine year old standing in line for the double loop roller coaster at an amusement park. I spotted my sign. I got out of the Jeep and took a picture of it, then of the mountain and of all the area that was mine. I'll be corrected to "ours" when I tell the story to friends and relatives, but this weekend, it was mine all mine.

The tent smelled musty. After getting it put together, I opened all the window flaps and the front door panels. I was hoping the mountain air would help. I stepped inside and it dawned on me, I forgot a sleeping bag. Fortunately one of the kids left theirs inside. It was a Scooby Doo bag. No one was going to see it, and I didn't care if they did.

I heard a sound just outside the tent. When I went to look, there was nothing there. I looked up the path to the side of the mountain.

Something was passing through the shadows. It was almost like smoke. I grabbed my canteen in case there was a fire that maybe a worker forgot to put out before they left for the weekend. I wasn't far when I saw a white blur pass through the trees again. It was fast as the wind. It must be smoke and the fire was spreading. I kept looking for anything smoldering, but I was unsuccessful. It was getting dark. I went back to the tent and got ready for a good night's sleep.

In my Scooby Doo bag, I was thinking about what to do in the morning. The sound of crickets, hoots from the owls and a lone wolf kept me up half the night. When the clouds covered the moon, they all got quiet at the same time. I made a mental note to get good insulation in the house to keep out the sounds of the forest dwellers.

When I woke the next morning, there was something staring at me. I wouldn't have minded all that much, but it had nested on top of me. Evidently it was trying to stay warm. I grabbed a towel and put it over the critter and took it outside. I shook out the towel, and this big old lizard of some sort, leisurely strolled away. Apparently he'd been thrown out of better places and wasn't all that upset about it.

The Wild Side of Camping

Hunger set in. There must be something about fresh air and sleeping outdoors. I was famished. As an adult in my late thirties, well, maybe for a second time give or take five years, you would think I would know a thing or two about camping.

Truth be told, the only camping I had ever done was with the kids in our backyard. There, if you had to go to the bathroom you just went inside; if you were thirsty, you went to the refrigerator and if you were hungry, you sat at the kitchen table until your wife had the pancakes with bacon. Mrs. Butterworth would be soaking into the cakes like a sponge. Mmm good.

After watching the lizard waddle away, I turned to get my cooking supplies out of the Jeep. I had packed a Bunsen burner along with a couple pots and pans to cook with. Everything a man could want to eat was neatly placed in a cardboard box. There were quick and easy canned stuff to cook, some snacks, chips, Twinkies and soda pop. The ice chest wouldn't fit with all the other junk, so I planned to pick up ice at the convenient store in town. I forgot to stop on my way in last night. I guess that will have to be added to my agenda for the day.

No one told me that Brown bears and raccoons don't need an invitation to a picnic. With the weather being on the warm side, I left the windows down and the doors unlocked on the Jeep.

The Jeep was completely emptied of everything. My clothes were strewn everywhere, most of them shredded into pieces. All the food had been consumed. Even the canned goods were forcibly opened with either claws or teeth. The mess spread over the open land with a trail leading into the woods. These guys must have known the Hansel and Gretel story. They left little bits and pieces of things so they would be sure to find their way back. I couldn't figure out why they pulled off the interior door panels and ripped out the headliner. I found the back seat over by the stream that ran along the edge of our property.

The only thing I could do was take pictures and laugh about it.

I laughed right up to the moment that I discovered something very large had tried to eat my tires. All four tires had been bitten and were flat to the ground. Now I cried. I cried like a baby. I didn't know what to do. With the construction crews gone for the Holiday, it was likely I wouldn't see anyone until Tuesday morning.

I looked for my cell phone to call a tow truck. "Oh Shit!" The battery was dead. I looked into the Jeep for my charger. All that was left of it was the cord. The charger itself had been chewed off.

"Double Oh Shit!"

The only thing to do was to walk to the Realtor's cabin. If Al were in, I could get a ride to town. I took off my fuzzy slippers and started looking for my tennis shoes. They were nowhere around, but I did find a clean pair of underwear hanging on a bush. It never occurred to me to look up. As the sun was rising, so was the temperature. I was wiping my brow when I spotted one of my shoes about thirty feet up in a pine tree. Alright, one shoe, that meant, maybe the other would be nearby. Sure enough, it was floating down stream.

The nagging question in my mind was do I wear a wet shoe, with or without a sock? I started throwing sticks and rocks at my other shoe in the tree. My pitching arm just wasn't what it used to be, every attempt at knocking it down was unsuccessful. It was getting hot and I was parched. I walked over to the stream and cupped my hands to get a couple sips of water. It felt cool and soothing going down, but tasted a little funny.

The walk down the dirt road to the cabin was nothing short of an adventure. My right foot with the wet shoe would make a squish sound with each step that I took. My left foot with the fuzzy slipper had a hole in it. I stepped on a sharp rock.

"Ow!" Squish "Ow" Squish "Ow. Ow" Squish.

Not only was I quite a sight, but now I had sound effects to go with it.

Just before going up the steps to the cabin, I sniffed my arm pits to make sure I wasn't too offensive. I couldn't be sure that the smell of the wet tennis shoe didn't overpower any body odor

I may have been generating. I was trying to discern the smell, if it was the shoe, my socks or the water?

I've always had the best of luck. Bad luck, that is. A sign on the door said: Closed for the Holiday. I sat on the front steps and started to sniffle a little. That caused me to breathe in the toxic fumes emitting from my shoe. I verped, the taste of vomit stuck in the back of my throat.

Desperation was setting in. I decided to break a window and climb through to get a drink of water. Wouldn't you know it, not one rock anywhere around. Ah, but I did have a heavy wet clunky shoe. I threw it at the plate glass window. I then crawled into the office. With only a couple small cuts and minor scrapes, my mission was accomplished.

I went directly to the water fountain. No water. I went into the bathroom. No water. I was totally frustrated. Freaking out, I yelled,

"Jiminy Christmas, can't a guy catch a break?"

A light from the heavens shone through the broken glass. The sun settled in on a white box. It was Al's refrigerator where he kept beverages for his guests. I fell to my knees in front of it praying that there would be something inside to drink.

I opened the door slowly. Inside was a treasure trove of treats. Orange juice, sparkling water, prune juice, two pieces of chocolate wrapped in tin foil and one half of a tuna salad sandwich with a bite out of it. I had hit the mother lode.

The orange juice tasted like Al's famous elixir. A bite of the tuna then a piece of chocolate, another sip of juice, a bite of tuna and the second piece of chocolate. After my feast, I was ready for a nap. I pushed two chairs together and stretched out. In an instant I was asleep. My rest was interrupted with a dire need to go to the bathroom. I managed to sit before soiling my britches.

"Boy that was close."

I was talking to myself and then realized that the X on the chocolate probably wasn't because it was extra dark or extra good. The sparkling water with prune juice may have tasted like a poor man's chardonnay, but it loosened me up so much I think I may have lost a few pounds during the colon cleansing.

"Oh Shit! No water."

Misery Loves Company

Things just kept getting better. The prune juice and chocolate were doing their thing. I couldn't get off the toilet, and there was no water to flush. What else could happen?

I heard a car pull up and two car doors slam shut.

"Careful now, Jeb, whoever or whatever might still be in there."

"Roger that Sheriff."

Okay, so now I know what else could happen. The two officers walked slowly up the stairs.

"Whew wee, what the hell is that smell?"

"Damned if I know, Sheriff, but whatever went through that window must have died in there."

"Can't be no burglar, 'cause they would have gone through the front door. Al never did put a lock on it."

"Roger that sheriff, but what if it ain't dead yet?"

"Better go get the shot gun out of the car. If it ain't dead, we'll have to put it out of its misery. Hey, while you're there, grab me one of them swine flu masks. The smell in this place is horrid."

The situation wasn't getting better. I didn't know if I should yell for help and surrender or clean myself with my shorts and make an escape through the bathroom window. The two officers continued their investigation. Their voices were muffled wearing the surgical masks.

"Look, there's some hair and blood on the glass. It must be injured."

They walked into the office.

"Hey, Sheriff, maybe it's that bear that invited itself to your daughter's backyard birthday party and ate her cake while everyone was in the pool."

"If that basterdly beast is in here, I'm gonna shoot it, stuff it, and have it mounted. My little girl still cries about not having her cake."

"Shh, I think it's in the bathroom. The smell is permeating through the door and wilting my eyebrows."

"Back me up, Jeb. I'm going in."

The bathroom door was opened slowly with care. When it was

fully opened, the sheriff was in the ready position with his forty-five pointed right at me. His deputy was peering around from behind with the shot gun pointing through the door. I threw my hands in the air.

"Don't shoot. Don't shoot."

While looking at two masked officers with weapons drawn, I had no problem finishing the job I'd started. The expression on their faces when they saw me was priceless. The whole episode would have been a You Tube sensation if someone had been filming the event. They both took two steps back. The sheriff closed the door. The next thing I heard was two guys bustin a gut laughing. When the sheriff was finally able to talk,

"Sir, if you'll clean up in there, air the place out, and promise to pay for the replacement of the front window, well, I reckon we can just forget this event ever took place."

As the front door closed, all the way back to their car, I could hear more laughter. The only good thing was, I didn't get arrested and hauled off to jail. The bad thing was I still needed to get to town. Now, more than ever I needed a change of clothes and a pair of shoes.

Squish "Ow." Squish "Ow."

I was hoping the walk into town wasn't going to take long.

A Return to the Local Hotel

Jeremy was standing at his usual lookout station. When he saw me walk up to the counter, immediately his hand went in the air. His index finger was pointing upward indicating he would be just a minute.

A couple started towards the desk to check out. They were no closer than three feet when they did a one hundred and eighty degree turn and headed into the hotel bar.

"Geez, what the hell, they aren't going to let that guy stay here, are they?"

"I don't know. I'm just glad we're leaving and not getting his room when he checks out."

Jeremy was getting a whiff of me every time the lobby doors

opened. He tucked his nose into the sleeve of his uniform and walked over.

"John, John Fellows, is it really you?"

"Yes. It's me, long time, no see."

"What in the world happened to you? You look a total wreck. Were you mugged, rolled and left for dead?"

"No. Nothing like that, it's a long story. I'd just like to get a room and take a shower, then soak in a hot tub. My feet are killing me."

"You smell like something else is killing you."

"Yeah, well, someday I'll tell you the story. Right now I need you to do me a favor. There's a fresh fifty in it for you."

"Anything for you sir, I am at your service, Mr. Fellows. Fire away."

"I need you to go to the local haberdashery and . . ."

"The Haber-whatery?"

"Men's Store, I need you to go to the closest men's clothing store."

"Why didn't you just say that in the first place?"

"Never mind, pay attention, you might want to write this down. Pick up three pairs of jeans, 34" waist, 30," inseam. Get three polo shirts M/L. I need a sweatshirt too, in case it gets cold at night. Make that a large. Oh, and a pair of deck shoes, or some camping boots."

"What size?"

"Um, an 8 ½ or a 9 and I'll need three pair of white tube sox. Oops, I need underwear.

Three pair size 34/36."

"Cotton or silk?"

"Cotton or silk what?"

"Boxers, what kind of fabric do you want? I don't do polyester. They don't let you breathe."

"Nothing down there has to breathe. Besides, I wear all cotton briefs, white."

"I should have known. You want to keep the family jewels close in case of a squirrel attack."

"If you can dispense with the jokes, there may be a bonus in it for you. Now, how about that room?"

"Your wife made reservations for tonight with a late arrival guarantee. Shall I give you that room?"

"NO! I mean no, I won't be staying overnight."

"I get it sir, mum's the word,"

"It's nothing like that."

Jeremy winked at me, with one of those, "I know what you're doing." It wasn't worth discussing.

"I understand. Room 632, it's all the way to the back and upstairs away from our other guests. Your odor won't bother them. Here's a can of Lysol. Use it liberally, please."

I went to my room and undressed. I threw my clothes into a dry clean bag and tied a double knot in it.

With the water getting ready, I looked in the mirror. This was the first time I actually saw myself since the break-in. I was horrified. There was a three inch gash in my forehead with a clump of hair missing. I had other small scrapes on my cheeks, and there were blood stains on my hands from the glass when I crawled through the window. With my shirt off, I could see I had scrapes across my shoulders and back, I was a total mess. I hopped in the shower without checking the water temperature. I jumped out as fast as I got in and adjusted the water from ice to refreshingly warm. Now soap and scrub and soap and . . .

"Uh oh, what was I thinking? I must have lost my mind for the moment. My wife was going to be here tonight. I had to get back to our property as soon as possible and re-assemble the tent, clean up the mess, and start a camp fire so it looked like nothing happened. I don't want the "told ya so" conversation. Not tonight anyway, just not tonight.

Fellows Folly Continues

Jeremy got me back to the home site before sun down. The tent was still intact. It was one less thing to worry about for the moment.

Since I hadn't packed much in the way of clothes for the weekend outing, that part of the clean up was easy. Jeremy helped clean up the rest of the mess and offered to take the garbage back to the hotel to throw out.

"Thanks for all your help. One more thing before you leave. I need to push the Jeep behind that bush. I don't want my wife to see the flat tires. Just knowing we have bears is one thing, Knowing they can bite through steel belted radial tires is frightening. I don't want her to get scared off by the local critters."

"No problem, Mr. F."

"Here's a crisp Franklin for your efforts today."

"What's a crisp Franklin?"

"Duh, it's a one hundred dollar bill."

"Oh, right. Thanks, thanks a lot."

"You've still got my credit card. If you want, take your gal pal to the Black Hawk Tavern for dinner tonight."

"The Black Hawk, are you sure? It's a pretty fancy place."

"Then you'll have a nice time. Leave the card and the receipt at the hotel desk. I'll pick it up when I leave. There's nothing to spend my money on out here."

"Okay, um, is wine included?"

"Wine, beer, whatever you want. Oh, don't forget to send a tow truck as soon as possible. If you can find someone to work on a Sunday, there could be a bonus in it for you."

"You're the best, John. Is it okay to call you by you first name?"

"Sure, why not?"

"I'll have someone out here before noon tomorrow. You can count it."

The sun was setting when we said our final good-byes. Never had an artist painted a scene so beautiful. I went into the tent to get my camera. I was glad I had digital, because I would've hated to run out of film.

When the sun was fully behind the mountain, it was lights out. I should have thought about starting a fire earlier. I gathered some wood for a real old fashioned camp fire. Since I gave up smoking a pipe, all I had were matches instead of my trusty Zippo. Without paper or kindling, I was going through matches fast with no success of a fire.

The genius light bulb turned on in my head. I took the Sterno can from the portable stove and placed it under the firewood. After only one match, I had instant fire. The logs were turning a glowing orange and the flames were brilliant blue. I kicked back to relax with nothing left to do, but wait for my wife to show up. It wasn't a question of would she; but when?

One thing about camping that no one ever told me was that compressed oil cans are for heating and should not be placed inside a raging fire. I was toasting my toes getting all snuggly and warm. With the blue skies above speckled with stars, it was nothing short of a perfect evening. The only sounds were of the crickets chirping, owls hooting and the crackle of the fire. I started to nod off when . . .

KABOOM!!!

That damned little can blew up like a hand grenade. Burning logs were flying everywhere. By best estimate, some shot up thirty to forty feet in the air. Cinders were burning the dry grass. I was running and ducking trying to take cover.

It was raining burning embers and sticks. I felt like I was in the middle of Dante's Inferno.

Fire and brimstone was falling all around. When I thought it was over, the can, came sailing down from the sky like a meteor and thumped me in the head. Not that getting hit in the head with a hot can wasn't painful, but my hair catching on fire was a sensation beyond description. I ran to the stream to put myself out. I could feel steam rising from my scalp.

From out of the middle of the water I went running over to the campsite to stomp out all the brush fires that I could find. Before another mishap I decided to go to bed. I still haven't figured out how the brimstone rain missed the tent, but thankfully it did.

It was after midnight, I hadn't fallen asleep, my adrenaline was pumping, my head was thumping, and my scalp still felt like it was on fire. There was a rustling sound outside of the tent. Too bad there was no food left for the bears to eat. The flap of the tent opened and someone snuggled up next to me. I thought it was my wife arriving for a midnight rendezvous. I never knew her to have hot breath and a stubbly beard. I rolled over for a little smooch only to discover a mountain lion lying next to me. Even though it appeared to be friendly, I still jumped up screaming. It got startled and began growling. We both tried to be the first one out of the tent.

After it ran off into the woods, I went back into the tent and zippered shut the door and all the windows. It was getting a little clammy, but I wasn't going to have anymore uninvited visitors.

Even though I was dead dog tired, it took awhile for me to finally fall asleep. From inside the tent, I woke up to the sound of: Cuckoo, cuckoo

Outside a voice was calling:

"You who. You who."

Now what? I couldn't figure out if it was night or day. There was no light with the tent sealed shut. It sounded like one of those damn noisy owls again:

Cuckoo, cuckoo

Second thought, it might be a morning dove. The sound was a little softer and less annoying than an owl.

From outside:

"You who."

Now I was really getting irritated, I yelled at the top of my lungs.

"SHUT THE HELL UP! Can't a guy get some sleep around here?"

There was silence. I closed my eyes and then opened them when I heard a throat clear.

"EXCUSE ME."

Uh oh, I knew that voice.

Think, Listen and Spin

Peeking out from the tent flap, the first thing I saw was a tapping foot. Following the leg up, there were folded arms. I stopped before looking into the eyes of the woman I had loved and adored for more than thirty years. I was hoping she was just cold. If so I would invite her into my humble abode and we could cuddle until warm. That was not to be the case.

"John, come out here, this minute! Are you totally out of your mind? Why in the world are you out sleeping in the kids Ninja Turtle tent in the middle of a mountain wilderness?

"Well, I- -

"Don't answer. I'm not finished. Did you know there are brown bear, cougars and poisonous snakes and lizards living all over the area? Any one of those horrible creatures could have visited you in the night, and you'd be dead meat right now."

"Well, I- -

"I'm not finished. You can just hold on to your lame response and excuses. I booked a flight out after working on a report that's due Tuesday. I was hoping we would catch up with each other and have a romantic evening. The flight was delayed and I didn't get in until 11:30. I had guaranteed the room for a late arrival. I just wasn't expecting to be that late."

"I'm sorry, - -

"There's more, so again, let me talk. You'll have plenty of time for your side of the story. By the way, start collecting your thoughts, because it had better be good. I arrived at the hotel thoroughly exhausted. Thinking that I would enjoy a nice hot bath in the spa tub before retiring to bed, I was comforted with that thought. The hotel clerk said, "We had to close the west side of the hotel due to plumbing problems. Since the hotel is booked solid, the only room left is a studio room with a fold out bed. We'll have the issue fixed in the morning and get you into your suite as soon as possible."

"Gee Honey, I - -

She held her hand up signaling me to hold my tongue.

"John, I had to sleep on a sofa bed. The support bar was right in the middle of my back, I thought I was going to die, tossing and turning all night. And the worst thing, the person who had the room before me apparently didn't know the meaning of soap or physical hygiene. The odor left in this room was straight from the pits of hell itself. I had to get out of there as quick as possible. Yesh, I think I can still smell it. It's clinging to me like a foreign entity."

"Boy, you've had a rough night, I w - -

The hand went up again. We were still standing just outside of the tent. Since we were using hand signals, I gestured to the log that I had been using as a stool at what once was a campfire. She sat down and I sat next to her on the ground.

There was a warm cinder still glowing on the ground where I was sitting. I felt it might be inappropriate to scream in pain at that moment, so I shifted my butt away from the burning ember.

"That feels better. Go ahead with your story. I'm still formulating mine, cause you're not going to believe what's happened to me over the last twenty-four hours."

She glared at me.

"Sorry, go ahead."

"Thank you. As I was saying, this putrid smell of fish and manure was just lingering and I think it's in my hair and on my clothes. Can you smell it on me?"

"Smell it? Me? No, I don't smell a thing other than your beauty. I'm so happy you could make it out for the rest of the weekend. Maybe we should go to town and have some coffee and a little breakfast. By the time we finish, the room should be ready and you can have a nice hot soak in the whirlpool. How's that sound?"

"It sounds wonderful. But, don't think you're off the hook. I got a call during the flight from our bank."

"Oh?"

"They thought we might be victims of credit card fraud."

"Wh-why, would they think that?"

"Well, the first call, they asked if we were traveling. I said yes. They said there may be a mix up, because there were two reservations made for the same hotel on the same day. I said it was a little strange, but maybe the wilds of camping had gotten to my husband so he checked into the hotel. He doesn't know I'm coming. They were satisfied with that, and I was hoping it was true."

"I can explain. I- -

"You'll have your turn. I'm not finished. A half hour later I received a second call. This time it was from a fancy designer men's clothing store. They wanted to know if they should allow a charge for 725.00 dollars to go through. The bank thought if we were vacationing, we would be bringing clothes not buying them.

I asked what the person looked like.

Strangely, they described the hotel clerk Jeremy to a T. I asked them to see if the fellow using the card knew what the middle initial on the card stood for. I would find out then and there if it were stolen or not. Without hesitation the name John A. Fellows came out, I could hear him clearly over the phone. I told him to go ahead with the charges and if there were any issues, I would call to dispute them later. Now, how would a hotel clerk now your full name?"

"I can explain. I - -"

"I'm not quite finished yet."

"Uh, oh."

"You'd better believe uh-oh. I was starting to think you were coming out here to have some sort of an affair, but I never expected it to be with some gay lover. John, how could you?"

"I couldn't, I mean, I didn't, I - -"

The hand went up again to silence me for the last time.

"I got a bill this morning from a dinner at the Black Hawk Tavern."

"I can explain . . . how did you get the bill?"

"John, while you may live in some sort of dream world where people still use tin cans with a string to communicate, I on the other hand use the latest in technology. When the bank called for a third time, I had then email a copy of the bill to my Blackberry."

"Oh"

"Eight hundred and fifty dollars for a bottle of 1930 vintage Chamblee imported from the south of France."

I gulped.

"One hundred and thirty-five dollars for surf-n-turf, and a side of escargot with turnips salad, mind you that was plate number one. The second order was the same, but with an added filet. This dinner was almost two hundred dollars."

"I gulped again."

"There's more. Dessert must have been served in golden goblets. Seventy-five dollars for flaming jubilees' and here's the real topper, a twenty-five percent tip. John, this bill is over fifteen hundred dollars. Go ahead, it's your turn."

I wasn't prepared for the restaurant bill, and I hadn't a clue about the fancy pants store, although the sequins on the shirt should have been an indicator that these weren't your run of the mill outfits.

"John, before you start, I need a cup of coffee. Let's go back to town and get something from that quaint little shop across from the hotel."

"That sounds like a good idea. Where's your car?"

"I had Al from the realty company drop me off. He was checking out a break-in at his office. I thought we could just take your Jeep."

Truth or Sympathy

"Give me a second to get my watch, my keys and my wallet."

With the accusations of being gay, and thinking about the bills Jeremy ran up on the charge, I hadn't given much thought to the four flat tires on my Jeep. The instant I picked up my keys I realized I had to tell her what happened. I wasn't ready for the reaction I would get. We were only three payments into the loan on the Jeep. I was pretty sure the finance guy didn't include the wild crazy-assed bear damage insurance.

"What's taking so long? I'm hungry and I have a headache from no caffeine yet this morning."

"I'm trying to find my cell phone and my wallet seems to be missing."

"I don't know why you need either. Your cell phone is either off or has a dead battery, and your gay lover spent all your money. He probably still has your wallet."

I looked back at my wife through the tent flap.

"Look, I'm not gay, so stop saying that. I can explain everything as soon as we get out of here."

Last night I was so busy straightening up the camp site, I failed to notice the pants that Jeremy had bought for me. I knew they were a tad snug up top, but I just figured the size was a little off. What I didn't know, was that they had sequins running down the sides with flared bell bottoms. My butt was sticking out of the tent while I was still trying to find my personal effects. I heard my wife say something somewhat muffled.

"Not gay huh, I can't wait to hear all about these flouncy pants of yours."

I looked at the rhinestone-lined zipper and pockets. Jeremy had me in a flamenco dancer's outfit. That would explain the high heeled boots with the pointed toes and taps on them. Now I was starting to feel about as gay as I looked.

"John, if you don't mind, leave the other dance wear in the bag. some of the money. I must say those pants do have a way of reshaping your We're taking back what you haven't worn yet. We can try to recoup figure."

"Don't worry. I fully intend to take back the other outfits and get some real clothes."

I had started talking while backing out of the tent. It was warm enough to take off the waist length jacket that matched the pants. I had a tee shirt on that I thought was a stylish white and tan. When I came out and turned around, my wife gave me a look, and then covered her mouth while saying,

"Oh, My, God"

The next thing I knew she was falling off her stool and rolling on the ground laughing. She was totally covered in tears and almost choking with laughter. I couldn't imagine past the pants and shoes, what could be so funny. I looked down at the front of my tee shirt. It had a picture of a man's hard body chest with a six pack of abs. On my somewhat bulging mid-section, I looked like a pregnant guy on steroids. I couldn't help but laugh at myself too. I stopped laughing when I saw the Jeep behind the bush and knew we had to get to town in it. Do I tell her, or let her find out for herself? After all, it wasn't like it was my fault, well not exactly anyways. Maybe we'll get in and since we're on a dirt road, it won't be all that noticeable.

"When you're done laughing, can we get going? I'm getting rather hungry myself."

"Oh, alright, I'll try not to laugh again until I hear your story of why your buddy dressed you up like a darn fool. Didn't you get one of those lampshade hats to go with the outfit?"

She started laughing again. I wasn't going to give her the satisfaction of seeing the hat lying on top of my sleeping bag. I closed the tent flaps and headed towards the Jeep.

"Come on, honey, if we hurry, we can make the coffee shop before they start serving lunch."

The Moment of Truth

The moment of truth was on the other side of the tent. I helped my wife up from the ground where she was still in full snicker. I was the perfect gentleman as I escorted her to the Jeep. When we got close, we could see the claw marks of the bears. They were all the way down the side from the front fender to the rear bumper. Somewhere in the night you would think I would have heard the clawing. It had to sound ten times worse than fingernails scratching on a chalk board.

Jillian's eyes widened, her mouth dropped open, but not a word was spoken. I held my tongue as we continued to the passenger side. This side of the Jeep had even more damage. The back glass was shattered and the sheet metal had puncture holes from the claws.

Once again my wife's eyes widened, her mouth opened and not a word, not even, so much as a peep. I couldn't believe how destructive these animals were. My beautiful candy apple pearl paint was ruined. My mouth dropped open and I almost cried. I managed to keep my composure for the moment.

I started to open the door. Stuffing from the seat fell at our feet. When the door was fully open, the door came unhinged and fell to the ground.

"Um, we can get that later. (Referring to the door) You may want to buckle your seat belt."

I nonchalantly walked around the back and got into the driver's side of the Jeep. My wife was staring out the windshield when the recliner on her seatback broke. Now being a bit startled, she was on her back looking at the ceiling. I put the key into the ignition to start the engine and was hoping we could somehow make it to town.

221

Curiously I had more room in my driver's compartment than I ever remembered. Something was missing, but I couldn't quite figure out what?

"Are you looking for this?"

Jillian was holding the steering wheel that was lying in the back next to her head. One of the bears must have been teething there was still drool on it. I graciously took the wheel and placed it on the column.

Gingerly I started the car rolling. So far, no more parts falling off, I felt confident that we would make it to the main road, and it would be clear sailing from there. I was surprised with how well my wife was taking all this. She still wasn't saying a word. I looked over, and it was one of those times when I knew I should have kept my mouth shut, but I couldn't resist.

"You look comfortable. I didn't know the seats reclined that far."

I looked at her, and daggers with flames on them were shooting out of her eyes. If looks could kill, I would have been dead where I sat.

Fullup up up. Fullup up up. The flat tires were making a sound so unique I wished I could have recorded it. The ride was bumpy, and without stuffing in the seats, it made it all the more uncomfortable. I smelled something burning. Smoke was coming out from under me. Apparently I had inadvertently hit the heated seat button. My fancy pants were on fire and the rhinestones were melting. Jillian looked at the flames that were shooting out of my ass and roared with laughter.

"Do you want to pull over and put yourself out? I'll wait."

Well, that was a relief. I thought we were going to go the rest of the day without her talking to me. I jumped out of the Jeep before it came to a full stop and found myself sitting in the stream next to the back seat of the Jeep that the bears had dragged over. I still couldn't figure out how they got it out and then pulled it a hundred feet away into the water. But it was cool and comfortable. My wife got out of the car a minute or so before the whole thing went up in flames. Then;

Ka boom!!!

The Jeep exploded. There were pieces parts flying all over. My wife joined me as I flipped the seat over to take cover.

Déjà vu All over Again

When the last of the shrapnel fell from the sky, we crawled out from under our protective cover. I flipped the bench seat over. We sat in the middle of the stream. We were laughing, and crying while clinging to each other still shaking with fear. All of our emotions were just pouring out of our bodies. It seemed appropriate for what we had just witnessed.

"John, I swear, only something like this could happen to you. I was so angry when I first arrived that I didn't want to say anything, but, you look like hell. What happened to your forehead? That cut could probably use a few stitches. And look at the back of your head, there's a clump of hair missing and the scalp is nothing but blisters. You used to have such a beautiful head of hair, now it's a gnarly mess. It you didn't look so damned pitiful, I'd wrap my hands around your throat and choke the last breath of life out of you."

I was ready to start telling my side of the story from the very beginning starting on Friday night. It was the most logical place and it would keep everything in chronological order.

My mouth opened, but the sound coming out was silenced by another much louder sound. I recognized it from TV and the movies, though I had never seen one of these contraptions in person. Coming over the ridge behind us was a Black Hawk Army helicopter. Our heads turned in unison to see this monster bird flying towards the charred wreckage of the Jeep.

While it was hovering over the area, a squad of Army Jeeps followed by six police cars, two ambulances and a fire truck were racing towards us down the dirt road. Dusty billows were floating into the sky causing hazy grayish brown clouds to block the sun. They circled the Jeep and a swat team got out and began surveillance of the surrounding area.

They were dressed in black flak jackets, each one carrying an assault weapon. So far no one had spotted us. The Jeep had landed a hundred or more yards away, so we weren't too close to the action as it were. When the all clear signal was given, the rest of the troops along with the cops got out of their vehicles. I heard a guy with a bull horn yell.

"Check the area for survivors."

We both slumped into the water then crawled behind the bench. Hiding didn't work. We were spotted by the chopper.

"Stand up and put your hands on your head."

Immediately we were swarmed by the troops, cops and even a couple of FBI agents. Peeking cautiously from behind the front line of defense was the local sheriff and his deputy.

"Jeb, isn't that the feller from the latrine at the realtor's office?"

"That's a big ten four, Sheriff. I'll never forget that nasty cut on his head. He should probably get that stitched."

After a weapons search we were handcuffed and taken to the police station by special agents Maddox and Schmidt. Now, I'm not blaming my wife, but we probably could have talked our way out of being arrested, if she hadn't kneed one of the officers in the groin while he was doing a full body search for guns and assorted weapons of mass destruction. Every time we tried to offer up our defense, we were told,

"Shut up and wait for an attorney. Anything you say can and will be used against you in a court of law."

Apparently, when the wiring of the heated seats started the cushion materials on fire, one of the wires of the fuel injection system heated up.

That wire went into the gas tank, which created the internal combustion which caused the Jeep to explode in a ball of fire with clouds of thick black smoke that could be seen from five miles away through the front window of the diner downtown. The sound was heard for some distance farther than that, because the Army base isn't anywhere close to here and they heard it loud and clear. Air raid sirens were going off in every major city within a fifty mile radius.

Special agent Maddox turned around while we were still in the car. He slid the safety glass window open.

"If you two didn't set that car on fire, you're lucky to be alive.

If you did set it on fire, you'll be lucky if you don't get three to five in the state penitentiary."

Jillian turned in my direction. Her eyes glared at me. I could see those fiery daggers shooting out at me. I even think she tried to break out of her handcuffs so she could choke the life out of me.

Public Enemy, Numbers One & Two?

We were taken to a holding cell upon arrival at the station. There were six other detainees. Most of the men were in sleeping off a drunken binge the night before. One woman looked like she might be the local hooker, and then there was the guy who had committed the crime of the century, until we arrived. We were now Public Enemies one & Two. I was already envisioning our photos on the post office wall if we were to escape. Maybe we would make "America's Most Wanted Special Edition."

"So, what are you two in for? Having a little flirty time in the park, or something kinky?"

The alleged criminal was the only one curious about why the two of us were joining him in being incarcerated.

"We're not really sure. They haven't formally charged us with anything yet. Our car exploded, and we thought we were being rescued. Instead we were arrested."

The gentleman took a step back.

"I heard the explosion and saw the smoke. Then there was a lot of commotion in the station. The TV down the hall said something about a terrorist car bombing."

Well, that explained the Army and all the troops being deployed to our campsite. I asked the guy what he was in for, just to make small talk.

"My neighbor caught me copping a squat on her front lawn and called the cops. Her dog shits on my front lawn every day and I told her to clean up after it, or I would call the dog warden. She refused saying it was fertilizer and if I didn't like it I could clean it up myself. Well, paybacks are a bitch. What comes around goes around. I don't have a dog, so I decided to do the deed myself.

Unfortunately she came out earlier than usual."

My wife and I took a step back from him after hearing his story. One by one everyone was called to the desk to pay a fine or to schedule a court date. It was our turn. Special agent Maddox called us to come forward.

"Mr. Fancy Pants, step out. Mrs. - -

"Don't even think about calling me Mrs. Fancy Pants unless you want to sing lead in the Jersey Boys quartet."

My wife was threatening to knee another cop. I gave her an elbow and told her to behave and just follow orders so we could get out of jail and go home. I got the usual glare, but she settled down, and we followed the agent and two officers into the interrogation room.

"I thought we were supposed to get a phone call and have an attorney present?"

"Depending how this goes, you shouldn't need one."

Special agent Schmidt was very positive, and was giving us a glimmer of hope that we wouldn't be spending the night in the gray bar hotel. We looked at each other, and confidence was building, until they separated us. They wanted to see if our stories would match. Only one problem, Jillian didn't know about the bears and the wires and the reason that the Jeep exploded. She wasn't going to be able to tell my side of the story.

"Shit!"

I sat on a hard wooden chair waiting for the FBI agents to return. More than a half hour passed and no one had come in to talk with me. I was getting nervous and started to perspire. Sweat was pouring out of everywhere. My shirt was soaking wet, my forehead was dripping, and then they walked in.

"Why so nervous, John? Is there something you want to confess?"

They knew my name. They must have finally let Jillian talk. She probably told them who we were and that the whole thing was a big mistake.

"You'll be somewhat pleased to know that the charges against your wife have been dropped."

"Yes, that's a relief, but what were the charges?"

"Three counts of public endangering. One count of damage to private property. One count of dumping hazardous waste. One count of endangering the wild life and natural waters, forests and grass lands with fire and threats to the environment. She told us that she had just arrived and knew nothing of what had been going on. She said she thought you were suicidal and that you needed treatment, that somehow you were trying to take her with you, which would add attempted homicide to your charges."

"What? How could she? I can't believe she would accuse me of such a thing."

"She didn't. When the event went on the news earlier today, the hotel clerk came over and told us about the bears and how you had to walk into town along with all the events that preceded that. He also told us he was supposed to send a tow truck to get your Jeep, but before he could do that, the thing blew up. He told me to tell you, that you and your wife can stay the night in the spa suite at the hotel.

You're free to go. Oh, there will be a small charge for the rescue. The Army escort and the police, fire department and ambulance will all send you an expense report for services rendered. They'll be added to your hotel bill. Have a nice life, sir."

THE END

Book 11

The Green World Travelers Guide
Publishing Since 1979
Holiday Traveler's Edition

Get the Best Holiday Fares to Anywhere.

Page 12 has the exciting last minute details on an all inclusive trip to the Paradise Island Resort & Spa. This trip includes airfare, ground transportation to and from the resort, three meals a day and all beverages. (Except alcohol) We guarantee the lowest prices of the year if booked through the Green World Traveler's Agency before October 30, 2008.

"WOW! That sounds great."

I was talking to myself sitting in the barbershop waiting for my monthly hacking of the hay, or what was left of the patch on top of my head. The magazine on the table in front of me caught my eye. I couldn't help but pick it up to read about this fabulous trip. After all, it had been a stressful year for my wife and me. We deserved a break. For once I was going to stick to my guns and plan a holiday retreat. No relatives, just my wife and the kids.

Pg. 12

Three – Five and Seven sun drenched days on an Island so far off the map we can't tell you where it is. It's our private Island in the tropics. There's Sun, Shopping, Fishing and Fun. The average temperature year round is 88 degrees. You'll enjoy a restful day on the beach or at the hotel spa. The service is fit for a King and his Royal Family. Come play all night at the Merchants' street festival. There is music for dancing, food, games and the shops are open till midnight on Saturdays. This is the vacation you will tell your friends about for years to come.

I couldn't control my excitement. It would have been in my best interest to sit still while under the shears. I wiggled like a little boy in the chair. My haircut was uneven, and my barber's apologies for clipping my ear were as sincere as his laughter when I walked out. As soon as I got home, I fired up my computer.

"Come on, come on. Why does this thing have to be so slow?"

"John, is that you?"

"Yes, dear, I'm in the office. Wait till you see what I found at the barber's today."

I had ripped the ad from the magazine so that I would have the website and something to show my wife. Jill walked in to see what I was up to and what all the excitement was about.

"I hope it was the piece of your ear that the barber cut off. What the heck happened to you? And your hair, did you piss him off again or what?"

"Never mind that, it'll grow back. I'll just wear my hat."

"Not the one that says, my other hat is a Stetson?"

"No, I think you threw that one out after we went to the fair and there was that incident with one of the vendors."

"You're right, I forgot. So, go on. Tell me all about your great discovery."

I pulled up a chair so that Jill could sit in front of the computer screen with me. It was magic when the screen came on showing the Resort. We both gasped. The falls were breathtaking. The ocean water was bluer than any we'd ever seen. And the rooms, well, they were beyond description. "Fit for a King" was an understatement. Jill was as excited as I was. She was at the edge of her seat.

"When can we go? I'll start packing. Are we taking the kids? No. We'll maybe we should. No, oh, I'll leave it up to you. No, wait this could be our second honeymoon."

"Um, I was thinking of the week of Christmas. It would be a get-away from all the holiday meals and the hustle and bustle of the Mall. The kids will be out of school, and we can have a vacation to remember and talk about for years."

"John Alan Fellows, what in the world are you thinking? Christmas is all about family and sharing and snow. It's the most wonderful time of the year. I don't care how wonderful a tropical vacation would be, we are not going for the holidays."

"I - - well I just thought. . .

"Not another word. I won't hear of it. Besides, we probably can't afford a place like that anyway. Get ready for dinner."

Dinner was quiet. The kids weren't home. I got the dagger stares. One would have thought I did something horrible deserving possibly the death penalty or worse.

"I. . .

"If you are going to start up again about that stupid Island vacation, you can stop now. I told you I won't have you steal my Christmas with my family, and yours. Don't forget we see your family too."

"Yes dear, my family too. Can I help with the dishes?"

"You can do them yourself. Just wrap the leftovers for the kids. I'm taking a bath then going to bed."

"Good night, dear."

"Good night, to you too, take the garbage out. The fish bones stink. There's something green with hair in the refrigerator that smells funny. Take that too. "

The phone rang before Jill's tub was ready.

"Hi, Grace. Yes, Jill's home. No, I'm sure she would love to talk with you. What's that? Oh, that would be delightful. I'm looking forward to it. Hang on. Jill, it's the phone for you."

"Tell whoever it is I'll call back."

"It's long distance. Your sister Grace is on the phone. I think you should talk to her. She has some important news."

I just got in from taking out the garbage when Jill walked into the kitchen. She was in her robe getting ready to take her bath and head for bed. I could immediately tell something was wrong.

"Don't ask and I won't tell. Book the damn flight for five. We should leave on the twenty-third. I don't care if we don't come back till New Years."

With that said, she turned and walked away. I didn't see my wife until dinner the next night. The kids were all present and accounted for. There wasn't much to talk about other than school and homework. The usual gossip about who was dating whom was the topic of conversation with our daughter on her cell phone. The boys were more interested in the mashed potatoes than talk.

Elise was our oldest followed by Martin, and the baby of the family was Lewis. Lewis hated being called "the baby." His thirteenth birthday was this past August. In his mind he was a junior adult.

Elise was seventeen, and our 'tweener, Martin, was fifteen. He was waiting to get his temporary drivers license in the spring. I was hoping he would be a better driver than his sister. I swear I had more hair before she started driving.

The Best Made Plans

Planning our Vacation

I don't know what I like most, the research, the planning or the vacation itself?

If all went well, this would be the vacation of a life time. According to the travel agency, we could swim with Sea Turtles or MANTA-Rays. That sounded like cool beans to me.

"Daddy, I need to use the computer. Will you be done soon?"

"Oh, sure, honey. Do you have a project for school? ''

"No, I'm filming a phone call to broadcast to my friends."

"I hope it will be tasteful."

"Daddy, just what kind of girl do you think I am?"

"A very good one I hope."

My evening of planning the perfect vacation was put on hold for a couple of hours.

"Daddy?"

''Yes, Eli?''

''Are you and mom planning a trip? I saw the resort you have on your desk top. It looks sensational. You two will have a great time."

''Do you really think it looks sensational, because, you'll be coming too."

"No Way.'"

"Is that a good No Way or a bad No Way?"

"It's like No Way am I going on another gay vacation with you and Mom."

"Not just me and your mother, but your brothers are coming too. This will most likely be our last family vacation together."

"Ew! Even worse, I'm not going and you can't make me either."

Elise stormed out of the room slamming the door behind her. She passed her mother in the hall.

"You had better have a talk with your husband. He's totally out of control . . . again!"

Jill walked cautiously into the office.

"What was that all about?"

"I just told Eli about the vacation."

"You didn't?

"Why?"

"I would think you would know by now. There is not one teenage girl in the world that wants to be seen with her parents. The last thing on earth they want is to go on vacation with them."

"So, what do we do? Let her stay home?"

"What? Are you crazy! There's no way she stays home. It's a family vacation. Your little Princess is coming. She can be miserable with the rest of us."

Jill left to talk to Elise. I got back to booking a few day trips while on the island. I was thinking about how to break the news to the boys. I didn't need another door slamming episode with Martin and Lewis.

Free is Good

Not All Announcements Come at the Right Time

October 29th

The travel arrangements were made before the deadline.

Because I booked by the 30th, I got a free room upgrade. I also received one complimentary bus tour of the island. I was so excited I wanted to call Jill at the office and give her the good news. Calling my wife while she was at work was somewhat forbidden by the management of her company. I was only to make personal calls at lunch or on breaks. It was only 10:30, not even break time for another half hour.

"Gee, I sure am hungry today. I think I'll take a stroll to the candy machine. Do you want anything, Phil? I'm buying."

Phil gave me the, what are you some kind of queer look.

"No, I'm good. Sally packed me a slice of homemade apple pie. I'll have that at break. Isn't it a little early for a snack?"

Phil was also the house mouse. Anything that could be construed as gossip, Phil would take it straight to the department manager. I had to be careful that he didn't see me on my cell phone as I walked down the hall to the candy machine. I was paranoid, looking back every once in awhile. Phil poked his head out of the office door. I knew it, he was watching me. I quickly put my phone away hoping he didn't see it.

"Hello, hello, HELLOOOO."

Jill's voice was muffled in my coat pocket. I had forgotten to hang up. Now she was getting mad that there was no answer. I could only hope she didn't check her caller ID. My phone rang. I had to answer it even though the weasel Phil was now standing in the hall after hearing the cell phone.

"Hello, this is John. How may I be of service? No, sure a lot of my clients call my cell, so what can I order for you? We have some great specials running through November 19th."

I went into the bathroom and locked the door behind me to get out of view.

"What was that all about? Did you just butt dial me? This better be important. I walked out of a meeting with the Sr. Executive and a new recruit."

"Jill, I'm sorry. I had to call. We got a free room upgrade and one free bus tour of the island."

"You're an idiot."

Click.

"Jill? Jill?"

"John, is that you?"

I looked around and saw two feet in one of the stalls.

"Yes."

"John, would you mind getting me a roll of toilet paper and sliding it under the door?"

"No not at all."

"Uh, John, congratulations on the room upgrades and bus tour. Women have no idea what we men go through to save a few bucks on a vacation."

"You got that right, brother. How 'bout a courtesy flush."

I got out quickly. Whoever was in there must have had something rotten for dinner the night before. My eyes were watering. Only one good thing came from my encounter in the bathroom. Phil had given up waiting for me, and the coast was clear to go back to work.

October 31st

Halloween

I hated Halloween. Ever since the kids grew out of the dressing up and walking the neighborhood begging for candy, I lost my enthusiasm towards the holiday. These days the kids went to costume parties. If I got home from work early, I would have to pass out candy to the rotten hoodlums that came around. Half of them didn't even dress up. They just came by holding a pillow case then complained if you didn't have the "Good" candy. Last year one of the punks tossed the candy back in the bowl. He said it wasn't high enough in caloric intake for the likes of his intestines. As he turned away laughing, I bonked him in the head with it.

I decided it was better not to lie to my wife. I would just tell her I was stopping at Kelsey's bar for a beer with the boys and I would be home after the government mandated two hours for Halloweening was over. My cell phone rang as I started to pull it out of my pocket. It startled me.

"Yes hello. Oh hi, Jill. Yeah, I got stuck at the office. I have so many new client files to get ready. I'm sorry I probably won't make the passing out of the candy this year."

"Say hi to Kelsey and Joann for me. Pick up your daughter at 11pm. She's at Felicia's. Do you need the address?"

"Wait, I said I was working late, how do you know I'm going to Kelsey's?"

"I was heading home after dropping the boys off at the Junior high school Halloween Hop. I spotted you turning into the parking lot. I assumed you were going in for a beer."

"Oh. And why is she "MY daughter" tonight?"

"The Princess and I had a little conversation about staying out until midnight. I told her 10pm on a school night and she argued. We settled on 11pm, so don't be late."

"Jill, for once I can almost see her point. It's Friday."

"They went to school today, right?"

"Yeah"

"Then it's a school night. One discussion of the subject is enough."

When Jill said it was enough, I knew to shut my mouth. It took twenty wonderful years to learn, but like all good husbands, I learned. I couldn't wait for the earful I would receive from my daughter on the way home from her friend's tonight. Maybe two beers wasn't going to be enough.

The Ride to Felicia's

Driving Under the Influence or the Bump and Feel Method

"I've never driven while intoximated. Let's me shet the record star-raight. I have never droven while interrogated. There, now pleash tell ny wife I left an hour. . .

They told me I passed out, but I think someone slipped something in the punch. I had left the bar and went to pick up Elise at her friend Felicia's party. Her mother invited me in while Elise got her coat. She gave me a cup of cider, and I heard some of the girls gasp and say,

"Oh no, Mrs. J., maybe he doesn't like apple cider. I think

Elise said her father is allergic to it or something."

I said, "Don't be silly."

And that's all I remember. Jill had to come and get us both. When I woke up Saturday morning, my hair was wet from my head hanging in the toilet.

"Well, look who's up. I hope you're proud of yourself. What a great example you set for your daughter. What were you thinking?"

"I swear Jill, I only had two beers. I went to pick up Eli, and Felicia's mom gave me something to drink. I think the punch was spiked."

"If your daughter hadn't gotten up at three this morning puking her guts out, I may have doubted you."

"Oh, good, like father like daughter. Neither one of us can hold our liquor."

"I just better never find out that you remember anything that happened last night."

"Why? What did I do?"

"On your way to the floor, you were grasping for anything to keep from falling."

"Oh, boy"

"You betcha, oh boy. You went face first into Felicia's mother's Elvira costume. I think you may have popped a boob. Anyway, you ripped off her dress and she lost her fangs somewhere. She called and said you owe her forty bucks."

"I didn't think I remembered her as being a size double D."

"Trust me, she's not. Now go get a shower. You're taking Lewis to his soccer match at 1pm this afternoon."

I did as I was told. The whole time I was snickering. It must have been quite a sight. I just hoped no one had their video phones recording the incident. It would be one of those U-tube movies that would probably go viral.

"Marty, are you coming with us to your brother's soccer practice?"

"Do I have a choice?"

"No."

"Then why'd you ask?"

Marty was the middle child. He was the only one that I still had a little parental control over.

"Lewis, we're leaving in five minutes. Get your gear and bring it to the car."

Jill was still attending to Eli. She was at the stage the day after when all she could say was,

"I'll never drink again. I swear, I'll never even have so much as a sip of wine or a Red Bull and Vodka shooter."

"Be glad I don't know what that last one is, or you'd be grounded for more than just the weekend."

"Mom, that's not fair. I'm sick. I shouldn't be grounded too."

Elise didn't always have the best argument to receive leniency, but she was good at begging, whining and getting her way when she wanted something. At the moment she wanted nothing more than to sleep without the bed spinning around.

Marty was squirming around in the front seat on the way to the soccer match.

"Is there something you want to talk about, son?"

"I heard all about the vacation. Gerry, my friend from school said the islands have nude beaches. Is that true, Dad?"

"I suppose it is, but I don't know for sure."

"If they do, are you and Mom going to go?"

"Well, it's a family vacation and we would all be going together. Do you really want to see your old man and mother naked?"

"Um, I guess not. What if you and Mom just go to the hotel pool, and Lewis and me go to the nude beach?"

"That's fine with me, as long as you understand it's a participation only beach. That means you have to get naked too."

"Maybe I'll just go to the hotel pool with the family."

"That's my boy. Here we are. Help Lewis get his gear to the field."

The rest of the afternoon and evening was uneventful. Sunday came and went. The Thanksgiving holiday was one week away. That meant a little over a month and we would be on our way to Paradise.

Thanks Giving 2008

The Bird, the Potatoes, and the Family

The family gathering had outgrown our house. We had to rent a hall at the Civic Center to hold all the guests. What with the In-Towners, Out-of-Towners, In-Laws and Out-Laws, Cousins, Aunts, Uncles, Nieces and Nephews. Grandmother, Father Mother, you name the relative add a couple homeless people and you got our Family for dinner. We had seventy-eight RSVP's this year.

My wife and her mother would make the birds. Three twenty-five pound turkeys would be doing the honors. All of the Aunts and sisters would bring side dishes and desert. It was a veritable smorgasbord, a cornucopia of epicurean delights. We feasted like there was no tomorrow. After a second round of dessert, I often wished there would be no tomorrow.

With the top of my pants unzipped, I joined the men to watch football on the rented big screen TV. By big I mean 72 inches of nothing but Jerseys and helmets crashing together in the mud. It was heaven.

"Turn that thing down. We're trying to talk over here. Ain't you guys got no manners, or is you deaf or something?"

Jill's mother had an eloquent way of expressing herself. She would also belch to compliment the chef. That would always get my mother started on comments about growing up in a barn. One year they threw mashed potatoes at each other. This year I was waiting for the annual argument to start. I just didn't know what was going to light the fuse.

"So, Jill honey, have you made the reservations for Christmas yet?"

"What? What reservations are you talking about, Mom?"

"For the hall, have you reserved the hall yet?"

I just found the fuse. Now I was waiting for Jill to light it. All hell was going to break loose if she told her mother there was not going to be a Christmas dinner this year. I was getting ready to lock myself in the bathroom.

"I usually book the hall the day after Thanksgiving. That would be tomorrow, Mother."

"Oh Good, ya know your sister from California is coming this year, don't cha?"

"Yes, she called to give me her travel arrangements and complete itinerary of her stay and daily events."

"That's just like Jennifer. She is always so prepared. I don't know why none of the rest of you girls turned out like her?"

Jill had that red glow starting to brighten her cheeks after hearing her mother's comments. I'll give her credit, she held back. I did see her hand drop to the table and fumble around as though she was looking for something to throw.

"By the way, dear. . .

The beginning of that sentence by Jill's mother never ended well.

"You might consider booking earlier next year."

"Why pray tell, why would you say that, mother dear?"

"Well, the poster on the door in the hallway with upcoming events says that the 24th of December is reserved for the Reynolds family. On the 25th a festival of Christmas is being held in this very hall by the Dorner-Schmeggie Family. I don't see how we can join them, do you, dear?

Oh boy. Steam was coming from Jill's ears. Not that she didn't love her mother, it's just her mother had a way of making her feel inferior. I wondered how much longer she would be able to constrain her emotions. And then;

"Mother, John and I have decided to surprise the family by having Christmas elsewhere. Fully catered, nothing for anyone to do, but eat drink and be merry."

The entire room went silent. Not a peep from anyone. An even stranger phenomenon, the TV went mute with no one touching the remote. I could feel the tension in the room. It was like a dark ominous cloud hanging over. I was waiting for the lightning and thunder to start any minute. The first words to come out of anyone's mouth were from Jill's mother.

"Well, why don't you just shoot me now and get it over with? We might as well not have Christmas at all."

"Mother, you're being over dramatic and making a scene."

"I disagree. I think your mother is right. Go ahead and shoot us both."

My mother has never agreed with anything that Hazel, (Jill's Mother) had to say.

"I'll handle my daughter. You find your good for nothing son. I'll bet he's behind this."

"My son would never commit treason against his own family. Besides, he loves Christmas and the gathering. Why he wouldn't miss it for the world."

My little princess Elise almost choked on her Coke when she heard that. She knew the Christmas vacation was my idea. I continued to watch the elder women argue. I am convinced that Jill's mother has a pair of small horns hiding under her bouffant hairdo.

I was about to try and calm things down when one of the teenagers got the group chanting

"Grinch Grinch Grinch Grinch. . ."

Before the mashed potatoes started flying, or an all out food fight started, I grabbed Jill by the hand and pulled her into the bathroom.

"What were you thinking telling your mother that we were going to have Christmas catered somewhere else? Where, do you think we can book a dinner for eighty at this late date?"

"I don't know, and don't yell at me."

"I'm sorry. I just want to leave here with our heads still attached. Did you see Aunt Sophie pushing the potatoes towards your mother so she could load up?"

I suggested escaping out through the bathroom window. Jill wouldn't have anything to do with it, so we walked back in. The party had settled down. Everything was back to normal. The guys were watching TV and the women were spreading gossip. If it were fertilizer, we'd have the best darn garden this side of Lake Superior.

Apparently Elise didn't have her fill of the family feud. She pulled me aside.

"Daddy, do you think Grandma will give me spending money for Christmas if I tell her I want to go shopping on the island?"

"You wouldn't dare?"

"I wouldn't if I can stay home."

"That's blackmail. I'm your father. You can't blackmail me."

"Watch and learn, Daddy, watch and learn."

"Elise, wait- - let's talk about this for a minute"

Her smile wasn't very angelic, that's for sure. She had plans and thought she was going to get me to cave on her joining the family for vacation. She actually thought I would let her stay home. Well, she was going to learn that Daddy's little princess wasn't too old to get a spanking.

Sunny Side Up or a Red Bottom

Elise, our first born, was my little girl. She was my Princess. I often told her that all through her formative years and even into her teens. She had me wrapped around her little finger from the time it was pink and wrinkly until now. Elise knew how to get me to do anything she wanted. At one point she could have had the moon, were it mine to give. Tonight she crossed the line. At 17 she was in for a rude awakening. A father can only handle so much before he cracks. Trying to blackmail me was low, even for her. I had to make a stand. No pouty face, arms crossed foot stomping little girl of mine was going to push me around, huh uh, no more.

"Jill, can you come in here for a minute?"

Elise might win the battles with me, but the war was over when her mother stepped into the room. Momma didn't cut no cotton when it came to disciplining our three children. Not that they needed much. I mean, they weren't like the spoiled rotten brats they called children that lived next door. There were several occasions I would have liked to drop kick the lot of them out of our yard. I voted to have their whole family excommunicated from the neighborhood. City council didn't have room on their agenda to take a ballot count, so they were permitted to stay.

"Jill, your daughter and I were discussing the possibility of asking your mother for a Christmas gift of money to spend on vacation. Do you have any thoughts on the matter?"

Elise glared at me. She couldn't believe I would play the trump card. I felt a burning in the middle of my forehead. She didn't dare look in her mother's direction. Elise knew if she did the conversation would be over before it began.

"NO!"

Only one word and Jill squelched the whole conversation. Eli and I looked at each other. She still had the evil glare going. I stuck my tongue out and followed Jill back into the dining hall.

People were starting to pack plates to take home. That meant clean-up. I volunteered to take out the garbage and fold the chairs. As we were saying our good-byes to everyone, I couldn't help notice that both of our mothers were missing. It was midnight before we finished and headed for home. The kids walked with their eyes closed to the car. Fortunately we lived only ten blocks away or I would have been sleeping in the car with them.

There was a red light blinking in the kitchen when we arrived home. The children dragged themselves to bed. Jill went upstairs with them and started her bath water. I was still unwinding. While putting the food away I found a small piece of pumpkin pie. Feeling guilty that it might go to waste, I decided my waist is where it should end up.

The blinking red light was the message machine on the phone. I wondered who might have called since the entire family and then some was gathered together today. I played the first of two messages.

"Jill dear, thank you for helping me create a beautiful dinner to serve to our wonderful family and what's his face's family too. I'm just sorry that you ruined it for your father and me when you made that ridiculous announcement. Having thought it over, we are declining the offer to attend. Your sister booked us a last minute cruise. We saved over seventy percent off the regular price, and we'll have all we care to eat with people from all around the globe. I imagine they will enjoy our company as we shall enjoy theirs. Good night, dear. Sleep well."

There was only one thing that came to mind as I listened to the recording. I can't let Jill hear the message. Well, actually there were two things that came to mind, but as a good Christian man, I couldn't say the other without putting a quarter in the swear jar.

Fortunately for Hazel, I didn't have any change in my pockets. The red light was still blinking. That meant another caller left a message.

"Honey, I don't blame you a bit for wanting to get away from those lunatics. I told you when you get married it's not just the girl you get, but her whole damn family too. Thanks for a wonderful day. We should get together more often. Maybe next time just the two of us for lunch or a weekend at the cottage. That would be fun. Good night. Love ya."

One thought came to mind when I heard that message. Jill definitely cannot hear this. I hit what I thought was erase, but it turned out to be just the pause button. I found out the next day when Jill got up to start her annual trek to the mall for Black Friday sales. She came into the bathroom without so much as a knock or an excuse me. I covered with the newspaper that I was reading while on the commode.

"You forgot to make the coffee."

"Gee, I'm sorry, shall I go down now and make it for you, or can it wait for a few more minutes?"

"I think you know that's not the reason I'm interrupting your time with the comic section and sports."

"No, I don't have a clue as to what's got you so fired up."

"Try telling me you didn't hear the message from my mother last night."

I was thankfully sitting in the right spot.

"Oh, shit."

"Oh shit is right. Now what are we going to do? She'll be telling everyone about her rotten no good for nothing Son-in-Law that stole her Christmas."

"Why am I always the bad guy? Can't you be the bad guy, just once?"

Jill was pacing across the tile floor in the bathroom. At one point she looked at me then walked out.

"My, gosh, that's disgusting."

The rest of the morning was non-confrontational. Jill took the kids to the mall, and as traditions have it, I hung the Christmas lights up on the house.

Running a Christmas Con

With the rest of the afternoon to myself, I stretched out on the sofa and feigned watching TV while taking a nap. I awoke to darkness. It was 7pm. The family was still shopping. I took the opportunity to use the time wisely. There were a few final plans that needed to be addressed before we would leave for vacation.

The Paradise Resort and Spa was located on a small island, somewhere between Jamaica and Aruba. The only way to get there was by boat after a one day stay in Jamaica. I couldn't wait. The garage door was opening. The family would be ascending on the home front like locust. I sauntered down the stairs to meet them.

"Hello, family. What do you think of the lights and decorations this year?"

"Dad, you're so gay. Besides, the decorations are the same every year. Can you drive me to Felicia's? We're having a sleepover."

"If it's okay with your mother, it's fine with me. Where is your mother anyway?"

"Beats me, she was in the car when we came home."

"Jill, are you still in the garage?"

I got the wave to hush. She was on her cell phone talking to someone who was carrying on and on about something. I decided to get dinner started for me and the boys.

"You two hungry? Did you have a good time at the Mall and find any bargains?"

"I'm hungry. Short stuff ate too much cotton candy and puked all over. It was great!"

"Stop calling your brother short stuff."

"Yes, Sir."

"Okay, pizza it is."

I threw a frozen pizza in the oven then set the timer for twenty-five minutes. Frozen dinners was about it for my skills in the culinary arts. The boys and I finished eating. Jill was sitting in the cold garage with the phone glued to her ear. If the conversation goes any longer, I swear her ear will fall off the side of her head.

"Princess, your chariot awaits. What time are we leaving for Felicia's?"

"Give me ten, Daddy."

"Okay."

My favorite movie of the Holidays was coming on at 8pm. I was trying to rush Elise along, so I wouldn't miss the beginning. I've been watching White Christmas with Bing Crosby and Danny Kaye since I was about eight years old. It would be on every Christmas Eve while we decorated the tree at my grandparents.

"Eli, come on, I don't want to miss my movie."

"Daddy, I swear you and that stupid movie. Like how many times can you watch that same movie year after year? I'm ready. Can we please just go now?"

"Just let me tell your mother that we're off."

Once more I was waved off. I could only guess by the tone of the conversation that she was talking to her mother or her sister. If it were Jill's sister, there would be no living with her for the next day and a half. If it's her mom, we will all suffer for the next week, if we're lucky.

When I got back from dropping off Elise, which would have been alright, except for the awkward moment when I had to face Felicia's mother. I was hoping she wouldn't bring up Halloween and the costume debacle. BUT . . . she did.

"So, John, are you off the sauce for good now, or do you only fall off the wagon when the moon is full?"

She laughed and I tried to laugh along with her. I was embarrassed still about the incident. When I got home I grabbed a soda pop and headed for the living room. The introduction to the movie along with the first round of commercials was on. I barely got my butt situated when Jill walked in and shut off the TV.

"John, we have to talk."

Whenever Jill started a conversation with, "John, we have to talk" it was never anything I wanted to talk about, and it usually didn't end well. The last time we had this conversation, I ended up in a hotel room for the weekend.

"Yes dear, what's on your mind?"

"I figured out a way to accomplish a holiday vacation and keep peace with our families."

This should be interesting. Somehow I knew it was going to benefit her mother and not so much me, or my parents.

"That's wonderful, honey. What's the plan?"

"First, we get the Dorkey-Schmukeggs to cancel at the hall…

"That would be the Dorner-Schmeggie's."

"What's that?"

"Never mind, go on with the plan."

"Okay. Once they cancel, we book the hall and have Christmas like every other year. After all, it's tradition."

"That's all I needed to hear. There is no fighting tradition. Not with Jill or her family. And there is no sense starting the argument about having our own family traditions. Until Mother Hazel passes or Hell freezes, we have got to go along with her families tired old traditions.

"Consider it done."

"Really?"

"Sure, all I have to do is the impossible and push back the flight or cancel."

"Honey, if you pull this off, which I know you will, I'll make sure there's something a little extra in your stocking for Christmas."

"Oh Boy, I can hardly wait."

I went to the garage and started the car. I ran the garden hose from the exhaust into the window of the car. I closed my eyes and hoped that death would be swift and painless. A light bulb went off in my head. I had the perfect plan. First thing Monday morning I would call the hall and make arrangements for both families to attend Christmas dinner together. After all, what's twenty more when you have seventy or eighty to begin with? The bigger problem was convincing the Dorner-Schmeggie's that they wanted to join our family's traditional holiday dinner. The next issue was exchanging non-refundable airline tickets to a different departure date.

Monday December 2nd 2008

"Good morning. May I speak with Hartmut Dorner please?"

"Who's calling?"

"This is Tall Ted from WHJY, your holiday fun channel 101. Is this the Mrs.?"

"Yes."

"So, is the big guy home?"

"No. He's at work. Is there a message?"

"Gee, I'm sorry. Your husband has been selected to be the Grand Prize winner of our first annual holiday vacation give-a-way."

"What did he win?"

"It's an all expense trip to an island resort. Can you believe it? Your husband and four guests can go with absolutely no obligations. Have him call this number within 30 minutes to collect his prize"

I was deaf in one ear from all the excited screaming. The only way I could get the hall was to get the Dorner-Schmeggie family to cancel. I gave them our vacation to keep the peace.

Communication is the Key

Speak Clearly or Bad Things Happen

"You, what?"

Jill was not as thrilled as I thought she would be when I told her how I accomplished getting the hall for Christmas.

"I did what you asked. I thought you would be pleased. The hall is ours. Yippee!"

"You're an idiot. I didn't say to give our vacation away. I just said to postpone it for a couple of days."

"Jill, the whole idea was to appease your mother, sisters and the rest of the family, I got the hall, isn't that a good thing?"

"I suppose. I'll call Mother and tell her everything is set for our annual Christmas dinner at the hall."

I was somewhat off the hook. Well, for the moment, or so I

thought. Jill walked into the living room and turned off the TV. Once again, I knew the conversation wasn't going to be without consequence.

"John, we have to talk."

Oh boy, here we go. I always hate when she says that.

"Yes dear, why don't you have a seat and you can tell me what's on your mind."

"If you think patronizing me is going to make things better, it's not. I just got off the phone with my mother. She said her tickets were non-refundable and she couldn't afford to give them up. She said and I quote. (*Sweetheart, it's only one day out of the year. I'm not getting any younger and your father isn't either for that matter. How often does a woman my age get to go on seven sun filled days in the Bahamas on a cruise at Christmas? You enjoy yourself and tell the family we'll send a postcard. Oh, and everyone gets a T-shirt. Love ya, bye-byes for now.*) The nerve of that woman, I have half a mind to call her back and tell her off. I can't even think straight, I'm so - - so angry."

"Jill, it looks like your mother's won again and at our expense. Do you want me to call the Dorner-Schmeggie's and tell them the trip was just a prank? We might as well make someone else miserable for Christmas too."

"John, you're not going to ruin a perfect stranger's vacation. Just let it be. I'm going up to soak in the tub to let off some steam."

I turned the television back on. A White Christmas was airing again. Maybe this time I would be able to watch it without interruption.

"Ring ring, Ring, ring"

I was hoping if I ignored the phone, whoever was calling would leave a message. Beep.

"Johnny dear, I have some news I want to share, but I don't want to leave it on a tape machine. It's rather personal. Don't worry, nobody's dead or anything like that. We won't be able to make it for Christmas dinner this year. Your father is taking me on one of them deluxe cruises with all the food and shopping, I'm so excited. Call me. I don't want to go into details. Someone else might pick up the message."

I quickly went to the phone and hit the delete button. This was one message Jill didn't have to hear until, well maybe some other life time. I went to the garage and turned on the car. I placed one end of the garden hose in the exhaust and the other in the window. I closed my eyes and hoped for a quick and painless death.

Wait, I could book a cruise too. We could still go on our holiday vacation as planned. It might not be the Paradise Island Resort & Spa, but it wouldn't be two feet of snow either. I ran like a little kid to my computer to see what kind of last minute deals there were.

On a whim I went to The Green World Travelers website. There was a 24 hour hot line. I dialled the number. I was so nervous with excited anticipation. What if I could book the vacation of a life time all over again? What if. . .

"Green World Traveler, hold please"

I was on hold for more than five minutes when a woman with a thick southern accent answered.

"Good Even-ning, I hope ya'll are having a simply wonderful night, how may I help you?"

"My name is John A. Fellows. I had a vacation to the Paradise Resort & Spa booked for five, but I had to re-assign them to some other travelers. It's a long story. Anyway, my family can go now, so I wanted to see if there's a possibility to re-book."

"What was the date of your departure, please?"

"December 23rd."

"Checking December 23rd. One moment. Still checking. Hold one moment, Mr. Fellows."

I was breathing heavy. What if. . . I had my fingers crossed. I even crossed my legs for extra luck.

"Sir, still checking. Ah, I have it. We had a cancellation this morning. A villa suite, with adjoining room, sleeps a total of six adults. Will that work for you?"

"Yes. Oh my yes. That's fantastic. Book me right away."

"Do you still want the all inclusive rate?"

"Yes."

"Mr. Fellows, I see you have a day reserved for the spa for

your wife, and a trip to the Sea Turtle swim, is that correct?"

"Yes, I want everything just as before."

"That's it. I have your vacation confirmed. Have a happy holiday, sir, and ya'll call me if you need anything before you leave. Good night."

"Good night."

I was so excited I couldn't contain my emotions. I even think I may have peed a little. I ran to tell Jill the good news. I knew she was going to be as excited as I was. She was just getting out of the tub.

"Jill, Jill, hurry come out of the bathroom, I have something I have to tell you."

"What, did something happen? Are the kids okay?"

"It's nothing like that. Another family cancelled and we're back on for the vacation of a lifetime. I was able to get everything the same as before including swimming with sea turtles."

"You're an idiot. I'm going to bed. Tell me about it in the morning."

That wasn't the reaction I thought or hoped to get. I was feeling a bit rejected. I went downstairs to watch the end of my movie.

"Sheesh."

If at first you don't succeed

Or Failure is Not an Option

A full week had passed, not a single mention of the vacation, the plans, or the time when we would be leaving. A full week and we hadn't discussed the Christmas dinner at the hall. It was Monday morning and I was getting ready for work. I went into the kitchen. Jill had her back to me while she cleaned up the dishes from the kids' breakfast.

The sports page was open next to a cup of coffee by my spot at the table. I couldn't imagine what I had done to deserve such royal treatment. Never mind the fact that I was King of my castle. Jill never saw it quite that way. Oh, there was no doubt she was the Queen, but I, well let's say my wife allowed me to think I was

King.

Jill turned on a dime. There wasn't a dancer in the world that could have made that turn and stayed on their feet. I was sitting dazzled by her brilliance and grace. Of course the moment ended with,

"John, we have to talk."

Those words were becoming all too familiar lately. I often thought I heard them in my sleep. I once thought I heard my boss say the very same thing just before he gave me a briefing on the advantages of downsizing the company from the top down.

"Honey, I only have time to drink my coffee. I have a meeting at eight and I can't be late. So, if it can wait till tonight, I will guarantee you my undivided attention."

"Sure, dear, it can wait. You run off to your little meeting and do whatever it is you do. I'll just go to work as I always do and count the hours until we can share a moment of your time together."

That was a signal that I should call into work to announce that I've been diagnosed with typhoid or some other communicable disease that would keep me home for at least an hour or death, whichever came first. I looked at my watch.

"Jill, if it's important I can call to postpone my meeting until 9 or 10."

With a look that would have melted a puppy's heart she sat in the chair across from me at the table. I didn't know what to say. I felt tears welling up in my eyes.

"Jill, what's wrong?"

"Where did the money come from to book the vacation a second time?"

Uh-O, I knew the question of money would come up sooner or later. I was just hoping it wouldn't come up until we were in our late eighties and I could declare myself incompetent to answer.

"I, ah, well I borrowed it from the boys' college fund."

"YOU DID WHAT?"

"Come on Jill, we both know the boys probably won't go to college. Its money that's just sitting in a fund waiting for us to do something fun with it."

"You took money from the boys, what about from your daughter, did you steal from her too?"

"First of all, it's not stealing. Second, ever since your daughter found out she had a fund, she watches it like a hawk. If the deposit into her account is a day late, I get a text asking why I don't love her anymore. Followed by, do I want to see my only daughter suffer socially by attending a community college? So no, I didn't take money from Elise."

"I thought we were settled on having the Christmas dinner and foregoing the vacation?"

"Well, we were until our parents pulled out and booked a vacation of their own."

"What do you mean, our parents? I know about my mother and father, but this is the first I'm hearing about your parents. John, you have some explaining to do."

"Umm, I well, when I got a call that my mother was going to take a cruise on the same boat as your mother, I thought wouldn't it be fun if we all went? Then on a whim I called the travel agency. Someone cancelled and we got our trip back."

"You would have stayed home for your mother, but not for mine. You better go to your stupid meeting. I don't want to talk about this anymore."

"Okay, dear, see you later. Would you like me to bring something home so you don't have to cook tonight?

The cold icy stare said, no, but I knew she wanted me to bring something home. A good husband learns to read between the lines. After twenty years of marriage, I'd learned that no means yes, yes means yes and anything in between means I had better come home with flowers and a box of chocolates. Tonight would be that night.

I got to work in time to greet everyone coming out of the meeting. No one looked happy about the outcome. I decided to head to my desk and look busy. Maybe no one noticed I wasn't there. I got a cup of coffee. My message board showed that I had a call from Elise, it said urgent. I could only imagine what it might be about. Before calling I checked to make sure her college fund deposit had been made.

"Daddy, I heard the trip was canceled. I'm sorry to hear that. I was so looking forward to going. I know how disappointed you must be."

"Princess, did you call to tell me that?"

"Why yes Daddy, I thought you might want some words of condolence."

"Well, to tell you the truth, it was canceled, but now it's back on. So, you don't have to be so down in the mully-grubs."

"WHAT? You booked that stupid trip again. I HATE YOU." Click.

That wasn't the reaction I thought or hoped to get.

"Sheesh."

Charity is a Gift from the Heart

Playing Santa for Another Family

December 13, 2008

The day was dragging. Every time I looked up, the wall clock said ten. After an hour I realized the battery was dead.

When the day ended I rushed to my car to try to get to my favorite florist before it closed. I loved the place. The Petal Pusher was an eclectic shop with flowers, gifts, flavored coffees and candy. It's a one stop apology shop for men. I especially liked that they knew my name. They had a card filled out with my wife's favorite flowers and candy. When I went there, I didn't have to worry about forgetting anything.

"Shit, I mean shoot."

The lights were off with a closed sign hanging in the window.

I threw a quarter into the ashtray. The ashtray was my mobile swear jar. When it was full I knew from experience that there was enough change in it to buy a large pepperoni pizza from Papalardo's. It seemed as though we were having pizza more frequently as the Christmas Holiday got closer.

I had two options. One: Go home empty handed. Visions of sugar plums were not dancing in my head following that thought.

Two: Go to Jungle Jim's International Market in Fairfield. Jungle Jim's was billed as one of the largest grocery stores in the world. He had delicacies from over 80 different countries. Why, the cheese section alone had 1400 entries. His wine collection has over 900 labels. If you couldn't find what you wanted at Jungle Jim's, well you might as well be from another planet looking for Kryptonite. My problem was the place was so big it would take half the night to find the floral garden and the rest of the night trying to decide which ones to buy.

Oh, and forget the chocolates, the Chocolate Kingdom was overwhelming.

When I was a kid things were so much easier. You would go to the corner drug store. There were three chocolate companies to choose from: Russell Stover's, Fanny Farmers, and Whitman Chocolate Samplers. I preferred the latter because inside the top of the box was a map of where the good candies were in the tray. You didn't have to poke a hole in the bottom with your thumb to test it and then put the yucky ones back. I still laugh at the vision I have every time I think about the second brand's name. What were they thinking when they came up with that?

Since I only had two items I was able to get in the express check out. The guy in front of me was having trouble with his credit card. Naturally I was irritated. If you don't pay your bills they cancel your card. What an idiot. Then he tried to write a check. It was refused. I could see the cashier was frustrated and didn't know how to politely tell the guy to go to the ATM and come back with cash. I looked at the things he was trying to buy. He had a box of diapers, some baby formula and a canned ham. I needed to move things along.

"Miss, put his tab on my bill. Sir, just pack your stuff and have a good night."

He didn't know what to say. A perfect stranger was being nice.

"Thank you, thank you very much."

"Don't worry about it. I was going to put something in the red bucket with the bell ringer. I guess I'd rather see the recipient than worry that my portion of the take was being skimmed off the top."

"Well, thanks again and have a Merry Christmas."

I was almost out of the grocer's when the man walked back up to me.

"Ted, Aren't you Tall Ted?"

I had to think for a minute. This was the guy who had won the vacation. I put on my best radio voice.

"Why yes, sir. And you're Warren Dorner of the Dorner-Schmeggie family, right?"

"That's right."

"You and your wife have got to be pretty excited about your big vacation coming up next week?"

"That's an understatement. She was excited alright, but not happy. She told me I was stupid for signing up for the contest. Once we found out what the taxes would be we had to turn them in. I wanted to say I'm sorry, but I couldn't find you or the station. We thought you could give the tickets away to someone who would be able to use them."

I hadn't thought about the 1099 that he would have to file. Nor could I tell him that the tickets weren't going to be reported because they were mine and not the stations. It was too late for that.

"The worst thing of the whole deal, Ted, is that I don't even listen to WONE 101 the fun station. No offense, but I didn't sign up for the contest. My wife and I lost the hall at the civic center for our Christmas dinner, and it's too late to book elsewhere."

I felt like the creep from the black lagoon. Not only did I almost ruin his marriage, but I ruined his families Christmas dinner at the hall just so I could keep peace with my family.

"Look, Dorner, the Station is holding their annual Christmas dinner at that very same hall. Apparently when you cancelled they got it. We are having a number of needy families attending our Christmas dinner extravaganza. You and your family along with your extended family are welcome to join us as our guests."

"I don't know what to say."

"Don't say anything. Be there around 3pm. I always say the more the merrier."

"We'll be there. Thank you, Ted, you are the most generous

man I've ever met in my entire life."

I felt all warm and fuzzy. I did a good deed and I was happy. It felt like the Christmas spirit had taken hold.

I was ready to enjoy the Holiday, even with the big dinner and all the relatives. So what, it's only one day a year. I'm a survivor and I've been generous to a fault tonight.

My cell phone was ringing when I got to the car. It was Jill, and I was two hours late getting home from work. I could answer the phone and pretend that there's a bad connection, or I could not answer the phone and tell her that the battery was dead. I had to think fast.

When First We Learn a Web to Weave

Deception is Nine-tenths of Valor

I chose to ignore the phone that was ringing on the front seat of my car. Assuming Jill was still in the kitchen, I walked in holding my prized bouquet of flowers in front of me.

"John, what did you do?"

"What do you mean, what did I do?"

"It's not unusual for you to be late coming home from work. It is unusual for you to bring me flowers. They're even my favorites."

So far, so good, if I guessed right on the candy I'd be two for two. I pulled the box from behind my back that I had been hiding.

"Here honey, sweets for my sweetie."

"Geez John, I just cleaned the floors. With all the bull crap you're spreading, I'll need to watch where I step."

"Funny, you're a very funny girl. I bought these as an apology for this morning."

"John Alan Fellows - - if you think cheap candy and overpriced flowers are going to smooth things over from this morning, if you think- - second thought gifts will make up for you childish antics and selfish lack of consideration for others . . .well you're right"

Jill walked over to me with a silly grin. She kissed me on the forehead then took me by the shoulders and turned me towards the living room. With a swat on the butt, she said,

"John, go watch some TV or read the paper. Dinner won't be ready for another thirty minutes."

I now was the one with the silly grin. It had been a long time since Jill had gotten a little frisky with me. I sat in my favorite recliner. It was double stuffed with goose down and covered with naw-ga-hide. I don't know how to spell the word and I sure don't know what kind of animal it comes from. All I know is that it's the most comfortable seat in the house. I fell asleep before I could turn on the nightly news.

"Daddy"

I was startled in the middle of a tropical paradise. Jill and I were sunbathing and . . .

"Oh, Elise, what is it, Princess?"

"I was wondering about our trip. Will we be driving?"

"Honey, it's much too far to go by car."

"Then, what about a train? I hear they have trains now that can travel faster than a plane."

"While that may be true, they only have those in Japan and we aren't going to Japan. We'll be going to the other side of the world crossing the Atlantic Ocean."

"Oh, then we'll be going by boat. Are we going on the same cruise as both Grandmas?"

"Princess, you are just full of questions tonight. That's not like you to have a conversation with your dear old dad."

"Well, if I have to go on the "Family Vacation," then I want to know all about it."

"Okay, first we fly to Miami. We'll spend an overnight there before catching a connecting flight that will take us to Jamaica and then Paradise Island Resort where- - -"

"Wait, What? Are YOU nuts or something?"

"I, I don't know what you're asking."

"Daddy, you look at Billy sideways if he so much as holds my hand. But, you would think nothing of having a perfect stranger at an airport grope your little girl."

"Elsie, it's not groping, it's a security pat down."

"In your world it might be a "pat down." In my world the boys call it getting to second base. How could you?"

"It's not like it's my fault, ya know. There are bad people out there. Besides, if you don't want the pat down, you can go through the check in with the scanner."

Elise let out a shriek that caused the hair on my neck to stand straight up.

"Daddy, that's even worse. Every pre-pubescent boy in the world stands at the end of the line gawking at the naked hotties as they walk through the x-ray machine."

"Honey, it's not an x-ray machine and you don't walk naked through them."

"It's not? And you don't"

"No, now stop being silly."

"You don't think I'm pretty. You could care less if people will be looking, touching or doing other despicable things to me. I hate you. You're the worst father in the history of the world."

My little girl was growing up, and I wasn't handling it very well. She went running upstairs to her bedroom. I heard the door slam followed by another "I hate you, Daddy" and what might have been a shoe thrown at the wall. I yelled into the kitchen

"Jill, remind me no vacations with airport security."

"Okay, dear. Dinner's ready, call the kids to come and eat."

"Uhm, maybe I'll just call the boys tonight."

There's no Tree like a Christmas Tree

Pine Scent's Not Just for Bathrooms

Saturday December 18th

Our family's tradition was to put up the tree one week before Christmas. It was always fresh, never one that had been cut down who knows when with the needles falling off in the car all the way home. Not one that when you put the lights on, you worried it was so dry that you had to wrap a fire extinguisher as a gift and keep in under the tree. I wouldn't allow one of those store bought skeletal trees that you could see through while hand picking the needles out of the carpet. For me, a fresh cut tree was the best. It was our family tradition to travel to Pine Acres and pick out a tree from the forest. For fifty bucks they would drag it, tie it, bag it, and rope it to the top of your car. What a deal. They even rented chainsaws so I didn't have to get mine repaired for the occasion.

Jill and Elise were planning a mother daughter day, so this year it would be just me and the boys doing what we deemed as a man's job. I had been taking the boys to Pine Acres since before they were out of diapers. One year the snow was so deep we lost little Lew. I searched for nearly an hour to find his numb, frozen body buried in a six foot snow drift. I suppose if he hadn't had a scarf wrapped around his face, we may have heard his cries for help. Oh well, he thawed and all is well, except for one finger. The middle finger on his right hand stiffens up at the mere mention of hunting for a tree.

"Make sure the tree doesn't hit the ceiling this year. Last year the Angel got bruises on her forehead and there's still some clumps of her hair stuck to the ceiling from the year before."

Jill was giving me last minute instructions on how to pick a tree. I liked them tall and full. Lots of room for ornaments, lights and presents underneath. You can't find all that in a short stumpy one.

"Yes, Dear, I measured the room, and I know how big it should be. If it touches the ceiling, I can trim a little off."

"You've said that every year since we've been married. Once the tree is in the stand, it doesn't get trimmed. I think you say that to appease me. I'm warning you, nothing bigger than 6.5 maybe 7 feet. THAT'S IT."

"Six foot five or seven feet blah blah blah"

"What was that? I missed it, you're talking soft. I can't hear what you're saying.

"Nothing, I have to get the boys ready by seven or we'll miss out on the best selection."

"John, honey, if you wanted the best selection you should have gone on November 26th the day after Thanksgiving like everyone else."

I didn't want to see Jill's I told you so face, so I continued on my mission to garner the boys together. Elise passed me on the stairs. She still wasn't speaking to me after almost a week.

"Good morning, Princess. How are you this fine snowy day? Are you looking forward to your day with Mom?"

"I hate you."

Okay then, now's she's talking to me again.

"Marty, Lew, let's get a move on. The trees aren't going to wait for you two sleepy heads to come cut them, you know."

My boys Martin and Lewis came out from their room dragging like two Neanderthals. They looked pitiful. It was like watching two inmates do their final march to the electric chair. I was beginning to think that maybe they weren't interested in the trek and adventure of finding the family tree. I was beginning to think that they didn't want to go into the woods where there were no footprints in the snow and find the perfect tree. I was beginning to think that until Lewis said,

"Dad, how about if you go. Marty and me will stay home and unpack the lights to make sure all the bulbs light before you put them on the tree?"

"Yeah, Dad, remember last year when only half of the tree lit up and you had to hang a spot light from the ceiling? Remember Mom got mad at you because of the holes you made to put up the brackets to hold the lights? Remember the year before when. . ."

"That's enough. I want you two boys to go up in the attic and bring down all the lights and decorations. I'll go get the traditional family Christmas tree all by myself. If I freeze to death out there alone, tell your mother and sister that I love them both."

"Dad, come-on, if you get anymore syrupy Mom will have to make us some pancakes. Let's get our coats, Lewis, or we'll never hear the end of it."

"That's the spirit. I'll be in the car waiting."

It was only a forty minute drive to the Farm. I was singing Christmas songs. The boys were singing right along - - with earphones on while listening to music on their mp3 players. It was snowing, but not bad enough to detour me from our mission. I couldn't see the road through the whiteout conditions; however,

I had been traveling to Pine Acres for over twenty years, and I think the car instinctively knew the way.

"Yes I'll hold. I know the weather's bad. I'm in the middle of a blizzard. So how long before a tow truck can pull me out?"

The car forgot there was a turn on Rt. 4 and continued straight into a ravine. If the snow wasn't up to the windows I was pretty sure I could have rocked the car out, but, well. . . I turned the radio on and listened to Christmas music while waiting for AAA.

It was already dark by the time we got to the farm. I begged the curator to stay open for another fifteen minutes while we went to pick out a tree. He was nice enough to stay and only charged me double for his inconvenience.

"Dad, my feet are frozen. Can't we just take the first tree we see?"

As I turned I noticed the weather conditions were worsening. Poor Lew's finger was stiff and shaking at me.

"Don't worry, we'll find the perfect tree and then I'll treat you boys to burgers and fries at the Purple Pickle. How's that sound."

"Great, but I gotta go to the bathroom."

The Perfect Tree

Finding a Nest Can Bring Good Luck

The further we trekked into the woods the darker it got. We were losing the light of the moon. All the trees were starting to look the same. I pulled out my pocket pen light to try to get a better look at the suspect in front of me.

"Hey, boys, come over here. I think this is the one. This is the tree that will complete our family tradition. What do you think, Marty - - Lewis, hey where are you guys?"

"We're right behind you, Dad. Don't freak out."

"I'm not freaking out, Lewis. I just couldn't see you."

"Dad, this tree is like fourteen feet tall. Mom will throw a hissy fit just before she shoots you."

"Yeah, and she's not a very good shot. You'd better hide Marty if you don't want to get shot along with Dad."

"You two are regular comedians, aren't you?"

"Dad, we're supposed to pick out a tree that won't hit the ceiling. Mom made us promise we wouldn't let you bring home the biggest tree in the forest. Can't we just get a pre-cut tree from the barn?"

I clutched my chest feigning a myocardial infarction. Lewis threw in his two cents.

"I got a better idea, let's go to Jungle Jim's International Market and buy one of those trees that have the lights and fake snow sprayed on them."

With that, my knees buckled and I fell to the ground. I kicked my feet in the air, shook for a minute or two and then lay silently with my eyes closed.

"What do you think happened to Dad?"

"I don't know, maybe a heart attack?"

"Do you think it's from all the years of eatin Mom's bad cooking?"

"I suppose. I mean all those greasy meat dishes covered with cheese, it's gotta clog an artery or something."

"Marty, I'm scared. Should we leave him here in the snow while we try to get help?"

"Lewis, don't be stupid. He might get eaten by a bear or a wolf. That's after the raccoons come down and scratch his eyes out. They like eyeballs, I think. It's a delicacy for them or something."

I sat up and said,

"Boo!"

They both jumped out of their skin. I pulled them by the arms into the snow, and we all wrestled for a little bit.

"You know we knew you were faking, don't ya?"

"Oh, sure Marty, and your comments about Mom's food is our little secret. Now let's get that tree. I saw one back this way."

Three amigos walking back the way we came, frozen feet, hands and snot running down our noses. We were quite a sight, that's for sure. All bundled up and we could barely walk. Our feet were barely lifting off the ground. We trudged onward.

"That's it, that's the tree. Who has the saw?"

The two boys looked at each other. I knew that look. It meant, "I thought you had it."

"Dad, don't even say you don't have the saw."

"I won't say a word. However, I always come prepared. If you two go flag down the guy with the tractor, I'll start cutting this puppy down."

The boys went off through the field in the direction of the sound from the farm tractor. I pulled out my combination pocket knife. I've had it since I was eight years old. My father gave me this knife when I was in cub scouts. I was going to pass it on to my oldest son. However, he was never a scout, so I haven't given him the prized possession from my youth yet.

"Okay, let's see. Knife – spoon – fork - can opener – corkscrew - file, scissors – ah, saw blade."

I got down on both knees and started trimming around the base of the trunk. I found it was easier to bend them back and forth until they broke off. When the bottom row was trimmed, I started using the saw. I had just broken through the bark when,

"What's that smell? I guess they probably fertilize the trees to make them grow faster."

The guy with the tractor pulled up near the tree, grabbed a chainsaw and in less than three minutes it was down on the ground. Without so much as a word, he tied the tree up to the back of the tractor and headed for the barn. We ran to hop onto the back of his trailer so that we wouldn't have to walk all the way back. The diesel fuel smell combined with the pine scent created hallucinogenic memories of years gone by. Even with the aroma wafting up to my nostrils, I could still smell the fertilizer.

Our host from the farm bagged the tree and tied it to the top of my Jeep. We were on our way home with a stop to the burger joint as a reward for a job well done. If it were possible, I would have napped along the way just like the boys in the back seat.

The Joys of Fatherhood

Laughter May be the Best Medicine but Not at My Expense

The Purple Pickle was my favorite burger joint. I loved the pickles, the atmosphere, and most of all, the Angus beef burgers. The house specialty was a bacon and egg cheeseburger. I ordered it every time I went for dinner. The boys liked the more mundane burgers, just cheese no frills. The biggest deal of the place was the bottomless fries. The waitress would come around often to top off the drinks and refill the basket of fries. One order was enough for the whole family.

When we went in, I signed us up for a table. The waiting time was only 15 minutes. They gave us one of those vibrating thing-a-ma-jigs. I sat on the bench in the vestibule and closed my eyes. I was exhausted from the day's activities. When the lights started flashing and the vibrations started, I was rested and ready for dinner.

I couldn't figure out why people kept looking in our direction and then walking quickly away. The hostess sat us at a round table for four. She asked the usual questions about drinks and turned her head away to take a deep breath before asking another question about our dinner selections. I thought it was a very odd behavior. As we started to thaw, the fertilizer smell was getting more pungent. Lewis looked at me.

"Dad, you smell like shit."

I was taken aback by his blunt accusation.

"Me, I thought it was one of you."

People nearby were moving away from us. They were calling for their waiter/waitress, then complaining about something. I couldn't quite make out what they were saying, but they were pointing at us while talking.

"Marty, when you said you had to go to the bathroom while at the farm, did you go one or two?"

Marty sheepishly held up two fingers.

"Oh my God, it's me that stinks. I must have rolled in your excrement while trimming the tree. We have to go right now. We have to leave immediately."

The waitress was bringing our food. We had never been served so fast in all the times we'd been coming here.

"Miss, we need our food boxed to go."

"No problem Sir, I'll get you some boxes."

As she walked away I heard her say to herself, "Thank God they're leaving." Before she got back I looked in my wallet for cash to pay the bill so that we wouldn't have to suffer further embarrassment waiting for the charge card to be run.

"Shit, I mean shoot. I used all my cash paying for the tree."

Both boys held out their hands for a quarter from me to put in the swear jar. The head waiter and manager walked over to our table.

"Sir, it appears you may have had a little accident. If you would kindly remove yourself, we'll bring your food to your car. As our compliments for coming in tonight we'd like to give you this gift card. We apologize for any inconvenience we may have caused you and your boys."

"You are being most gracious, I understand. Gee, a hundred bucks to the Olive Garden, I didn't know you were affiliates."

"We're not. We just don't want you back, or at least not anytime soon. Pull your car around the back to the kitchen entrance. Your bag should be ready when you get there."

I was five shades of red with embarrassment. The boys were busting a gut laughing all the way out the front door on our way to the car. I called out to the manager.

"Uhm, can we get some extra pickles, I love your pickles."

"Yes, yes just please go."

The manager was holding his nose. As I warmed up, the smell was filling the entire restaurant. When I had pulled around to the back, one of the bus boys was taking my chair to the dumpster. As we drove away, I pulled off my pants and threw them out the window. That created another round of uncontrollable laughter from the backseat. All I wanted this year was a Christmas to remember. This wasn't what I had in mind.

The boys jumped out of the car with food in hand and ran into the kitchen through the garage entranceway. I was in such a panic to get out of my soiled clothing that I didn't think about lowering the garage door. A car full of Elise's girlfriends pulled into the driveway. I was frozen like a deer while staring into the headlights of the car. My pride had shrunk while I held my under garments at arm's length in front of me. Elise got out of the car.

"Daddy, I can't begin to think of what you're doing, but I've never been so humiliated in front of my friends like this. I hate you!"

She ran into the house and slammed the door. I pressed the remote on the garage door and watched as the headlights of the car with all her friends pulled out of the driveway. I found an old pair of waders and pulled them on, then went inside to face my wife.

"Hi Jill, you're really gonna laugh when you hear what happened today with the boys at the farm."

"I'd better, John, or I'm filing for divorce. Get a shower and put some clothes on. We need to talk."

"Uh-O."

Passing the Olive Branch of Peace

A Pine Branch Will do in a Pinch.

I ran upstairs feeling like a child that just had his punishment doled out by his mother. Truth be told, I couldn't wait to get in the shower. I wanted to crawl out of my skin to get away from the smell. I think the stink was even in my hair. used an entire bar of my wife's French lavender soap. The Loofah By the time I finished washing, rinsing, and washing again, I had no longer had any loof left. My skin was red, either from scrubbing or an allergic reaction to the soap. Watery eyes and a runny nose was part of my discomfort, but the stink was gone and I could deal with the rest.

Martin and Lewis had managed to get the tree off from the top of the car. They dragged it into the front room and began setting it up. I was proud of the way my little men were taking responsibility. I overlooked the snickering when I walked in the room. I had to admit the entire event was pretty darn funny.

"Dad, Mom wants to see you. She said to march right into the kitchen as soon as you came down from your shower. We told her what happened. I think the warden will go light with her sentencing."

"Thanks. And thanks for helping with the tree."

"Can we put the lights on too?"

"Sure Lew, you and Marty can decorate with Mom and me, if she'll let us."

"You're a funny guy, Dad. Even if she lets us, you know she'll be fixing it tonight when we go to bed."

"I know Marty, but it's her thing and that's what mothers do. If you hear anything coming from the kitchen that requires a 911 call, just ignore it and let me die in peace."

The boys both laughed and continued with setting up the tree. When I got in the kitchen, it appeared that Jill had been crying. I feared the worst was yet to come. She wiped her mouth while holding the remains of my burger.

"I swear John the Purple Pickle makes the best darn burgers on the planet. Thanks for bringing one home for me. I was starved. Elise and I went shopping for vacation clothes and found the most darling bathing suit for her. I dropped her off at her friends' and never had time to eat."

"Vacations clothes and a swim suit, I'm surprised."

"John, while you may have been practicing for the nude beaches in the garage, your daughter and I are a little more modest."

Jill started laughing at the thought of me getting caught in the garage by Elise and her friends while I was trying to get out of my poopy pants. It was then that I realized that her tears were from laughing so hard at the story the boys told her and not from anything else. I was relieved.

"Mom, Dad, come quick. Come see the tree."

Jill and I looked at each other. First thoughts were the thrill of seeing this year's tree for the first time, the second thought was fear that it might be lying on its side, setting the house on fire. We quickly got up from the kitchen table and ran into the front room to see what all the commotion was about. Lew was pointing to the top of the tree while Marty was holding the branches apart so we could see in.

"Look, Dad, a bird's nest. You've always said it is good luck to have a tree with a nest in it."

"Yeah, it looks like we picked out the right tree after all."

The Angel was on top with an inch of room to spare from the top of her hair to the ceiling. My wife was beaming with joy. We pulled the boys over to enjoy a group hug. The Kodak moment didn't last long. Elise came down from her throne and looked into the room to see us all together in a warm embrace.

"Gay! I'll be home by eleven. Larry and I are going to the movies, K – see ya."

When the cars horn in the driveway honked twice, she was gone in a flash. The boys pulled away after their sister's comment. After all, being teenagers they couldn't be seen hugging their parents. I was surprised and pleased that they stuck around to finish trimming the tree. It was the first time in a long while that I felt all was well with the world.

Monday December 21st 2008

On the twenty-first of December, it was the company's tradition to give every employee a Holiday bonus. Some people considered it a fifty-third pay check. Others thought it was part of their pay plan and they deserved it for all the hard work they did throughout the year. I, on the other hand, did not live or die by the bonus. It was just that. Whatever they gave me was fine. It was their gift to me. Some years it would be a couple hundred bucks, other years it was over a thousand dollars. This year I decided whatever it was, I would divvy it up amongst the family to use as spending money on the Island.

My family had grown accustomed to the fact that I was a last minute Christmas shopper. The children knew that they would be showered with gifts, but that most of what they got, they had never heard of. Possibly that no one ever heard of.

"Anyone can get the most popular toy advertised on TV, but you boys have something none of your friends have."

I would tell them that every year when their little pouty faces looked up at me and asked,

"Why Dad, why, why can't we have a Nintendo game station or a Sony blue ray player? Nobody plays electronic Scrabble or

Star Wars Monopoly with action Jedi figures. Why can't we have something that at least moves with a remote controller or does something on video?"

This year was going to be different. I had it all planned out. Marty was old enough to have a cell phone, Lewis was going to get an MP3 player, and Elise was getting a portable lap top. I would have more time to myself for my writing if she wasn't face booking all night.

The best thing about the week before the holiday was the food. Every morning there would be a tray of cookies, muffins, pies or some other sweet treats brought to the office from home. We would have cheese trays with crackers, veggie trays with dip, shrimp with dip and an assortment of other munchies and dip. It was a foodie's paradise of epicurean delights. If I were to die prematurely, let it be January third of any year. Just let me eat my way through the holidays and into my grave.

My envelope with the Holiday bonus was on my keyboard when I came back from lunch. I thought it was a little odd. Usually they were given with a hand shake and a wish for a Merry Christmas. Oh, well. I didn't look at it. I put it in my jacket pocket to save it for the vacation as planned.

The Christmas Bonus

Surprise!

December 23rd 2008

It was my last day of work this year. The office was closing for three days over the Christmas Holiday. This was the first time in seventeen years that we were going to be closed on Christmas Eve. That would give me a full day to do my shopping.

Ernie came over to my cubicle. I wasn't fond of Ernie. I think he knew it too. He was the corporate suck-up. He just rubbed me the wrong way when he started more than ten years ago and we've never quite connected since.

"Hey John, are you packed and ready to go?"

I felt obligated to talk to him since he was standing in front of me asking a direct question.

"I've been ready to go for weeks. The packing I leave to my wife."

"I'll bet she's excited. So where are the kids going to be staying while you two are away?"

I looked at Ernie with a strange inquisitive look.

"Why, they're coming with us. We booked adjoining rooms."

"How quaint, I'll bet that set you back a couple nickels?"

"Ernie, are we talking about the same vacation that I've been planning for almost two months?"

"I don't know, unless you got your bonus early this year."

"No, I didn't. So what are you talking about?"

"Uhm nothing, I just wouldn't wait to open your envelope this year. Bye-bye now."

Ernie left me scratching my head. I assumed he knew about the Paradise Island Resort vacation, but he seemed to be indicating that there might be something else. I blew it off as a practical joke.

When the day ended, I rushed to my car. I was going to pick up a burger that I missed out on the other night. Jill was at a bon voyage party for her mother, so I was on my own for dinner. The kids were somewhere, I know I was told, but at the moment their where-a-bouts were the last thing on my mind. I pulled up to the Purple Pickle Drive through and disguised my voice so they wouldn't recognize me.

"I'll have the bacon egg and cheeseburger. Eggs over easy a little runny and two pickles on the side please."

"Would you like fries and a Coke with that?"

"Fries yes, Coke no. I'd like a Jamocha shake with a shot of espresso in it. That's all."

"Your total is $17.33. Would you like to add a tip?"

"Sure, whatever the customary amount is, will be fine."

"Please pull around. Your order will be at window three. Have a Merry Christmas, Mr. Fellows."

"The same to you."

I didn't think about the voice in the box knowing my name

until I started to pull around the building. I had to ask the check out girl how she knew who I was.

"That's easy. We run your plate when you pull up. That way if someone tries to pull away without paying we can report them to the police for petty theft."

"Oh, that's pretty high tech."

"Yeah, we like to think we're a progressive company. Have a happy holiday, sir."

"Thanks, you do the same."

I couldn't wait to get to my burger. I wasn't going to take a chance that someone would be home and try to eat it before I got to it. I couldn't believe the nerve of my wife giving the toppings to the dog. If she would have thrown the eggs and bacon in the garbage, I'd have been tempted to go dumpster diving and retrieve them. There was no getting em back from Rufus.

I unwrapped half of the sandwich so that I could hold it and drive. The gooey mess of the eggs and cheese were like a taste from heaven. I was thoroughly enjoying myself when I entered an intersection, missing my turn. Not paying attention, I continued driving taking a bite of sandwich, a handful of fries and a big gulp of shake.

"Ooh ooh, brain freeze, ow."

I ran off the road and dropped my sandwich in my lap while knocking over my shake. The car swerved into a snow bank then stopped. My whole life flashed in front of my eyes in a split second. I sat for a moment looking at the mess in my lap and on the floor. There was no saving the shake mixed with dirt and salt, but the burger was not going to waste. I finished scraping it off my coat and then backed out onto the road and drove home.

The front of my coat looked like I had a run in with a flock of chickens; it was covered in egg yolks. I wasn't going to make the same mistake and take it off in the garage. I placed my soiled coat on top of the dryer and continued on my merry way into the front room. I turned on the tree lights then reclined in my favorite chair where I fell asleep.

My family is most considerate when it comes to me sleeping in my chair. I woke up at a quarter past one. It was officially. . .

December 24th

At eight o'clock I set sail for the mall. I wanted to get there early to make sure I got what I was after and got out. The first thing on my list was a phone for Marty. He'd been begging for three years, and this year he's going to be so happy, I'll probably get a hug. The electronic store had the pay as you go phones, no contract and no high bills. You just pay a fee and when you use up your minutes, you buy some more. I got him a nice one with big numbers so that there would be no misdials. It came with everything including ten minutes of free air time.

Lewis's Mp3 player would be a snap. I went over to the gadget department and found the perfect one for him. It was brilliant blue with five-hundred mega byte capacity. The box said it could hold up to thirty songs. Sheesh, how many does a person need anyway? Now for the laptop, that would take a little more thought and comparison shopping. They had a sale on a ten inch ultra thin jobby. I liked it right away. Without further ado I took my prizes and headed for the check out. Jill would be the last on my list to shop for. Her presents always took the remainder of the day to find. However, a nice mocha latte' was in order before anymore shopping.

No more Jean Nate

Re-Gifting is a Family Tradition

Time was passing by so quickly I couldn't believe it was three o'clock already. With the variety of stores in the mall, you would think I'd come up with at least one idea for my wife. I ended up at Sears. They had a big sale on home gym equipment. Jill had been suggesting that she might want to join the Y and maybe I would like to join too. That made me think that maybe she would like a stair-stepper or stationary exercise bike. I decided on a NordicTrack Recumbent Exercise Cycle GX4.0 Now, that's an exciting gift. I couldn't wait to see the look on her face when she opened the box tonight.

After going to the gift wrap station, I took all my "Santa" gifts and loaded them into the car. I sure hoped that there would be room under the tree for Jill's gift. The box was four feet long and almost as wide. One more stop to make, then nap time before getting ready for Christmas Eve's mass at the Church. Our tradition was opening gifts after church and then a midnight dinner. That's why I always took a nap; it was to be a long night.

"John, is that you?"

"Yes dear. Can you go upstairs for a couple of minutes? I want to put the presents under the tree."

"I promise I won't peek. I'm busy getting dinner ready and I have stuff in the oven for tomorrow. Go around to the front if you think it will spoil your surprise."

"Okay, I just didn't want to drag snow in on the carpet."

"Oh sure it's okay to drag snow in on my nice clean kitchen floor."

"That's not what I was thinking. I'll be back in a flash. Something smells pretty darn good in here, and it's not just the food."

"John, don't be thinking about getting frisky. The kids are home and I'm busy. By the way, a package came for you today, special delivery. I had to sign for it and everything."

"What was that? I can't hear you from in the garage."

I took the presents and placed them under the tree. Someone had already been organizing the gifts by name. There was a pile for each of the kids along with a couple for Dad, and Mom. The box that came for me had me curious. Who would send me something special delivery? It was probably from my mom and dad. Maybe it was a souvenir from their vacation or something like that. I went upstairs and set the alarm for seven pm.

"Elise, Martin, Lewis. Let's get a move on. You know how Father McAlister hates when his parishioners are late. I don't need to get honorable mention for being in church twice this year with the distinction of being late both times."

"John, who are you yelling at? The kids are in the car. We're just waiting on you."

"Oh."

It was a festive Yule tide ride to church. We sang jingle bells Santa smells and all the kids' favorite songs. When we arrived, we quietly walked in hoping to find a seat in the back. No such luck. We had to go almost all the way to the front, and that's when…

"Welcome, I'm so glad that you could make the service tonight. Please have a seat up front. The communion wafers are always fresher when you get them off the top of the plate.

"There was a big roar of laughter from the crowded cathedral. I wanted to find a hole and crawl into it. However, Father wasn't finished with us yet.

"All things come in their own time. John, we are glad that you and your family could make it tonight. This night we celebrate the coming of the Christ Child. He was on time you know."

We sat right up front where the whole congregation could see us and Father kept an eye on us making sure we didn't leave early. It was the most embarrassing hour in church of my life, well maybe second most. Easter was pretty bad too.

"Thank you, Father. Have a Merry Christmas. You are welcome to stop by the hall tomorrow to enjoy a meal with our family if you have nowhere else to go."

"Jill, that's very nice of you to offer. I understand your mother won't be there, so maybe some other time when it will truly be a family gathering."

I got an elbow in the ribs like it was somehow my fault that her mother and father decided to bail on us for the holiday and take a cruise. Sheesh!

The Christmas magic came back when we arrived home. The lights on the house twinkled under a light coating of snow. Inside the tree lights and decorations were like being inside Santa's castle. The kids rushed to the tree to start opening gifts.

"You kids wait to open presents until I put the food in the oven and come over to watch."

Jill's request fell on deaf ears. Elise took charge of the gift retrieval and dispersion to their proper recipient.

"To Martin from Lewis, to Elise from Lewis, to Lewis from Lewis, hey, you can't give yourself a gift."

The process of calling names and passing out gifts went until they were all out from under the tree. Next came the ripping off of the wrapping paper. Bows and ribbons were sailing in the air. Some landed in the tree and some landed on me. You would think these kids had never gotten a gift before.

"Okay, gang, now it's time for you to open your presents from Santa."

They knew the gifts from Santa were from me, but they played along. By this time Jill joined us for the unveiling of the "Special" gifts.

Martin opened his box with the cell phone. He was just about ready to thank me when he pulled the phone out and saw it had over sized numbers. I had apparently picked up the geriatric version that was for people with poor vision. Lewis opened his Mp3 player. He looked it over and then placed it under the tree. I could see his disappointment, but I wasn't sure why. After all, thirty songs with a one hour play time was a big deal, well at least I thought so. I turned to see how Elise was doing with her compact lap top.

"Daddy, the opening screen is in Chinese. How do I convert it into English? Why is the screen so small?"

She too placed her gift back under the tree. I heard her mumble something about spending too much on the vacation and not enough on her and her brothers' gifts. I felt ignoring the comment was in my best interest.

"John, open your envelope from the company."

"Okay."

"*Dear John,*

We have appreciated your long tenure with the company and your loyalties. You have dedicated yourself to many of our charitable causes and you're to be commended."

I stopped for a minute and looked for my bonus check. There wasn't one.

"John, you look upset. Is your bonus not as much as you hoped for?"

"I think the bastards are firing me."

Lewis held out his hand. I reached into my pocket looking for some change for the swear jar.

"Why do you think that dear?"

"Let me finish and I'll tell you."

"Over the last five years your department has grown to a level no longer sustainable by the company. We would like to visit with you in person and discuss your options for the future with Able Wright & Schmick."

"I can't believe they're downsizing my department. They want to discuss my options for staying with the company."

"Oh, John, I'm so sorry. Couldn't they have waited until after the Holiday for such an announcement? And no bonus either? You're right, they are a bunch of Bastards."

This time Marty's hand went up for the quarter.

"I'll have to owe it to you. Put it on my account."

"Oh, good there's even a second page. I can hardly wait. Maybe they'll just kick me in the ass while they're at it."

Three hands went up in unison.

"Here's five bucks. That should take care of me for the evening."

"John,

Please be home on December 24th to receive a special box that will be coming to you requiring a signature of acceptance.

The Management Staff"

"How flipping impersonal can you get? It takes a lot of nerve to put a letter like that together. I guess I don't have to wonder why they didn't hand it to me like in years past."

The whole family sat staring at me with their mouths open. They were as stunned as I was. I wanted to scream. I even thought about calling my boss and giving him a piece of my mind. I picked up the phone and started to dial, then thought better of it.

"John, see what's in the box that is so special it had to be signed for."

"Maybe they wanted to be sure that I got my pink slip so that I don't show up for work on the Second."

"The box is too big for a pink slip."

"Gee, ya think?"

I ripped the box open. I was so angry I could spit nails. Inside the box there was a gold colored letter. It said:

Salutations, Mr. Fellows,

You are cordially invited to the Executives Dinner Reception where you will receive a key for your new office on the 15th floor. Below are some essentials that you will want to bring with you.

"Holly Crap!"

I threw the whole contents of the box in the air and yelled at the top of my lungs,

"Holly Crap, I'm getting promoted!"

Christmas Eve comes to an end

Christmas Morning Begins Early

"Jill, we haven't forgotten you. Now that all the drama's over, it's your turn to open presents. Open the ones from the kids first. I want you to open the one from Santa last."

"Here, mother dear, I hope you don't already have one."

Elise handed her mother a box. It was store wrapped and about the size of a blouse. There was a lot of winking going on between the two of them. I suspected that they picked something out together the other day when they went shopping.

"Oh, Princess, it's adorable. Thanks so much, I don't know how you knew I would need a bathing suit for our trip?"

There was more winking.

"Now open this one. Marty and I got it together so we wouldn't get you two cheap things."

"Lewis, how thoughtful, I wonder what it could be."

"Don't guess, Mom. Just rip into it."

"Oh, but I might want to save the lovely paper."

Jill's expression was priceless. I could tell she had no idea what the boys had gotten for her. It was a square black box with no writing on it. She almost looked afraid to open it in fear it might have one of those springy snakes jump out at her. The top was all paper. After pulling out all the stuffing, in the bottom of the box was a nice French bath set containing, soaps, lotions and a body fragrance splash.

"Boys, this is wonderful, I haven't had Jean Nate since your father used to buy it for me when we were dating. Come here. Let Mommy give you both a big hug."

"Gee, Mom, if we knew it was going to make you cry, we would have gotten the Nintendo Family game instead."

"Okay and now for the grand prize. . ."

I struggled to pull the box from under the tree. It was heavy and almost toppled everything over.

"Ta Da!"

Jill glanced at the children's faces, each with a look of anticipation. Everyone was curious as to what could be in the big heavy box. She had to get off the sofa and kneel next to it to unwrap her gift.

"What is it, Mom?"

"Yeah, come on, what is it already?"

"Why, it's a- - it's time for dinner, that's what it is."

As Jill walked into the kitchen to get the dinner out of the oven, she whispered to me.

"We'll talk about this later."

I knew what that meant. Dinner was solemn. Not much was being said about anything. Then a low sheepish voice broke the silence.

"Dad, did you save the receipt for my Mp3 player? I might want a different color or something not so flashy. You know how kids are. They might want to steal a cool unit like this, so maybe black or silver wouldn't attract their attention."

"Why of course, Lewis, it's in the drawer by the micro wave."

"What about the receipt for my phone. It's a nice one, but I think I might want one of those texting phones and one that will fit in my pocket and not just my book bag."

"Well, Marty, if that's what you would prefer, sure. The receipt for it is with the others."

"Elise, if you want to take your gift and exchange . . ."

"Daddy, it's perfect. It fits in my purse and I just love it."

My little Princess came over and for the first time in weeks, she gave me a hug and a kiss on the cheek.

"Good night, Dad. Good night, Mother dear."

"Good night sweetheart."

With the children up in their rooms playing with toys and trying on the clothes that they weren't going to return, I was left alone in the kitchen with my wife. I was waiting for the conversation about the home gym.

"John,

She started out with a very soft, but firm tone in her voice.

"May I explain my reasoning behind the gift?"

"If you think that will help, have at it."

"Well, Jill, you've been talking about joining the Y. I thought it would be easier and save time if you didn't have to travel all around town after a hard day at work."

"I know you meant well. However, let me just say that going to the Y is a social event not to be confused with a desire to tone, or lose weight. Not saying that I need either, even though your gift would suggest otherwise."

"No, no it doesn't suggest otherwise. It doesn't suggest, well, otherwise at all."

"Then would you like to tell me why I would want or need a home gym?"

"It's actually just an exercise cycle."

A glare with flames came shooting across the table.

"Um, the receipt is in the envelope with the rest of the Christmas receipts. We can take it back tomorrow as soon as the stores open and before we have to leave for vacation."

"Shit, the damn trip. I haven't started packing yet. Clean up down here before you come to bed, I have to get the suitcases down from the attic.

Jill gave me the evil eye again as I started to hold out my hand for her contribution to the swear jar.

"John, if you hold your hand out for a quarter, you'll be wearing that damn jar on your head."

The Feast is ready for Consumption

Celebrating the Holiday with Family & Friends

279

December 25th Eight AM

I made my way downstairs to the kitchen using the bump and feel method. My eyes were glued shut with sleepy dust. Instinctively I found my way to the coffee pot. With my empty hand, I felt around for the back of a chair then sat down at the table.

"John, you look like something the cat dragged in. Only the cat didn't drop it off at my kitchen table."

"Thanks."

"No, seriously, when you finish your coffee, pick up whatever that dead thing is in the corner."

That opened my eyes. I looked over to see what the cat dragged in. It looked like a dead rat with feathers.

"John, you look tired and distressed. What time did you finally get to bed?"

"It was a little after three."

"Why so late?"

"I was reading my promotion letter again and looking through the brochure with the information about our stay and travel arrangements."

"You must be excited. I'm so proud of my Pookey Bear."

Jill gave me a big hug and a kiss on the cheek. She hadn't called me her pookey bear since way back when we were still dating. I didn't have the heart then or now to tell her how much I hated that nickname.

"I'm sorry about last night. You can set the exercise equipment up in the basement. I've noticed your muffin top in need of a little trim. Feel free to use the bike whenever you want."

"Gee, uh, thanks dear."

Wow! A hug and an apology all in the same year, I was feeling like Mr. Lucky. I looked at my belly. Maybe I could stand to lose a pound or two.

"Would you like another cup of coffee?"

"Sure if you're pouring."

I didn't know how or when I was going to tell Jill about the travel plans for the executive meeting in Colorado. It was scheduled for the same time as our Paradise Island resort trip. I thought maybe I should just blurt it out now, or ease it into a conversation later. I even thought about letting it be a surprise at the airport. Since she had a hot pot of coffee I decided to let it wait until later.

Eleven AM

"Time to go, Elise, Martin, Lewis. Your father is waiting in the car. You know he's never first, so let's get a move on."

Jill was standing at the bottom of the stairs still yelling when I came walking down from our bedroom.

"What's with all the yelling?"

"I'm trying to round up the kids. I thought you were in the car already?"

"I was- - I forgot my wallet."

"Where are the kids?"

"I thought they were in the car with you."

"John, how can they be in the car with me, if I'm in here with you?"

"I don't know. Do you have your keys?"

"No. I'm not driving, so why would I need my keys?"

"Because I can't find mine and I don't want us to be late."

"John, I swear - - I'll get my keys, you make sure the kids are in the car and stay put."

We were off to set up the tables and chairs at the hall. The food would be arriving at one thirty with the guests following shortly after. At the entrance of the hall there was a marquee welcoming our families along with the Dorner-Schmeggie Family. I grabbed the sign and threw it into a closet. I hadn't told Jill about inviting the family whose holiday and marriage I almost ruined with my radio give-away scheme.

The food looked fantastic. The relatives were arriving right on time. I didn't think to ask Dorner how many he would be inviting, but there was plenty to feed a city block, so I wasn't worried. My luck was holding. Most of the hall was filled before the Dorner-Schmeggie's started to arrive. They would fill in the empty tables toward the back, and no one would be the wiser.

"John, I didn't think we could pull this off on such short notice. I can't believe how many people turned out this year. It seems like twice as many as last year, don't you think?"

I gulped and took a deep breath before answering.

"Do you think so? It seems about the same to me. Why don't you bang the gong to get every ones' attention, and we can get dinner started."

"I'll let you have the honors. After all, that stupid gong is your family's tradition. It might as well be a hog call to the trough."

"Thank you, my dear."

I rang the gong three times and then made a short announcement.

"We're glad you all could make it out today. Let us all enjoy being with friends and family and LET THE FEAST BEGIN."

"Nice touch, John, but really. Next year I'll do it."

"What, I thought it was fine."

"Let the feast begin? What kind of blessing is that?"

"Okay, I forgot my lines. It's just usually either my mom or your mom takes charge. I'm not used to wearing the pants at one of these functions."

"Yeah, I'll say, let's eat. Did you save us seats at the head table?"

"Jill, you told me to put names on the tables, and I put . . ."

I put my hand in my pocket and felt a card. It was our placard for the head table.

"Oops."

"Never mind, we'll just sit with your relatives at the back table. It'll be quieter and we might even get something to eat without a potato flying in all directions from one of our mothers."

"Sure, that sounds fine. What relatives of mine were you talking about?"

The Party is Boring

We Miss our Mothers Fighting at Dinner

Jill pointed to two empty seats at the Dorner-Schmeggie table. Mr. Dorner spotted me and was waving for us to join them.

"That must be one of your cousins. My family doesn't do plaid shirts and corduroy pants for the Holidays."

I frantically looked for another table. Marty and Lew were sitting at the head table with their Aunts and Uncles.

"Jill, why don't you start at the buffet table, I'll be along in a minute."

"Hey, guys, how's everything going? Are you two getting enough to eat?

I was making idle chit chat then leaned in to make the boys an offer they couldn't refuse.

"Look, there's twenty bucks a piece if you boys go sit at the table in the back, so that your mother and I can sit with her Aunts and Uncles."

Martin was quick to respond after assessing the situation and thinking over the offer. Mr. Dorner was still waving.

"Make it a hundred and we'll do it."

"One hundred a piece, are you nuts? You can't hold up your old man like that. Why, that's highway robbery."

I stepped back from the table for a minute to weigh my options when I spotted Jill heading to the empty seats. I made another offer.

"One hundred even. You can split it anyway you want. Make up your minds before your mother sits or the deals' off. Tell her you were saving us two seats over here."

Lewis chimed in.

"We'll need to see the color of your cash."

"Trust me, I'm good for it. Now hurry. Go - - Go - - GO!

The boys did as instructed. Jill came over to where I was standing. I pulled out a chair for her to sit next to Aunt Betsy and Uncle Walter. Before she could say anything about the table swap, I excused myself.

"I'll be right back, I'm starved."

I went to the buffet by way of the back table to say hello to the Dorner-Schmeggie family and to drop off the hush money to my boys. Larry Dorner was excited to have me grace his family's table with my presence. He still was under the impression that I was a radio celebrity.

"Ted, I can't believe the turn-out. This is fabulous. The food, well the food is top shelf. It's better here than dining at the Holiday Inn."

"Thanks, Larry. It does look like we have a better turn-out than anticipated. How many of these folks are with you?"

"I think just twenty or so of our kin showed. The rest don't know what they're missing. By the way, Ted, this is my wife Hannah, her sister Amy, my mother Wilfred, and at the other table are some of our cousins and . . ."

"It's been nice to meet you all. If you'll excuse me I have to mingle and join my wife for dinner."

"Oh sure, you go right ahead. And thanks a million for everything."

As I walked away, I mumbled.

"That's about how much it cost too."

When I finally got to sit, Jill was in the middle of an anxiety attack.

"John, no one is having fun. It's too quiet in here. You can hear people chewing their food."

"I know. It's not the same without our parents fighting. Wait, look, your Aunt Myra is about to fall asleep. If we're lucky she'll do a face dive into her salad and lose her blue wig."

"That's not a wig."

"Really, are you sure? Five bucks says it's a wig and it falls off."

"You're on."

Aunt Myra was teetering in her chair. Jill and I were on the edge of our seats hoping no one would disturb the moment.

SPLAT!

A perfect nose dive. Not only did it startle Myra, but it shocked the rest of the relatives at the table. When she picked her head up, there was lettuce in her hair, dressing dripping from her nose and she spit a cherry tomato half way across the table. The whole place erupted with laughter. Jill was thrilled.

"Okay, that's got the party started. You owe me five bucks.

Aunt Myra's not wearing a wig."

Jill was beaming from ear to ear. I looked in my wallet for a five; all I had were tens and twenties.

"Double or nothing I'll bet you I can lob a meatball into the gravy boat from here."

"Go for it."

I took my spoon and strategically positioned it with the handle hanging over the edge of my plate. Placing a meatball carefully on the spoon, I attempted to judge the distance to the center of the gravy boat where it would make a big splash.

"Okay, there are three tables end to end. Each table is seven feet long. The target is one third of the table length from the end. . ."

I hit the end of the spoon with just enough force to catapult the meatball. It went soaring into the air high above everyone's head. Jill and I were watching its flight. The meatball descended in what seemed like slow motion. It missed the center of the bowl by about three inches. Instead of a tidy splash it hit the ladle. A big spluggugin of gravy spewed forth from the bowl. A tidal wave of gravy hit three unsuspecting cousins and Uncle Floyd.

Uncle Floyd retaliated. He took the fat from his ham and flung it like a rubber band in our direction. It settled on Aunt Lucy's forehead. Lucy dipped her fork into her mashed potatoes and sent a plop flying. One of the cousins yelled;

"FOOD FIGHT"

And it was on. We were having the time of our lives. We tried not to laugh with our mouth open in fear we might catch a miscellaneous piece of mystery meat. The Dorner-Schmeggie family was horrified. The entire clan went running towards the hall exit to escape the insanity. Larry almost made it out when he slipped on a Jell-o square.

Mrs. Dorner tried to keep him from falling. She slipped too. The two of them fell into her mother. A moment later the whole family went down like human dominos.

There wasn't a dry eye in the place. I laughed so hard I think I may have peed myself.

When most of the food from the tables had landed on the floor, it was time for our guests to head for the door and go home.

December 25th

Seven-thirty PM

Clean up was always left to Jill and me. Our loving children pitched in while moaning and complaining the whole time. We sure had a good time this year. Our parents would have been proud that we carried on their tradition of the after dinner food fight. I videotaped the mess and forwarded it to my mother's email. It's not often that a son can make his mother proud, and I didn't want to miss the chance to do so.

At a quarter of nine we were finished hauling out the garbage. Jill was putting the mop and pail away while the kids got their coats and headed for the car. I was still glowing from the outcome when Jill asked the inevitable question.

"John, when are you going to tell me that your trip to Denver is the same time as our trip to the Islands?"

"You know about that?"

"John, how long have you been married to me? I looked over the brochure they sent while you were in the shower this morning. I thought by now you would have said something. The flight leaves in 10 hours."

"Well, I, a well."

"I didn't see any tickets for the rest of the family. Are you planning on attending by yourself while we go to the tropics?"

"Um, well."

"Don't stutter, John. Just think long and hard before you answer the question."

"Okay, Jill. I gave the tickets away since they were non-cancelable. I planned on booking the rest of the family to Denver in the morning."

"You WHAT? Are you nuts? You gave our tickets to the vacation of a life time in paradise, our tickets to seven sun-filled days in the tropics. You gave away my day at the spa so that we can all freeze to death and see you get some stupid promotion with a key to the executive latrine."

"Well, I, I."

"Just shut up. Let's go home. If Lewis's middle finger freezes permanently in an upright position, I hope he reminds you every day for the rest of his life. You've ruined his childhood. He and his sister and brother are bound to be scarred for life. I hope you're happy with yourself."

I was feeling pretty darn swell a few minutes ago. Now I just felt remorse and depressed. I didn't know what to do. I couldn't ask Larry Dorner for the tickets back. His family was so appreciative it would be devastating to them if I did such a thing. On the other hand, I might not have to sleep with the dog for the next unforeseeable future. Damn dog always has gas or fleas or both. I needed a plan.

With the ride home in silence, I was able to think without interruption. The kids were asleep in the back seat. Jill was nodding off too. A moment of inspiration struck like lightning. I came up with a great idea. I would call the travel agency in the morning. Denver wasn't far from Mexico. I could book a flight right after the ceremony and we could spend the rest of the week in sunny Mazatlan or Cancun. That would then give us two vacations in one. The sun and sand will thaw Lewis's finger and all will be well with the world. Or at least that's what I thought.

The Best Made Plans Part Two

Next Time Just Shoot Me

There was no way I was going to fall asleep while worrying about the travel arrangements for the rest of the family. I was pretty certain the agency would be open on the day after Christmas. I waited until a little after midnight to call.

"Thank you for calling the Green World Traveler. My name is Amanda. Where would you like to spend your Dream Vacation?"

"Hi, Amanda. This is John Fellows. I'd like to be spending my "Dream Vacation" at the Paradise Resort and Spa, but it doesn't look like that's going to happen this year."

"Oh, I'm sorry. Where will you be going instead?"

"I need to book four one way tickets to Vale."

"Colorado?"

"Um, yes, of course."

"Mr. Fellows, when will your party be leaving, and from where?"

"They'll leave Monday December twenty-seventh, from Cincinnati International airport."

"I'm checking four tickets from Cincinnati Ohio to Vale Colorado. Sorry, there are no flights from Cincinnati."

"Try Northern Kentucky."

"Yes, we have a 9am or a 3pm from Cincinnati/Northern Kentucky International airport. Will you need transportation to the airport?"

"No, I think we can get there. We live in Cincinnati."

"Would that be Ohio or Kentucky?"

"Ohio."

"I see, and where will you be heading to when you leave Vale?"

"On Thursday the thirtieth of December, I'll need a flight for five to Mazatlan in Mexico."

"I know where Mazatlan is."

"Good. I'll need reservations at the Aztec Resort through Sunday. Make it a two room suite. Then return to Cincinnati/ Northern Kentucky Airport."

"Mr. Fellows, may I ask if you are planning two winter vacations?"

"No, I have to go to Vale on business. The stay in Mexico is to be our tropical get-away."

"The temperatures in Mazatlan this coming week are going to be in the 50's during the day with dips in the 30's at night. It's the coldest it's been down there in over forty years."

"Ouch"

"May I suggest an all inclusive Western Caribbean cruise on board the Sojourn of the Seas with a stop in Dominica? The temps will be in the 80's and 90's all week."

"I'll take it with adjoining cabins. Outer rooms with a balcony mid-deck if possible."

"You've got it, Sir. Since it's last minute, I'll email you with a confirmation. Just print off your itinerary and you'll be all set. Have a nice trip."

"Wait, how much is all this going to cost?"

"Sir, do you want to have a special time with a trip to remember?"

"Yes"

"Then I suggest you check your American Express bill when you get home. It would just ruin things if I tell you now. Have a good flight, be safe and thanks for booking with the Green World Traveler today."

The Pleasures and Perils of Traveling

The TSA has Rights Too

I was exhausted from the party and the planning. In three hours I would be heading to the airport for my business trip. After typing a detailed travel itinerary for Jill and the kids, it was time to take a nap.

The flight was four and a half hours, so I would get plenty of rest before getting to Vale. This afternoon shortly after arriving, the company had plans for the junior executives to play a challenge round of snow golf. It would be groups of four playing against the seniors. I'd never played anything more than putt-putt golf and never in the snow. This was going to be a real test of my abilities. We would be traipsing around in the snow with a club trying to hit a brightly colored ball into a hole that is three to four hundred feet away. Not exactly my idea of a fun day. The only good thing was the temperatures were to be in the 30's, so we'd only be freezing not frost bitten.

The travel agency scheduled a limo to pick up the family on Monday at seven in the morning. Their flight was at eleven, and they would arrive by five at the hotel. I planned dinner for five at the Red Flag Steak House. It had a favorable review and was within walking distance of our hotel. The alarm went off, and I dragged myself into the shower. I was trying to be extra quiet, so that I wouldn't wake anyone up at this ungodly hour of the morning. On my way downstairs I smelled fresh coffee. That meant Jill was up.

"Good Morning, John. I saw the itinerary you put on my dresser. That was very thoughtful of you. I see we leave tomorrow, so you have a whole day to enjoy yourself and get a little rest and relaxation before the family hits town."

"Good Morning to you, too dear, I don't think there will be much time for relaxation. The company has a full day planned for us newbie's. I'll miss you and will be counting down the hours until you arrive."

"John, you're so full of crap. Maybe that's why I love you. Even in the worst of times, after a big fight, you still have a positive attitude and can make me smile."

We hugged, we kissed and I was off to the airport. With all the snowing and blowing, the wind was pushing my car all over the road. The bridge over the Ohio River had a coating of snow with a sheet of ice underneath.

At four in the morning there wasn't enough traffic to warm the roads. The salt trucks were ineffective with the cold temperatures that plagued our Cincinnati area for the past week. Sliding all the way across into Kentucky was the scariest ride of my life. Every inch of the way, I thought I'd go over the side and into the icy water below.

I could see the signs for the airport, with less than a mile I was going to make it. Upon entering the airport the first thing I heard was the announcement of flight cancellations. One after another the announcements were filling the terminal sound system. People were walking in circles swearing about missing a plane, or that they couldn't get home. I was trying to see the board or listen for my flight number. The sign flashed that the flight to Vale would be delayed for two hours. Compared to some that were canceled completely, two hours was nothing to complain about.

Starbucks, here I come. After spotting the coffee sign, I thought it would be something to tied me over along with one of their famous blueberry muffins.

"How can you be out of Machiatto's? It's your signature drink."

"I'm sorry, Sir. Our supply truck got stuck on the road in a fifty car pileup. We are almost out of coffee period. If you want something, you had better order fast, or it'll be gone."

"Fine, I'll have a Tall coffee double cream, with vanilla and caramel syrup. Oh, and a blueberry muffin heated."

"Will that complete your order?"

"Yes."

"That'll be twelve-fifty. Correct change if possible."

"Why so much?"

"Because we can. Do you have change or not?"

"Yes, I have change, but you can bet I won't be back."

"Sir, you're at the airport. We don't expect you to come back. Next, can I help the next in line please?"

Not only did I get ripped off, but the muffin was old and the coffee was cold. I ended up throwing both out and got bottled water from a machine that didn't have an attitude and gave change.

Two hours passed. The sign above my gate changed again. This time it said my departure would be at two-thirty. That was four hours from now. I went up to the already frazzled attendant to ask if there were any other flights to Vale or even Denver. She had the most fascinating expression of wonderment I had ever seen on an adult before.

"Sir, before we engage in an oral duel to the death, let me just say; there are no flights to anywhere in or out of this airport for at least four maybe six hours. So, unless you want your ass handed to you, I'd suggest you sit it somewhere and wait like a good little man along with the rest of the rude ignoramuses'."

I put my head down and walked slowly away from the desk. I felt like a puppy that had just been hit with a newspaper. Sitting down on a bench as far away from the agent as possible, I found a wrinkled magazine to hide my face behind.

It was midnight. I was tired and hungry. People were starting to hold vigilante meetings. I think they wanted to tar and feather the agents. It wasn't exactly their fault. I mean, they were only trying to do their jobs in the best way possible in an impossible situation. However, they all had attitudes that made the ladies at the DMV seem like the tooth fairy.

"Attention. May I have your attention please? All passengers please check the current status of your flight. The boards will be updated momentarily. We will begin to release planes in limited numbers. The flights that are scheduled to leave in the next forty-five minutes will be leaving at their regularly scheduled times. Any prior flights will begin departure shortly depending on their final destination, starting with flights to western destinations such as California, Colorado and Nebraska."

Finally some good news, my flight was back on the board, and we would be leaving in an hour. I checked my watch for the time. It was six o'clock Monday morning. My flight was twenty-three hours late. As I was boarding the plane, I could swear I heard a familiar voice.

"John, hey John, I think we're going to be on the same flight. John, over here, wait, John."

I must have been hallucinating from being over tired. It sounded like my wife. I was stuck in the middle of an anxious crowd and couldn't see who might have been calling me.

The Rage Within

Ready to Explode Any Minute

I couldn't believe after all the time I had been in the airport sitting through the worst winter storm in more than ten years, that I was finally boarding my plane to Colorado.

"I'll need to see your boarding pass, Sir. Oh, I'm sorry. You have a ticket for Sunday's seven o'clock. We're currently boarding Monday's flight. We'll be announcing the previously scheduled flight sometime this afternoon. I'll have to ask you to step aside and find a seat."

I didn't know whether to cry or find a rope and strangle someone. Maybe right after I hang myself. It was everything I could do to remain calm. I spotted the person behind the voice calling me. It was my dearest wife Jillian and my loving family.

"John, I didn't expect for you to wait for us. It would have been okay if you went earlier and had your fun in the snow without us. Were you able to get us seats together?"

I didn't have the heart to tell her what had happened and that they would be traveling without me.

"Jill, honey, what's that?"

"It's a Skinny Caramel Macchiato from Starbucks. I'm surprised you didn't see it on your way in. Everything was so fresh, especially the blueberry muffins. I had mine warmed up, and the berries just burst with flavor in my mouth."

"I think I'm going to be sick."

"What's wrong?"

"Nothing"

"Well, you should have stopped in. I made a point of writing the young girl's name down that served me. Her name was Bridgette, and she was the sweetest thing. She gave me extra whipped cream without me even asking. You know how I love my whipped cream."

"Yes, dear, I know."

"John, you look like you're about to cry. What's wrong?"

"My flight was delayed because of the snow storm. I'm not scheduled to go until later today. The airline is keeping today's schedule and then filling in the missed or delayed flights this afternoon."

"Well, that's just ridiculous. You come with me, mister."

Over the last twenty years, there is one thing I learned, and that was to follow my wife whenever she called me mister.

We walked together to the counter as they were making the last call for all boarders.

"Miss, there has been a mistake, and I'm sure you can take care of it for us. We have five travelers going to Vale, Colorado. My children have already boarded the plane. As you can see, they booked my husband for Sunday instead of Monday. Now that's not possible since we are all here together today. I would suggest that whoever fat fingered their key board filling out his reservation make the appropriate corrections."

"I'll take care of it for you, Mrs. Fellows. You can board now. We will be taking off in just a few minutes."

I was impressed to say the least. When Jill has a mind to get

293

things done, don't stand in her way. As we were approaching her seat, I heard her talking to the man that was in what would turn out to be my seat.

"Excuse me, sir, but I would like to sit with my husband during the flight. I noticed you're flying alone, so you might want to take the seat next to the cute little blonde in row thirteen. You'll have the aisle so you can stretch those long legs of yours."

"Jill, I didn't see any cute blonde on the way to our seats."

"How could you miss him? He was about five, jumping up and down. There was no way I would be able to deal with that for four and a half hours."

The guy was glaring back at Jill. The old expression "if looks could kill" was definitely applicable to this situation. Somehow Jill was able to ignore it. I, on the other hand, hid behind the backrest of the seat in front of me, out of view.

At this point after a restless night, I was hoping to get some sleep before we reached our destination. Hoping was the key word, but wishing and praying were more like it, and none of those things were going to happen.

"John, you are not going to believe your daughter at the security station."

Any statement starting with "your daughter" meant that Elise did something to embarrass her mother. I was about to find out what rather quickly. Hoping I could stay awake through the whole story, I leaned in and said,

"So what happened that's got you all fired up? I haven't seen you this angry since I started the kitchen ablaze while trying to deep fry a chicken."

Jill started her rather lengthy story.

"We checked in at the counter and all was well until we got to the security station. The boys and I were taking off our shoes when I noticed Elise was not with us. Of course I was panicked thinking something may have happened. You know there is a lot of abduction of children for the slave trade? Well anyway, I spotted her staring at the Transportation Security Agents. I called out to her. Elsie, get over here, I don't want us to get separated."

"I can't decide whether to go through the groping line or be humiliated by having my naked body broadcast to the world by way of that scanner machine."

"First of all, it's a pat down, and second, no one is going to see you naked. It's a skeletal projection. Now let's go."

"A woman of your age may be used to sexual assault, but I'm still a virgin, in case you needed to know."

I walked over to your daughter. The conversation was getting loud, and people were starting to stop what they were doing to listen.

"A woman of my age, what's that supposed to mean? Choose your words carefully, young lady. You may be your father's little Princess, but right now you're a thorn in my side."

"Mother, dear, you're getting over dramatic. I merely meant that woman of a certain age can feel comfortable with a stranger touching them, but I just can't let anyone but the man I marry touch me in my – well, you know- - private zone."

"Go over through the scanner, and don't say another word."

Jill started mumbling.

"A woman my age, I'll give her . . .

Just then a security guard approached the two of them.

"Is there anything wrong?"

"No, officer, my daughter doesn't want to go through the pat down. She feels it's a violation of her female sexuality."

"I understand. I have a teenage daughter that has determined that she too will not go through the pat down process. How about if we take a walk over to the scanner and go through the x-ray instead?"

"The officer made one big mistake. He attempted to grab your daughter by the arm and escort her through the line and into the "Machine." The next thing I knew she kneed him in the groin and went screaming into the bathroom. I had to shield my face with a magazine to hide my embarrassment. A shuttle came and carted the officer to the med station. I threatened Elsie with bodily harm if she didn't cooperate. A nice woman came to my rescue with one of those electro-magnetic wands and scanned both of us and then brought us personally to the gate. And that's when I saw you. The rest, as they say, is history. John- - John are you awake?

Did you even hear a word I said? Don't make me start over."

"Attention: May I have your attention please? There is a lot of cloud cover as we head west. We are being diverted south over the gulf and then up through California. The skies are clear coming into Denver from the west. The circle around will add a landing delay of approximately two hours. There will be complimentary drinks, beverages and snacks. Please fasten your seat belts and remain seated until the safety light turns on."

"I heard that."

Are We Almost There Yet?

The Four Hour Flight That Took Two Days

We were already two hours into a four and a half hour flight when they announced we would be circling over LAX to get to Colorado from Cincinnati, Ohio. Another two hour delay, this time in the air. All I wanted was a little nap. It didn't have to be a full resting sleep with snoring and drool, just a little nap.

"John, did you see our children when we got on the plane?"

"No. I just assumed you did when you told the ticket agent that they were already on the plane."

"You're such an idiot. I told her that so that I could get you on the plane. I left the kids on the bench and told them not to move until I got back. I told the boys not to even think about leaving their sister alone to use the bathroom. If they had to go, they were to use a cup."

"Jill, you don't think that we left them behind, do you?"

"I don't know what to think. Right now I'm trying not to have a panic attack."

Jill started looking through her purse for an antacid. I was trying to look around the plane for any sign of our children. The headrests were too high. With the stewardess coming my way with the beverage cart, I couldn't get out in the aisle to check behind us.

"Hey, Marty, have you seen Mom?"

"No."

" Elli. . .

"What do you want, ya little puke? Can't you see I'm busy? This phone battery better not go dead. It's the only contact I have with my friends that haven't been abducted by their parents to go on some lame ass vacation."

"Ahem, that'll be a quarter for the swear jar."

Elise reached into her purse for a quarter.

"Here, take this and put it where the sun don't shine."

"Okay. Now that I have your attention, have you seen Mom?"

"Yeah, she's five rows up on the left with Dad."

"Dad, when did he get here?"

"You amaze me. How do you make it through life without noticing what's happening around you. See the woman with the seventies style hairdo, that's Mom. The guy next to her trying to be a cowboy with the leather hat, that's Dad."

"Gee, I think you're right. I thought we lost her at the airport. That still doesn't explain Dad though."

"Look, if you want the long version, go ask. If you want my version, he was beamed in by Scotty."

"Really?"

"Lewis, you're an idiot. Now leave me alone."

Martin and Lewis leaned into the aisle to check out what their sister told them. She was right, but they didn't believe the beaming in part about their father.

"John, I'm worried. Do you think my cell phone will work up here? I want to call the children and see if they're alright."

"The phone should work fine. Look, three teenagers in an airport together. I'm sure they can figure out how to call a cab and get back home. Just have your sister Edna meet them, and tomorrow they can try again. This way we will have one night to spend together."

"John, if we left the kids in the airport, I'm not going to be feeling frisky. You can get that thought out of your head right now."

Just then Marty tapped his mother on the shoulder. Jill just about jumped out of her skin.

"Hey, Mom, how much longer till we get there? I'm bored."

"Martin, you made it. Are your sister and brother with you?" Jill looked back to see Lewis and Elise waving at her.

"Yeah, Mom what'd ya think? We wanted to stay in the airport and wait for you guys to come home? No way!"

"I'm just glad for once the three of you didn't listen to me and stay put."

"Hey, they wanted to stay, but I told them I wanted to learn how to ski, and then Lewis said he wanted to learn how to snow board and Elise said there would probably be cute guys by the fireplace, and well, here we are."

"Good. Now go tell your brother and sister that they're grounded for not following orders. If you pull it off without laughing, I'll let you pick out tonight's restaurant."

Emergency Landing

How Far can a Plane Fly on Low Fuel

Our flight was approaching its seventh hour in the air. When Jill stopped talking, I was able to fall asleep. I woke to the pilot's voice making the following announcement:

"Ladies and Gentlemen, we are currently flying at an altitude of ten thousand feet. Below us is a lot of cloud cover with two feet of snow on the runway in Vail. After circling for more than two hours hoping for a weather change, we are experiencing low fuel. We will be making an emergency landing at the closest airport where there is no snow or ice to contend with.

This is not a panic situation; however, we need everyone to remain seated and fasten your seatbelts. It may get a little bumpy on our descent through the clouds. Again, stay seated and don't panic."

Before I could say a word or a prayer, Jill was rushing down the aisle to check on the kids. She was giving them instructions, telling them not to be afraid and everything would be alright, when she was apprehended by one of the stewards.

"Ma'am, you have to return to your seat."

"I just want to talk to my children for a moment before we fly into uncertainty."

"Ma'am, everything will be just fine. Your children will be just fine. I need you to take your seat."

Just then the plane dipped and then rolled slightly. Jill was now in the steward's arms as he tried to keep her from falling. This caused a bigger stir with the kids than the plane possibly crashing.

"Get your hands off of me you, well, you pervert. I'm old enough to be your Moth- - Aunt."

"Excuse me Ma'am, but I didn't want you to fall and hurt yourself. Now go sit down before we have another little mishap."

Jill was still defiant, but headed towards her seat. Another gust of wind hit the plane. This time the nose went up causing Jill to fall one more time into the steward's arms. The only place he could get a grip was around her bust. Needless to say, this was not going to end well.

"You did that on purpose."

"Ma'am, I merely kept you on your feet. I had no intentions of . ."

"What, of copping a feel? Let go of me before I have to hurt you."

That went better than expected. Jill was finally sitting. Not happy, but sitting. When the steward came by to ask her to fasten her seat belt, he almost took one for the team in the gut with Jill's coffee cup.

"I'll have a refill please."

I was ready to say something when the Captain came over the intercom system again.

"We have clearance to land at Dallas/Fort Worth. We should be on the ground in twenty minutes. You can all relax. We have plenty of fuel to make Dallas. Please remain in your seats when we land. It will be just a few minutes to refuel and we'll be back in the air. It appears that there has been a break in the clouds, they will have the runway cleared in Denver within the hour. Anyone that would like to get to Vail tonight, there will be a Blue Ribbon courtesy bus to take you there."

Dallas: Monday December 27th Seven pm

The refuelling went according to plan. We were back in the air in less than forty-five minutes. Almost everyone on the plane was asleep. I was staring out the window when I was blinded by a strange orange ball in the sky. For the first time in four days I could see the sun. It was a beautiful sight watching it set behind the mountains. With a fog rising off the tops, it looked like it was melting. I nudged my wife, so we could share the moment together.

"Jill, look the sun."

"Which one?"

I was confused by the question, but she was half asleep with her eyes still closed.

"Not one of our sons. The Sun."

"Jesus is here? Are we dead?"

"NO, open your eyes. It's the sun."

Jill opened her eyes, saw the sun, closed her eyes to go back to sleep, then said,

"John, you're an idiot. Wake me up when we get there."

I continued warming my heart with thoughts of fun in the sun later this week. While I was dreaming of our four day cruise, the Captain came over the intercom with another announcement.

"Ladies and Gentlemen, I have good news. The latest storm has moved through, we will be able to land in Vail after all. Our E.T.A. is forty-five minutes. You can use your cell phones and other electronic devices until we start our descent. Thank you for flying the Friendly Skies this evening."

"Yippee!"

I was jumping for joy in my seat. Everyone in the cabin started waking. There was a stir of activity. People were on their cell phones making travel arrangements to get to their hotels. Taxis were going to be at a premium. I was glad I had reserved a rental car.

I called to let my supervisor know that I would be in by 11pm. If anyone was still at the bar, I'd stop by for a nightcap.

"Johnny boy, I'm glad you are finally going to make it. We are having a very good time. Too bad you're missing Ernie's bachelor party."

"You're kidding, Ernie's getting married?"

"Oh, God no. Who'd want to marry him? He just happens to be the only bachelor, so we decided to throw him a party. Ooh, gotta go. The cake with the stripper just arrived. I'm supposed to take pictures. See ya when you get in."

I was starting to think that maybe these parties were a weeklong celebration and that monkey business was the only thing going on. That's probably why the wives weren't invited. Now I'd have to try to keep Jill away from the promotion ceremony. The gold keys might be given to the recipients by some shameless hussy. I felt like I was already in trouble, and I wasn't even there yet. Maybe I could get out of going to the dinner somehow . . . but how?

To Ski or Not to Ski

You Take the Kids, I'll be Waiting by the Fire

While the plane was taxiing to the terminal, people were standing, stretching and retrieving their bags from the overhead storage compartments.

"John, what's wrong? You look stressed. Did they cancel the dinner because of the weather?"

"I'm fine. As far as I know the dinner is still on for tomorrow night."

How stupid. I could have told Jill the dinner was cancelled. Then I wouldn't have to worry about making something up for her not to attend it with me.

"Jill, maybe we should plan something for you and the kids to do tomorrow. I'm sure you don't want to sit through a boring awards ceremony. It's probably not a good idea to leave the kids on their own for two or three hours either."

"If you don't mind, John, that sounds good to me. I was planning a migraine anyway."

"Oh. Well then it will work out just fine. We'll plan a ski trip with a tour guide and meet back at eight after the dinner. I'll skip ceremony so we can pack for Thursday's flight to the land of sun, blue skies and sandy beaches."

"That sounds wonderful."

The five of us went together to the baggage claim, then to the rental counter to pick up our car. The hotel was only twenty minutes from the airport. My eyes almost popped out of my head when I saw the lodge we were staying in. It was a humungous log cabin with a two story fireplace in the atrium. You could feel the warmth of the fire upon entering. The check in area had ten attendants standing behind a rock-based counter with a solid granite top.

"Jill, can you believe this place?"

"I feel like we're in the middle of a Hollywood movie."

"Dad, look, an outdoor swimming pool, can we go?"

"Sure, As soon as we check into our rooms. I don't want you two boys stripping down right here in front of everyone."

I heard a faint voice coming from the peanut gallery.

"Why not, you do it in front of my friends?"

Elise was referring to the time when I got caught in the garage with my pants down trying to get out of a stinky situation.

"That wasn't planned. I don't make a habit of changing in the garage and certainly not when your friends are pulling up the driveway. Can we try to forget that ever happened?"

"I only wish I could. I've been scarred for life."

Jill found the direction of the conversation entertaining, but refrained from laughing out loud. When we got upstairs to the room, our breath was taken away for the second time tonight. It was spectacular. The company had spared no expense when it came to booking the event. All I could say was,

"Wow! Will you look at this place, I've gotta find my camera and get some pictures. Too bad we will only be here for a day. I'd have liked to be here for a week or two."

"Don't get too comfortable. It's nice, but I'm looking forward to the beach."

"Me too, if you want my opinion. . ."

"Princess, if it's not positive. Keep it to yourself. I'd prefer to savor the moment."

The boys could have cared less. They found their swim suits and were heading back downstairs to the outside heated pool. Snow was falling, and it was the coolest thing to see the steam rising off the water. There were underwater lights that lit up the pool. It was a beautiful shade of ice blue.

"You boys be back upstairs by midnight."

"Okay, Dad."

Martin and Lewis were off and running to the elevator. Now it was Elise's turn to make a request.

"I'm bored. Can I go to the gift shop and pick out a souvenir?"

"Sure honey. Here's ten bucks. Be back by midnight. No talking to strange boys while you're down there. You don't know where they've come from."

"Daddy, you're a real killjoy. I'm only leaving the room so you and mom can have some quality time. Put a scarf on the door handle so I'll know when it's safe to come back in."

"Don't worry, you won't be interrupting anything. We have to unpack. We'll probably watch the local news and be in bed before you kids get back."

"Okay Dad, whatever you say."

When the door closed, I looked at Jill and she looked at me. It had been a long time since we had been alone together. We had an hour to get frisky.

"I'm going to grab a shower. Do you care to join me?"

The Dinner Party

What was I Thinking

Jill and I missed our opportunity for intimacy. We got out of the shower, put on our onesie pajamas and fell asleep as soon as we hit the bed. A little after twelve midnight, I heard the boys come in. They were trying to be quiet, but not doing a very good job at it.

At twelve-fifteen the door opened again. That would be Elise. I was impressed that the three of them were back before one o'clock.

"Dad- - hey, Dad, we're hungry."

Lewis was loudly whispering through our half opened bedroom door.

"Dad, can we get a pizza?"

"Lewis, where are you going to get a pizza at this hour?"

"There's a menu under the phone. The hotel has twenty-four hour room service. It says they have the best pizza in all of Vail."

"Well, if it says so, I guess you can order it. Make sure you ask your sister if she wants some too, so that you have enough."

"Okay, should I ask her friend too?

"Her friend? What friend?"

"Some dude she picked up downstairs at the bar."

"Some dude she picked up at the bar?"

At this point Jill and I sat straight up with our eyes wide open.

"Dad, why do you keep repeating everything I say?"

"I don't know."

I walked over to the bedroom door and looked into the living room. There were two bodies relatively close sitting on the sofa in front of the fireplace.

"Lewis, go order your pizza and tell your SISTER I WANT TO TALK WITH HER, NOW!"

I said the last part loud enough that Elise and her "Friend" could hear me. They separated faster than Lewis could run to the phone. Our daughter slowly came to the door, probably dreading the conversation that was about to take place.

"Eli, I thought I told you to stay away from strangers? And then you have the nerve to bring one up to the room in front of your brothers. What in the world is wrong with you?"

"Daddy, calm down. He's not a stranger."

"He's not? Then who is he."

"His name is Randy. He's in my Geometry class at Brentwood. His family is staying here through the weekend. Isn't that great? The Fyfe's invited me to go skiing with them tomorrow. Is that okay? I said yes."

"I suppose, but what about the bar? You aren't old enough to go to a bar."

"Daddy, Lewis left out one little detail. It was the snack bar by

304

the pool. We were watching the two idiots jumping in the water and acting like seals. Oh, and they have burgers to die for, much better than the dumpster burgers at the Purple Pickle."

"Really, they're that good, huh? I guess I should have trusted you. Don't stay up too late."

"We won't. Randy has to be in by one o'clock. His parents have a curfew for him too."

"They sound like fine, respectable folks. Good night dear."

Jill chimed in behind me. Good night, sweetie. Tell Randy to have his mother call me in the morning to confirm their plans so we can make arrangements for later in the day."

"Okay Mom, goodnight."

"I guess we can go to sleep now."

"Are you nuts? While out daughter is out there in front of a romantic fire with a teenage boy."

"But, I thought since she knows him, you'd be fine with that?"

"Are you kidding? It's worse. Now they can carry the torch back home with them and pick up where they leave off here. Open the door a little wider. I want to keep an eye on them."

"Yes, dear."

We sat in bed with our arms crossed on our laps. Sitting in our footie pajamas, we didn't dare go out where we could be seen and laughed at. When the clock struck one, Randy left as promised. Finally I could get some sleep.

"Daddy, are you still awake?"

"Of course Princess, what's up?"

"I need to talk with you privately. Can you come into my room?"

"Sure."

I went quietly into Elise's room. I didn't want to wake Jill. This would be our first Father Daughter talk in many weeks. I felt it was a special moment that I would remember and cherish for a long time.

"Okay, here's the deal. Randy saw a stripper going into a cake just before it was pushed into a corporate party. Guess what the company name on the outside marquee was?"

"Getmore Marketing, Products and Services, Inc.?"

"Bingo. The way I see it, you would have been at that party if the plane hadn't been delayed, right?"

"I guess so."

"Yeah, you guess so. And mommy dearest, the trusting soul that she is, would be none the wiser, right?"

"I guess so."

"Right again, Daddy-O. So, all I want is to stay through the weekend and fly home with the Fyffe's instead of clinging along with the fam on your lame-ass vacation."

Out of habit I held out my hand for a quarter to put in the swear jar.

"You've got to be kidding. I'm blackmailing you and you're worried about a stupid quarter?"

"Elise, Princess, let me explain to you how families and marriages work. . .

"This ought to be good."

"Oh, you better believe it will be. First of all, there will be no blackmailing me. Second there will be no skipping out on the lame-ass vacation that I have planned for the family. Thirdly, and last, you will be grounded from the moment we walk in the door upon arriving home."

"You can't do that. I'll tell mom all about you and your pervert buddies having a stripper."

"I already told your mother about Ernie's bachelor party that the guys had tonight."

"Uh-O"

"Uh-O is right. I have half a mind to put you over my knee and give you the spanking you deserve, but you're too old for that. I'll think of an appropriate punishment and let you know in the morning what it is. Good Night, Sweetheart."

"Yeah, sure, goodnight, father."

To the Mountain Top We Go

Up was Easy - - Down, Not so Much

The overnight forecast was calling for up to four inches of

snow. With the severe winter storms we'd been through this year, four inches was like sneezing at the salad bar. No one was going to notice.

Jill was up with the sun. She had her feet propped up on our balcony rail with a cup of coffee in one hand, a magazine in the other. From our room you could see the atrium with the two story fire place blazing. I could feel the heat as I stepped out to join her.

"Mmm, that coffee smells good. Any left?"

"I would suppose so, I ordered room service. It's a vanilla caramel latte."

"Oh, I thought maybe you made a pot. They have all the stuff in the kitchenette."

"I'm on vacation, John. You're not helpless. Make a pot if you want one."

"I think I'll have what you're having."

I went into the other room to call in my breakfast order. Someone had their crabby pants on this morning with the belt pulled tight. I needed to tread lightly so as not to start World War III.

"I'm ordering a pancake and egg breakfast. Do you want anything?"

"Just another latte, and tell them to double the espresso. I need a little pick-me-up this morning."

"Okay."

After placing the order, I took surveillance of the perimeter to see where the children were. They were all still in bed. It was seven-thirty. I suppose I shouldn't have thought that they would be up yet. Following my rounds I went back to join Jill.

"Ya know, your daughter tried to blackmail me last night?"

"I heard."

"You did? How?"

"Ah, we're in a hotel with paper thin walls."

"Oh, yeah, right."

"By the way, you did a nice job putting "your" daughter in her place."

"I learned how to handle her from you, dear."

"I am curious about one thing though?"

"What's that, Jill?"

"When were you planning on telling me about the bachelor party and the strippers?"

"Umm, well, I - - -"

"Never mind, John, at least you weren't there. You get into enough trouble without help from your corporate buddies."

"I suppose that's true."

"Just so you know, I'll be going to the dinner tonight after all. It's not that I don't trust you, I don't trust them."

"Well, I'll be pleased as punch to have you with me when I accept my award and promotion. Do you think I need to prepare an acceptance speech?"

"I wouldn't. You're at your best when you come shooting off the cuff. The way you pull sh - - I mean stuff out of your backside is amazing. Hilarious, I might add, too."

"I guess. Thank you?"

The doorbell rang. It was breakfast, and not a moment too soon.

"Thank you. Here's a little something for you."

"Gee thanks, sir. The hotel adds a twenty percent gratuity for room service, so a tip isn't really necessary, but I sure do appreciate it."

"Oh, well, hey, wait. Wasn't I supposed to get two lattes?"

"You ordered the Big Breakfast and a latte."

"But, the Big Breakfast is supposed to come with orange juice and coffee. I didn't get those either."

"Look, we serve over two hundred rooms every morning. Occasionally a mistake is made. Do you want the tip back?"

"No, I just want what I ordered, that's all."

"Fine. When I get back to the kitchen, I'll place your order for a latte and an orange juice with coffee. Anything else while I'm at it?"

"No, that'll be all."

"Swell, my buzzer is going off, which means I'm late for my next delivery. Thanks a lot."

I closed the door and headed towards the balcony with the food tray.

"Geez, does everyone in this place have their crabby pants on?"

"What's that, John? I can't hear you from in there."

"Nothing, they forgot to bring your latte."

"Oh, don't worry about it, I'm going to take a shower before the kids get up or I won't be able to get in the bathroom."

I thought Jill was going to throw a hissy fit about the coffee; however, she was distracted with the shower, so I was spared a verbal assault that I'm sure would have been aimed in my direction. Even though it was clearly the kitchen's fault. Or maybe not, oh well, there will be another cup hot and ready when she gets out of the bathroom.

One by one the children woke up and strolled out of their bedrooms. They were in various stages of apparel, half clothes, with the other half pajamas and in Elise's case, just the top half of an oversized two piece.

"Elise, the Fyfe's called a few minutes ago. If you are still going out ski doing, Mrs. Fyfe said to meet downstairs in front of the fireplace about nine-thirty."

"Daddy, why didn't you wake me up? How do you expect me to be ready in only an hour and a half? Geez, Dad, could you like wait until the last minute so that I have to go out un-cleansed and without make-up. You want Randy to see the real me, so that he hates me, don't you?"

"Princess, you are beautiful just the way you are, all natural. You don't need make up for some boy to like you. Now hurry, the water just turned off, which means your mother is out of the shower."

"Order me something for breakfast, I'm starved."

"That won't be necessary, honey. The Fyfe's are going to take you with them to the Chalet for brunch before they hit the trails."

"Daddy, I don't want Randy to think I'm some sort of freakish pig. I need to eat before I go, so that I just have a nibble or two. Don't you know anything about first dates? The girl doesn't let the boy know she's hungry. Sheesh!"

"It's been a while since I've been on a date. I guess it must have slipped my mind. We certainly wouldn't want young Randal to think that you eat. What do you want for breakfast?"

"Okay, write this down. I'll have the Big Breakfast with extra pancakes, a side of hash browns, two extra slices of bacon, a blueberry muffin and a tall orange juice. Did you get all that? I'm starved."

Elise was heading for the shower when I confirmed her order.

Yes, I think I got it, one piggy platter for the young lady. How about you two? Do you want something to eat too?"

The first one to speak was Marty.

"Not right now, Dad. I don't like to eat while on vacation until around eleven or twelve. I like lunch for breakfast."

"What about you, Lew? Do you want something now or later?"

"I'll wait."

"Okay, then, one breakfast for my favorite daughter and none for my favorite sons."

I got a phone call from Ernie. He was checking on all the inductees to make sure they knew the times for today's events. From one o'clock until three this afternoon there was a marketing meeting. The awards banquet was tonight at seven. We were supposed to wear black tie formal attire for the big promotion. Nobody said anything about that until now. I needed to find a tux rental somewhere in town and hope they had my size.

"Jill, I have to go into town to rent a suit for tonight. I'll meet you and the boys on the bunny slope in a couple of hours."

"Okay, dear. See you in a few."

I was off in a flash. Half way down the hall I realized I was still in my pajamas and had to turn came back to the room to put some clothes on. It was another Kodak moment as I stood in front of the door in my red flannel Onesie without a key to the room. It wouldn't have been so bad, but the waiter with our breakfast arrived. He was starring and holding back a gut buster laugh.

"Would you like me to call maintenance, or do you have a key somewhere in that get-up of yours?"

"Someone will open the door. They just have the TV a little loud. Give it a minute"

"Sir, I can give it all day. I'm not the one everyone is laughing at."

The door opened and Jill grabbed me by the arm. She took the food tray from the waiter and kicked the door shut.

"I swear, John, if I'm not watching you every minute of the day, you're somewhere embarrassing me."

"I didn't do it on purpose you know. I stepped out to get our free paper and the door closed behind me. I think there must be a draft in the hall."

"Get dressed. I'll see you later. That's if you don't get arrested for flashing. Did you know the trap door on you PJ's is flapping and you have no underwear on?"

A Little Too Much Too Late

It was 11 o'clock before I was able to catch a bus into town. Understandably there was only one Tux shop, and even more, that their standard sizes had been reserved earlier in the week by all the guys attending the big ceremony tonight.

If I wanted to wear black, I had a choice between a 52 long or a 44 short. I wear a 38 regular. I decided to go with the 44 short. I bought a pair of black cowboy boots and tucked the pants into them to cover my white socks. I had them staple the waist to fit; however, the lower portion was somewhat in a bunch and uncomfortable to sit on. The jacket was a problem all the way around. It was big enough for a second of me, but the sleeves stopped 4" from my wrist. I could only hope it would be dark in the hall for dinner.

I arrived back at the hotel around 3pm. Jill and the boys were still at their ski lesson. Elise was nowhere in sight. A nap seemed appropriate. At 4 o'clock I heard the boys come in. They were stripping out of their snow suits all the way to their bedroom. The next thing I saw were bare butts on the way to the pool. I was hoping they got their swim trunks on by the time they got to the elevator.

Next in was Jill. She was dragging herself straight to the whirlpool tub in our master bedroom. I heard a groan hello as she passed me. It was time for me to go downstairs for the business meeting before dinner and the awards ceremony. I was thinking of what to say for my acceptance speech.

The meeting was cut short. Most of the guys were still on the slopes and didn't make it in on time. I decided to loosen up with a couple of beers at the bar before going back to the room to get ready for dinner.

Ernie and some others from the office were sitting at the bar. When I walked in, the there was a round of applause and some hollering;

"Hey John" Followed by "John-E, John-E, John-E."

Phil handed me a drink.

"Salute!"

I downed the drink along with the group. Immediately another drink was put before me. Ernie mumbled a few words followed by every hand raising with their drink.

"Salute!"

After three of whatever they were giving me I had to sit down. That was a mistake. I had three more shots and then fell face first on the floor. There was a round of applause followed by laughter. Two of my fellow office partners picked me up and took me to the elevator. They pressed my floor and then put me in by myself.

I was holding on to the hand rail for dear life. The elevator was traveling at normal speed, but my mind and body were operating in slow motion. When the elevator door opened, I was afraid to let go of the rail. By the time I leaned forward to exit, the door closed and I was on my way up to another floor.

Up and down, with my head spinning round and round. I was trying desperately to keep the contents of my stomach contained. The elevator settled on the first floor. I exited quickly. Realizing I was in the lobby, I turned around but missed my opportunity to get back on, before the doors closed.

Swaying like a palm tree in a gentle wind, I waited for the next elevator going up. When the light indicated a car was going in my direction, I stepped forward before the doors opened. I didn't want to miss another opportunity to get on the next car going to the 3rd floor.

I was somewhat self absorbed not paying attention to anyone riding with me. The person to my left was tapping their foot.

They were either impatient or annoyed. When the doors opened on the 2nd floor, a couple exited leaving me and the tapper to continue our ascent to the 3rd floor.

"Daddy, you're drunk."

"Prin-chess, ish that you?"

"Yes, it's me. If that door opens and more people get on, try not to embarrass me. I honestly don't know how your wife puts up with you."

"My w-wife ish yor ma-mother."

"I know the relationship. However, she has a choice and I don't."

"That's mean to shay. I'd give you a spankin, but my hans feel numb."

At that moment the jalapeno poppers that I had at the bar were trying to make an escape by way of an audible flatulent. I wasn't able to squeeze my cheeks long enough to hold it in until we got to our floor. The emission trumpeted an alert before the noxious gas hit our nostrils.

"Holy crap, dad, that's disgusting."

Out of habit I held out my hand for a quarter to put in the swear jar. The elevator doors opened. Elise ran out as I fell to the floor.

The doors were hitting my legs trying to close and then re-open. This happened several times until Jill came to my rescue. She dragged me to our room, swearing under her breath. I was holding my hand out when she slammed the door to our room shut.

I slept through dinner, the awards ceremony and the celebration party that followed. Phil brought an envelope with a key to my new office along with my Holiday bonus.

The flight to Mazatlan was quiet. Jill and Elise weren't talking to me, and the boys were a few rows behind. All in all it turned out just like the advertisement in the travel magazine said.

"A Vacation to Remember for a Life Time."

THE END

Book 12

The Smallest Traveler

A Famous Explorer Finds a Real Fairy Tale

As a world traveler in search of treasures both new and old, I've covered the globe, four times, no make that five. Each time returning home, I was more dead than alive. Body parts to heal along with mental and physical fatigue translated into a recovery time of more than a year.

I was still cataloging relics from my last journey some fifteen months earlier, when the bug to get back on the road bit me. It bit so hard that I dropped everything and booked a flight to Ireland. I didn't know why Ireland, but my gut instinct told me I was going to make a discovery that would change my life.

On the flight overseas, I started reading through my memoirs of the last trip I had made to the land of green clover and Leprechauns. The four leaf clover of Kilkarny was legendary. The locals tell of the fortune one will garner if they find the clover and present it to a Leprechaun. It is said that he must turn over his pot of gold that sits at the end of a rainbow.

Upon arrival, I had a cabby drive me to the oldest pub in Kilkarny. Old pubs are known to have the city elders in attendance most nights of the week. They were full of Blarney and told the best stories. It was the ciphering between tale and truth that made the best of conversations over a warm pint of beer.

My notes said to go to the Blarney Tavern of Kilkarny to find a man of substantial years. Ask for Shueshowme. I didn't remember writing that, or what it meant. Was Shueshowme a name, or was it a question I was to ask the old man of the tavern?

The man of substantial years was easy to find. He sat at a table near the fireplace and had a clan of both young and old sitting at his side and on the floor.

All eyes were fixed upon his reddened face as he told a story of times gone by. His hair was white with a beard that strolled from his chin to his chest. He was a robust man will a twinkle in his eye. He very much reminded me of my childhood ideas of what Santa would look like if I were to see him in person.

"There I was walking one day through the field of blue and gold. As I entered the forest, to the left of the tallest oak in the wood, there grows a portabella mushroom the size only one's imagination can hold."

Immediately I was captivated by this man's story and how enthused he was with the telling of it. He seemed to be recalling with fine detail all that had happened as though it were yesterday.

"I rested me weary bones against the oak. If I were to have a burger in my right hand, the mushroom would have been in my left. I was hungry beyond belief. I started to pull a piece of the fungus off to appease my stomach's demands. That's when I heard a voice calling out to me."

"Beware, my fine fellow. If you eat the roof off a fairy's castle, you will be enslaved to her for the remainder of your days. Being that of a young man, I'd be careful if I were you. The stomach can wait for another time. You must leave the mushroom alone and hurry back across the field of blue and gold."

"I looked around and there was no one to be found, so I ate the mushroom until I could eat no more. Well, I'm here to tell you, it was a curse. I fell deep into a sleep that kept me still for nigh unto a hundred years. When I awoke, there was this town, the forest was gone and I stumbled in here. A beautiful red-haired waitress offered me a beer, and I've been here ever since."

He laughed so hard he almost fell out of his chair. Everyone around laughed with him. He had us all hooked, and we fell for every line he threw out. What a great story. It was late and I decided to get a room for the night and come back for another story tomorrow.

The Legend of Kilkarny

The winds were blowing all day. I was on my way to the library to look up some history of the town. There was only the registry of when it was named and that of the man who first settled here. Founded in 1821, this lovely little hide-away called Kilkarny sat quite a distance from the bigger cities. Surrounded by glens and brooks there were fields of grass and flower scattered throughout the area. The flowers were both blue and gold and smelled of cinnamon and rose. I could breathe the air till it lifted my thoughts straight from reality to fantasy. It was hypnotic to say the least.

After my day of study, I went to the tavern to listen to the man of substantial years spin another tale. He was a master at captivating his audience. He talked softly to bring the folks close to him and then would erupt with a loud voice to push them back in their seats or fall onto the floor. I don't think I've ever seen a better showman anywhere in my world travels. His stories started in the same fashion every night.

"There I was walking one day through the field of blue and gold. It was nigh about the noon hour when I spotted a wee fellow sleeping under the clover. Legends have been told of magic falling on the flowers of blue and gold. It was to be my luck if I could catch me a leprechaun and receive a gift of his magic. It was all I could do to sneak up on the sleeping wee one. I took off me bonnet and put it over him. Then I covered the bottom and scooped him up in me hands. To be sure he was a fighter, but he settled down when I started talking blarney with him."

A twinkle in the aged one's eye sparkled as he talked about the magic of the wee one. The recounting of the tale appeared to bring him back to his younger days. He was excited more than any other time during his telling of the story. I was starting to almost believe he was telling of his youth and an actual event that took place some many years ago.

"The wee fellow's name was Tu Shome. He took me to the rainbow's end and filled my pockets with gold. When I could carry no more, Tu Shome placed a spell on me that kept me asleep for a fortnight. When I awoke I was broke."

The name of the wee fellow was very similar to the name/phrase I had in my notes. I wrote it down phonetically and hoped to look it up in the library in the morning. I may have been looking all this time for the wrong spelling of this very same leprechaun.

The old man sat quiet for a moment. He took a sip of his beer as the last of his listeners headed for home. It was almost midnight. Tomorrow would be Saint Patrick's Day. A few more minutes before the bells of St. Mary started to ring in the new day. When he finished his drink, his eyes rolled back in his head. He started to fall out of his chair. The old man opened his eyes and looked directly at me;

"Find Tu Shome, you must promise me . . . find Tu Shome."

He clutched his chest and fell forward onto the floor. At the strike of midnight he was dead. I tried to revive him with CPR, but to no avail. The swirling winds of the night caused the door of the tavern to open. I was startled and looked away only to find the old man gone when I turned back.

The bar maid and I held each other and cried.

Heed the Call

When That Still Small Voice Speaks - - LISTEN

Catherine was the bar keeper's daughter. She was Irish to the bone with long flowing hair and emerald eyes. Her ageless beauty made her stand out in a crowd. She had the eye of every man walking in the door. Upon finding she wasn't a flirty lass, their attention turned to the story telling of the man of substantial age.

We sat together reminiscing over the old man's stories. The morning sun shone through the smoke covered glass of the front window. It was time for me to go. I asked her if she knew what the old man's name was.

"I'm not exactly sure. He sat in that same chair since the day I started tending bar at the age of thirteen. My dada told me stories of him from the time I stopped wetting me diapers. I suppose we never thought to ask him. He was just always here and that was that."

"Huh, well, I guess I'll see you later tonight."

"By the way, before we wait too long, what is your name?"

"Gee, I'm sorry, I suppose I haven't introduced myself, have I? My name is Jack. I only know yours because you were mentioned in some of the old man's stories, plus the guests all call you by your first name."

"Well, Jack, then I'll be looking forward to seeing you as the sun sets, like usual."

"Good day, Catherine. I'll see you in a bit."

I decided to go into Limerick today. Limerick was the closest city with a sizeable library. I was going to need something more to look through than the few historical records that were held here in Kilkarny. I gathered up my notes and my lap top then hopped the first bus out of town. The napkin that I had written on last night before the old man passed away had changed colors. Last night it was white with green letters. Today it was green with white letters. I would have thought I was mistaking, but I had another napkin from a previous time, and it was white with the name of the tavern in green.

The name of the leprechaun that I was supposed to look for was no longer written down on the napkin. It had disappeared. My notes were still legible, but when it came to the name, there was only a blank spot.

It was a strange occurrence to be sure. The Library in Limerick was one of the oldest buildings in the town. At one time it was an Irish castle with a rich heritage until it fell under siege by the French.

During the war it was burned almost to the ground. When the castle was restored, the family feared it to be cursed, so they donated it to the public trust to become a library. Where the family is now, no one knows, and the record of their names has been long since removed to protect them from future attacks.

The bus ride to Limerick would be over an hour. With little sleep the night before, I thought it to be the perfect time for a nap. I tipped the driver to alert me when we arrived, so as not to wake up somewhere else. I headed to the back of the bus where I was less likely to be disturbed. On the seat was this morning's paper left by a previous traveler.

We were waiting at the station for a few more passengers. Before settling in for my nap, I glanced through the paper and found an article about a museum exhibit that was to be open through the weekend in Limerick. The name Alice Pleasance, being the curator, caught my attention.

Some of you may know the name too. She was the little girl that alleged she went to a strange and wonderful land. I always thought it to be just a story made up by someone who had taken a few too many hallucinogens as a child. Yet, here was a traveling museum of artifacts from young Alice's journey to a place she called Wonder Land.

As the bus pulled out of the station, I rolled my jacket up to make a pillow and shortly after fell asleep. I can't remember ever resting so completely. The ride to Limerick was over before I knew it. I was hailed by the driver to come forth and exit.

"Thank you. I appreciate you calling me. I fear I was in such a deep sleep, I would have been to the end of the line and heading back before waking."

"No problem, have a great day, sir. Be sure to catch the exhibits while you are here. I understand them to be fascinating and educational as well."

"I plan to. Maybe I'll see you when I head back to Kilkarny tomorrow."

"Ey to be sure, I'm the only driver between here and there. Where will ye be staying the night?"

"Gee, I hadn't given it much thought. Is there any place you'd recommend?"

"Sure, if ye want a good comfy room and a hot meal, stay at the Siobhan bed & breakfast."

"I'll do that, to be sure."

We parted company, and I headed directly to the library to start my research. I had a full day planned, and now I had a museum exhibit to fit into it. I wasn't sure about the hotel that the driver recommended, as to whether or not I would need a reservation. I decided to call ahead just to be safe. The librarian told me that the Siobhan had been closed for over twenty years. I couldn't believe the high praise from the driver for a place that no longer was in business. Maybe I was pronouncing the name wrong. I wasn't fluid in Irish, so my accent may have been throwing the interpretation off a bit.

The Magic of Leprechauns and their Spells was the first book I pulled from the shelves. It was a large leather-bound book with gold leaf pages. The glossary held the names of over four hundred known magical spells that had been documented. It also contained a list of Leprechauns that had been found in the field of blue and gold. This was the book that I thought might have some answers as to why I came to Ireland in the first place and where I might find Tu Shome, the Leprechaun.

The Museum of Limerick

Fantasy Found a Home

I couldn't have been more excited about anything. I checked out the book from the library and went straight to the museum to see Alice's collection from Wonder Land. It had my curiosity piqued all day. The museum was only a block away from where I stopped for lunch. I had a quick snack and then ran the whole way only to find that they were closed due to lack of interest.

Well, I had an interest, and I wanted to see inside. I went around to the back of the building and found a broken window large enough for me to crawl through. I didn't know that it was a basement window, and I fell eight feet to the floor. The fall was a bit of a shock to the body along with a twisted ankle.

There were no lights on except the night lights for security. I had to bump and feel my way to the exhibits while hobbling a bit with the bad ankle. The showroom with Alice's display wasn't very large. There was one table a length of twelve feet by ten wide. It was an understatement to be sure, and no wonder, no one was interested. Tiny little trees to make a forest, a doll house sized castle and itsy bitsy characters that could hardly be seen with the naked eye. I felt my enthusiasm for the trek had been wasted.

I was about to leave when I saw a sign pointing to a staircase. It indicated for better viewing of Wonder Land see it through the looking glass. My curiosity was tweaked once again. I slowly made my way up the metal winding staircase. The upper floor had wooden rails that one could look over to see the displays below. In the middle there was a spy glass pointing in the direction of Alice's Wonder Land table. I peered through the dusty old scope.

To my amazement, the display was bursting with activity. Everything through the looking glass was life size, or so it appeared.

I spied a white rabbit with a blue jacket running to and fro. There were all the scenes from the story taking place before my eyes. It was like watching the movie all over again. I couldn't understand why there was no interest. This was the most fantastic thing I had ever seen in all of my world travels.

I stepped back for a moment to rub my eyes to make sure what I was seeing was real. It was fantasy coming to life. I sat on the floor under one of the night lights to read my book for a couple of minutes. In a chapter about a Leprechaun prince, I found the name Tu Show-me. Finally I struck pay dirt. Here was the name that the old man of substantial age told me to find. There was a poem about someone, maybe the old man himself:

There once was a man from Kilkarny
His stories were full of Blarney

One story he told
For sure to be true
He told to you and me

The story of a Leprechaun
By the name of Tu Show-me

Tu Show-me
Had a spell to cast

Your life
If you caught him
Would forever last

I wasn't sure what that might mean in the scope of things. The old man said he caught a Leprechaun and then slept for a hundred years while being robbed of his gold that was given to him by the same wee man. If the wee man was Tu Show-me, then the old man was not to die, but have ever lasting life.

I started to laugh. I was starting to believe all this stuff. These were the tales of dreamers and not real.

They were fantasy not reality. I packed up my book and notes and went out to find a place to stay for the night. It was after sunset, and most of the businesses were closed for the night, except of course for the pubs. On a side street that may have led somewhere out of town was a broken sign hanging from one side while the other touched the ground. The sign said one mile to Siobhan's Bed & Breakfast. I don't know why, but I decided to go even though I was told it had been closed for many years.

I could smell a fire place burning and saw lights shining brightly at the end of the road. It must be coming from the hotel. Now I was confused. Who was right, the bus driver or the librarian?

Built in 1843

An Irish Inn or so it Would Seem

I walked up the marble stairs of the Siobhan Inn. The porch was lined with large white pillars, and the front doors were oversized glass with brass trim and handles. All of it was sparkling clean as though they had just finished polishing before I arrived. I stopped for a moment before I pulled open the door. There was music playing in the grand ball room. As I entered I could see the dining room was virtually filled to capacity. I was worried with all these people that I wouldn't get a room. Ringing the bell at the front desk, I was in awe of the grandeur of this historic building.

"Yes Sir, may I offer you a room for the evening?"

"Why, yes of course. I didn't think I would be able to get in. Is it always this crowded on a weekday?"

"My good man, we are filled to capacity every St. Patty's day."

"That's right, I forgot it was St. Patrick's. Well, I'll take a room. How late is the restaurant open?"

"We are open until eight, but you can still get dinner while seated in the ballroom. Tonight we have the Tu Ra Lu Ra orchestra. They are the last of the original Irish bands that still play here every St. Pats."

I wasn't connecting at this point the word "original" as it was used describing the band. I just thought he meant authentic.

"I think I'll just freshen up a bit and come back down before the dinner hour is over."

"You'll be in room 105 at the top of the stairs to your right. Have a pleasant stay."

As soon as I turned, the desk manager disappeared. I looked back to ask a question, but he was nowhere in sight. It was odd that someone well into his seventies would be so spry. Entering the room was a splendid treat. In the center of the room was an old canopy four poster style bed. There was a fireplace already burning with the tub water running. Now that's service.

I dipped into the tepid water that had bubbles floating across the top. The smell or roses and cinnamon filled the air. I remembered the fragrance, from another time and place, but I didn't know from where or when. It was so relaxing that I fell asleep.

I woke to the sound of the hall clock as it made its last strike of the midnight hour. The fire had gone out long before I got out of the tub. There was a chill in the air. The room felt damp with a musty smell. The bubble aroma had left the room when the fire went out. I crawled under the covers to warm myself. The sheets were not as fresh as I thought they should be. I tried to turn on the floor lamp standing next to the bed. It wasn't working. There was a sharp clap of thunder with lightning parting the skies. It was probably a power outage due to the storm. I was fortunate to be able to fall asleep with the rhythm of the rain falling over head.

The sun shining through the roof woke me up. I couldn't believe my eyes. There was a hole the size of my bed in the ceiling. Everything in the room was covered with dust and cob webs. There's no way all this happened over night. I was frightened beyond belief. I ran out of my room heading for the stairs when I grabbed the handrail before falling to the first floor. The steps were nothing but a decayed pile of wood lying in the lobby. This place looked like it had been abandoned for years, maybe twenty years just like the librarian had said.

What a strange occurrence. I tied the sheet from my bed around the top rail to use as a rope to get to the lobby. When I attempted to open the front door, it wouldn't budge. I was locked in. All the windows were boarded shut. There was virtually no way to escape. This was quite a pickle I had gotten myself into. I was starving. I was wishing I had taken up on the shepherd's pie for dinner. Mmm, mashed potatoes, green beans and sweet baby carrots all smothered under a blanket of gravy. Thinking about it wasn't helping the growling of my stomach.

When I exhausted all avenues of escape, I retreated to the lobby and plopped down on one of the sofas. It was clear I was going to be here for a while. I needed to get back upstairs to get my library book. If nothing else I could make use of my time and continue reading the history of Leprechaun's from the area. The only way up was the way I came down. I gave the sheet a good yank to be sure it was tied tight before starting my ascent to the upper floor.

Upon entering the room, I assessed the possibility of climbing out through the hole in the ceiling and then jumping down from the roof. I used to do something as a kid in every hotel I ever stayed in. That would be bouncing on the bed. If I could bounce high enough, I might catch the edge and pull myself up. I tucked the book into the back of my pants and began jumping on the bed. These big old beds were not much more than coil springs, wood frame and a thick mattress for comfort. I kept sinking into the mattress instead of bouncing skyward. With every bit of strength I had within me, I pushed the king size mattress to the floor exposing the box frame and springs. I ran from the side of the room, leaped onto the bed and bounced through the hole in the ceiling.

"Weee heee! Boy that was fun."

Okay, so now I was on the roof, I needed to get down. There was a big pine tree that was fairly close. If I could grab a branch, I'd be home free and on the ground. It was just a little out of reach, but that wasn't going to stop me. Well, it wouldn't have until I spotted a ladder that was leaning against the building. Apparently it had been left there during a repair or gutter cleaning. No sense risking a leap of faith when I could take a sure bet.

The first building at the end of the street was a little breakfast diner. It was as good as any place to get a meal and read while waiting for the bus to return me to Kilkarny. It was already a half past one o'clock. The bus was due at two, so I had some time to spare. My reading took me to a chapter on famous recipes. There was one for short cake. I hadn't had short cake in years, especially with fresh strawberries and cream on top. I asked the waitress if they could make me a small piece of short cake using the recipe from the book.

"I think we can arrange that for you, sir. I'll have me chief put a plate out for you straight away. Would you like a topping to go with it?"

"No, I'll have it plain, but with another cup of coffee, please."

It wasn't long before the waitress brought me a plate of the leprechaun's shortcake. I saw the bus pulling into the station, so I asked for my check. I wrapped the cake in a napkin after taking a bite, then stuffed it into my pocket.

As I started to run to catch the bus, I tripped on my pants. They seemed to have gotten a little stretched from sleeping in them. As I waved my hand to get the attention of the bus driver, I noticed that the sleeve of my shirt had also gotten longer. The closer I got to the bus, the larger it was getting. In fact, everything around me had grown ten times its original size. I got to the station in time for the return trip. The bus driver was making his last call. I could barely see the tops of his shoe. Frantically I was jumping up and down trying to get the driver's attention before he closed the door of the bus. I ran as fast as I could to the curb to avoid getting run over.

I don't know what happened, but either I was the size of a

peanut or the town had grown into a village made for giants. It must have been the "shortcake." Now what was I going to do? I sat on the curb until I spotted the world's largest dog. He was sniffing, snorting and drooling, something I didn't want any part of. I slid just inside of the drain sewer and out of sight. Too bad I wasn't out of sniff. This monstrous beast would breathe in, and I would have to hold tight to the side of the drain. Then he would snort, and I almost fell into the sewer. In and out and in, I was exhausted trying to keep from being sniffed up his nose and then blown out into who knows where. When he left to find something worth eating, I climbed back onto the curb to rest.

"Whew, that was too close for comfort."

Finding Alice

Riding a Dog Wasn't in the Plans

There are times when I wished I wasn't right. Like for instance right now, I wished that a person's clothes and possessions did shrink along with them like in the movies. I always thought there was no way for that to happen, and I was right. Of course, in the children's movies they can't have naked people running around, especially if they were to have a sudden growth spurt.

I stopped shrinking at the size of a gnat. All I could do was sit on the curb and watch my clothes get run over in the street by all the cars passing by. My worst nightmare was returning. I could hear the panting of the pooch from earlier. At my current size, he wasn't as much of a threat. I was curious how well trained this mutt might be. When he was close enough to crawl on, I headed straight up and climbed in his ear. Knowing that dogs have great auditory reception,

I began to shout a command to go fetch. His ears perked up, but he wasn't sure what to do.

There was going to be a slight learning curve for the two of us. I needed to think of a way to communicate my needs, and he had to figure out where the voice was coming from and what it meant. I decided on pain management. I would bite his ear, and then give a command. If he did what I said, he would be pain free. If he did something else, I would bite him again until I got the desired reaction. It wasn't long before my furry friend figured out how to divert discomfort.

First, I had him drag my clothes and library book out of the street and toss them gently behind some shrubs. Now came the hard part. I needed to get to the museum to find Alice's growing potion. Getting to the front door was only part of the problem, if they were open; the museum curator wasn't going to allow a dog in. The next issue was getting onto the display. Actually, forgetting my size, getting in wasn't going to be a problem at all. I was small enough to walk proudly and straight away through any hole or crack in the door.

I whistled loudly into the dog's ear followed by a command to run. He took off like a bolt of lightning. We were leaping and bounding at top speed. I was tossed up and down until I fell into a waxy spot in his ear and got stuck. The rest of the ride to the museum was smooth but uncomfortable. Not only was I a sticky mess, but it smelled bad too.

When we got to the museum, the wild ride with Mr. Fur came to an abrupt stop. He sat in front of the doors wagging his tail. I think he was hoping for a treat, which unfortunately I couldn't provide. I did, however, give him a few, "You're a good dog" in his ear. I think he accepted that. After hopping off my faithful steed, he remained out front for awhile and then went off to do whatever it is dogs do.

Getting to the top of the table display that held Alice's Wonderland was like climbing the Empire State building. It was a mile high at my size. I wasn't expecting to see everything life size. I guess I really didn't know what to expect. I found a piece of tissue to gird my loins so that if I ran into anyone within the display, I wouldn't be totally embarrassed.

The activity of the day before was nowhere in view. There wasn't a single animal or person in sight. I found the table of the infamous tea party. All the places were set, but not a soul to be found. It occurred to me that they might be at the Red Queen's castle. There was only one path through the woods, so that was the direction in which I went.

I stopped just a few feet into the forest. I remembered seeing a perfume bottle on the table at the tea party. It looked like the bottle of Alice's elixir from the movie. If I were right, that bottle held the potion that would return me to my normal size. I ran back as fast as I could with a newfound excitement for the first time today. The bottle was taller than I. With all my strength I knocked it over, spilling its content onto a platter.

With the first sip, before I could blink I was the size of the bottle. With a second I was sitting in the middle of the display almost breaking the table it sat on. To my chagrin I was in front of a small crowd with nothing but the forest hiding my private parts. I picked up the bottle, put the top on and then ran out of the building yelling;

"Fire - - Fire!"

I don't know why I decided to yell fire, but it created a panic, and I was no longer the focus of attention. I ran down the block to find my clothes. The last bus to Kilkarny from Limerick was pulling into the station as I zipped up my pants. What an adventure. If I had found Alice, we could have shared notes and started another chapter in Wonder Land.

The ride to Kilkarny wasn't filled with any more excitement, I was glad for that. I couldn't wait to get to the Tavern to tell Catherine all that had happened. I continued reading where I left off in the book of Leprechauns. It was a fascinating book to be sure, but I hadn't found anything about the one they called Tu Shome. There was a reoccurring symbol throughout the pages of the book. It wasn't anything I had ever seen before in my travels. Maybe Catherine would be able to identify it for me.

When I got back to the Tavern in Kilkarny, there was music playing with the bar filled to capacity. I was surprised to see so many people. In the corner by the fireplace a small group of people had collected to listen to a story being told by a man of significant age. It was as if I had never left and everything was the way it was when I first came a few days earlier.

The only change was Catherine. She was thirteen years of age and just starting to wait tables for the first time. Her father was behind the bar. In my travels, I had gone back in time more than forty years. The old man, however, was the same age as the day he died. I wondered how many times this had happened before.

The old man looked at me and stopped his story telling for a moment. He said to me;

"Boy, many a man has traveled the sea, and many a man has looked for me. Ye must go back four more times, if ye want to find Tu Shome and end the curse. Are ye up for it? I hope you are, cause I'm tired and almost out of stories."

I said to the old man. . .

"Don't bet your bottom button against me, I'll be back."

THE END

www.ingramcontent.com/pod-product-compliance
Lightning Source LLC
Chambersburg PA
CBHW062026170626
46813CB00001B/308